The Heat
of
Ramadan

The Heat of Ramadan

Steven Hartov

Harcourt Brace Jovanovich, Publishers
New York   San Diego   London

Requests for permission to make copies of any
part of the work should be mailed to:
Permissions Department, Harcourt Brace Jovanovich, Publishers,
8th Floor, Orlando, Florida 32887.

Library of Congress Cataloging-in-Publication Data
Hartov, Steven.
    The heat of Ramadan/Steven Hartov.—1st ed.
        p.   cm.
    ISBN 0-15-139858-5
    I. Title.
PS3558.A7146H43   1992
813'.54—dc20   91-41305

Designed by Lydia D'moch
Printed in the United States of America

First edition

C D E

This book is dedicated to:

Philly and Oren

for always being there

———

and to the memory of
Mike "Nachum" Katzin

He loved his family,
he loved his work,
and he loved his country.

Author's Note:

Although *The Heat of Ramadan* is essentially a work of fiction, certain details are fact-based. Therefore, in order to protect those professionals who must continue to operate in a precarious world, I have changed certain military unit names, intelligence terms and operational techniques. For the sake of the drama, I have also moved some locales and altered dates. Finally, the entire work has been reviewed by the IDF Military Censor, which is a requirement with which I must comply, given my background.

New York
January 1992

RAMADAN: The ninth month of the Islamic year, often falling at the height of the summer's heat, and observed as sacred with fasting practiced daily from dawn to sunset.

There's crazy people walkin' round,
With blood in their eyes . . .
Wild-eyed pistol wavers,
Who ain't afraid to die.

Bogenhausen

January 1985

FROM THE MOMENT ECKHARDT PULLED THE TRIGGER, he knew he was killing the wrong man.

In the universal concept of time, it was merely a bisected second. Yet it was also one of those horrific moments of a man's life when another dimension seems to encroach upon reality, cruelly elongating a seizure of pain so that it might be experienced in all of its tortured glory.

Ecstasy seems to be gone in a flash.

Agony goes on and on and on.

It was, as Eckhardt would always remember, a moment full of sorrow. Swollen with hatred at first, then a sudden instinctive withdrawal as the realization began to surge from somewhere within his brain. And suddenly the portent of the error smacked against the inside of his eyes like a judo student being slammed to the mat.

Yes, he had killed before. He had done so in combat,

with the fury of the charge and the smoke and the gunfire and the screaming. And yes, he had killed in other ways, stealthily, with the dark heart of the saboteur, removed from the scene but accepting that the deed was his own. And yes, this was also not his first elimination at close range.

But before, Eckhardt had always been sure that his cause was righteous, his aim was true, his victim deserving of his fate. And in the past, in those face-to-face encounters, the Team's human targets had displayed many instinctive reactions to their precipitous demise. Shock. Horror. Anger. Certainly dismay before dying.

Yet now, if there was a God in heaven or hell, and if nature and Eckhardt's vision were not deceiving him, *this* man's twisted visage registered something frighteningly different . . .

Complete and utter *surprise*.

So once again, Eckhardt's aim was true. Too true. For he knew that as sure as the night would soon devour Munich, he was making the mistake of his life. But it was too late. The bullet was flying from the gun. It could no more be recalled than could the finest, most well-disciplined racehorse once the bell had clanged and it was out of the gate, dashing for the finish.

Still, ever the professional, committed to the battle, trained to suppress all self-doubt at this crucial juncture, Eckhardt pressed on with the attack. He could feel, rather than see, Rainer Luckmann beside him. The barrel of Luckmann's Beretta hovered inside his peripheral view, bucking slightly and spewing grey smoke as Rainer emptied his pistol. And Eckhardt watched his own weapon, trembling at the end of his arms. He registered, against his will and for all eternity, the face of the *wrong man* as the victim covered it with his hands and then sat down hard on the sidewalk, his brown paper parcels of fresh rolls spilling over the legs covered in fine tweed trousers.

Eckhardt stepped forward, seeing his own fists drawing his Beretta down toward the man's chest, hearing the distant scream of someone else, someone witnessing the pornography of violence. Knowing that person, too, would forever share his horror.

He fired three more rounds.

"*Genug*," he whispered to Luckmann. Then he said it again, louder, almost booming, so that the language would register to witnesses. "*Genug!*"

He turned to walk across the street. He knew that Luckmann was keeping pace, he did not check; he saw nothing but the blue Ford Fiesta waiting for him. He longed for its comfort, the whine of its small engine. Unthinking, his hands their own masters, he released the clip from the Beretta, put it in the pocket of his leather coat and reloaded the pistol with a fresh magazine from his belt.

As he reached for the door handle of the car he thought, *How the hell could it have all gone so wrong?*

For up until that very moment, *Operation Flute* had, as they liked to say at Headquarters, "Ticked over just as it must."

———

It was cold in Munich that morning. Raining, but without snow. It was still early, yet the light would remain the same all day, like mottled pewter or a North Pole night.

Tony Eckhardt sat at a small table in a safe house in Unter Sendling. The table was ugly, a stained round formica top and peeling brown metal legs, but it was good enough for a student. At the moment, Eckhardt wished that he *were* a student.

He looked out the small, lead-glass window, yet he could see nothing of Unter Sendling, for the kitchen faced the stone facade of the other half of the building. The flat had been carefully selected. Second floor—you could jump from the kitchen if you had to. Wooden stairs—you could hear anyone on the landing. There was only one set of "scenic" windows, and they were at the front of the salon facing St. Stephen's Pfarrzentrum. If you set up camp across from a church, anyone who wanted to observe you would first have to get past a Bavarian priest.

These things were always well thought-out.

Eckhardt sipped at a cup of Alvorada. But he could not eat.

Rainer Luckmann, on the other hand, seemed to be having no trouble at all. Luckmann's side of the table looked like a ravaged Konditorei platter. He had finished a half-liter of orange juice and was on his third cup of the rich coffee. Before him sat a large dish with two half-boiled *Eier im Glas*, into whose bright yolks he was violently jabbing the buttered stump of a Semmel roll. Adding to Eckhardt's gastronomic disbelief, Luckmann punctuated his "light" breakfast with gnashing bites from a greasy *Weisswurst*.

"Guten Appetit." Eckhardt's tone was veined with disgust, though he knew that he was simply jealous. He wished he could eat too.

Luckmann looked up. He swept his shaggy brown hair back over his forehead and stared out innocently from his bright green eyes. His mouth was full.

"Bist du nicht hungrig?"

Eckhardt smiled and shook his head. *"Du bist eine Sau. Wirklich."*

Luckmann shrugged, taking no offense. "Okay, so I'm a pig." He returned to his plate. Then he reached across the table, picked up his packet of Schwarzer Krauser No. 1, and began rolling a cigarette. That was another thing that Eckhardt could not fathom. Food that could sink a battleship, tobacco that could burn through asbestos. Iron stomach. Iron lungs.

Then as if to dispel Tony's envy, Rainer glanced up again, grinned sheepishly, and said, "I guess I'm nervous."

"Ja." Tony nodded, pleased to be once more in the company of a human. *"Ich auch."* You see, everyone had his own way of dealing with pre-combat jitters.

Eckhardt pushed his cup away, got up, and walked through the salon to the front window. He looked at his watch for the twentieth time. It was still only 9:00 A.M.

He put his hands on hips and stared through the freckled glass at the St. Stephen's Church, whose red peak wavered like a dream castle behind the smoky sheets of water that coursed over the window. He blew out a sigh and turned to gaze at the small flat.

Everything was German. The furniture, the books, the piles of *Stern, Der Spiegel, Süddeutsche Zeitung,* and the dichotomous volumes of Goethe, along with the occasional Heinrich Böll. His clothes were German, and Luckmann's as well, right down to the underwear.

The only foreign items were their Italian Berettas, yet these too were accompanied by forged licensing documentation associating both men with GSG9, the West German anti-terrorist team. Even the subsonic ammunition was West German—designed to kill, but not to penetrate the Target and possibly injure a wide-eyed passerby.

Someone was brilliant enough to think of everything, which allowed Eckhardt a certain relief from responsibility. Yet it also caused him to feel rather primitive.

The Doberman at the end of a leash.

Something was gnawing at the pit of Eckhardt's stomach. He swore to himself, for the hundredth time, that he would give up drinking that corrosive poison as soon as the mission was over. He was too damn jumpy. He had to begin changing gears, closing down emotions. The mission's team leader had to command with cool objectivity and sharp reflexes, all the

5

while seeming to his subordinates to be in complete self-control. As he had done many times in the past, Eckhardt now searched for a focus which would help him attain this Zen-like state.

On the far wall of the flat was a large poster framed in glass and aluminum. It was a soft-focus photograph, warm and colorful, of the lush green lawns and bird-bedecked ponds of the Englischer Garten. Stroked across the picture in bright pastels were the words of the poet Eugen Roth:

> *The chance, the luck, of a Munich address*
> *Spares you half of life's storm and stress.*

Eckhardt had seen the poster countless times, but it was only now that he really noted the irony. He laughed out loud.

"Was ist los?" Luckmann called from the kitchen.

"Sssshhh." Eckhardt continued to stare at the poster. He had broken his mood.

He dropped his hands to his sides, willing the arms to relax, the fists to open, the fingers to dangle. He narrowed his eyes and saw his own reflection in the glass. Short blond hair, grey-blue eyes, a strong neck, and below that, the mid-length black leather coat.

His image reassured him. Smoother, calmer now, he directed his mind to *Operation Flute*.

Amusing, that Hans-Dieter Schmidt had chosen such a name for this mission. In Arabic, the word for flute was *halil*, and the sound of that word was really too much like the Target's real name. But since you never, ever, chose an operational code that remotely resembled reality, Hans-Dieter had surely done so intentionally. In this business, to be predictable was to be finished, and Schmidt was never predictable.

By now, Eckhardt was sure, Hans-Dieter would have been in his office for over two hours. Eckhardt was equally sure that the mission commander had been "arriving for work" at that hour since he had rented the vacant import/export suite, if for no other reason than to quell any suspicions regarding his early arrival on this particular day.

The office was situated close to the expansive Munich Trade Fair and Exhibition Company, the MMG, for obvious cover reasons. But the precise choice of SchiessStatt 13 seemed to have been selected to satisfy Hans-Dieter's sense of the comical-ironic. For Hans insisted on calling it *ScheissStrasse,* in keeping with his oft-repeated opinion that espionage was a "shitty business."

Eckhardt began to review the pre-mission details.

Ettie Denziger would be moving into position, setting up her easel on her glassed-in veranda, which overlooked Barbarossa Strasse in the quiet borough of Bogenhausen. Eckhardt had not, of course, ever set foot in Ettie's flat, but her detailed descriptions enabled him to picture the environment.

Wearing a voluminous green cardigan, she would encamp in her large wooden rocker. A telephone—not purely a social device—would be at her side, next to a large pot of black coffee. Her petite blonde head would sport a number of items—dangling chain-and-ball silver earrings, the earphones of a Walkman, and on her crown a pair of half-spectacle, half-opera glasses. The veranda would not be heated today, so that the window glass would remain clear. Ettie would shiver, along with the leaves of her veritable greenhouse, as the cold January wind invaded through the sill cracks.

As befitted an art student, she would have tens of brushes, tubes, trays and inks surrounding her legs. And as befitted the Team's Communications Officer, her artwork would suffer today as she looked and listened in a coldly unaesthetic manner. After a month of work the large canvas of Bogenhausen's Barbarossa Street was still only half-finished. Had Ettie not been quite so attractive, friendly and aggressively eccentric, her neighbors might have asked why it was taking her so long.

Eckhardt did not allow his thoughts to linger with Ettie, for he had feelings for her that were somewhat less than professional. . . .

Peter Hauser. Now, there was a man who could not possibly sit and wait; and fortunately for him he would not be required to do so. Hauser's triple duties as Transportation Officer, Primary Tail and Back-Up would keep him moving all day long.

Already at dawn, Hauser would have commenced his check of the "motor pool." There were, to the dismay of the Department's comptroller, ten rental vehicles involved in *Flute*, as well as a purchased truck and an ambulance. Each vehicle had to be inspected for fuel, oil and water, then started and warmed to attest to its health.

All of the rental vehicles had been hired from different firms with one of three Swiss VISA cards, which were linked to relatively small cash accounts in Geneva banks. Throughout the early morning, Hauser would have gone systematically from glove compartment to glove compartment, inserting typewritten notes into each rental agreement. Long after the cars were abandoned, and hopefully recovered by their irate owners, the messages in German would intentionally appease:

"Terribly sorry for the inconvenience. Please forgive and charge our account."

Eckhardt had developed a consummate respect for Hauser, and he trusted his technical judgments implicitly.

He could picture the diminutive, muscled ex-motorcycle racer gleefully flying through the rainy streets of Munich, flitting from one machine to another, fretting like a pit manager at Le Mans. . . .

Then there was Francie Koln.

As Secondary Tail and Emergency Decoy, Francie was

going to have an extremely unpleasant day. She would spend all morning outdoors, within five hundred meters of the Marienplatz, wearing her Walkman, waiting for her cue. If she had ever harbored fantasies about the romantic life of an espionage agent, today she would surely be cured of such notions.

Francie's tasks were somewhat more difficult than Ettie Denziger's, inasmuch as she was the Team's "character actress." Inherently she possessed all of Ettie's dynamic qualities, yet she could play against her own type and was therefore called upon to do so with regularity. Her specialty was going completely unnoticed, and she had practiced donning this cloak of invisibility until details of her physical and personality traits were obscured, and encounters with her quickly forgotten.

Her form was lithe and athletic, so she wore bland, oversized shirts and fatigue-like trousers. Her hair was dark brown and of a naturally groomed texture, so she refrained from washing it much while in the field. She would pull it back into a tight bun and don thick glasses to dull the liveliness of her hazel eyes. Everything suggested such a total lack of sexuality that men would look at her and fairly grimace when she topped it all off with an expression that her mother would have called "*farbissiner.*"

Today, Francie would fairly disappear within her operational area. Wearing a dull raincoat, a floppy hat and her Walkman, she would be forced to listen to blank static. She would read passages from a mundane work on the life of Wagner, and she would move from café to café, never lingering for more than half an hour, yet constantly forced to order food for which she had no appetite.

She would wait, and by midafternoon she would be sick to death of eating. . . .

Eckhardt moved forward through his mental checklist,

arriving at the image of one of his favorite comrades. Harry Webber was the elder of the primary field team, and thoughts of him were always sure to improve Eckhardt's mood.

Austrian born, Webber frequently amused the younger members of Special Operations with his tortured dialect of a working-class Viennese. He was close to forty, tall, bony, stooped and mostly bald. His sharp eyes were creased with smile lines, his sideburns going grey. His hawkish sly nose and quick smile completed the demeanor of some sort of comic cabaret master, constantly on the verge of tossing off one-liners which served to levitate even the gravest of situations.

On *Flute*, Harry Webber would be serving as the Team's Janitor, with a secondary function as Emergency Decoy.

As with all complex military missions, *Operation Flute* had a window within which it would have to be executed. After a certain amount of elapsed time, the operation could no longer be considered secure, and it would have to be abandoned until some future date and place. Today was *Flute*'s final day.

Whether or not the mission was on, at given intervals this morning the primary team members would take to the streets of Munich. Harry Webber would appear at the first of the five safe houses. In one hand, he would have the long fingers of a tall, blonde resident female agent, compartmentally ignorant but quite beautiful. On his rain-soaked face, Harry would sport a lurid grin, suggesting an early morning dalliance.

It would take the couple less than fifteen minutes to sanitize each house. First, wearing surgical gloves, they would sweep for "giveaways," incriminating items forgotten under pre-combat pressure. These were seldom if ever found, and part of the reason that Harry's comrades loved him so was that his admonitions to transgressors were always executed, post-operation, in a quiet place far from the sonar ears of Hans-Dieter Schmidt.

Next, from his leather shoulder satchel, Webber would remove two cans of Vichy Basic Homme after-shave spray. In recent years, Department had decided that it was dangerously time-consuming to thoroughly wipe a safe house for fingerprints. Instead, a liquid had been developed by the Magicians. Applied with an atomizer, the substance served to break down the oils left by wayward fingers, making it nearly impossible to lift a latent print.

Like housekeepers on Benzedrine, Webber and his partner would quickly spray nearly everything in the room that had a nonporous surface. They would do table legs, telephones, chair arms, picture frames, door handles, bathroom fixtures and even magazines. Granted, for a time each flat would smell like a cathouse in Port Said, but soon the odor, along with the initial stickiness, would fade.

At last, after a final once-over, Webber would deposit a fat envelope on a conspicuous tabletop. As with Hauser's cars, it would contain a typed note of apology to the owner and five hundred deutsche marks.

By midmorning Webber would have sanitized all of the safe houses and dismissed his partner. Then, he would spend all day if necessary, sitting in his truck in a private garage in Schwabing, listening to the radio. . . .

Eckhardt, still lost in the half-reveries of pre-mission review, did not realize that he was smiling stupidly.

"Warum bist du so glücklich?" Rainer Luckmann had finished his *Frühstück* and washed the dishes. He had removed his black leather alpine parka, and with pistol on belt was down on the floor. With shoe toes on the yellowed kitchen linoleum, hands on the grey salon carpet, he was doing push-ups.

"Thinking of Webber," Eckhardt explained.

"*Neun . . . Zehn . . .* He's getting too old for this work."

"*Du Arschloch . . .* he's at his peak. Relaxed, unlike us. And don't do too many. Spoil your aim."

Luckmann obediently switched to sit-ups, but first he took a drag from his cigarette, which was perched in a metal ashtray on the kitchen table.

The stench of the tobacco made Eckhardt want one too. He reached into the pocket of his coat for a pack of Rothmans and lit up with a disposable lighter. The Great Game—as the British liked to call the intelligence business—took its toll. All of the primary team members were fit, but all of them smoked. Tony wondered if the entire team were rounded up for questioning and deprived of their cigarettes, they might all begin to sing like a flock of California lovebirds.

Hans-Dieter Schmidt, Eckhardt was sure, would also be smoking at this very moment. He would be hunched over his desk at Kinder-Spiel GMBh, his bogus toy import-export firm, staring at three black telephones like an optimistic vulture. The small office, filled with maps, catalogs and shipping forms, would be foggy with smoke. Schmidt would not move from his chair, the only evidence of his anticipation the ravaged red-and-white packs of Krone filters at his fingertips.

Schmidt's usually optimistic expression would be devoid of all humor as he waited for word from a team of Casuals. The Casuals were local resident operatives whose only function would be to identify the opening moves of the Target, report in, and then quit the mission.

Eckhardt sighed as he marveled at the complexity of the operation, the number of personnel involved. In modern times, the idea that a lone assassin could successfully tail a well-protected quarry and then execute the mission solo was a concept relegated to works of Fleming fiction. To do the job properly and, most important, to survive the episode, you needed support. There were very few world-class intelligence apparatuses which could work as noncompetitively with their own national counterparts. Eckhardt took pride in his fellow countrymen's abilities to cooperate, compartmentalize, maintain security, and still execute a sophisticated mission. Today, *Operation Flute* would involve the facilities and personnel of Diplomatic Security, Civilian Intelligence, Military Intelligence, Air Force Intelligence and Special Air Operations.

If *Flute* succeeded, the credit would be ravenously consumed by all. But if it failed, everyone would also eat his "helping of straw."

Perhaps this attention to operational detail somehow served as psychological compensation for the Missing Factor—the Unknown Quantity. That single nebulous entity was inevitably the Target, for while preparation might be perfect, everyone in proper position, you never knew precisely what HE was going to do.

Amar Kamil.

Was he still in his room at the Continental on Max-Joseph Strasse? The Watchers had been at it all night, sealing the hotel as best as they could without blowing the mission. At last report, 0120 hours, Kamil had retired. But who could be sure?

And then, if and when he finally appeared, would Kamil play the game? Would he proceed as he had done for four days running, to his "office" beneath the Stachus? And if he did so, when he finally emerged, would he still have the sexual appetite for a risky call on his paramour in Bogenhausen?

So many variables. So many chances. So much reliance on luck and fate. It all began to seem suddenly foolish to Eckhardt. Bordering, in fact, on the impossible.

They had been tracking the terrorist across Europe for nearly three months, yet he always seemed to evade their grasp, like an evil magician. At times, Eckhardt had to remind himself of the importance of the mission, and he would hark back to the initial briefing, when the Team was assigned to *Operation Flute*.

"What did he do now?" he had asked Schmidt when the commander first announced their target. Kamil certainly had a bloody resumé, but he had not yet committed an act nefarious enough to warrant execution.

"He blew an American airliner out of the sky."

"Hornesby?" Rainer Luckmann had asked breathlessly, whispering the name of the sleepy Scottish town into which the flaming wreckage had slammed, along with its 262 passengers.

"Yes."

"Then why don't the Americans get him?" Eckhardt had posed.

"Because they would have to have an eyewitness, Kamil's fingerprints, and an Act of Congress to do it," Schmidt had said with a mixture of pity and scorn.

Eckhardt needed no more reasons, for Kamil was now responsible for mass murders that cut across international lines. But he also wondered whether the Team had finally met their match.

He sucked on his cigarette, watching Luckmann perform his exercises, and his stomach began to churn again.

The telephone rang.

Luckmann stopped in mid sit-up. Eckhardt flicked his head toward a corner of the salon where the dirty white instrument sat on a small wooden table.

It rang again.

Luckmann sprang to his feet, but Eckhardt was there first, snatching up the receiver. He forced himself to produce a normal tone, even a touch of drowsiness.

"Morgen."

"Grüss Gott." It was Hans-Dieter's basso voice. "Is this Herr Adler?"

"I'm sorry." Tony was already nodding at the expectant Rainer. "You have the wrong number."

"Entschuldigen Sie, bitte."

Schmidt hung up and Eckhardt's receiver clattered into the cradle simultaneously. He was already moving to pick up his small overnight bag. Luckmann threw his jacket on and pulled a black leather cap onto his head. Neither of the two men spoke as they examined the rooms, quickly, one last glance. They had done it twice already. It was just habit.

"Ready?" Eckhardt faced Luckmann in the middle of the salon. Rainer patted the small bulge under his jacket.

"Ready."

"Wir gehen."

———

The splattering of the cold rain sounded suddenly like ball bearings on steel plate, but Eckhardt, hatless, ignored it. Alone, he walked slowly across Kossener Strasse to the dull blue Fiesta parked in front of the church, opened the door, slipped into the front seat, deposited his satchel in the rear, briefly warmed the engine and eased out into the street. The rain was bouncing up white halos around the parked cars in Unter Sendling, and hardly anyone else was driving. He swung around the church, headed north on Zillertal and stopped fifty meters up the block.

Luckmann waited by the apartment-house door, as if reluctant to brave the downpour. He counted to a full thirty seconds and, satisfied that no other vehicle had followed Eckhardt, went out into the street. He walked casually toward the corner, headed up Zillertal Strasse and jumped into the passenger seat, welcoming the growing warmth of the engine.

"Ein dreckiger Tag," Luckmann spat, complaining about the weather. He stuffed his bag into the rear seat while Eckhardt pulled away, taking a slow right onto Otztaler and heading east toward the center of the city.

"It's going to stay this way," said Eckhardt, concentrating on keeping his speed down. *Nothing above third gear,* he told himself. "Better get used to it."

Luckmann blew out a breath and looked at the little cloud. "Can I at least take an umbrella?"

"As long as you don't use it." Eckhardt smiled.

"Fuck you."

They were already on Lindwurm, only a block away from the Theresienwiese. During the Oktoberfest, the massive playground had been filled with revelers downing ten-liter pitchers of beer and then happily regurgitating kilos of broiled oxen, grilled fish and pork sausage after wild rides on the Tri Star or the roller coaster. Today it was only an empty grey flattop crossed by the occasional pedestrian trudging through soggy snow.

"The radio," Eckhardt ordered.

"*Jawohl, Hauptmann,*" Rainer sarcastically obeyed.

The Fiesta's cheap Sanyo had been extracted from the dash and deposited in the trunk. In its place, as with all the primary team's vehicles, was a creation of the Department's Magicians.

On the outside, the black, high-tech AM/FM was a Blaupunkt Frankfurt. On the inside, it was all Tadiran. "A German radio with a Semitic soul," as Hans-Dieter described it. The receiver contained some unusual features uncommon to simple car stereos.

Below the tuning display were six preset buttons. The three on the right functioned normally and could be preset to choice commercial stations. The three on the left were set to engage only the operational frequencies of *Flute.* While the "Blaupunkt" contained no apparent tape player, inside was a sixty-minute, continuous-loop microcassette.

Pushing the radio's power knob, rather than turning it, activated only the cassette and the operational frequencies. The tape played a prerecorded local pop station, from which all references to time, day and date had been edited. The disc jockey was a female.

From her chilly veranda in Bogenhausen, Ettie Denziger would control all broadcasts to the primary team. Through her modified Walkman, she would monitor Munich police traffic. Her telephone, seemingly one of those push-button, clock-radio extravaganzas, served a dual function. It received incoming calls, yet through it Ettie could also broadcast to the Blaupunkts over a powerful UHF transmitter. She could switch operational frequencies with numbered combinations on the push-button handset.

Ettie's coded messages would be brief. When necessary, she would override the sultry taped disc jockey with a "weather report" or a "birthday greeting," offering team up-dates, instructions or frequency changes. Excepting a special alteration to Eckhardt's Blaupunkt, there were no provisions for two-way conversations.

Ettie liked it that way. No one could talk back to her.

Rainer reached over and punched the power knob on the radio. Immediately the tape engaged in the middle of a Dire Straits recording of "Private Investigations." Luckmann laughed, but Eckhardt was concentrating on the traffic. He was following a green-and-white Audi police car, and his knuckles tightened under his leather gloves.

Luckmann pushed the far left preset button, engaging the first operational frequency. It added no static to the taped broadcast, as only Ettie's voice could actually open the wave.

Eckhardt stared past the droning wipers of the Fiesta. He blew out a breath when he turned onto Kapuziner Strasse, as the police car continued on Lindwurm. Traffic was still light, and he wondered if the massive hangovers of January's *Fasching* festival had kept most of Munich in bed today. It was not good. No traffic meant less police work, and he wanted the police to be very busy today.

The Neuer Sudl Friedhof appeared ahead, the grey stones

of the cemetery pressed under a white curtain of steamy fog. Eckhardt turned onto Thalkirchner and stopped the car.

"Go see your poor Tante Hilde," he said.

Luckmann groaned and walked off into the cemetery.

Eckhardt moved on, quickly found a space, and parked. He left the engine running, the radio on. He turned off the wipers, opened the window a crack, and lit a cigarette.

After a moment, there was a knock on the passenger window. He opened the door to admit a tall redheaded girl, who fairly fell into the front seat, shivering under her long woolen coat.

"Liebchen." Tony leaned over to kiss the girl. She looked startled at first, then she remembered and kissed back. Tony mentally shook his head, but he said nothing. He might have to kiss her all day long, and there were worse ways to wait.

Long ago the Department had decided that a single man waiting in a car was a suspicious sight. Two men was sacrilege. However, a loving couple usually elicited nothing more than a smile.

The girl was a resident consular employee, totally compartmentalized, knowing virtually nothing. Her cover was light, and to an inquisitive policeman she would respond with blushes and confess to no more than a recent one-nighter with 'Franz,' as she had been told to refer to Eckhardt. She opened her coat, then the top button of a cream silk blouse, and moved closer to Tony, who stretched one arm around her shoulders.

"Could be worse," the girl said, smiling shyly. "At least you're good looking." It would probably be the most exciting day of her diplomatic career.

"Shh," Eckhardt whispered in her hair. "Let's listen to the radio."

He wondered if this couples routine might be wearing thin. He was certain that Department must be aware of it too. *Soon they'll be using pairs of children,* he thought. *Or worse than that, midgets.* The image brought a smile, quickly quelled by a glimpse of Luckmann in the cemetery, mourning no one in the rain.

At 10:10, Amar Kamil had finally left the Continental, prompting his grateful Watchers to make a public telephone call to Kinder-Spiel GMBh in Westend. In turn, Hans-Dieter Schmidt had promptly dialed 551570, got the desk at the hotel, and asked for room 210. He held his breath for five rings, and when no one answered he hung up and began dialing again, sending all of the primary team members into the streets.

The chase was on, but from this point forward it had to be played as a courtship rather than a pursuit. The Department's military psychologists had made extensive studies. Animals in the wild sensed when they were being hunted. Sentries guarding enemy bases seemed to feel it when they were about to be taken down. Even in the crowded streets of a major city, Targets could often smell a tail.

Amar Kamil could not now be followed in the classic sense. He would be picked up by Casuals at various points, the sightings not even reported, and left to go on his way. If he did not reasonably adhere to the pattern required by the mission, *that* would be reported and *Operation Flute* would be postponed. This was where luck would become a major player in the game.

So far, Kamil was cooperating. He walked out of the Grand Hotel Continental and stood under the large green-and-gold awning, seemingly sniffing the weather, or perhaps expecting some other scent. He was wearing an expensive, olive, Calvin Klein raincoat. It was long and supple. A royal blue silk scarf with delicate paisley ends was wrapped around his throat. His short, wiry dark hair was covered by a soft,

19

brimmed grey cap. He carried a briefcase in one hand and a folded umbrella in the other. It would be fairly easy to track him today, if he did not alter his attire.

He went into the hotel's underground lot and came out driving an immaculate, black four-door BMW 316. He switched on the wipers and moved down Max Joseph, making a right on Otto Strasse, at least seeming to be heading for the Stachus. That was when the first set of Casuals made their call, describing Kamil's dress for the day.

While the primary team hurried out to assume their first-stage positions, Kamil continued driving. Now, as long as he did nothing totally unexpected, there would be no more Casual reports to Schmidt until the second stage.

On the corner in front of the Justizpalast a middle-aged man was walking a shivering German shepherd. He watched the BMW as it *passed* the Karlsplatz, but he was not alarmed. The wide double thoroughfare of Sonnenstrasse was one-way on this side. Kamil would have to make a U-turn at Schwan-thaler, cross the tram line and double back if he was indeed headed for the Stachus.

The man crossed over onto the broad median strip of Sonnenstrasse. His shepherd seemed happier to be among the tall trees, though they were winter-dark and threadbare, drip-ping with water. The man stood, staring up at the huge white Mercedes-Benz sign over the curved set of five-story stone offices on the north side of the square. He looked as though he longed for such a luxurious vehicle, though he was actually counting the endless seconds.

When the black 316 passed him, heading back the other way, he smiled and bent down to pat his grinning companion.

For the past four days, Amar Kamil had been coming from his hotel to the Stachus. Sometimes he made elaborate detours through the Innenstadt, but he always arrived at the same place. Even in winter, the Stachus was one of Europe's most frenetic squares. Above ground, there was a large circular fountain, with hundreds of jets ringing the circumference, spraying white arching fingers into a central geyser. Lining the stone square on its north and southeast were two massive, semicircular business edifices of an unappealing mustard color.

Grand access to the Stachus was from the east, through the grey medieval arches of the Karlstor, which looked like the entrance to a moated castle. Below the Stachus, accessed by wide stairs and escalators, was a sprawling shopping center and pedestrian mall, spidered with passages leading to the trams and the S-Bahn station.

It was into this subterranean world that Kamil had descended each day. One of the many mall shops was a small jewelry concern—by appointment only. It was owned by a man named Friedrich Hart, who was actually Horst Schmitter, a senior intelligence officer of the Red Army Faction, more commonly called the Bader-Meinhoff Gang. Apparently Kamil had some interesting business with Schmitter, but as far as the *Flute* personnel were concerned, at this point that information was irrelevant.

On the first two days, after spending some hours with Schmitter, Kamil had gone to visit a woman in Bogenhausen. He had been seeing the woman on and off for a year, and by the nature of her appearance—blonde, buxom and athletic—the encounters were assumed to be sexual. An extremely loose tail was placed on her, although no electronic surveillance. Yesterday, she had been out of town, visiting a girlfriend in Freising. Today she was back at home, and it was hoped that Kamil's appetite had caught up with him in the past forty-eight hours.

The Casual and his canine companion watched as Kamil's BMW passed the Hypobank on the northern corner of the Stachus. The car pulled into the indoor parking lot. The

Casual knew that attendants received the vehicles there, so the Target, whose name and function he did not know, would shortly emerge. He waited for a break in the traffic on Sonnenstrasse, then hurried across the road with the shepherd. The downpour had receded into a chilly drizzle, and he sat down on one of the large stone stools next to the fountain. He began to play with the dog, who happily responded to cuffs on the ears and short *woofs* from his master.

This Casual was no amateur. In his youth, he had worked for British Intelligence during World War II, as a deep cover agent in Berlin. Though long retired, over the past ten years "Johann" had performed thirteen brief but essential tasks for Hans-Dieter Schmidt. He had a vast wealth of street experience, and could "watch" a target almost without looking at him.

Kamil emerged from the parking garage, crossing the Karlsplatz, using his black umbrella as a walking stick. Johann was confident that Kamil was headed for the stairs leading down to the subterranean mall. In a moment, his role would be over, another clean entry in the weathered old intelligence diary he kept in his head.

But Kamil made a sharp left and headed straight for the arches of the Karlstor.

Johann continued playing with the shepherd, yet he blinked in the rain as he watched Kamil's receding back. The quarry was passing below the large Zeiss sign on the east side of the square, heading for the endless expanses of the pedestrian way on Neuhauserstrasse, where he could disappear in a half-minute.

Johann walked quickly to the Wienerwald at the south end of the square. He stepped into a yellow-framed telephone booth, threw 20 pfennig into the slot and dialed Kinder-Spiel. The shepherd whined, sensing its master's discomfort. It was 10:32.

Hans-Dieter answered before the first ring had stopped.

"Kinder-Spiel."

"*Morgen,* Hans. This is Johann."

"How are you, Johann?"

"Fine, fine. Listen Hans, I know we were supposed to meet Leo for luncheon, but he had to go east for the day."

"Really?" Hans's voice barely betrayed his concern. "Are you sure?"

"Oh, yes. I'm sure. Sorry about the inconvenience."

"Not at all. Perhaps some other time. I guess you'll have the day off, then."

"Yes. *Wiedersehen*, Hans."

"*Wiedersehen.*"

Both men terminated. Schmidt now had a difficult decision to make. Kamil had deviated, had not entered the Stachus. He was moving east on Neuhauser. Johann had used the word *go,* so Kamil was on foot. He might return to the Karlsplatz, or he might do something altogether unexpected. If he had already sensed a tail, then *Flute* was blown anyway. Schmidt decided to move in a pawn.

He called Ettie in Bogenhausen. When she hung up with him, she made her first broadcast on Frequency A. Her voice, as languid and as casual as that of the female disc jockey now chattering over the Blaupunkts, cut in with a brief commercial announcement.

"Now, all you lovely *Münchner* girls, I know it's raining a bit today, but there is a big sale on at Berlmeyers on Neuhauser. You really should not miss it. Hats, business cases, umbrellas and coats 30 percent off for *Fasching!*"

The message was intended for Francie Koln, as Innerstadt was her operational area. But every one of the primary team knew what the relay meant.

Still parked next to the cemetery, Eckhardt recoiled from the redhead and lit up a cigarette. She did not immediately realize what had happened and took it quite personally.

In an open parking lot in Marstallplatz, on the eastern

side of the National Theatre, Peter Hauser sat in a maroon Audi 80. It was the only "power car" in the primary fleet, and as Hauser heard Ettie's first report, he realized that all of his motor pool work was going down the toilet. He slammed the steering wheel with a fist.

In Schwabing, Harry Webber was inside a large, leased private garage. The cab of his long, green Mercedes delivery van was open, and he sat on the running board, listening to the radio and munching on a sandwich of sliced *Schinken*. Hearing Ettie's report, he did not even miss a bite. He had been on too many missions. It was still early in the game.

Francie Koln stopped short when she heard Ettie's announcement. Her Walkman used the same three operational frequencies as the mobile Blaupunkts, but it played no decoy tape, so the voice startled her as it boomed through the blank static to which she'd been listening all morning.

She was two hundred meters from the Marienplatz, walking north through the pedestrian mall on Theaterinstrasse. She cursed herself for having lost concentration, wandered too far from the first-stage area. She quickly spun from the distant vision of the Siegestor triumphal arch, smothered in smoky fog, and she hurried back toward the spoke of her assigned compass. She cut west into Schaffler, willing the twin gold spires of the Frauenkirche to grow larger, loom over her, and then she was past them, nearly running.

If she reached Neuhauser quickly, she might beat Kamil, if he had not yet turned into a side street. Her stomach was bloated, the Wagner biography heavy in her bag. She was sweating, panting, and she struggled to remember what Ettie had just said—"Hats, business cases, umbrellas and coats." All right, she had seen over twenty recent photos of Kamil and now she had a good description of the accoutrements as well. She *had* to try and pick him up. . . .

Perhaps only two minutes had passed and Johann was

still standing in the phone booth at the Stachus, miming a conversation into the dormant instrument. He squinted through the fogged glass at the medieval teeth of the Karlstor, and he began to smile. Yes, Kamil was now strolling casually *back* through the gate, carrying a newspaper.

Amar Kamil was no amateur either. He had simply engaged in a brief detour before he descended to visit Schmitter. If he were being classically tracked, he would feel the resultant shake-up, sense the panicked moves in the environment.

Johann called Hans-Dieter, hoping that his relaxed appearance was a sufficient mask to his hammering heart. He began to laugh, gesturing grandly and making his presence in the proximate booth seem completely innocent. "My God, I'm such a fool Hans," he said. "I was looking at the wrong date! Of course we'll have lunch with Leo today."

"Are you sure, Johann?" Schmidt asked. "You can make me crazy sometimes."

"I am sure, my friend."

Within seconds, Ettie was excusing herself to her "radio audience," announcing a correction. The sale at Berlmeyers was for *tomorrow*.

Already on Neuhauser and close to panic, Francie suddenly snapped her head up to the gorgeous sound of Ettie's voice. She sat down on a metal bench, leaned back, closed her eyes and then let the rain pound her face. . . .

———

For the next two hours, Amar Kamil stayed beneath the surface of the Stachus, which, despite the continuing rain, became effervescent with Munichers on lunch hour. Excepting a "mother-and-daughter" team who had immediately replaced Johann and his dog, all of the Casuals had been called off. Now, the only operatives remaining on *Flute* were the primary team and a few emergency backups. The local residents who had briefly participated would only learn of the mission's nature if it succeeded and the news reached the morning papers.

The two remaining non-primaries sat in the Wienerwald, taking an extremely long *Mittagessen*. The "mother" was not really a Casual, but a photoanalyst from Department. The "daughter" was a clerk from the embassy cipher room. They were happily engaged in addressing invitations to the daughter's upcoming wedding, and no one bothered them.

On a signal from Ettie—a reference to a possible improvement in the weather confirming Kamil's return—everyone else had gone to his Stage Two position.

Eckhardt reluctantly dismissed his parking companion, who he had belatedly come to realize was really quite attractive and used an erotically disturbing eau de cologne. He honked twice, and Luckmann came trotting out of the cemetery, looking not too much worse for wear. Rainer had found a tomb with a suitable overhang under which he had properly engaged his grief.

They drove to the Prinzregenten Theater in Steinhausen, moved the car every thirty minutes and took turns grabbing something to eat and relieving themselves in public restrooms.

Peter Hauser happily put his Audi in gear, left the open lot in Marstallplatz and drove east to the Isar. He moved north on Widermayer along the river and parked by the sloping bank, fifty meters short of the Luitpold Bridge. He sat in the car, studying the enormous grey statues on the arched structure, watching a single elderly woman as she leaned on the metal fence near the steel-colored water, feeding white winter geese.

He did not dare leave the radio unattended, so he munched on various *Schmankerl* from a paper bag and drank black coffee from a thermos. On occasion, he slipped over to the passenger side, opened the door and peed onto the grass from a sitting position.

Harry Webber left the garage in Schwabing, drove across the river, and parked the delivery truck on Schönberg Strasse in Herzog Park. The neighborhood was dead quiet, and he went through two copies of *Stern,* one of *Quick,* saving the German edition of *Penthouse* for last. The bogus "letters" to the staff seemed that much more obscene in *Hochdeutsch,* and Harry actually laughed out loud at some of the more raucous "real-life" exploits.

Francie Koln, bereft of transportation, walked to her next station at the Odeonplatz, where Hitler had staged his abortive Beer Hall Putsch in 1923. There, near the high yellow facade of the Theatinerkirche, she found a small *Konditorei.* For the first time all day, she was happy to be inside a café. She went to the washroom, took off her sopping hat and dried her hair as best she could with a paper towel. Then she took a table near the front, readjusted her Walkman over her ears and actually managed to read a newspaper as she sipped coffee from a porcelain cup. She had already eaten enough for a week.

Hans-Dieter remained perched over his desk at Kinder-Spiel. He did not eat or drink, but he finished another pack of Krone.

Ettie made contact once, to change frequencies, and everyone switched to Channel B.

They waited. It could happen in the next five minutes, or not for five hours.

At 14:10, Amar Kamil appeared at the top of the Stachus escalator. He walked around the fountain and headed for the parking garage.

The women timed it perfectly. They collected their invitations, exited the Wienerwald and strolled arm in arm across the Karlsplatz. They walked slowly, further reducing the pace as they crossed under the Hypobank sign, chatting and giggling like schoolgirls. The nose of Kamil's 316 poked from the parking garage, offering a momentary side view of his face through the smoked glass as he eased out into traffic and headed north on Sonnenstrasse.

The two women quickly turned toward a bank of telephones.

"Kinder-Spiel." Schmidt must have snatched at his phone like a cat after a bird.

"Hans? It's Trude," the elder woman said, not even bothering to conceal her pleasure. "Don't forget to pick up Uncle Fritz at the station."

"Has he left yet?"

"Yes."

"Did you see him off?"

"Yes, yes."

It was a critical moment. Schmidt had to be absolutely sure that the target was positively identified. If 'Trude' was really convinced, then *he* could be as well.

"Okay, just tell me again what he looks like."

"Olive raincoat, grey cap, briefcase, umbrella." Trude added a touch of drama. "I told you, dear. You're so forgetful."

Hans ignored the playacting. "What was it you said about his skin?" he asked.

"Light, dear." A Circassian ancestor had given Kamil a somewhat non-Semitic complexion.

"Earlobes?"

"Detached."

"Yes." Now he tried to trick her, just to make sure she wasn't being overly enthusiastic. "Did he limp?"

Trude hesitated for a split second. Then she said, "No, silly. Of course not!"

"You're a good girl." Hans's voice was smiling.

"I know. *Wiedersehen*."

"*Bis später*." He hung up, made his decision in a micro-second, and called Ettie Denziger.

———

"Just a short interruption before we get on with some *fantastischen* tunes. Believe it or not, Münchner, tomorrow looks to be a sunny day! *Wirklich*, maybe even good enough for a Fasching picnic!"

At her café table, Francie Koln lifted her eyes from the paper. *Picnic*. That was it. Kamil was mobile.

She dropped a few coins onto the table, gathered her bag, pulled on her floppy tweed hat and left the *Konditorei*. The rain had almost completely let up, and it was now turning to a light, powdery snow.

Francie walked briskly north on Ludwig Strasse. She had to make the intersection with Von der Tann before Kamil got there. The midday traffic was thickening, and she was sure to beat him, but she kicked out a pace anyway.

In planning sessions, Peter Hauser had made a strong case for this route. He had been over it in his own car possibly thirty times, at all hours of the day and night. If Kamil was going to cut through the Innenstadt and cross the river toward Bogenhausen, this was always the best route. If he had other plans, what the hell did it matter?

Francie waited at the corner, fiddling inside her large handbag, her eyes shifted under the brim of her hat toward the Oskar von Miller Ring. Three minutes passed. Nothing. Then, suddenly, the BMW appeared right next to her, having come from behind up Ludwig. Kamil turned the corner onto Von der Tann, heading east. Francie ran her checklist: black BMW 316, single passenger, last four license digits 5734.

Hauser was right. Kamil was following the pattern. Francie would make no report. Now it was up to her comrades.

She had one more assignment, and she walked happily

after Kamil's car, watching it blend into traffic as it headed toward the river. Her steps were lighter now, her enormous tension fading as her chilled neck muscles began to relax.

She reached the American consulate at the corner of Königinstrasse. The Americans had great respect for their flag, and it had been pulled in from the desecrative weather. A pair of Marine guards stood outside at the main entrance to the old stone structure. Francie felt sorry for them.

There was a trash receptacle at the corner of Königin. She reached into her bag, came up with an apparently empty can of Tuborg and dropped it into the trash container. Then she walked across the street to the Englischer Garten, down to the large pond near the Japanese Teehaus, and stayed there, watching the ducks, keeping her eye on a pair of public phones not twenty meters away.

Peter Hauser picked up Kamil as the 316 cruised onto the Luitpold Bridge. He allowed three other cars to follow the BMW, then he cut into traffic and crossed the river. He smiled tightly as he drove. He had read the bastard's mind.

Harry Webber had already left Herzog Park and driven down to the west side of Bogenhausen. He swung the truck around a large high school, the Max-Joseph Stifts Gymnasium, and parked thirty meters south of the intersection of Bruckner and Röntgen. Traffic from the west side of Bogenhausen flowed naturally to the east side through this narrow funnel. Harry was smoking now; he used a plastic cigarette holder, something he could bite down on. To the west up Röntgen, he could see the low red-brick facade of a small hospital. Farther to the west, but not far enough he knew, was the Bogenhausen Police Station.

On the icy veranda at Number 1 Barbarossa Strasse in Bogenhausen, Ettie Denziger's body began to go rigid with tension. She had heard nothing since 14:17, when she had issued her last operational order. While she knew that no contact meant that Kamil was following the *Flute* plan, the waiting was torturous.

She turned her rocker more to the west, reached over and wiped the porch window with a soiled rag. Below her, the red roofs of Bogenhausen stretched away like gingerbread housetops in a fairy tale. The quiet borough was being dusted with light, flour-white snow, the narrow streets traversed by the occasional cautious driver. A few hunched figures emerged from the quaint houses and neighborhood shops. In the distance, Munich's spires stabbed at a slate-grey sky beneath the already fading daylight.

No one had arrived yet. It was a good time to change frequencies. Then she thought better of it. At this crucial juncture, someone might have a microchip failure.

She removed one of the Walkman's pronged phones from her right ear, leaving the left one in. She turned up the volume. In a few minutes, she would be monitoring the Munich Police band and simultaneously transmitting through the telephone handset.

She chewed on the wooden shaft of a paintbrush. Barbarossa Strasse, the main street of the neighborhood, stretched away to the west until it curved around the little Nazareth Church and disappeared. Traffic was one-way coming toward her. From the north, the small side streets were also one-way, cutting south across Barbarossa. Traffic-wise, it was a good spot for an entrapment.

Eckhardt's blue Fiesta was the first car to appear. It came cruising down Barbarossa and parked in the middle of the next block, south side, between Vogelweide and Wagenbauer.

Ettie worked her telephone handset, switching briefly to normal function. She called Hans-Dieter on the speed dialer.

"Kinder-Spiel."

"Are you open today?" Ettie asked quickly.

"Tomorrow. We're closing early."

"Yes. Maybe the weather will be better. Thank you."

Hans-Dieter hung up and opened a desk drawer, removing a Walkman similar to Ettie's. Yet with his device, one earpiece was tuned to the police band, the other to *Flute*'s operational frequencies. He had learned to be "ambi-aural." He pushed the headphones onto his dry bald pate.

The next car was Peter Hauser's Audi. Like Eckhardt, Hauser had detoured in order to overtake Kamil and arrive in the operational area first. He cruised past Eckhardt and Luckmann, quickly swung north to Stuntz Strasse and came down the one-way Walpurgis, parking halfway down the block facing Barbarossa.

After a few more seconds, the black BMW turned the corner near the Nazareth Church. Ettie dropped the opera-glass spectacles down over her eyes. A single driver. Last four plate digits, 5734.

Her breath was coming faster; she tried to calm it, the heat would fog the window. She worked the telephone handset and said, "Here's a birthday greeting from Inge Schwartz-kopf in Stuttgart, to her Uncle Oscar in Steinhausen: *'Herzlichen Glückwunsch zum Onkel Oscar.'*"

In their Stage Three positions all over Munich, the backs of the primary team members went stiff. *Flute* was about to go down.

Kamil parked his car on the north side of Barbarossa, almost directly across from Eckhardt's Fiesta. Tony mouthed silent nonsense to Rainer, and Rainer watched only Kamil.

Amar Kamil's paramour lived in a small apartment house on the northwest corner of Barbarossa and Walpurgis. Next to that was a small bakery shop with a yellow awning. On all of his visits, Kamil never went directly into the apartment. Sometimes he would just sit in the car for a bit, but usually he would enter the shop, take a table, watch the street for a while and then exit with a freshly baked gift.

Kamil got out of the BMW.

"*Er geht*," Luckmann whispered inside the Fiesta. Both men eased back on their door latches.

Kamil went into the bakery shop.

"Could be a few minutes now," said Luckmann, but now Eckhardt was also watching the shop, his muscles wound like steel suspension springs. His heart was hammering against his leather coat and his breathing was ragged. Inside his tight leather driving gloves, his hands were soaked. He quickly pulled the gloves off, threw them on the dash and smeared his palms on his slacks.

In less than sixty seconds, Kamil came out of the shop carrying two long paper bags. But he did not turn left toward the apartment. He turned right, and his keys were dangling from one hand.

"He's going for the car," Luckmann hissed.

"*Raus*," said Eckhardt, and he was out of the Fiesta, spinning quickly as he left the door ajar.

He stepped quickly across the road, registered a small blond child as the scarfed figure darted out of his way. He knew that Rainer was keeping pace as both their right hands flicked open their coats, emerging with the glistening Berettas.

They mounted the sidewalk and closed on Kamil's back. Fifteen meters. Now ten. Now five. They cocked the slides.

It was then that Kamil turned, and Eckhardt expected to see the snout of the Makarov pistol that he knew Kamil carried. But instead, what faced him was an expression of initial greeting, that quickly turned to surprised horror, and would haunt Tony Eckhardt for the rest of his unnatural life. . . .

It was over in six seconds, and then Eckhardt found himself walking back toward the car. His hands, entirely their own masters, worked the mechanism of his Beretta, reloading. He heard Luckmann breathing behind his left shoulder, the footsteps too quickly stamping the light dusting of new snow.

"*Nicht so schnell*," Tony said to Luckmann, though he, too, was staring at the growing form of the Fiesta, longing for its comfort, its shelter, its *speed*.

A tune played itself over in Eckhardt's mind, a litany of instruction: "Walk Don't Run." He had used it to calm himself under many similar pressure situations. He had never revealed his secret mantra to anyone, lest they think he was mad.

At the moment, he certainly *felt* the onset of insanity, for he was convinced that his target, now lying in a pool of blood on the sidewalk, was a victim of tragic misidentification. Yet, in the eternity of that moment, he had no choice but to behave as if the operation had been executed to perfection. He was responsible for the follow-through, the safety and escape of his people, and any incursion of self-doubt could mean doom for them all.

But he did not feel stable enough to drive. He suddenly shifted trajectory, walking around the front of the Fiesta. Luckmann took the cue immediately and jumped into the driver's seat, coming up with his own keys. Eckhardt got in, closed his door, said, "*Langsam, Rainer. Langsam.*" Luckmann nodded, pulling gently out of the spot. He turned right down Wogelweide, hissing a sigh of immense relief as he achieved second gear, then third.

It was at that moment that the Bulgarians appeared. No one had seen them. Not Ettie, Tony, Rainer or Peter. They had been sitting in a white Opel Kadett, two blocks back on Barbarossa. The perfect loose tail, they had not followed the Team. They had been there all day.

Peter Hauser started down Walpurgis, seeing Tony's car moving up ahead, knowing that they had *done it*. But as he reached the intersection with Barbarossa, a screaming woman came running across the road from where she had just had a close look at the bloody corpse. Peter was forced to slam his brakes; the nose of the Audi swerved in the slick snow and a white Opel Kadett jumped the intersection and went careening after Tony's Fiesta.

Ettie Denzinger knew that something was not right. Her heart fluttering like a trapped bird's, she watched Tony and Rainer take Kamil down. Yet almost immediately the Munich Police Band began to chatter like a cageful of apes.

"Bogen One, this is Ettstrasse. We have a reported shooting in your district, Barbarossa and Walpurgis."

It just couldn't have happened that fast. Even the most vigilant citizen would be temporarily shocked into inaction. Ettie reacted quickly, putting out a Public Service announcement.

"Münchners, driving conditions are worsening. Please be on your best behavior this afternoon."

As soon as Harry Webber heard *driving conditions*, he moved. He could already hear the hee-haw of a police siren approaching from the west, and he knew that ambulances would momentarily emerge from the hospital on Röntgen. His task was simple, yet exposed and dangerous.

He spun the wheel of the truck and drove the big Mercedes down toward the intersection of Röntgen and Bruckner. He gathered speed, hesitated as a Volkswagen crossed in front of him, then stabbed the accelerator and almost simultaneously stood hard on the brake pedal. The wheels locked and the truck swerved, its nose dipping toward the slick pavement. The left wheels rocked up for a second and Harry thought he might flip it, but then the vehicle settled perfectly, completely blocking the fork as car horns blared all around him.

He cut the engine, reached down and yanked the choke handle all the way out. It had a modified cable and valve, and in two seconds the carburetor was irreparably flooded.

Three green-and-white Audi police cars came speeding down Röntgen from the west, their beacons turning and sirens hawking. The first car, with a large number 96 painted on its hood, stopped just short of the side of Harry's cab. A young *Leutnant* jumped from the cruiser, throwing his arms up and screaming all at once.

"*Du blöde Sau!* Move that goddamn thing!"

Harry obediently reached for the keys. He turned hard and the engine whined, coughed and gurgled. But it did not start.

Webber rolled down his window, shrugged at the *Leutnant*, and smiled a stupid smile.

Ettie had also seen the white Opel cut in and follow Eckhardt. Just to make sure, she ran over the operational fleet in her mind. *We have no such car.*

She called Kinder-Spiel.

"*Ja*," Hans snapped.

"It's Hilde, Father."

"What film did you rent, dear?"

"Marlon Brando. *The Chase*."

"Sounds lovely. I'm looking forward."

"See you later then."

Hans-Dieter had also been monitoring the police band, and he also knew that things were happening too fast. But *The Chase?* Someone, other than the police, was after his team leaders. He called a number in Baumkirchen.

"Kentworth Air," a man answered in clipped British English.

"This is Mr. Harrington," said Hans. "Are you flying today?"

"We can be, Mr. Harrington."

"Thank you. I may have a delivery."

"Very good, sir."

Tony, Rainer and Peter each had four tickets in their possession for four different commercial flights. But if things were really too hot, the outgoing flights covered by German security, then an alternate was in order.

Kentworth Air was owned by Air Force Intelligence, its facilities available to all branches of the clandestine services. One of their aircraft, a modified DC–9 "cargo and medical" transport, had been sitting on the repair runway at Munich International for two days, a victim of mechanical difficulties. Within minutes, it was going to experience a miraculous recovery.

Francie Koln's code had popped in her ears less than a minute after she heard Harry receive his *go*. Ettie's voice sounded rather pleading.

"Münchner girls, now please listen carefully out there. We have a sad request from Martha Houe's mother in Blumenau. She misses you Marti, wherever you are. Please call her and all will be forgiven."

Francie had hoped that she would not be required to perform this next bit. She liked Americans so, they were always so friendly and generous, wanting to be everyone's best buddy. However, things were apparently not going too well, and besides, no one would be harmed by her gambit.

She had already reached the phones at the Japanese *Teehaus*. Thanks to the weather, no one was in the area. She reached into her coat pocket and removed the body of her Walkman. She opened the cassette player door, which was empty, and she pulled the plastic sprocket off the left-hand nub. There was a small button underneath.

She turned toward the American consulate; the grey stone hulk could be clearly seen through the trees. She pulled the earphones off her head, for she had been told that they might squeal madly, and she pressed the button.

Inside the Tuborg can, lying in the trash receptacle, the

gunfire simulator went off. It issued frightening reports, one after another, although it hardly gave off smoke. Both of the Marine guards instinctively went to their knees.

Francie could hear the dull popping as it echoed through the morning air. She was already on the telephone, dialing 110, the police emergency exchange.

"Munich Police. How can I help you?"

Francie was breathless; she needed no encouragement. "For God's sake come quick! Someone is shooting at the Americans!"

"What's that? Please, *Fräulein*, calm yourself."

"*Das amerikanische Generalkonsulat,* on Königinstrasse! Gunfire!"

She hung up the phone. Her hands were shaking. She began slowly walking north. There was a car waiting for her in a lot in Schwabing. She was trying to remember what *kind* of car.

In Hans-Dieter's ear the police band went mad. Half of the Munich fleet spun from their positions and headed toward the Englischer Garten. In response to requests for clarification, a captain at Ettstrasse came on the frequency and briskly announced that the security detachment at the American consulate had indeed confirmed gunfire, and if they didn't want to have another Munich Massacre on their hands, every available unit should get its ass over there.

But Hans-Dieter was still terribly concerned about his team leaders. Through the wild radio traffic, he realized that a certain ambitious Lieutenant Hess, Car 96, was still at his position at Bruckner and Röntgen. Hess was about to arrest the driver of a Mercedes truck and then ram the stalled vehicle out of the way.

Schmidt made a dangerous decision. He picked up the third black phone on his desk, punched the "hold" button, and cut into the police band.

"Hess in 96! Forget about the minor street crimes, you idiot, and get to the American consulate *now!*"

There was a moment's hesitation, and then the young *Leutnant*'s challenging voice broke over Schmidt's earphones.

"This is Hess in 96. Who the hell is that?"

"This is PERGER, you stupid swine! And if you ever want to see your family or your pension, you'll move! NOW!"

Perger, as Hans-Dieter well knew, was the Munich Chief of Mobile Control. He was also on vacation somewhere in Bayern, but hopefully in the confusion no one would immediately recall that fact.

Leutnant Hess radioed the other cars in his convoy. They backed out of the intersection and headed west for the American consulate.

Schmidt sat back and lit another Krone. His bald head was finally glistening. Thank God the Germans had not lost their penchant for obeying orders.

At Bruckner and Röntgen, Harry stepped down from the cab of his stalled truck. The only official remaining on the scene was an angry ambulance driver. His vehicle stood behind him, its beacons winking in frustration.

"I'll just go and call the office," Harry apologized. "They'll have a service truck here in five minutes."

"My patient will probably be dead in five minutes!" The attendant snapped.

Harry just shrugged and walked away. *Hopefully, your patient is* already *dead,* he said to himself.

He walked across the intersection to a small grocery store and lunch counter. Peter had checked it all out for him. He asked to use the bathroom, made for the facilities in the rear, then kept walking to the back of the store and went straight out the delivery door.

He crossed to the Bohmerwaldplatz and got into a dull beige Volkswagen Golf. He would drive the car to his garage in Schwabing. There, he would eat and change his clothes from a supply in the trunk. He would also switch the plates, from rental to civilian, and then wait a full twelve hours. No matter the crime, Munich Police did not maintain serious, traffic-disturbing roadblocks for longer than twelve hours.

In the morning, he would begin the long drive to Berlin.

Eckhardt and Luckmann knew they were being pursued, but they did not know by whom.

They were already out on 94, heading for the airport, passing the huge rail yards of the S-Bahn-Abstellbanhof. The white Opel was maybe a hundred meters back, but it was gaining. Turning in his seat, Eckhardt could see the two occupants. They might have been plainclothesmen, but their white faces had that squared-off, slabby look of Russian Intelligence muscle. The passenger was sitting in the *rear* seat, and seemed to be holding a mobile phone. That was not a good sign. Shooters rode in the rear seat.

If they *were* Germans, Tony and Rainer would have to lose them, or give it up. There would be no battles with West German authorities.

Hauser's maroon Audi was behind the Opel but still blocked by one car between them. As the Opel gained on Rainer, Hauser swung dangerously out into the right lane around his civilian interloper, pulling back in behind the white Kadett.

"Who are they?" Rainer asked, flicking his eyes from the rearview mirror to the road. He was concentrating on making the next leg without having an accident. Traffic to the airport was picking up.

To Eckhardt's dismay, he peripherally noted a spectral oscillation from the south. He turned again in his seat to see three police Audis approaching up the access road from the train yards. They were clearly in a hurry.

"I don't know who the hell they are, but they're using a radio phone and they're not calling my mother."

Then the Bulgarians floored it.

"Here they come," Rainer hissed. He had his own foot to the floor, but it didn't help. "Tell Peter from now on I want a goddamn Mercedes."

The Opel swung into the open right lane, growing larger. Eckhardt could see now that its rear windows were open.

"Do you have a plan?" he asked hoarsely.

"No, but I'll do *something*."

The Opel pulled alongside and Eckhardt saw the pair of meaty hands holding an ugly object.

"Scorpion!" he yelled.

Rainer slammed the brakes as the machine pistol began to chatter. The Opel dashed by and the shooter had to shift quickly and awkwardly, but the burst of 9-millimeter parabellums punched low through the right side of the Fiesta, the first three hammering into Eckhardt's right leg and knee as he screamed, and a fourth bullet shattering Rainer's side window as he snapped his head back.

Rainer immediately floored it again, turning the wheel hard to the left, nearly denuding the steel median rail, and he shot out around the nose of the Opel before they could get off another burst.

Peter Hauser saw the whole thing, and like a good backup man, he did not hesitate. The Opel driver had pumped his own brakes, swerving tail to the right, giving Hauser a perfect target. Peter punched the gas, aimed for the left front wheel, touched the brakes once before impact so that his bumper would dip, and smashed into the Bulgarians at eighty kilometers per hour.

It was not a deflecting blow. He drove straight on, hurling the white Opel off the right shoulder, where it impacted with a metal light pole.

Peter regained his course. He shook his head. Some-thing was dripping onto his left eye and he swiped it away with a glove. He had not remembered to attach his seatbelt, and he looked at the steering wheel top. It was deformed. *Some racing driver,* he thought, and he actually smiled. The car was still functioning. That was why he loved German cars.

He looked in the rearview. Three police cars. He looked ahead. Luckmann was fading. Peter would not get away, but he could make sure that Rainer and Tony did.

There was a *Strassenarbeiten* sign up ahead on the left. The guardrail was down, and a few trucks and tractors sat collecting snow on their roofs. Hauser spun the wheel, dashed madly across into the oncoming traffic, and headed south amid a cacophony of car horns, back toward Munich.

Obediently, the police followed him.

Hans-Dieter and Ettie both heard the radio chatter of the massive police convoy that went after Peter Hauser. They lis-tened helplessly as it closed on him, south to the Innsbrucker-ring, then onto E77 and west to the Perlacher Forest. From the frantic exchanges of the hunt, they could visualize his mad dash, not knowing why he was performing it, but only that Peter Hauser most certainly had a good reason. The voices of the German policemen took on the heated excite-ment of the kill.

"This is Two-Nine. He just drove right into the trees."

"Forty-Seven, take your men to the north."

"This is Ettstrasse. Don't lose him now."

"Two-Seven. He's out of the car. He's hurling something away."

"What is it, Two-Seven?"

"Six-Two. He's into the *Forst.*"

"Don't lose him Six-Two! Or we'll be in there all god-damn night!"

Hans-Dieter had no time to despair, for something else crackled over the police band. Something worse.

Tony Eckhardt's blood was collecting in a pool on the floor of the car. He could not move, and he didn't dare touch his leg, not even to apply an improvised tourniquet.

Rainer had reached back to his bag and dragged it into the front seat. One-handed, he extracted an electric razor and cracked the cover off it against the dashboard. He pulled the right knob off the Blaupunkt and seated the razor's cord plug in the open receptacle. It was a last resort. He spoke into the microphone, breaking directly into the police band.

"Hier ist 101. Es ist ein Unfall passiert."

Hans-Dieter fairly bolted from his chair at Kinder-Spiel. It was Luckmann's voice, and in this case *road accident* meant a badly wounded soldier. Hans immediately picked up his police line and slammed the hold button.

"One-Oh-One, you may investigate." He hung up and called Ettie.

"Guten Abend," she answered.

"Liebchen, it's Father. There's been a road accident or something. I'll be home late. Why don't you get some rest."

There was silence on the other end.

"Liebchen?" He had no patience for the delay.

"Yes, Father. Fine."

Hans hung up and dialed on another phone. When it rang through he said, "Hello, this is Kinder-Spiel. I'd like a Janitor in here to clean up please. Yes, now."

He collected his things and left the office.

Eckhardt was gripping the dashboard with white-knuckled fingers. His eyes were squeezed shut, but he made no sound. Luckmann was looking for the prearranged exit, only a kilometer from the airport. He snatched a glance at his partner.

For the first time since leaving Tel Aviv many months before, Luckmann suddenly burst into Hebrew.

"Tagid li, Eytan. Ma karah lanu?"

Eckhardt, despite his pain, admonished his partner in German.

"My name is Tony Eckhardt, Luckmann," he groaned, "and I don't *know* what the hell happened. But you will speak German until we're either dead, or at home. Understood?"

"Okay, *Eckhardt*." Rainer spat the name. "But fuck you, because in ten minutes we *will* be either dead or on our way home."

They pulled off the highway and drove straight down an industrial road for half a kilometer. It was growing dark. The ambulance was waiting, its rear doors yawning. The beacon was unlit.

It took the doctor and his assistant less than twenty seconds to lift Eckhardt into the rear of the ambulance. They were not gentle, and he tried not to yell.

In the meantime, Rainer stripped the Fiesta. He took the bags, the Blaupunkt, the microphone, Tony's gloves, but there was nothing to do about the blood. He hoped that it would snow hard for days, and no one would bother about the abandoned car.

Then they were all in the ambulance and it began to move slowly toward the airport. The doctor was a combat surgeon, an ex-paratrooper, and he worked quickly, snapping at his male assistant.

"Morphine."

"No morphine," Eckhardt grunted.

"Shut up," the surgeon barked. Then he turned to Rainer. "It's bad, but he'll live. Strip him."

Eckhardt lay on the folded gurney. The blood had stopped flowing, mostly due to the cold. Rainer began to gently remove his clothes.

"Get them off him! We've got ten minutes!"

They worked quickly, injecting Eckhardt with a double dose of morphine extract and changing his clothes to hospital attire from a small wardrobe. The doctor dressed his wounds, covered the leg with a plastic sleeve, then quickly wrapped both limbs in elastic bandages as if the patient suffered from circulatory problems. He attached an infusion bag to one arm and hung it from a steel stanchion on the gurney.

"Shave his head," the doctor ordered.

The assistant hesitated.

"Shave it! He has to look like it's his last cancerous week, not like some fucked-up commando!"

A portable razor came out, and in two minutes Tony's hair was nubbed down to the scalp.

"And clean it up. Every hair."

The assistant bent to his task. From a black satchel, the surgeon removed a pair of ugly steel-rimmed spectacles. He roughly placed them on Eckhardt's face. Then he snapped a plastic medical bracelet onto one wrist.

"There's a uniform in the closet," the doctor said to Luckmann. Rainer stripped out of his clothes and destroyed his airline tickets, keeping the British passports, one for himself and one for Eckhardt. He donned a white lab coat, white trousers and a stethoscope.

Eckhardt's pain was becoming tolerable, but he hated the helpless drowsiness that was engulfing him. He felt the rolling of the ambulance, but he did not register the crucial, dangerous juncture as they arrived at Munich International's cargo gate.

He heard the driver say, "Kentworth Air. We've got one has to go to London."

When the security personnel, with their hard faces, grey

uniforms and dangling Uzi submachine guns, opened the rear doors, Eckhardt closed his eyes.

"Sshh," the doctor said to the intruders. "He's not long for this world."

A customs official checked their passports in silence.

Eckhardt dozed off for a short time, then he awoke inside a hazy grey tube as the DC–9 taxied down the runway. He was strapped to a mobile stretcher. There were regular airline seats to his right.

A door opened up forward. He managed to lift his head. Hans-Dieter appeared from the cabin, stonefaced, dressed as a flight engineer. He lumbered down the aisle.

Schmidt fell into a seat next to Eckhardt. He threw off his hat and tore open his tie, as if it might kill him like some poisonous constrictor.

"How are you?" Hans asked in Hebrew.

"Okay," Tony slurred. "But I might be gone again in a moment."

"Who were they?" Hans asked. "Kamil's people?"

"No." It was Luckmann's voice, from somewhere else. "Europeans. Maybe Eastern Europe."

"Where is everyone?" Tony's own voice sounded strange to him, a fragile echo.

"Mostly away," said Hans. "Ettie stays on, of course, but she'll be fine." Schmidt lit up a Krone, unhappy to have to relay the rest. "Peter took the police off you and headed for Perlacher Forest. Took them on a wild-goose chase, but they have him now. He did it for all of us. It's the only reason we're in the air now."

Tony stared up at the ceiling. He was weak; still he tried not to let the tears well up. The aircraft banked heavily to the right. It was flight-planned for London, but it would not see England tonight.

"Benni." Eckhardt suddenly called Hans by his real name.

46

He was not sure if he should go on. In this state, he knew that his judgment was hazy, his logic distorted. "It didn't feel right," he said. "The Target, I mean."

"I know," said Benni Baum. He patted Tony's hand. "You and I, we may be opening a fruit stand together."

Eckhardt was suddenly very awake. He stared at Baum, his eyes asking the question that was stuck in his throat.

"I just had a report from Ben-Zion." Benni smiled painfully. "A team of Watchers just made positive I.D. In West Berlin."

"Let me guess," said Luckmann's tired voice.

"That's right," said Benni, and he blew out a wreath of smoke. "Amar Kamil."

Eckhardt turned his head and stared back up at the ceiling, and this time the water filled his eyes and he blinked it onto the sheets.

He was alive, and he was going home. But he was leaving too many things behind.

A captured agent. An operational fiasco. A political bombshell . . .

And a murder.

Part 1

PASSED-OVER

I

Jerusalem

Late Spring 1986

IN A CITY OF ANCIENT KINGS, ringed by sunburned hills from which Jesus once preached, dangerous wadis where Mohammed had raced his white steed and intrepid ruins stained by the tears of Abraham, certainly the Talpiot Industrial Center was not the ideal place in which to culminate a career in government. In fact, as Eytan Eckstein was realizing on a morning scented with the coming of summer, this large parcel of subsidized, nonprime, hardly historical real estate might well have been serving as an unkindly hint from the Prophets of Employment. The Industrial Center's leprous ugliness, and Eckstein's banishment to it, seemed to suggest that here was a place for terminations rather than auspicious beginnings.

For the rest of Jerusalem was nothing if not majestic. Any human who had ever been there, for a single day or for half a century, was forever captured by its beauty. Jerusalem, no matter its cinemas, cars and computers, could not be modernized, would not be dragged into the unaesthetic twentieth century. Jerusalem's face was of stone; stubborn, it chose its own light from the spectra of sun and sky, reflecting it back to the breathless eye.

Connoisseurs of architecture say that you can read the character of a city by the shadows it throws. Jerusalem streets are painted with silhouettes of high arches rather than angled steel, with domed mosques and sand-roughened spires instead of the cold synthetic fingers of tempered glass. It is true, of course, that among the towering ramparts of the Old City you can see the lines of tanned legs and short skirts, suit coats and soldiers' rifles. Yet they are interspersed with the cloaks of nuns, the *jallabieh*s of Arabs, the long frocks of the Hassidim. In the streets below, the automobiles also project their modern angles, yet they seem somehow temporary, as if horses and camels might regain the day at any moment, to no one's consternation or surprise.

There are very few places in the City of David which breach the code of aesthetic pleasure. But certainly the Talpiot Industrial Center is one of them, and that is why Eytan Eckstein hated it so.

The Center itself had been banished to the southern outskirts, lying in a valley well beneath the skyline, a dusty bowl between Bakka and the Hebron Road leading to Bethlehem. Jerusalem had an abundance of holy men, ministers and philosophers, yet it failed to attract exporters, developers, or manufacturers. So the T.I.C. was the city's compromise.

"We need it," the mayor had said. "I just don't want to have to *look* at it."

The Center was built around three huge horseshoe-shaped structures. Their four-story sides were slapped with the requisite Jerusalem stone, but this was merely a token gesture to the civil architectural regulations. Most of the walkways, walls, stairways, and doors were of sheet steel, painted in an unflattering rustproof blue. On the eastern perimeter were the storefronts—toy outlets; furniture warehouses; pizza, fellafel and even pancake restaurants. On the interior, rental space was expansive and inexpensive, attracting scores of carpentry shops, metal workers, photo studios, and ceramic manufacturers.

Inexpensive was the descriptive element which had attracted the Department's eye, and certainly the comptroller could not be blamed for doing his duty. Anonymity was an equally important requisite, for when interviewing prospective Special Operations agents, you allowed them to see nothing significant until they'd been thoroughly vetted.

Intellectually, Eckstein accepted all of this, yet emotionally he felt somehow excommunicated. But then he had been feeling that way for a very long time.

The leg was almost healed, a fair miracle considering that the doctors had come within a hair's breadth of amputating. Nearly sixteen months had passed since that rainy January night when he'd arrived at the military wing of Assaf HaRofe Hospital in Ramla. Recostumed in standard IDF fatigues, one trouser leg dramatically ripped away, he had been admitted as the casualty of a firefight in southern Lebanon. The nerve, bone, cartilage and muscle damage was extensive, oxygen-starved tissue having resulted from clottings despite the attention of an aggressive field surgeon.

For a while, it was touch and go with the leg; surgeons from the Orthopedic and Micro departments performed two five-hour operations in quick succession. To their discretionary credit, the hard-pressed doctors did not acknowledge or discuss the patient's delirious ramblings in his pre-op or post-op medicated state. He had been admitted as Captain Eytan Eckstein, 202nd Paratroop Brigade, a company commander who had suffered his wounds near Sidon. Yet he muttered on about Germany, someone named Kamil who apparently frightened him, and a lost comrade called Peter. Odd name for a fellow Israeli paratrooper.

One of the surgeons had a son serving in the 202nd, so he knew that they were presently on maneuvers in the Negev, nowhere near Lebanon. Perhaps the presence of a burly bald major, steel-blue eyes observing the progress from one corner of the operating theater, prevented the doctor from mentioning this discrepancy.

Eckstein had spent over half of a painful year at Assaf HaRofe. At first, and for a long time, he was bedridden—bored to near madness during the days, haunted by thundering, sweat-provoking nightmares after dark. He watched his plaster-encased leg for a near eternity as an ingenious hydraulic brace pumped it, slowly, to and fro, bending the knee, stretching the calf, like some medieval torture device.

To the staff, it was strange that no family appeared to visit the handsome Paratroop Captain, and perhaps that accounted for his lonely, brooding moods. For how could they know that his parents were still receiving postcards from him, once a month, addressed from the historic capitals of Europe? The other wounded soldiers were fairly exhausted by the influx of visitors, dusty rifle-bearing comrades in from the field, fretting girlfriends, food-laden mothers and fathers. Eytan's few visitors, though apparently young compatriots, were usually out of uniform. Inside the wards, their small talk was hollow. Sometimes they whispered to the patient. Briefly.

When Eckstein achieved his first breakthrough—wheelchair status—the Others began to appear. Older men, with the postures of officers in casual street clothing, briefcases in roughened hands. The patient would disappear with them, sometimes for hours, having been wheeled outside into one of the hospital's remote, sunny courtyards.

For Eckstein, the debriefings were much more painful

than the mending wounds left by the bullets and scalpels. However, out of these sessions evolved clarity.

As a result of discussions with Eckstein, the postmission investigators had cleared most of the Team of responsibility for the Bogenhausen Fiasco. Eytan himself could not be fully exonerated, for he was Team Leader and had in fact shot and killed an innocent Arab chauffeur called Mohammed Najiz. Much of the blame was placed at the feet of a photo-recognition specialist named 'Trude,' who was rapidly put out to pasture. Benni Baum, as overall commander, had asked for, and received, most of the lashings.

Of course, the long stay at Assaf HaRofe had had its benefits. Eytan Eckstein had imposed upon him a much-needed rest. So long an animal of field instincts, he slowly reacquired some of his humanity, as well as his identity. He began to respond naturally to the sound of his own name, and the tight springs of conditioned reflex began to unwind. He knew that he would never again be a field agent in Special Operations, and at long last, he began to accept this.

Finally, and certainly best of all, he had met Simona. She had never probed, never pushed, a young nurse who had clearly been born to give. It took Eckstein some time, but eventually he became aware of her coal-black hair, her piercing green eyes and the wide, quick smile. Their romance developed slowly, traditionally, and over the course of half a year it was forged into a bonded love. They had been married soon after Eckstein's release.

And so he was back, though never again to be a real participant in The Game. Perhaps only a fringe player, a tired contestant, forever an observer of the chess masters at work. He tried often to count his blessings, suppress his memory; in fact, today was the day when he had decided to put away his cane. The doctors said that he would always walk with a strange gait.

Unfortunately, as Eytan secretly knew, he would also forever limp in his mind.

The office was located in the central horseshoe of the Industrial Center. It was up on the third floor, all the way at the end of the southwesternmost prong, facing the inside of the shoe. To get there, you had to walk up three flights of cement stairs inside a dark well and then hike another fifty meters along a balustraded catwalk which overlooked the interior delivery courtyard.

The blue steel sliding doors reminded Eckstein of a hospital morgue freezer. There was a small sign on the outside which said *Jacob Bar-Zoar Ltd.—Exporters and Shippers of Israeli Citrus*. Inside, the narrow concrete space was divided into two rooms. One of them held piles of empty wooden fruit crates. The main office held a desk, two chairs, and a telephone. Behind the desk, covering the entire wall, was a ZIM Lines shipping map of the world, criss-crossed with trade routes to exotic ports of call.

There were no further set dressings in *Bar-Zoar Ltd.*, as it was purported to be a start-up business. The company, if asked, was looking for a few enterprising young men and women to work in its overseas offices. The appearance of healthy youths in uniform would raise no eyebrows, for it was common in Israel that as soldiers neared the ends of their tours of duty they began to job-hunt, hoping for adventuresome travels abroad.

Eytan sat behind the large steel desk, looking every bit the young Jerusalem executive. He wore blue jeans, sneakers, and a white, long-sleeved epauletted shirt rolled to the biceps. His only visible extravagance might have been the black Breitling dive watch he had once purchased in Switzerland, yet only the initiated would realize its value. The tools of Eckstein's present trade were few—a pile of yellow legal pads, a cup full of pencils and a sharpener. Naturally, there was an overflowing ashtray and the ever-present packs of Time. He had had to give up the Rothmans. They were no longer part of a cover, and he would not be reimbursed for their expense.

Eytan was not really an Interviewer, per se. That task had already been accomplished at General Headquarters in Tel Aviv. Having passed that initial stage, agent candidates were now going through an intensive vetting period. Their minds and bodies would be poked and probed for months on end by doctors and psychologists.

In the meantime, Eckstein's assignment was to record, by hand, every detail of the candidate's life from birth to the present day. Subsequently, with Eckstein's report in hand, teams of Vetters would roam the country, often traveling abroad to confirm the veracity of the candidate's claims.

Although it was certainly a crucial task, on the tall totem of Special Intelligence assignments this job was at the bottom of the pole. Though officially forgiven for his part in the Bogenhausen Fiasco, Eckstein would probably never "come in from the heat"—a popular Department twisting of Le Carré's phrase—meaning an agent who remained in professional limbo.

Eckstein was ruminating over his career options when the steel door clanged with the rap of knuckles.

"*Kaness*," he called above the rumbling of a central circulation system.

The big door slid back to reveal the tanned face of a young soldier. He poked his head inside.

"Is this Jacob Bar-Zoar Ltd.?"

Eytan stared at him, expressionless. "Isn't the sign still up?"

The soldier blushed and swung the door wide, entering the office. For a moment, the whine of table saws on wood planks echoed from the lumber shop in the courtyard below.

The soldier closed the door and turned to Eckstein. He squinted, trying to adjust from the harsh sunlight to the gloomy shadows of the room.

"*Shev.*" Eytan pointed to the chair.

The young soldier sat. He was a corporal in his early twenties, wearing the light khaki dress uniform of the Air Force and carrying a Galil assault rifle. His short brown hair was sun-streaked at the edges, his clear eyes still painted with a certain innocence. *A year with us, and that look will be gone forever,* Eytan wanted to warn him.

"Name?" Eytan asked.

"Ehh," the soldier cleared his throat. "Folberg, Gerard. 31–51–024."

The boy's nervousness was as blatant as his pleasing French accent. Eckstein smiled.

"You're not a prisoner of war, Gerard. You can relax."

The corporal smiled. He looked down at his hands and crossed one leg. Eytan offered him a cigarette, which he quickly accepted.

"Now, we're just going to talk," Eytan continued. "It will take a while, we'll begin at the beginning, and you might even have to come back here again. *B'seder?*"

The soldier nodded. "Okay."

Eckstein picked up a legal pad and poised a pencil to write.

"Let's start with your birth, and we'll do the first ten years. Don't leave out a detail. I'll select the items I wish to record. *Tatchil.*"

The soldier began to speak.

"I was born in Toulon, in 1964. . . ."

It always began the same way, as it had begun with Eytan himself, nearly eight years before. They were almost always Europeans, having been born abroad and then made Aliyah to Israel. Or if not, they had been raised in the homes of

European Israelis and spoke at least one language other than Hebrew. They had become good soldiers, maintained exceptional records and were usually from elite units. This Frenchman was serving in 996, the Air Force's pilot rescue unit. You had to be good to get in, and even better to remain.

Even as Eckstein began to record the details, he felt the familiar stab of envy. He remembered his own first months of vetting, the excitement of the unknown. He recalled the thrill of the first tastes of intelligence work: the mysterious interviews, strange exams, clandestine meetings in obscure cafés with tough-looking "civilians" who examined your every twitch.

Perhaps the *Gibush* was his fondest memory. It was the army's test of a soldier's teamwork ability. It was there, in the field, that he had first met Serge Samal, Zvika Pearlman and Mike Dagan, still not knowing that in time he would think of them only as Rainer Luckmann, Harry Webber and Peter Hauser. For months they had studied together, trained together, carried each other in mock stretcher drills, all the while watched carefully by their hawkeyed recruiters. And even then, when only the calm, the brave and the talented remained, the adventure had only just begun.

The romance of the birth of an army intelligence agent was incomparable. The secret training, the documentation, the covers. The shedding of uniforms for the guise of civilian clothes, the tracking in the streets of Tel Aviv, the weapons instruction, Intel history, sabotage, communications. And the secrets from friends and family that bound the compatriots together, even more than had the years in the field with fellow paratroopers.

And finally, the first missions.

How Eytan wished that he could go back there again, could once more be the admired officer, the hero. And how he wished he had quit the game early, while every operation was still a smashing success. Long before he had ever heard the name Amar Kamil.

Well, at least Eytan's was not the only career apparently stunted by Bogenhausen.

Almost immediately after being spotted in Berlin—on the very afternoon when Eytan was supposed to be killing him in Munich—Amar Kamil had disappeared from the face of the earth. At first, no one "purchased the ruse," as the Brits liked to say. For months afterward, the Western intelligence services searched for him. Mossad, AMAN, CIA, MI6, SDECE—they all sniffed around the alleyways of Europe, the *shuks* of the Middle East. Ciphers and cables were intercepted, informers and deep doubles scoured, and nothing came up. Rumors poured in—Kamil had retired to Libya, he was training in Yemen, he had gone underground in Central America. Eventually, the most recurring piece of information came to be accepted by the managers of Western intelligence. Where AMAN—Israeli Military Intelligence—had failed, Kamil's own brothers had succeeded. He had been killed by a rival, even more radical—if that was conceivable—faction. Abu Nidal, George Habash, Ahmed Jabril, one of them had disagreed with, or been jealous of, Kamil's activities. Within the terrorist brotherhood, internecine squabbles were most often settled with gunfire.

When Eytan first heard the news of Kamil's death, mentioned casually by Benni Baum as the major pushed Eckstein's wheelchair along a sunny sidewalk at Assaf HaRofe, he experienced a flood of emotions. Kamil's demise could not erase Eckstein's murder of Mohammed Najiz, but there was a sense of joyful retribution in hearing that an enemy's career had also taken a "downward turn." Then, almost immediately, Eckstein also felt a strange pang of commiseration. For what was Amar Kamil if not a mirror of himself? Yes, the Palestinian had been ruthless, seemingly indiscriminate, a killer.

But had the man been a Jew instead of an Arab, restrained by the shackles of government as opposed to free-lancing his own network, he might well have been something else. He could have been Eytan's partner.

The months of quiet recovery had certainly softened Eckstein's professional acumen, but his ingrained training had made him a skeptic, and he did not succumb to the sense of relief. Amar Kamil disappeared? Dead? How many times had such reports flowed in from all over the world, about so many of the opposition leaders, only to be rebuked by a signatory hail of gunshots in an airport lounge? What percent of intelligence reports were "quality products" and what percent "rejects"? How much was disinformation?

Eytan knew the answers to those questions. The Chief Rabbi of Israel could swear on his precious beard that Amar Kamil was dead, but Eytan would have to see the cold corpse before he'd believe it. He knew that this feeling of an "unsettled account" would probably stay with him until he died.

"I'll believe it when the check clears," was all he said to Benni Baum.

In the meantime, Eckstein was experiencing his own slow "death" in the Service. Sure, the salary was good, plus disability payments; in less than two years he could get out with a partial pension. Yes, the humiliation factor was high, but thanks to the enduring secretive nature of his work no one save his peers was privy to his failures. He was almost thirty-three years old, and he had nearly half the credits toward a university degree. He and Simona were trying to have a baby. He could have some kind of a future.

If he could just bite his lip and stick it out. . . .

The midafternoon arrived quickly, despite the mundane nature of Eckstein's tasks. He had to listen, concentrate, record, question, and that made the clock move. By 3:30, he had interviewed five candidates, four men and one woman, having taken a half hour to eat Simona's chicken-schnitzel sandwich in pita and read through the important articles in *Yediot*.

He was sipping a cup of *Nes* and waiting for the last candidate when the telephone rang.

"Bar-Zoar. Shalom."

"That's it for the day," a voice said.

"Where's the last man?" Eytan asked.

"Canceled. You can come on in."

"*Litraot*," Eytan said and hung up.

Eckstein sat back against the steel office chair. He was glad to be done for the day, yet he felt the familiar crawling in his stomach. At one time the butterflies had only appeared near the climax of a dangerous operation. Now they arrived whenever Eckstein was about to head down to Headquarters.

He stood up, felt the rough click in his right knee, ignored it and began to sweep. The legal pads were full of his scratchings. He placed all of them in his briefcase. Then he checked all of the desk drawers and the floor for every bit of extra paper. He pulled the plastic bag from the wastebasket and tied it shut.

It might have seemed paranoid, but Eckstein suspected that certainly one of these nights Colonel Ben-Zion would send over a pair of *Portzim*, the Department "burglars" who could open anything from a child's piggy bank to the Prime Minister's private safe. They would break in quietly, scour Bar-Zoar Ltd., and if they found even the smallest scrap of incriminating evidence there would be hell to pay. The Colonel did not like Eckstein. The brooding Captain's presence was a constant reminder of Bogenhausen, and Ben-Zion did not appreciate having this limping personification of Failure stalking around the Department.

Colonel Itzik Ben-Zion was Eytan's butterfly-maker. And the hostile feeling was mutual. Eytan hoped that he could complete his business at H.Q. without even seeing the commander.

The scuffed wooden cane was leaning against the cement wall, waiting for its master. Eckstein debated throwing it out with the garbage, but that seemed a cruel demise for a loyal friend. He picked it up, gripped it horizontally along with the handle of his briefcase, and walked out with the trash onto the sunlit catwalk.

His first few unaided steps were painful. His right hip seemed to be grinding at the ball and socket, but the strong afternoon sun helped and soon his muscles warmed and he was satisfied with his progress. The three flights of stairs were the most difficult. He used the handrail, and when he reached the bottom he was sweating and quite pleased with himself. A photographer who used the office next door passed him in a hurry.

"*Ma nishmah?*" The man asked after Eytan's welfare.

"*Al hakefak.*" Eytan smiled.

His shiny black Fiat Panda was baking in a lot off Bethlehem Road. It was small and boxy, like a little jeep. Eytan was always pleased by the sight of the car, mostly because he had affixed a decal to the rear window. It was a small pair of red-and-white parachute wings, with the bold "Follow Me To The Paratroops" printed across it in high letters. For so long he had been forbidden to display such egotistical amulets. But he was never going back into the field, so he had said to hell with it and slapped on the bright sticker. What could Ben-Zion do? Send him to Lebanon?

As he approached the Panda, Eckstein was barely aware of the fact that he was a creature of strange habits, and would probably always be so. When he was out on the street, his ears pricked up, batlike, scanning for the incongruous sound, the click of a weapon bolt, the patter of a pursuing footstep. His eyes automatically swept the lot, recording faces and matching them to his memory for noncoincidental repetitions. He glanced instinctively at the undercarriage of the Fiat, quickly running a checklist of natural automotive protrusions versus any freshly affixed shapes. When he finally reached the door handle, his fingers briefly hesitated as his eyes swept the lock for scratch marks, the space beneath the dash for inconsistent wiring.

Had he realized he was doing it, he would have felt quite foolish. He was no longer in Europe, on "enemy territory." This was his hometown, and the dangers virtually non-existent. Yet it was not a conscious indulgence, no more so than a pilot's instinctive preflight check.

Still, on occasion, Eckstein was made painfully aware of the insidiousness of his training. Since leaving the hospital he had, on three separate occasions, identified himself by a cover name while trying to cash checks. Naturally his Israeli Identity Card had contradicted him, causing the suspicious bank tellers to angrily refuse his business. Blushing, Eckstein had been forced to excuse himself and quickly withdraw, whereupon he would find himself outside in the hot sun, breathing hard and crawling with chills. He had never, ever, made such a blunder while in the field. It was the cruel price of recovery.

It was not yet summer, but the inside of the Fiat was as hot as a brass *finjon* on an open fire. Eckstein folded up the cardboard windshield guard, which didn't do much except keep the steering wheel from melting. He rolled down the passenger window as well as his own, strapped in, lit a cigarette, and put the car in gear.

Driving did not bother the leg at all. The seat had been slid back as far as possible, and the clutch, brake, and gas pedals custom-adjusted, so Eckstein really only used his feet. He liked to drive. It was one of the few times in which he felt totally in control of his fate.

It was already close to four o'clock when he neared the

center of town. He could have taken King David Street, the most direct route, but at this hour the walls of the Old City would be turning a seductive, burnished umber. So instead of turning left off Derech Hevron and swinging through the train station, he made straight for the intersection at Abu Tor, down and around through the Sultan's Pool and out onto the Jerusalem Brigade Road, receiving a sweeping breath of the towering walls as they flowed past the Fiat's windows. He checked the rearview mirror, somewhat more than was necessary. He did not bother to deny to himself that the detour also delayed his arrival, albeit for only a few minutes.

Too soon he found himself on Jaffa Road, descending toward Zion Square. Traffic was light, the banks and shops and cafés not having reopened yet after the midday *hafsaka*. He took the sharp uphill right onto Heleni Hamalka, feeling the tension, hoping that Colonel Ben-Zion would be out of the office.

The Russian Compound, with its myriad of religious archives, prison cells, courts, and government offices, was like a small city in and of itself. It sat on a large flat hill, just to the north of Jaffa Road, but seemingly on another planet altogether. While only a few meters away Jerusalemites engaged in social peccadillos at outdoor cafés and spent their overtaxed earnings on *schwarma*, ice cream and swimsuits, inside the Compound Orthodox nuns prayed for redemption, muscular *Shabak* agents planned counter-intelligence missions, and Palestinian terrorists tried not to succumb to interrogations.

On Jaffa Road lovers were planning illicit rendezvous. In the Compound, angry judges were pounding gavels.

And unknown to all but those who worked there, AMAN's Special Operations had also taken up temporary residence.

Up until two months previously, all of the major intelligence branches had operated out of the Tel Aviv area. IDF General Headquarters was located in midtown T.A. at the *Kiria,* and the Joint Chiefs liked to have operational information at their fingertips. The Middle East was a place where missions and wars developed quickly, their outcome depending on lightning reflexes. If you needed something fast—a file, a cable printout, a recon photo or an expert—you didn't want to wait until it arrived from out of town.

Special Operations had had its own building, too small really for the Department's rapid expansion. Colonel Itzik Ben-Zion kept pushing for a larger space, but the comptroller kept protesting over lack of funds. It was during a routine check of the building, and coincidentally in the midst of a heated budget debate, that the Sweepers found a *tzatat*—a bug in the Cipher room. Ben-Zion threw a fit, grabbing his seconds-in-command and rushing over to G.H.Q., where he stormed into the office of the Deputy Chief of Staff and pounded on his desk for half an hour. In Israel, the man who screams the loudest is often the one who gets what he wants, and Ben-Zion did his melodramatic best, raging about the two Russian electronic intercept trawlers just outside of Haifa, how he couldn't even take a shit without Moscow counting the splashes, and it was no fucking wonder that his people couldn't carry out a simple elimination when his own Cipher room was as penetrable as a Yarkon whore.

He needed a new, solid, *Koos eema shelachem*, SECURE facility. And he needed it Now!

While the IDF real estate people sheepishly began to shop, Ben-Zion was allowed to clear out of Tel Aviv and set up temporarily in Jerusalem. The people who knew the Colonel well smiled, for he had played it perfectly. Itzik Ben-Zion was an empire builder, and he had just laid his cornerstone. A couple of his agents wondered too indiscreetly about who had really planted the bug, and they quickly found themselves working an extended surveillance job in Uganda.

Eytan entered the long parking lot, now half-full of civilian and police cars, yet he kept driving into the Compound itself. The Russian Orthodox church was the centerpiece, its majesty incongruous amid the flat, bullet-scarred governmental stone barracks. The church had varied stone spires, topped by brilliant green domes and gold Orthodox crosses flashing in the sunlight. Surrounding these spires of faith were the towers of vigilance and fear—massive radar antennae, radio intercept grids, microwave dishes.

Eckstein drove past Police Headquarters, where a group of young Arab men was being escorted by burly detectives toward the Central Court Building on the other side of the Compound. A swarm of Arab fathers, mothers and children anxiously trooped after their sons and brothers, kicking up small clouds of dust. Just below the courthouse was a small dirt parking area. All of the vehicles were military cars, yet without exception all had civilian registrations. Only the occasional extra radio aerial served as a giveaway. Eytan joined them, just one more civil-service employee.

Special Operations had chosen an appropriate building for its temporary residence. The courtyard was dirty, the entrance doors peeling. The stained brass business shingles were singularly uninteresting, even discouraging. One said, International Association for Truth and Responsibility in Journalism. Another said, University Research Center for Incurable Venereal Disorders. The three floors ended in a flat-topped roof, and the weather-beaten walls barely met the minimum aesthetic standards set by Jerusalem civil district planners.

There were no aerials on the roof, as all of the telex, scrambler, burst and satellite cables had been run under the Compound through communications tunnels and parasited off the massive police and postal towers. The windows on the north side of the building faced the Central Courthouse, obviating the problem of prying civilian eyes. The southern windows faced Jaffa Road, but there the massive facade of the Central Post Office served as ample screening from that purview. Even so, every window had curtains, and each pane of glass was affixed with a suction cup containing an oscillating diaphragm operating at random frequencies set by a central transmitter. The vibrations would foil attempts to "read" the internal sound waves off the glass, either by laser or parabolic devices. Granted, the entire building hummed like a muffled bees' nest, but one soon acclimated and it no more disturbed than the air conditioners, which were only run on the most unbearable days, and only then to keep the computers cool.

Eckstein got out of the car, a bit stiff in the knee, but he left the cane inside and took his briefcase and the small bag of garbage. He inhaled a breath of the cooler late-afternoon breeze, straightened his shoulders, and walked.

Security at the main entrance seemed superficially light. Almost all public Israeli buildings use private security firms to guard their doors, old men in rumpled uniforms who check through briefcases and pocketbooks for weapons or explosives. The man at the SpecOps desk inside the cool hallway seemed no different. He was in his mid-fifties and wore a wrinkled, baby-blue epauletted shirt with a black patch of crossed church keys on his left shoulder. Actually, he was an ex-*Shabak* agent named Shlomo Bornshtein, once chief of security for three different embassies abroad. He was heavy with the oncoming years and too much foreign food, but there was still a lot of power hidden beneath the seemingly neglected uniform. He was also an expert shot with the Browning Hipower resting on his hip.

Shlomo glanced up as Eytan approached the desk.

"*Shalom,* Tony." The big man smiled. "How goes it?"

"Every day an adventure." Eckstein produced a laminated pass. It was the IDF's top security clearance, allowing its bearer entry into any military facility in the country, no questions asked.

Shlomo continued to smile. He did not even look at Eytan's card. He glanced up at a small television camera, pressed an intercom button and said, "It's Tony," to an invisible employee. A buzzer vibrated and the lock on the steel entrance door clicked and Eytan had to grab it quick before it closed again.

Eytan was somewhat offended. Shlomo should have examined his pass, no matter the familiarity. For a moment, he instinctively became the field commander again.

"I know you know me, Shlomo," he said as he held the door. "But you really should look at this thing." He still held the pass in his fingers.

Shlomo looked up with the expression of an impatient parent. He extended his hand, grabbed the card, exaggerated his perusal of it, matching the picture *twice* with Eckstein's face, and handed it back.

"After all, I could have been fired last night," Eytan continued. "Had my clearance taken away. Hell, I could be coming in here just to *kill* Ben-Zion."

"Smartest career move you'd ever make," said Shlomo as he returned to his roster work.

Eytan flushed, speechless. *Ya'Allah,* he called silently to God in the common Arabic exclamation, *Does* everyone *know my goddamn business?*

He entered a "submarine" chamber, pulling the door closed behind him. It was a steel closet with a large two-way mirror inside. A hollow voice spoke to him.

"*Shalom,* Tony. What have you got?"

"Today's interviews, trash for the burn bag."

"Armed?"

"Yes, but barely dangerous."

There was a snort from the speaker and the secondary door lock buzzed.

The headquarters of AMAN's Special Operations Department looked surprisingly like any other suite of Israeli government offices. All of the walls were of plaster-covered cement, painted a dull light-grey, their stubborn surfaces making it difficult to hang pictures, posters, charts or diagrams. Expansion screws didn't last long, so masking tape had seized the day, though the glue quickly dehydrated in Jerusalem and people were constantly sticking things back up on the walls. The floors were of the typically cheap, freckled slate tiles. God help the extravagant officer who dared to order carpeting. The harsh lighting was either industrial fluorescent or bare hanging bulb, so even the most tanned, rested employees looked sallow at their workplaces.

Because the occupation of the premises was still fairly new, the Department was undergoing a period of controlled disarray, if not chaos. The halls were narrow, leaving no room for reception desks or comfortable waiting chairs. Rickety wooden tables, piled with unclassified daily reports and periodicals, made passage difficult. Cipher cables, telephone and computer lines snaked from room to room, giving the hallway floor the look of a frigate deck under repair. The inevitable glass teacups and saucers found their resting places wherever employees had decided that they were overcaffeinated. Nervous Sweepers went about their fussy business virtually ignored, so in addition to the flurry of intelligence officers bouncing from room to room, there was the strange presence of spectacled men crawling on hands and knees, inspecting the cables, wall joints and every electronic accoutrement, as if the place also harbored a nursery for retarded wunderkinder.

Eckstein took the cement stairway up to the second floor, one at a time, left foot first, then resting on the right as he carried the briefcase and trash bag in his left hand and pushed off from the steel rail with his right. A young man was sitting at a steel desk on the second-floor landing. He was muscular, armed with a pistol, a telephone and a small cup of steaming

Turkish coffee. He looked like a receptionist at a maximum-security prison.

"Hello, Bavaria." He was extremely serious, and called everyone by their Departmental code names, even though that was only required for field operatives.

"Hi, Moshiko," said Eytan. He pointed to an object that looked like a netless basketball hoop, a grey steel frame standing next to the desk. "Where's the burn bag?"

"New rules." Moshiko raised a dark eyebrow. "Ben-Zion wants everything cleared twice a day now. They're bringing fresh bags up." He extended a hand toward Eckstein's trash. "I'll take it."

Eckstein hugged his plastic bag to his chest, mocking Moshiko's solemnity. "That's a break in regulations."

"Break this," said Moshiko, pointing down at his crotch.

Eckstein laughed and dropped the bag on the desk. "Don't worry," he said. "You get out in the field you won't have to put up with this shit."

It was Moshiko's dream to work as an operative in Queens Commando, which was the coded title for the Special Operations teams. But he was a Czechoslovakian immigrant, and both men knew that it would never be. The Mossad civilians occasionally used Russians, Hungarians and Czechs, but the risk of penetration was too high and AMAN tried to avoid recruiting East Bloc Jews, no matter their sincerity.

"*Alehvai,*" said Moshiko, looking briefly up to God, and he went back to reading a Hebrew translation of a Graham Greene novel called *The Human Factor*.

Eckstein moved on down the hallway. He passed the "News Room," where telex machines spewed unclassified terror-related reports from the world's major news agencies and the unencoded machines of Israeli embassies in major capitals.

Next was the Cover Room, where a trio of bright,

attractive young women chose titles for missions and operatives. They were hard-pressed to keep the humor out of their work, the only witness to their optimistic youth being a sign on the door in Old English calligraphy that read, "What's in a name? A rose, etc., etc., etc. . . ."

There was a glass window in the door and it suddenly popped open. A pretty, freckled redhead called Pnina stuck her head out and beamed at Eckstein.

"Bavaria, my dear!"

Eytan stopped short. Pnina's smile always forced him to respond in kind. "Hi."

"Wouldn't you love a new name?" she offered mischievously. "It's cycle time. You can have it."

"Don't think it's necessary," said Eytan, betraying his self-effacing mood.

"Oh, come on. *Bavaria*'s so, so . . . *dark*."

"Yes. Well, I'll think about it. Thanks."

"Okay," Pnina replied without taking offense. She closed the door.

Even back when he was a paratroop non-com, the seriousness with which Eytan undertook his tasks had resulted in his acquiring the nickname 'The Brooding Bavarian'. Somehow he took it as a compliment, and it had resulted in his choice of Bavaria as a Departmental code. *Might as well keep it,* he thought. *Like a souvenir*.

He continued on. So far, no one had noticed that he was without his ever-present cane. Well, he decided, it was like smoking. Nobody realized it when you finally quit.

He suddenly started when a captain called Heinz came storming out of the Cipher Room. Heinz was about Eckstein's age and had white-blond hair, dead grey eyes and the distinct look of a mad youth whose parents must have hated him.

"Well, get the goddamn thing down! Now!" Heinz had one hand on his hip and was gesturing angrily at a large diagram which had been posted on a bare wall. It was obviously a practical joke, a layout of the floor in black marker on rough beige planning paper. All of the offices were delineated and bore caustic comments in the square blueprint spaces, such as "Cipher Room—best coffee, worst conversation," and "Covers—three Lovelies—two single, one married, all easy," and so forth.

"*Koos och tahk,* what the hell do you think this is, the goddamn Tourist Bureau?!" Heinz stood there fuming while the Cipher Room's pair of ever-present guards jumped to tear the poster down. A middle-aged woman from the room stood by blushing, yet clearly insulted at having been reprimanded by Heinz.

"Too much coffee?" Eytan smiled at Heinz as he passed the scene. The temperamental captain ignored him.

He carried on and passed the small canteen, from which someone called to him, "Eckstein! The Creme Bavaria is great today!" He waved but kept on, feeling the knee a bit more but ignoring it.

All three levels of the building were Security Floors, but perhaps it was the presence of the canteen on Floor Two that gave the area a more relaxed atmosphere. It was here in the small *miznon,* with its coffee and sandwich bar, scuffed formica tables and orange plastic chairs, that personnel came to take a break, blow off steam, bitch about their assignments and their bosses. You could have a good laugh in the canteen, which you certainly could *not* do on Floor Three, where Itzik Ben-Zion held intricate, grueling planning sessions until well into the midnight hour on most days. And below, on Floor One and in the basement, there wasn't a hell of a lot of levity either. The Wizards, Watchers and Scouts worked down there, sweating over tool benches, handling microelectronic gear, weapons, explosives. They didn't joke much. An effective punch line could cost the Department a fortune.

So Floor Two was the People Floor, as the employees called it, and the canteen was a bustling hangout, its atmosphere spilling over at times. It could have been any small cafeteria in any public building, except for the fact that, on occasion, when a stranger would enter, the multilingual shop talk would come to a dead halt. A few seconds' delay, and suddenly everyone would switch subjects—basketball scores, troubles in the flower garden, pride in the children's progress.

As Eytan turned into Personnel, he caught the echoes of an argument as two men emerged from the canteen behind him.

"You can't do that, you *tembel!*"

"Why not?"

"You'll overload the relay. It'll burn and jam open, then you'll have an irrevocable fuze. No safety."

"So, we'll put a governor on the circuit."

"It's supposed to be *light,* you asshole. By the time you're done we'll need a fucking truck to move it!"

The conversation faded down the hallway as the men receded to the lower floors. Eytan smiled. The sounds of Operations.

Personnel was one midsize room, the walls lined with tall grey filing cabinets, shelves for computer disks and programs and roster lists for assembling training teams. There were three desks. The one on the left was for the Personnel secretary, upon which sat a cream-colored IBM-PC. Yudit, a bright-eyed, curly-headed brunette barely twenty, sat inputting Eckstein's previous interviews. The right-hand desk was Zvika's, a happy-go-lucky sergeant whose function as Personnel's runner, driver and gofer kept him out of the office all day long. His blotter was pin neat. The largest desk sat at the far end, against the windows. That was for the head of Personnel.

Eckstein did not have a desk.

Yudit looked up and smiled at Eckstein. He growled at her, a low, sexy wolf noise, and she blushed as she did every day when he greeted her thusly.

"Hey!" Yudit peered around her CRT. "Where's the cane?"

"You noticed. I love you," Eckstein said solemnly and continued on to the windows. He plopped down in a chair in front of his boss's desk, relieved to be off the leg again.

Danny Romano looked up from his work and gestured for Eytan to wait one moment. Eytan sat patiently, looking at Romano, examining the Italian Jew's high forehead and slick black hair. Romano was nearly forty and always had an empty pipe clutched between his teeth. He had given up actually smoking, but he saw no reason to abandon the pacifier altogether. His nature was absurdly pleasant for a man who had been working under the pressures of Intelligence for nearly twenty years. No one knew Romano's real name, for he was occasionally sent back to Italy or Sicily to undertake short roles in special missions. Apparently his cover was extremely vulnerable, and he was rarely used in the field anymore.

Danny threw down his pencil, sat back, folded his fingers behind his head and smiled over his pipe stem.

"How'd it go today?"

"A thrill," said Eckstein. "As usual."

Romano shook his head slowly, with some sympathy. "I keep telling you, Eytan," he said gently, probably using the same tone as when explaining the cruelties of life to his three sons. "You're lucky to be walking at all. *Breathing* even. Accept it. You were a Comet."

Romano often referred to Eytan that way, harking back to the officer's once-glorious field reputation in a wistful way.

"I know, I know," said Eytan. "But oh my friends . . . ," he began in English.

"And oh, my foes . . . ," said Romano.

"It leaves a *lovely* light," Yudit chirped from behind her IBM, having heard the banter a few times before.

"Hey you!" Romano wagged a finger in her direction. "I told you, no eavesdropping, and no flirting with my married men."

Yudit giggled and continued to type.

"So?" Romano switched to business. "How did they look?"

Eytan opened his briefcase and passed the legal pads over the desk. "In my opinion, two *Go*s and three *Never-Make-It*s."

"Why the three?" Romano frowned as he took the pads.

"One too cool, one too nervous, one too eager."

"Ah, so you're a psychologist now."

"Professional pessimist," said Eytan, but his tone displayed some hurt. "You don't want to hear it, don't ask."

"My dear friend," said Romano, smiling slightly yet dead sincere. "If I could, I'd dispense with the doctors, shrinks and polygraphs and just let you take them through from first interview to acceptance, or rejection. You know that."

Eytan bowed his head with the apologetic compliment. He stood up. Suddenly the knee was throbbing and he wished he'd brought the cane, if only for moral support.

"Well, I'm off."

"Hey," said Romano, staring at the legal pads. "You think Yudit can decipher this handwriting?"

"She reads my mind," said Eytan without looking at the secretary. "Besides, she can always call me at home."

"Oh, I'm sure Simona would *love* that," said Yudit from behind her screen.

"She trusts me," said Eytan as he made to leave.

Yudit laughed again as Eytan opened the door.

"No interviews till Wednesday," Romano called. "But come in and help out with the bios."

Eytan acknowledged with a thumbs up, then he went into the hallway, clearly taking a left instead of heading for the exit.

"Hey," Danny called. "Where to?"

"To see Benni."

Romano clucked his tongue. "I wish you could stay out of trouble, Bavaria."

"Yeah. Me too," said Eckstein.

He should have gone straight home. Ben-Zion had ordered Eckstein to stop ruminating over the Kamil case, and that meant staying clear of Research. But Benni Baum was still a close friend, and you could not order a man to terminate his friendships. It wasn't Eytan's fault that Benni now headed up Research, was it?

In comparison to Personnel, the Research Department at the end of the floor was a madhouse. Benni Baum liked it that way, and his people joked that even if forced to retire to being headmaster of a kindergarten, he would run it similarly, snapping out orders, planning activities and jumping from recess to finger paints like the field commander he would always be. Within the Israeli Intelligence community, AMAN's Research Department in Tel Aviv was uncontested as the brain trust of gathering, computation and analysis of raw information. Benni Baum's department in SpecOps was just a smaller version of the same. He could call on resources at will—from Mossad, AMAN, Shabak, or even the National Police. His private lair was bursting at the seams with files, computer printouts, cipher booklets, videotapes. There was room for possibly three desks and as many varied terminals, supporting a maximum of five analysts. Yet Benni Baum had accounted for every centimeter of space. He had four different computers, a multi-head VCR with a color monitor, a Tadiran shortwave and a massive cross-indexing file in four ceiling-high steel cabinets. Baum had no desk of his own, because he worked better on his feet. Besides, it allowed him to put two more people into the room, which usually harbored no fewer than seven in addition to himself. The atmosphere was always choked with smoke. Despite the anticigarette wave gripping the Western world, Baum encouraged the habit, contending that the puffing and fidgeting enhanced the mental reflexes.

Thanks to Colonel Ben-Zion's skewed concept of crime and punishment, Benni Baum had been suspended from Operations after Bogenhausen. But he had managed to twist things around. Now Operations could not function without him.

There was no lettered sign on the door to Baum's department. The Mechkarim Vechakirot (Research and Investigations) shingle had not survived the transfer from the Tel Aviv quarters. Instead, Baum had somehow acquired a large, black-and-yellow wooden sign from a road gang. It exhibited no words, but simply showed a muscular silhouetted figure bending over a large black mound of earth, applying leverage to a shovel. For that was how Benni Baum viewed his assignment, and also how he wanted his staff to view it—sweat-provoking, roll-up-your-sleeves, laborious digging, rather than a purely intellectual, chair-bound endeavor that could make your ass flabby and starve your inspiration.

Eckstein pushed on the road sign; the door swung open and he was immediately greeted by a cloud of cigarette smoke, the smell of *helld* in Turkish coffee, a cacaphony of computer printers and Benni Baum's thundering bass.

"*No,* Gadi." Baum was nearly shouting. "I don't *want* that now. Just give me what I asked you for."

"But Benni," a woman's voice sounded obstinate, nearly insubordinate, "we've got a 20 percent increase in verbs and nouns. We should start from the beginning of the file and fill in some blanks."

"*Ya'Allah!*" There was the crack of Baum's palm against

his own forehead. "How many times do I have to say it, Shoshi? We've got over three thousand transmissions. If you correct every page, Arafat will be living in Haifa by the time you're halfway done!"

"Okay, okay," someone else said.

The voices of opposition died down and the clatter of computer keys increased. Eckstein closed the door and Baum turned from where he had been posed like an orchestra conductor, waving his arms, demanding production from his various "sections."

Benni Baum was only five-foot-eight, somewhat shorter than Eckstein, but he had the wide body of a rugby player. He was forever battling a stomach which was addicted to his wife's German cooking, yet he believed that once he increased his trouser size it would be akin to a wartime surrender. He was constantly hitching up his belt. He smoked incessantly, but he still played soccer every weekend with his two teenage sons, and it was said that he could victoriously arm-wrestle any field agent in the Department.

As Hans-Dieter Schmidt, he had been overall commander of *Operation Flute*, and ultimately responsible for the murder of Mohammed Najiz. Yet unlike Eckstein, Baum's spirit had not been dulled by the Bogenhausen Fiasco. He viewed intelligence work as an extension of open warfare, and in war you made mistakes, accepted them, paid for them and carried on.

Benni was wearing a white short-sleeved shirt with light blue pinstripes, epaulettes and a host of buttoned pockets. His big bald head and jug ears were shiny with perspiration, and the shirt was dark under the armpits. He extended a beefy hand.

"Eytan!" He boomed as if he hadn't seen Eckstein in months, though they'd had breakfast together only the day before. "Why won't these people listen to me?"

Eckstein took the hand and squeezed hard to match Baum's power. "Apparently because they don't respect you."

"We respect him," someone said from the hazy atmosphere. "We just don't *like* him."

"Shut up and work," Baum barked without turning around. "How was it today?" He looked at Eckstein with some sympathy.

"Be serious." Eytan smiled.

"*You* be serious," Baum said, "and *take* it seriously. Only way you'll ever get out of it."

"Maybe I like it this way."

"Sure. And my father was queer."

"That's what's in your file," Eckstein said, and Baum clapped him on the shoulder. Benni suddenly turned back to the troops.

"*Nu!?* Yablokovsky, what's taking so long?"

"*You* wanted hard-disk backup, so now you have to wait," said a young bespectacled man laboring over an IBM compatible.

"Fucking insubordinates," Baum growled.

"Ah, the Israeli Army," Eytan sighed.

"Our socialistic flexibility will also be our demise," said Baum.

Eckstein searched the room. Something big was breaking; he could smell it in the atmosphere, he could tell by the frenetic concentration that gripped intelligence personnel whenever fresh information was coursing down the pipeline. All four computer terminals were occupied, the young men and women, who each had advanced degrees in the science, buckled over their keyboards like crows pecking at kernels of corn. Two additional men were fanning through the paper files in the ceiling-high cabinets, and one more brooding figure sat in the far corner by the windows, flipping through a small tattered notebook.

Everyone in the room knew Eckstein, and they were

always friendly. Though fallen from grace, he was still viewed as a field agent, a figure from that other world of daring and danger which they would never experience. He was usually regarded with a degree of awe, yet today the computer troops were fairly ignoring him.

"What's going on?" Eytan asked.

Baum raised a playful eyebrow at Eytan. Eckstein was out of his department, and was expected to respect the rules of compartmentalization which restricted access of information to a need-to-know basis. With a few selected individuals, such as Eckstein, Baum occasionally broke that rule.

"Is he cleared for this, Benni?" the small figure in the far corner asked without looking up from his notebook.

"I'm cleared for rumor, Horse," Eckstein said above the chatter of the printers.

Someone laughed. Benni Baum lit a cigarette, kept it between his teeth, and put his knuckles to his hips.

"Rumor is," Benni said, "Mossad has broken a big chunk of the Hyperion Codes."

Eytan's eyes bugged. "Mossad?"

"That's the rumor."

There was a historical, healthy competitive spirit between Mossad and AMAN, but cooperation on most matters was high. Many officers made career moves from one organization to the other, so the level of jealousies rarely got out of hand.

"Do you have it?" Eytan asked excitedly.

"By messenger, an hour ago, in black and white." Benni grinned. "Or in Mossad's case, grey and beige." He was clearly pleased, triumphant. Baum was nondenominational. He didn't care what outfit made the gains, as long as the war was going well.

"Isn't this Cipher's jurisdiction?" Eytan asked.

"*Jurisdiction* is just an excuse to do less work," Benni growled.

"Hyperion, huh?" Eytan said rather wistfully. "We could

have used that, Benni." He was clearly harkening back to their days together in the field.

"Someone *else* will use it," said Benni. "Take a chair." He had noted the missing cane and he gestured at Eytan's leg. "Shouldn't go too far the first day."

"That's okay. I'll stand."

The Hyperion Codes. All of the Research departments had been working on them for a long time, probably a couple of years. The Hyperion Institute had operated in Paris ostensibly as a language school. In fact, it had been a meeting place for French, German and Italian terrorists, as well as ETA, IRA, and PLO operatives. The Institute had been run by a KGB officer, identity unknown, but the gunrunning and operational planning activities were finally blown by the careless tradecraft of two Red Brigade members, Maurizio Folini and Oreste Scalzone.

Hyperion had been shut down upon the commencement of an investigation by an Italian court, yet the Israelis had managed to amass a huge file of cipher intercepts between the Institute and Moscow. Breaking the codes would uncover many tracks on the European stamping ground of international terror.

Benni Baum was not interested in all of the chitchat that had taken place between Paris and Moscow. He wanted the *names*, albeit coded, of the major players, ports of entry or departure, dates of operations. With cipher technology, no matter the sophistication, proper names could not be part of the random language. They were designated in code traffic by the prefix, SPELL, and the suffix, ENDSPELL. An additional twenty percent of the Hyperion traffic had been broken, so Baum wanted to run all the SPELL and ENDSPELL bits, and hopefully pick up some more clues by examining the freshly broken words immediately surrounding the proper names.

"I don't know, Benni," the female operator called Shoshi piped up again. "I still think we should run the whole thing."

"For God's sake!" Benni threw up his hands. Then, suddenly he calmed, folded his arms and said to the room, "You know what? We'll let Horse decide."

The little man in the corner looked up. He pushed his black-rimmed glasses back up onto his nose and swept a wisp of hair over his balding head. Horse was Baum's shadow, once a child chess prodigy, now a Ph.D. in geopolitical strategies, who was just thirty but looked forty. Benni used him as the devil on his shoulder, the operational pessimist. He had been with Baum for years, even accompanying the major on Special Operations. It was Horse's job to observe an operation from theory to execution, and then, when asked, to vocally envision all of the potential disasters which might foil the mission.

He had acquired his nickname as the result of an idiomatic fluke by an American-born agent. The operative had literally translated the English word for *nightmare* into incorrect Hebrew, calling the little man Benni Baum's *night horse*. When the laughter had subsided, Benni's little shadow had remained with the title, Horse.

During Bogenhausen, Horse had been laid up in Tel Aviv with a viral influenza. Afterward, he had followed Benni Baum to Research, where he continued to perform his same gloomy function.

"Nu, *Soos?*" Baum said to the brooding man. "The anticipation is killing me."

Everyone in the room waited. Horse would not be rushed. He rubbed his chinless jaw and stared into space. Finally, he turned toward the terminal where Shoshanah sat.

"Benni's right, Shoshi," Horse whispered in his squeaky rasp. "You're not Claire Sterling, and we are not writing a treatise on the evils of East Bloc logistical support of international subversive elements. Just pull the SPELLs and ENDSPELLs along with the five words preceding and following." He went back to reading his booklet.

"You see!" Benni Baum clapped his big hands together. "That's why he gets the big bonuses!" It was a joke, of course, as the IDF salaries were hardly generous and there were no bonuses.

"Okay, I'm getting a listing off the first three hundred pieces," Yablokovsky said from his terminal.

"Print it," said Baum.

The machine chatter increased.

"What about *Flute?*" Eytan suddenly asked.

Baum turned. He looked at Eckstein sadly, with a touch of empathetic reproach. "Now, Eytan. . . ."

"Why not, Benni? It can't hurt. Let the machines do it."

"You just can't give up the ghost, can you?"

"No, and neither can you, so don't pretend otherwise."

Baum bowed his great bald head and ran a hand over it. He blew out a cloud of smoke. He straightened up.

"Okay, Gadi." He jabbed a finger to the right. "Pull Yablokovsky's file, and then do an extraction for *Flute.*"

"Halil?"

"No, you idiot! That's *our* code name for him. Try GREGOR, ASWAN, and SIDON, but first just pull all the five- and six-character propers and create a separate file."

"Cancel that order."

A voice boomed from the open doorway, and except for the printer chatter, the room went dead and the Research staffers froze. The cloud of cigarette smoke suddenly shifted toward the opening, and amid the haze stood the tall figure of Colonel Itzik Ben-Zion.

The Commander of AMAN's Special Operations stepped into the room. He was too tall for the door frame and had to bow his head, but his cold stare remained fixed on Baum and Eckstein. Itzik Ben-Zion had that unfair advantage of unusually large men, especially in a land of midsize Jews. Even without uttering a word, he commanded power. In addition, his forty-six-year-old head still had every one of the coal-black hairs with which he'd been born, greyed slightly at the curled fringes, but looking like raw steel wire. His eyes were nearly black beneath equally dark brows, and his sharp nose jutted over tight lips like the beak of a hawk.

He slammed the door with one huge hand.

"Eckstein, what are you doing in here?"

Somehow, Eytan was not surprised at Ben-Zion's untimely arrival.

"Visiting."

The Colonel ignored the flippancy. "I have told you before, and I will not tell you again. You are not to wander from your own operational parameters, and you are certainly forbidden from interfering with the *important* work undertaken in this room."

Eckstein flushed. His knee was suddenly throbbing and he wanted very badly to sit down, but he just returned Ben-Zion's stare.

"I asked him in here," Benni Baum lied. Baum never gave quarter, not even to his boss, and he put his hands to his belt and hiked up his pants as if preparing for a fist fight. "As you may or may not remember, Itzik, I have authority to call upon any agent, at any time, for whatever needs required by my staff."

Ben-Zion ignored the major. He was not about to take on Benni Baum in a public forum. He continued deriding Eytan.

"Might I also remind you, *Mr.* Eckstein, that matters regarding *Flute* are no longer your concern. I will not have these people's valuable time wasted by your pursuit of a cold corpse." Ben-Zion's eyes were nearly glowing now, making

Eytan feel as if his own fair hair might suddenly burst into flame. "We have pending operations requiring immediate updates. The salving of your ego is *not* on my priority list."

Eckstein had had enough. He was not going to stand there and be Ben-Zion's whipping boy, nor was he going to wait to be physically thrown out. He picked up his briefcase and made for the door.

"I'm sure you have plenty of paperwork," Ben-Zion called after him.

Eckstein's blood was pounding in his ears. He heard footsteps following him as he limped quickly, white-lipped, down the hall.

"Eytan," Benni Baum's voice called. "Tomorrow night at seven, you and Simona. Maya is making Wiener schnitzel."

Eckstein kept walking, his vision half-blurred with fury and humiliation. He barely registered the curious heads which had poked from office doors, wondering who might be the target of Ben-Zion's wrath as the thundering voice still echoed down the hall from Research.

From the doorway to Cover, Pnina's concerned face suddenly emerged. "Bavaria?"

"Good night," said Eckstein as he hurried on, nearly staggering as he marched painfully down the cold, dark stairwell.

When by seven o'clock Eytan had still not arrived at home, Simona began to worry.

She of course had not known her husband during his tenure as a field agent, when he would often be gone from his apartment for days or would disappear from the country altogether without a word to friends or family. His present job, the one he fairly dragged himself to each morning, had very regular hours. He rarely came home after five. Still, during her regular military service Simona had been an Air Force radio-intercept operator in Tel Aviv. She knew from those two years "in the hole" that when something was brewing intelligence people often lost track of the time. She hoped that Eytan was simply engrossed in some important assignment. That would be good for him, for both of them. Naturally, all of the other, darker reasons for his delay also coursed through her brain, and she was tempted to call the office. But she would not do that. In Israel, military wives did not call the office *stahm*, unless they were in the advanced stages of labor or the house was ablaze. Everyone in the country knew that the real heroes of the Israel Defense Forces were the wives who waited, silently, stoically, and Simona was not about to shatter that image.

Simona had had a difficult day herself. She now worked in the children's cancer wing at Hadassah Hospital, and her face muscles ached from her constant attempts to smile, her feet burned from the endless tramping up and down the hard tile floors of the wards.

Yet she always looked forward to coming home, even climbing the three flights to their apartment in East Talpiot. Although it was only a rental, the flat was far beyond anything either Simona or Eytan had ever hoped for. By Jerusalem standards it was huge, with three bedrooms, a veranda and two bathrooms on the top floor. The main level had an expansive teak-lined salon which opened up onto another wide veranda, and there was a dining nook, American kitchen, and even a laundry room at the back. In addition, the living room had a fireplace, something Simona had only seen in American films.

Nowadays all Israeli rentals were listed in U.S. dollars rather than New Shekels, and the newlywed Ecksteins could never have afforded the $700-a-month fee. But Eytan's office allowed him $300 a month for housing, and upon seeing the place, and immediately loving it, they had agreed to skimp and save to come up with the balance.

So whatever the trials of their workaday lives, Eytan and

Simona were almost always calmed by the luxury of their living quarters. Family and friends always gaped in wonder at the extravagance of such a flat. But when they asked—in typical Israeli fashion—of the price of such quarters, Eytan would cryptically mutter, "You know, Ministry of Defense," and that would shut them up. If the apartment owner ever agreed to sell, Eytan and Simona both knew that they would rob a bank if need be, but they would somehow manage to buy Number 18 at 521 Maalot El Ram.

Simona had doffed her sweaty, hospital-permeated nurse's uniform. She had showered, washed her jet-black hair and pulled on a pair of jeans and a light cotton shirt. Barefoot now, she stood out on the main veranda, between her long rectangular pots of pink petunias and white magnolias. She had a glass of iced orange juice in one hand, and she looked out over the Judean desert, watching the Arab houses of Sur Bacher going purple with the coming of night. She tried not to look at her watch, one ear cocked for the ring of the telephone.

Eytan arrived at 7:20. He was using the cane again, and he was half drunk. He had stopped at the ridge of Armon Hanatziv, the Hill of Evil Counsel, where the UN was head-quartered. It was the most beautiful view of Jerusalem from any vantage, and when troubled, Eckstein often went there to sit on the hillside, watching the domes, spires and winding walls changing color with the trek of the sun. They were building a long promenade on the hill, and soon every tourist in the country would be trampling over Eytan's private pur-view, slurping ice cream and clicking camera shutters. But for now, there was only a tasteful restaurant dug into the hillside, barely visible from the road. Eytan had sat out on the grass, squinting at the distant Dome of the Rock, fairly inhaling three cans of Maccabee, trying to remind himself that he still had some things for which to be thankful.

But by the time he managed the three flights to the apartment, a hardship which he had stubbornly ignored when he signed the lease, he was sweating and the knee was on fire. Much of the anger had returned.

Simona hurried in from the veranda, greeting him like a faithful pup.

"*Todah l'El*," she said. "I was worried."

Eytan tossed his briefcase and cane onto the green Scandinavian couch. He fell into a black rocker and banged his head back on the wooden rest. He closed his eyes.

"No need. I'm covered for death and disability."

Simona ignored the stupid remark and kissed Eytan on his tight mouth. Her lips were soft and cold from the ice.

Eytan opened his eyes. "I'm sorry I said that." He reached under his shirttail and removed his holstered pistol, laying it on the wooden coffee table.

"No apology necessary." Simona was still smiling, but her wide green eyes showed concern. "Drinking so early? Very un-Israeli."

"I *am* very un-Israeli, thanks to my bloody career."

Simona sat down on the couch, holding her glass over her knees. Even in his cold, dark mood, Eytan could not block the incursion of his wife's warmth, her beauty, the lines of her full breasts beneath her shirt and the elegance of her long slender fingers.

"What happened today, Eytan?"

"God, I need a cigarette, Mona." He liked calling her that, and she loved hearing it. It was foreign, sexy. Simona took the cigarettes from Eytan's shirt pocket, lit one for her husband and put it to his lips. Her thoughts went briefly to the cancer ward and she dispelled them.

"I'm still listening," she said.

"Itzik Ben-Zion. That's what happened. That's what always happens."

"Ahhh." Simona sat back on the couch. She looked out through the white stucco archway to the dark hills and the brightening stars. This was a recurring problem, and it would not go away. Eytan had been a combat officer, and now he was "flying a desk," as they said. She had seen the syndrome before. In addition, that idiot colonel would not let Eytan forget something that had wounded her husband physically and crippled him mentally, something that had turned him into the vulnerable man she loved. But at this rate, he was not going to make it, would not last at least until his partial pension. They were trying to get pregnant, they needed the housing subsidy, their parents were not wealthy, and they would have to buy many new baby items on their own. If Eytan could not persevere, their fairy-tale nest would crumble.

"I'm going to quit," Eckstein said suddenly, propelling himself from the rocker. He listed slightly for a moment, then he stalked out to the veranda and leaned on the wrought-iron guardrail. The growing wind mussed his hair, the spring evenings were still rather cold, but he did not seem to notice.

Simona followed her husband, yet she stood back a bit, just listening.

"There's no reason to take it," Eytan said. "Be his punching bag. I'm young. I'll get something else. We'll manage." He suddenly dropped the cigarette and crushed it with his heel.

They both knew what *manage* would mean. Simona let the idea hang there for a while. Then she spoke.

"My husband always tells me, 'Don't grocery shop when you're hungry and don't make decisions when you're mad.'"

Eytan snorted. "But your husband's an idiot."

"Maybe he's just hungry?" Simona offered. "I was going to barbeque tonight. *Shishlik*."

"It sounds *yoffi*," said Eytan. "But I'm not hungry." He turned around and Simona saw the depth of the hurt in his eyes. "I'm just exhausted, Mona. Just damn tired."

She took his arm, put it over her shoulder and led him back inside as she squeezed his waist. "A nap then," she said as she led him up the staircase. "And then we'll see."

In the bedroom, Simona lowered the European window *treece*, putting most of the space into dark shadow, except for the brightening shafts of moonlight that sneaked through the cracks of the plastic latticework. She lowered Eytan backward onto the bed, took off his sneakers, socks, and jeans while he stared up at the ceiling. Then she kneeled on the mattress, bent over him and kissed him on the mouth. "You only have to do one thing for me," she whispered. "And I'll do most of it."

She stood up and began to unbutton her blouse.

Sex was the last thing on Eytan's mind, and he was about to protest. But then he remembered the baby. Simona had warned him, playfully, that these four days in her cycle were crucial, and no matter the moods, problems, fights, or lateness of the hour, they would be making love. Not that Eytan usually objected, since he was also anxious to begin adding to the family. Yet how could he have foreseen this day's insidious events? And how could he "perform" in this half-inebriated, dour frame of mind?

Yet he also knew, as he watched her, that he was captured. Simona's body still shocked him, as it had that very first time, alone together in an empty room at Assaf HaRofe near the end of his stay—her slim, permanently tanned figure, the smooth tone of her skin and the youthful curves of her chest. The black glistening hair at the peak of her sleek thighs could arouse him even if he were half-dead.

She came to him wearing only her panties, for she liked to start that way, leaving something to "peel." He felt himself growing hard, and he searched deeply in her soft mouth, the feel of her breasts against his skin, for a way to dispel all the pains of the day.

They had always made love with Simona above, for

Eytan's knee would not bear the pressure of other positions. Yet this time, with his growing passion suffused with residual anger, he once more "discarded his cane." He sat up suddenly, surprising Simona, gripping her shoulders as he kissed her neck, her breasts, the concave curve beneath her rib cage as she leaned back and moaned. And then he was rolling her over, and she did not stop him, helping him with her underpants and then his. And then they were one, rocking, gasping, crushing their mouths together until their fingertips dug into each other's flesh in a final arch of frenzy.

Some long moments passed while their breathing returned, slowly, Eytan above and Simona lying beneath, hugging him, contented. The alcohol, frustration, exertion and release had taken their toll. Simona slipped out from beneath her sleeping husband, kissed him softly on the ear and covered him with a sheet. Then she pulled on a robe and tiptoed away to make herself dinner.

He dreamed of many things, fitfully, twitching like a dog in the throes of his memories. He dreamed of the army, of parachuting into darkened deserts, of climbing the peakless mountains of Lebanon, of careening in brakeless cars through rain-slickened streets of anonymous cities.

But most of all, he dreamed of Amar Kamil.

2

A Small Town in Israel

YOSSI YERUSHALMI AWOKE AS HE DID ALWAYS, with the sun in his eyes. It was a calculated reception of the intrusive morning light, confluent with Yossi's lifelong practice of selecting bedrooms which would foil his poor nocturnal habits. All his life Yossi had battled the urge to sleep late, to linger in bed long past an acceptable hour. Forced to outwit his own metabolism, he would remove the slat-blinds from his windows, allow no curtains, and arrange the angle of his bed just so. Neither the banging of alarm clocks nor the persistent music of radios could penetrate his slumber. The only effective weapon was a blinding message from God.

Yossi's wife, Rina, was not terribly enamored of her husband's morning tattoo, but she had managed to adjust. After a year of marriage, the dawn's spectral and sonic cacophony of light and bird whistles careening off the bedroom walls no longer affected her. While her husband struggled with his

93

eyelids, she went right on sleeping. Unless, of course, the baby called to her first.

However, on this particular morning Yossi hardly even required nature's assistance. He had barely slept, yet he snapped up in bed as if he had had a full eight hours of rest. At long last he would be breaking the pleasant monotony of his existence, leaving for an extended business trip. He felt some pangs of guilt for leaving Rina and the baby behind, but he had not set foot outside of *Petach Tikva* since their wedding day. It was a welcome change, and he was suffused with anticipation.

The air in the room was cold, unusually so for late spring in Israel. Rina had kicked the blue woolen blanket down around her waist, and Yossi gently pulled it back up over her shoulders, where it covered the splayed ends of her long blonde hair. She did not stir, but her eyes were shut fiercely tight, as if she were already awake yet unprepared to face this day.

The bedroom door was propped halfway open with a triangular rubber stopper so they could hear the baby. Yossi slipped through, naked, hugging himself as he trotted across the cold tile floor of the salon toward the kitchen. The far end of the long salon had floor-to-ceiling windows; the sun streamed in through the collapsible metal blinds and threw wavy shadows on the floor as it passed the large leaves of hanging plants. But it was not yet strong enough to offer any warmth.

Yossi filled a steel *kumkum* with water from the kitchen tap. His fingers shook as he lit a match and ignited the gas stove. He set the water to boil and dashed back to the bathroom.

The Israeli method of solar heating is probably one of the most efficient yet unpublicized products of the Jewish State. The rooftop tanks bleed thin slices of water between aluminum sheets and plates of magnifying glass, and even after only a few minutes of sun Yossi had enough hot water in which to shave. He watched himself in the mirror as he lathered with a badger brush. He was satisfied with his thirty-five-year-old face. He had a full head of short, curly, reddish-blond hair. His jaw was wide and strong, his nose rather small and, except for a slight bump, barely Semitic. His lips might have been fuller, for they projected a certain lack of empathy, although his smile made up for that. The corners of his eyes were hardly wrinkled, and the irises so clear and so green they seemed almost unnatural.

He turned on the small transistor next to the sink, keeping the volume low. *Galei Tzahal,* the Army Network, was running its dawn wakeup program. It was a pleasant medley of old war songs from 1948. They were decidedly unmartial in tune and lyric and, like most Israeli war songs, expressed longings for home, family and peace. The signal was clear and strong, and Yossi smiled because his was the only neighborhood that enjoyed the superb reception of cable radio.

He rinsed his razor, leaving the swatches of lather on his face, and he began to hum along with Arik Lavie as he stepped into the shower. He turned the current on full and enjoyed the pounding of the hot water on his skin, and by the time he rinsed away the lather, soap and shampoo he felt more awake than he had in a month of mornings.

Rina was gone when Yossi returned to the bedroom. She was already with the baby, but Yossi did not seek them out. It would be difficult enough today, and he was putting it off. His small suitcase and briefcase were already packed, his clothes laid out over a chair.

He dressed, unusually for him, in a charcoal-grey suit. The new white shirt came fresh from its package, and it was stiff and coarse against his damp skin. He had some trouble with the dark blue pinstriped tie, for it had been so long since he had had to wear one. He briefly swept his new cordovan loafers with a rag and stood to look in the door mirror. Satisfied, if not exactly comfortable, he reached into his breast pocket for his glasses and set the tortoiseshell frames on his face. He squinted, then he smiled. He looked like a Geneva stockbroker.

At the end of the hallway, the door to the baby's room was closed. Yossi was about to enter, then he hesitated, turned, and made straight for the kitchen, fairly tiptoeing on the tile floors. From the refrigerator he extracted a bottle of *Mitz Paz*, more of a watery orange drink than actual juice. He took out a stick of margarine and a jar of strawberry jam, and picked out a fresh cucumber-sized roll from a basket on the kitchen table.

He made himself a dark cup of instant *Nes,* added some milk and sugar, and sat down to his breakfast.

He was really too excited to eat, but he forced himself to dress the roll. He did not know when he would find the next opportunity for a meal. It was strange, for the first time in so many work days, to not be going to the office. The people at the Bank Leumi branch were pleasant, and the conditions more than accommodating, yet he would not miss any of it. And although he took his studying seriously, spending his evenings in pursuit of a master's degree in modern Israeli history, the work and the learning took their toll on his family life. It was difficult to be a young father, so much responsibility. In truth, it would be good to get away, and he could justify his pleasure with the knowledge that the baby and Rina would want for nothing.

She came out of the hallway with her hair in disarray, wild around her face and over her shoulders. She was wearing her pink terrycloth robe, and she was clutching Katya to her, the baby wrapped in a white cotton shawl against the morning chill.

Katya was fussing, small hiccups as if she had been crying, and she reached her tiny hands up to Rina's face. Her mother gently pushed them away. She, too, looked as if she had been crying. Her cheeks were flushed and she had lost her ever-present smile.

On this morning, Rina was certainly not sharing her husband's optimism. And if he was actually indulging a certain joy, betrayed by his unusual morning alacrity, she was having none of it. The business trip was not a surprise, and Rina had been experiencing a growing edginess with the recent passage of time. Now, the panic of imminent abandonment was welling within her. *She* would be tasting no excitement, no thrill of adventure. She and Katya would be left at home. Alone.

However, Rina was mustering all her strength to suppress her emotions, check her tears. She still firmly believed that her role was that of Yossi Yerushalmi's loving wife, mother to his child, supportive partner. She was his only family, his roots, his moral support, and she would continue that role with a straight-backed martyrdom that seemed almost politically zealous.

Yossi looked up from his coffee, his eyes like those of a dog caught devouring the family chicken.

"*Boker tov,*" Rina whispered.

"No mornings are good mornings." Yossi repeated their private joke, but it fell flat.

"You look so strange," said Rina, her mouth twisting as she shifted Katya to the other side.

Yossi looked down at his suit. He swept some crumbs from his tie. "I *feel* strange."

Suddenly the baby began to cry. She reached up into the air and her face went red, until she finally let out the first long wail.

"*Ma yesh,* Katya?" Yossi stood up and walked quickly to

97

his family. He reached for the baby, but Rina said, "Don't. You'll mess the suit." Then she bounced the baby a few times, though it didn't seem to help.

"She knows us," Rina said. "She can feel it, that's all."

"Give her to me," said Yossi. "To hell with the suit."

Rina handed Katya over, and Yossi cooed to her. But he did hold her away at some length, keeping her tears from the grey wool.

"I'll get your things," said Rina.

She came back with the suitcase and the business brief. They switched, Rina recovering the baby, Yossi reluctantly hefting his bags.

He looked at Rina for a long time, wordless, completely at a loss.

"*Sa,*" she finally said, freeing him.

"*Ani etgageya,*" Yossi managed.

"I'll miss you too." Rina's tears were coming now, joining Katya's, soaking into her terrycloth.

Yossi kissed his wife on her trembling lips, tasting the salt. Then he kissed the baby on her pink skull, feeling the light fuzz of new hair.

He walked quickly to the door and was gone.

———

By the time Yossi reached the last of his four flights of stairs, he had switched emotional gears, recovering the optimism of the morning. The shock of the cold air, fresh and damp with the night rain, felt like a breath of pure oxygen after an evening in a smoky pub. He pulled his raincoat closed and buttoned it, briefly wishing that he had something heavier than the light olive trench. He turned and looked at his battered white Renault 4, parked in the open carport, hoping that Rina would finally learn to master the strange dashboard gear lever. He smiled at the little car and began to walk.

With a few long strides, he reached the street. Hannah

Senesh was not much more than an alleyway, a one-way road barely wide enough for the passage of a single car. It was a quiet place, lined with tall cedars and small apartment buildings, and Yossi had always felt affection for its name, dedicated to the bravery, self-sacrifice and near anonymity of a female Israeli war hero.

Although it was very early, even by Israeli standards, this part of *Petach Tikva* was already coming awake. Yossi could hear the dew-choked carburetors of small cars out on the roads, the voices of children on their way to *gan,* the low calls of businessmen as they beckoned to co-workers to come down from their apartments and join them in their walks into town. Yossi turned left and began to walk north on Hannah Senesh. He was tempted to look back at Number 7, up at the veranda from which he knew Rina would be watching. But he did not do so. An old man driving a watermelon cart passed him coming the other way; the shaggy driver and his donkey returned Yossi's nod with their own.

Halfway down the block on the left was a low, single-story cement building. The stucco house had a wide front window, its yellowed slat-blinds just rolling up into the wooden casing as Mrs. Grunwald hauled on the webbed lanyard like a ghostly sailor's mate raising roughened canvas. Mrs. Grunwald owned the local kiosk, as well as running a small children's playground. It was seemingly a strange combination, though her endeavors brought convenience and relief to neighborhood mothers.

Mrs. Grunwald bugged her eyes and smoothed her thinning white hair as she saw Yossi approaching in his suit.

"*Mar Yerushalmi!*" she croaked in a voice filled with years beyond estimation. "*Ayzeh chatich atah hayom!*"

Yossi bowed, accepting the compliment.

"Thank you. And good morning to you, Mrs. Grunwald."

As she did every morning, the old woman handed over

the first edition of *Maariv,* as well as two packs of Time. Yossi opened his briefcase and dropped the cigarettes inside. Then he took up the paper and scanned the headlines. As always, the edition was one day behind, but he was used to that by now. Events always reached *Petach Tikva* after the rest of the world had already absorbed them, as if the small town's opinion was unimportant vis-à-vis its impact on the international scene.

"Anything else?" Mrs. Grunwald asked, although Mr. Yerushalmi's response was always politely negative.

"Just a smile, please."

And of course the old woman complied, adding a slight blush as she smoothed her hair again. *"Shalom,"* she said as Yossi walked off.

"Shalom," he called over his shoulder.

"Going away?" She could not help asking the receding figure, and then she quickly put her fingertips to her naughty lips.

He just waved in the air.

Yossi reached Herzl Street and turned left again, walking more briskly, hoping to warm himself with the exercise. He passed some people on the road, children wearing brightly colored knapsacks and hurrying to school, pregnant mothers pushing prams, men his age and older wearing worn IDF winter jackets against the morning cold. The neighborhood Amizragas man who delivered the cooking gas bottles passed Yossi on the sidewalk. At first he failed to recognize Yossi due to the suit, but then he stopped short, winked conspiratorially and then waved as he entered a courtyard to one of the buildings.

Yossi arrived at the intersection, where on chilly days such as this, he would normally have boarded the Number 17 bus for the short ride down Haim Ozer to his branch of Bank Leumi. A policeman rode by on a white Vespa; soldiers carrying Galils and kit bags looked glum as they left their warm furloughs; pretty high school girls gossiped as they trotted to their early classes.

Yossi crossed the road and waited near the far corner. He lit up a cigarette and looked at his watch. He was not at a designated stop, but soon a red Mercedes bus pulled up, its visor showing the title SPECIAL in bold black letters on a white roller. Yossi boarded, the driver greeting him with a nod. He took a seat in the front. There was only one other passenger, a soldier who appeared to be sleeping on the rear-most seat.

The bus moved quickly south, away from the center of town, making no stops. It took a left on Rehov Pinis, traveling for another five minutes as the clusters of apartments grew more sparse and the traffic on the roads receded to the occasional army jeep or police car. The bus stopped at Sirkin Junction, the southeasternmost intersection of the town line.

"*B'atzlacha,*" the driver wished him success as he opened the doors.

"*Toda,*" said Yossi as he carried his cases down to the road.

He began to walk again, due east now, along the narrow highway toward the countryside. Here the grassy fields quickly fell off to unfarmed plots of flat mud. The trees were bare, excepting the occasional clusters of pines, and the spotty distant scabs of melting snow made the warmer memories of *Petach Tikva* incongruous.

After half a kilometer, Yossi reached a large mesh fence that blocked the highway. Its concertina-topped lengths drifted away from both sides of the road, disappearing over the distant hills. At its center was a gate in the roadway. A lone fatigue-capped figure in a green woolen uniform stood there, shifting from boot to boot, restraining a husky at the end of a leash. The man watched Yossi's approach and then wordlessly slid the gate back on its rollers, without raising his eyes again as Yossi passed through.

He walked another half kilometer, warm now with the exertion. Then, finally, at the crest of a hill where the highway ran between a pair of withered trees, he saw the car.

It was long, grey and boxy at both ends, parked across the two lanes as if confident that no other traffic would appear. Yossi's excitement rose, his heart faster now. He could not see into the car for its smoked windows, but as it grew larger the trunk suddenly opened like a genie's cave, hissing up on hydraulic hinges.

The engine was running; smoothly, barely audible, and Yossi stepped through the cloud of exhaust and put his cases into the deep trunk. He closed it, rubbed his chilled hands together, then walked to one of the rear doors and got inside. Immediately the big limousine began to move.

It took a minute for Yossi's eyes to adjust, for the sun had been so bright, and the car was gloomy with its black leather and photogrey glass. He was alone on the huge rear cushion; a thick plexiglass divider separated him from the driver's compartment. In the front right seat was a large figure, a husky man in a dark suit who appeared to be reading some papers. His head was wide, the short blond hair going grey with age. To the left, the driver's peaked cap stayed dead straight above the wheel, positioned between a pair of hands encased in black leather gloves.

The limousine was moving very fast now, fairly flying over the narrow highway. Suddenly Yossi was smacked with the reality that, despite his assurances to Rina, he was leaving. If all went well, he would not return. He turned in his seat and peered out the rear window.

On the flat horizon, he could still see his small *Israeli* town, its low plaster buildings, pointed cedars and plastic palms receding quickly in the distance.

Far to the south, and smaller than fingertips, he could just make out the wooden suburban houses and peaked roofs of the long-deserted *American Town*.

And to the north, not much more than grey dots on a low plateau, were the neglected stone facades and church spires of the *West German Town*.

He turned around and sat back against the high leather seat, releasing a sigh of wonder. It had been like living in Disneyland, for with the aid of satellite dishes, radio and TV intercepts, and the expertise of his fellow workers, everything above ground had been so *real*. Only the newspapers were always a day late.

He looked ahead, to the future, to the pinpoint end of the road that wavered at the next barren crest. And despite himself, he once more felt the growing excitement.

Though he would not be there for another six hours, he could almost *smell* Moscow.

The plexiglass partition suddenly slid down into its leather sheath, and the large man seemed to awaken to the presence of his charge. He turned quickly, throwing a beefy arm over the partition and smiling through a Slavic, gap-toothed mouth.

"Good morning, Aswan," said the man.

Yossi was momentarily shocked. It was the sound of Russian, which he had not heard in over a year. It would take him more than a moment to make the adjustment, and his eyes must have registered his surprise, making Major Vladimir Kozov think that he was admonishing the open use of his code name.

"Oh, don't worry about him," said the officer, pointing a gloved finger at the motionless driver. "He's deaf." The KGB man laughed heartily, a sound strangely accompanied by the gravelly singing of Vladimir Vissotsky as it boomed from a tape player. Many Russians had been imprisoned for listening to the dissident poet, but the KGB enjoyed whatever music it pleased. "It doesn't make for the safest driving," said the officer, still referring to his driver's handicap. "But it's perfect for security."

He was still laughing, but then it faded quickly, receding to a warm, sympathetic smile. He did not realize that his passenger's expression resulted from insecurity, a fear that his first utterance would gush forth reflexively in Hebrew.

The KGB man jutted his jaw toward the rear window.

"I hope you will not be too homesick," he said empathetically. "The *real* Israel awaits you." He smiled once more. "She is *longing* for you."

Amar Kamil smiled in return.

3

Jerusalem

ON TUESDAY MORNING, Itzik Ben-Zion was in a fine mood. Unfortunately for the Special Operations personnel, the Colonel's frame of mind was always directly correlated to the degree of his successes or failures. When operations proceeded with only a modicum of results, the commander was sullen, somber, somewhat like a burbling volcanic pit. However, on days such as this when his successes were no less than smashing, Ben-Zion's arrogance rushed to the surface like so much summer sea scum, and he was profoundly happy. And when Itzik Ben-Zion was happy, he was also supremely foul.

Eytan knew that it was coming, like a hunter smells rain on the wind, like a racing driver knows that on this day there will be the smack of steel against steel, the smear of blood on asphalt. Yet his insight was not exactly telepathic.

He had taken Monday off, calling in sick, and spent much of the morning in bed. He accepted Simona's advice and used most of the day to "cool off." He sat out on the large veranda at their round, white umbrella table, sipping iced coffee, catching up on the weekend papers, and soaking up the warm springtime sun. In the afternoon he met Simona at Machane Yehuda, where hand in hand they shopped for fresh meats and vegetables at the huge bins tended by friendly stall keepers.

In the evening, after Eytan canceled dinner at the Baums, they finally had their delayed barbecue, and with the aid of a couple of Maccabees Eckstein achieved an uneven keel approaching a relaxed euphoria that he had not known for many months. Simona went back to the hospital, having switched a shift with a co-worker. Eytan popped *The Living Daylights* into the VCR, and he laughed aloud at the Bondian shenanigans and whistled with respect at the riskier stunts.

At midnight, with the final TV news wrap-up, Eytan's state returned abruptly to stone-cold sober. There was a brief blurb, an early report about an assassination in Beirut. A PLO Chief of Operations named Abu-Mohammed had been executed in his flat, the details and perpetrators of the operation as yet unknown.

But Eytan had no doubt as to the identity of the executioners. He sat before the television for a good long hour, motionless, staring at the test pattern until it, too, faded into a blank screen. He filled that screen with a thousand images from his own history, hoping at once that there were no errors, that the mission was a total success, then guiltily wishing that it had somehow failed.

It seemed that a day could not pass without bringing some persistent reminder of Munich. His team members, though scattered now around the globe, made their regular appearances. Ettie Denziger, whose image he fought hardest to suppress, infiltrated his mind.

Beirut. He was glad that he had not been there, then felt

instantly and enormously depressed, somewhat like an injured goalkeeper who has just watched his team win the World Soccer Cup.

In the morning, after a night of fitful sleep, he was sorely tempted to take an additional sick day. Yet his pride finally propelled him from the bed. He was certain that his absence following Ben-Zion's tiradical reprimand had already fed the Department's rumor mill, and he wanted to quell any impressions that he might have finally succumbed to the Colonel's abuses.

Eckstein was in Personnel by eight o'clock sharp. Zvika, the driver-cum-runner, was already out on his errands, and Eckstein sat at the boy's desk correcting Yudit's typescript of his recent interviews. Yudit was not in yet and Eckstein borrowed the Walkman from her drawer and listened to the hourly news as he sipped a cup of *Nes* and smoked a cigarette.

The morning reports were already quite full of details. The sources were quoted as "foreign wire services," and indicated that Abu-Mohammed, one of the last surviving architects of the Coast Road Massacre of 1978 and known to Western intelligence sources as the Black Prince, had indeed been assassinated in Beirut. The execution was being universally condemned as perpetuating the cycle of Middle East violence, yet the operation was almost lauded for its surgical professionalism. Abu-Mohammed had been killed in his private quarters in the middle of West Beirut. His bodyguards had also been shot, but his wife and daughter remained unharmed, even though they had attempted to prevent the execution with their own bodies. The professional team of killers had arrived at the scene and departed within four minutes, leaving neither evidence nor casualties behind.

Almost without exception, "foreign sources" pointed to an Israeli operation. As Eytan removed the earphones from his head and dropped them on the desk, he needed no further proof of this assessment. He looked up at the ceiling, where the vibrations of moving feet from above caused the light bulbs to shiver on their wires. The Top Floor had been up all night long, and it was certainly not because they were holding a rousing poker game.

Eytan wished that he had brought along his pair of pistol range muffs. There was going to be a lot of unsubtle merry-making on the floors today, and he really did not want to hear it.

"*Boker tov.*"

He was snapped from his brooding by Yudit's greeting as she entered the room and closed the door. She was sprightly this morning, fairly bouncing on the balls of her feet, and Eytan could not help smiling at her.

"*Boker tov lach,*" he said and extended a hand to return her Walkman. "I borrowed it. Hope you don't mind."

Yudit tossed her black purse onto her desk top and retrieved the radio. "And if I did?"

"Then you wouldn't be Yudit," said Eckstein.

The girl almost blushed, but she managed to suppress it. She worked hard not to reveal the crush on her elder co-worker, but she wasn't fooling anyone. She examined the cassette-radio without really seeing it.

"So you've heard, then."

"What's that?" He feigned ignorance.

She knitted her brows. *Everyone* knew by this hour, every-one who had a radio or a television, from the top cabinet ministers to the Bedouins in the Negev. "You know. Beirut."

"Ah, yes." Eckstein sat back in his chair and blew out some smoke. "Used to be a lovely seaside city. Seems to me I was there once." He squinted up at the ceiling.

"Come on, Eytan."

"Yes. I heard." Eckstein gave up the game. Yudit was still very young, not yet bruised with the cynicism of expe-rience. He straightened the papers before him, as if bored by the whole affair. "Quite an operation," he said. "Must have been the Brits, or the Americans."

"Of course." Yudit was smiling at him again, and suddenly Eckstein realized that her look also harbored a degree of sympathetic indulgence. He always thought of the girl as a teenager, so much younger than himself, yet here she was already well-armed with those sophisticated psychological tongs with which women handled fragile male egos. It struck Eckstein that Yudit was certainly no child, probably long past virginity. She was a very pretty girl, and with her long black curls and blue eyes her form was reminiscent of Simona's.

"Yudit!" He suddenly sat upright. "For God's sake, you're wearing a uniform!"

All at once he was alarmed for her. It was one of Ben-Zion's strictest regulations. No one, no matter their military status, was ever to appear at Headquarters in anything but civilian clothes. And here she was, in olive *Class Alephs,* with her sergeant's stripes no less.

"I know. Don't worry so," she said, pleased with his concern. "Haven't you heard?"

"No, I haven't."

"New rules. All support staff have a day, once a month now, in uniform. I heard it was Benni Baum's idea."

"Naturally."

"Benni said it wasn't normal. Every building in the country's got soldiers going in and out, even if it's just personal business. Doesn't look right without them." She dug into her purse and came up with a buttered roll wrapped in sweating plastic. "Smart, huh?"

"Yeah." Eckstein tapped a pencil on the desk. "That's Benni." Indeed it sounded like Baum's reasoning. Baum had a chess master's mentality. He could always determine what the opposition would be thinking and then provide an appropriate bit of strategic doublethink.

Yudit stood up to make some coffee. "Want some more?"

"Sure." Eckstein watched her. The uniform was a drab, thick green cloth tunic that covered the top part of her slacks. The Supply Corps had recently replaced the old women's uniforms, which had been of light grey cotton, skintight miniskirts, blouses and slacks which revealed every delicious crevasse and curve.

"I liked the old uniforms," said Eckstein.

"That's what *all* the men say," Yudit answered a bit too quickly.

"Morning." Danny Romano came bounding in, his empty pipe clutched between his teeth. "Ah, coffee is what I need."

"Coming up," said Yudit.

"Morning," said Eckstein.

Romano dropped his briefcase on his desk by the window. "Feeling better, Eytan?"

"Walking wounded."

"I don't see the cane."

"And you won't again."

"Good man."

"Did you hear, Danny?" Yudit asked as she handed him a glass full of steaming black liquid. He took it by the top edges with thumb and forefingers, but it burned him anyway and he hurried to set it down.

"*Yo!*" He wrung out his hand. "Damned Russian Jews!" He cursed the Slavic tradition of placing hot liquids in glass receptacles, a painful habit which no government institution seemed capable of abolishing. "Yes, I heard. Itzik will be fucking insufferable today."

As if on cue, the door was pushed open and Heinz filled the frame. The captain's white-blond hair was wild, unwashed and hardly finger-combed, giving him a more-than-usual crazed look. Heinz was often referred to as Ben-Zion's *Stiletto,* for he carried out the Colonel's most morale-depleting directives, such as transfers, reprimands and rank-bustings, with cruel relish. Heinz's near-translucent blue eyes were shot through with fine pink lines. He had been up all night and was functioning on caffeine and adrenaline.

"Department heads upstairs in exactly fifteen minutes," Heinz snapped, and he looked at his watch like a platoon commander who wishes to frighten his green troops into punctuality. Then he glanced over at Eckstein and returned his gaze to Danny. "Just you, Romano," he said pointedly. "And bring a clean glass." He left and closed the door.

There was a moment of embarrassed silence in the room, then Eckstein emptied a pencil cup onto the desk and threw the plastic receptacle at the door, where it made a resounding crack and bounced onto the floor. "Good morning to you too, asshole," Eckstein shouted. He looked over at Yudit, who sat stiffly in her chair like a frightened cat. "Sorry," he said. He hated Heinz, primarily because the man had no mind of his own. He was an empty vessel, a pure reflection of his boss's moods and desires.

If Ben-Zion had liked Eckstein, then Heinz would have spent plenty of time kissing Eytan's ass. "And bring a clean glass," Eckstein muttered, imitating Heinz's self-important tone. He picked up a pencil and tried to return to his work. Things had changed too much in the department, and he prayed that it was merely a passing influence of an ambitious commander rather than an indication of growing national callousness. He remembered with melancholy clarity how, long ago after a successful mission in southern France, during which a pair of terrorists had been blown up in their car, his team had split up and reassembled a week later in Jerusalem. There, after a lengthy debriefing, they had spontaneously gone down together to the Western Wall to pray together—believers, agnostics and atheists alike. Now, in stark contrast, when Itzik Ben-Zion's people killed someone, the cold commander gathered his department heads together and poured champagne like the owner of a winning basketball team.

Exasperated, Eckstein dropped his pencil and sat back,

rubbing his forehead. Yudit had retreated behind her computer, tapping out the reports on her plastic keys. The clatter was grating. Eckstein pushed his chair back and stood up.

"I'm going to the canteen. Anybody want something to eat?"

Yudit shook her head.

"Eytan." Romano looked up from beneath his bushy eyebrows. "Keep an even keel, okay?"

Eckstein turned in the doorway.

"You know something, Danny?" He began to raise his voice, then realized that Romano was no target for his anger. He smoothed his tone to a low burn. "I don't mind being out of the action, I really don't." And he knew as he said it that for a long while that had been true, but it was quickly becoming a lie. "But I'm sick to death of having my nose rubbed in it."

He went out into the hallway and turned toward the cafeteria. Itzik Ben-Zion was coming briskly along the hallway, followed by a young man carrying a large wooden crate. Ben-Zion nearly tripped over a telex cable that snaked across the floor like a black asp waiting in ambush. He immediately stopped short and slammed his palm against the first doorway that presented itself. It happened to be Cover, whose personnel certainly had nothing to do with communications. But that did not matter to the Colonel. Victims were plentiful wherever his wrath would find them writhing in the corners of his kingdom.

He ducked his large head into the doorway.

"I want those fucking cables off the floors *today!* This isn't a goddamn movie studio!" He let the door slam.

"Could have fooled me," Eckstein mumbled to himself, "what with all the melodrama."

Ben-Zion continued his march, walking right past Eckstein as if his once unsurpassable team leader were merely an apparition.

Eckstein stopped, lit a cigarette and plugged it between his teeth. He jammed his hands into the pockets of his khaki chinos and concentrated on keeping his gait even. Down the hall, a small crowd was gathered around the long table that held unclassified reports and copies of the morning papers. The men and women were passing sections of newspapers to each other, reading headlines aloud from *Maariv* and *Yediot*. Eckstein started forward, feeling the click in his knee vibrate up to his groin.

He braced himself mentally as he passed the table, where no less than eight people were chattering excitedly about the Beirut operation. Pnina from Cover looked up at Eckstein and smiled broadly.

"Morning, Bavaria!"

Eckstein made sure to smile back just as hard. "Morning."

She held up the front page of *Yediot*. "Have you seen this?" she asked excitedly.

Eckstein waved a hand. "Read them all, cover to cover," he lied. As a young paratrooper in the late 1970s, he had once relished reading the after-action newspaper coverage of his own unit's operations in Lebanon. But he quickly came to realize how distant was journalism from reality. Later on, following team operations in Europe, he was amazed to discover that news reports of the events were mostly fiction, deduction and fantasy.

"Do you believe those French?" Pnina clucked her tongue as Eckstein passed.

He could guess at her meaning. The Europeans were probably widely condemning Israel for her assumed actions.

"What do you expect from the people who gave Paris to the Nazis with hardly a shot?" he said.

"Yeah," someone else concurred. "But under the table they're clapping their hands."

"Come on," another voice retorted. "Let's at least give the French credit for what they do well *under* the table."

Eytan strode past as the banter became pornographic.

He arrived at the cafeteria and plunged into a seat. The room was filled with the morning coffee crowd, many of whom had newspapers spread out and were happily discussing the evening's event. There wasn't a field agent among them, but they were all support staff and were proud of any successful Department endeavor. More than most days, Eckstein felt completely out of place, precisely because he knew that this was in fact now his peer group.

"*Café, mein Herr?*"

Benni Baum appeared from out of the crowd, his solid girth imposing like a rising planet.

"Morning, Benni." Eckstein smiled tightly at him. "No more coffee, thanks. Sit."

Baum took a place at the table. He sipped from a cup and took a drag from a cigarette. "How are you feeling?"

"Sorry about last night, Benni. Truth is, I just did not want to socialize."

"No apologies. Just answer the question."

Eckstein looked at his former field commander. There was no lying to Benni. When you did, he immediately called you on it anyway and then sucked out the truth.

"I feel like shit. Especially since Itzik is upstairs right now gloating like an idiot."

"That's honest." Baum smeared some sweat into his bald head with a thick palm. "Selfish, but honest."

"I'm glad the operation came off," Eckstein hastened to say. "But I don't know how long I can take it, being half in and half out like this. Days like today are hard, that's all."

"Who wanted the scrambled eggs?" a girl behind the coffee bar called out to the room. "They're getting cold."

Benni waited for her to stop shouting, then he leaned in close to Eckstein.

"Look, I told you we'd try to get your situation improved. You have to be patient."

"So Simona tells me too. I know, we want to be parents and I have to last until partial pension, at least. But I'd rather be some idiot's driver at this point. Limping around here like some crippled ghost is getting to me." Eckstein stabbed out his cigarette while Baum clucked his tongue and shook his head. "I've decided, Benni. I'm going to demand my rights. Today."

Benni's eyes widened. "To-day?" He jabbed a finger to his own temple. *"Hishtagata?"*

"No, I'm not crazy. It's the right time. Itzik will be peacocking and obnoxious right now, but it's probably the only window of magnanimity I'll ever find."

"Department heads!" someone in the room yelled. "Duty calls." A number of men began to leave the room.

Baum looked at his watch. "Eytan," he said. "You are a stubborn young bastard and I like you." He drew himself up and out of the chair, coming to a Prussian erectness. "But it is my duty to say, as your friend and superior officer, that I strongly recommend against this action."

"I'm doing it, Benni," said Eckstein. "Today. Now."

"I will back you up," Baum said almost instantly.

"I thought you might." Eckstein smiled up at the major.

"But wait for at least half an hour."

Eckstein looked at his watch. "Okay. Half an hour."

As he headed for the door, Benni put a meaty hand on Eckstein's shoulder. "If my sons turn out like you," he said, "they'll be all right."

"Benni," Eckstein called after him. "You forgot to take a clean glass."

"I don't drink at graveside," said Baum, and he left for the meeting with Itzik Ben-Zion.

The conference room on the top floor of Headquarters was not comparable to that of a major banking institution, but it was plush by Israeli governmental standards. The windows were curtained in long green brocade, and there were small brass chandeliers as opposed to flickering fluorescent lights. The floor was uncarpeted, but the long teak table, at which twenty officers could be seated comfortably, was shiny and freshly oiled. Instead of the usual metal folding chairs, there were expensive office swivel types, armless but adequately cushioned. There was a TV monitor at one end, a VCR and a pull-down screen for slide or film projections. A huge tear-off paper pad stood on an art easel, its brace of colored markers held in an attached blue plastic bin.

The room was filled with smoke—pipe, cigarette and cigar—and most of the tabletop was obscured by copies of the morning papers, empty coffee glasses and reams of telex, decode, and computer printouts. Someone's pistol had apparently been chafing his flesh, and it lay next to a half-empty glass of champagne, this single shiny black object altering the character of the room from that of Think Tank to Armed Camp.

There were two women in the room and eleven men. All of them were department heads or seconds-in-command. None of the field agents or team leaders were present, since anyone who had actually been on the ground in Beirut was now being debriefed at some distant safe house. The meeting, or rather the celebration as Ben-Zion would have it, was drawing to a close. The department heads had mostly risen from their chairs, were gathering their notes and printouts, many of them slightly euphoric from a night of intense work topped off by a morning glass of champagne. The Israelis by nature are not fond of alcohol, and it usually has a rapid and dizzying effect. Field agents actually have to be trained to drink.

Except for Ben-Zion's secretary, no one in the room was younger than thirty, and there was no rank below captain. Under normal circumstances, the exhausted officers would have been anxious to get back to their offices, where they might be able to steal an hour's nap. However, blatantly successful days such as these were rare, so they lingered. Three men were in a far corner, clucking their tongues and loudly expressing their sympathy for the commanders of the CIA.

The Americans had been asked for a favor vis-à-vis the Beirut operation, and a special vessel attached to the Sixth Fleet had jammed Russian communications off the coast of Lebanon for six mind-bending hours. But the much-to-be-pitied U.S. intelligence services were constantly taking a beating in the American press. So, when they did participate successfully in an anti-terror operation, they were not allowed to admit it.

In another part of the room, Benni Baum was chatting with a homely old woman named Sylvia who headed up encrypted telex and cable traffic. He was sitting on the conference table and waving his arms, and the woman laughed and suggested that he dismount before the cost of the new table was deducted from his monthly salary.

At the front of the room next to the white projection screen, Itzik Ben-Zion stood talking to a uniformed major general. The officer was as tall as Ben-Zion, grey haired and handsome in a rather regal manner. The man was Amnon Zamir, *Rosh AMAN,* the Chief of Israeli Military Intelligence. If Eytan Eckstein had been forewarned of Zamir's presence, he might not have chosen that moment to enter the conference room.

The wooden door swung open and an exchange could be heard from outside. The guard from the second floor desk had been posted to keep unauthorized personnel out of the meeting.

"It's department heads only, Bavaria," said a pleading voice.

"So, shoot me, Moshiko." Eytan stepped into the room

and closed the door. All heads turned to look at him, and he assumed an optimistic expression, if not actually a smile. He raised a hand as if clutching an invisible champagne glass. "*Kol Hakavod* to everyone," he offered. A couple of people said, "Thanks, Eytan."

Eckstein stalked straight along one wall, heading for Itzik Ben-Zion, who looked over at him briefly and returned to his conversation with General Zamir. Heinz, who was standing by Ben-Zion like a ball boy at a tennis match, glared at Eckstein with undisguised disdain.

Eckstein stopped close to Ben-Zion. Benni Baum eased himself off the table and edged closer to Eckstein.

"Excuse me, Itzik," Eckstein said.

Ben-Zion sighed and turned slowly to the captain.

"We're in conference, Eckstein."

"Just wanted to say *mazal tov,* Itzik." Eckstein smiled. "It was quite an operation."

Ben-Zion's ego was his soft underbelly. A twist of the lips indicated his minor pleasure at the compliment.

"Thank you, Eckstein."

Eckstein extended a congratulatory hand, which the Colonel was forced to take. The captain gripped hard and held on.

"This seems a good time to bring up a small problem," said Eckstein.

Ben-Zion immediately darkened. "It is *hardly* the place or the time."

The Colonel's meaning was clear, but Eytan purposely did not look up at General Zamir. The informality of ranks in the IDF could work to one's advantage if carefully played.

"I'll make it quick, Itzik," he said. "I need a change. I have to begin moving forward again."

"We'll discuss it later," Ben-Zion snapped, pulling his hand away.

"For once in your life, be generous," Benni Baum growled at Ben-Zion from over Eckstein's shoulder.

The Colonel pursed his lips. He could not be made to look petty in front of his superior officer. "What is it?" He fairly snarled.

Good, Eckstein thought. *He's nearly trapped now.*

"I need some activity. The desk is choking me. I have to get my mind and my body moving again."

The rest of the room had fallen dead silent. Eckstein's past reputation was well known in the department, and despite Bogenhausen, all who knew him still harbored a good deal of respect for the wounded warrior.

"There is nothing available at the moment," said Ben-Zion.

The head of the Training Department spoke up courageously from the other end of the table. "We could use him in the indoctrination course."

"The recruits don't need advice from a failure, Eli," Ben-Zion snapped.

"Now wait just one minute, Itzik . . ." Benni Baum's color was rising rapidly.

"Excuse me," General Zamir interjected, speaking directly to Eckstein. "Aren't you Eytan Eckstein?"

"Yes sir, I am."

"The Munich problem, correct?"

"Yes."

Zamir turned to Ben-Zion. "This man was a talented commander, Itzik. Baum here has a point about generosity, and it is certainly the day for it."

Colonel Ben-Zion was cornered. He was furious, but he had no choice but to relent.

"Okay, Eckstein. There are no positions available now, and I need you in Personnel. But you can begin some physical retraining." He snapped his fingers at Heinz, who still stood there glaring at Eckstein and Benni Baum. "Heinz, call Win-gate. Send Eckstein over there. He can start this afternoon."

It wasn't precisely what Eytan had in mind, but it was a small victory.

"Thank you, Itzik," he said, and then he pointedly looked up at Zamir. "And thank you, General." That sealed it. Wit-nesses, the C.O.'s backing—Ben-Zion could not easily retract the order. Eckstein turned to leave and Benni Baum clapped him on the shoulder.

The door opened and a communications officer entered. He was one of Amnon Zamir's personal staff, and he called out to the general.

"Amnon, the phones are ringing off the wall. Journalists, radio, TV. What the hell do I say?"

"Well, Gadi." The general lifted his head and looked at the ceiling. "We want everyone to know it was us, correct?"

"Fine, so what's the official AMAN response?"

Amnon Zamir smiled.

No comment.

"You played it perfectly, it worked and that's fine," said Benni Baum. "But now you have to back off."

Baum and Eckstein trotted back down the stairway to the second floor. Actually, Benni was bounding and Eckstein was hobbling with the aid of the handrail, but their steps were light considering Baum's girth and Eckstein's scars.

"It worked, thanks to you," said Eckstein.

"Nonsense. I just growled in the right places. Did you hear what I just said?"

"Yes, Herr Major."

"I'm serious, Eytan. You got your foot in the door and now you have to be a good boy. Just stay out of his way and maybe we'll keep you from being bored to death for the next year and a half." Baum was using his hands for emphasis, pumping his palms as if performing push-ups in the air.

"It's fine, Benni," Eckstein assured him. "I don't have to get out in the field again."

"And while Itzik's here, you never will."

"Good. I don't want to."

They reached the landing. Moshiko was back at his desk. When he saw Eckstein he shook his head in disgust.

"Thanks a lot, Bavaria."

Eckstein smiled wryly at the young security officer. "You shouldn't have let me through, Moshiko."

"As if I could have stopped you. You were like a goddamn freight train."

"Sorry." Eckstein passed through with Baum in close pursuit.

"I probably won't get leave for a month!" Moshiko called after him.

"I'll tell your girlfriend you're on a secret mission," Eckstein said over his shoulder.

"Your moods are dangerous," Benni noted. "Just like our Commander's."

"Don't insult me. I'm entitled to one good mood per full moon."

The hallway had emptied. The morning's excitement had dissolved into a normal day's work load, and personnel were back in their offices. A couple of electronics men were down on the floor, rerouting cables to atone for Ben-Zion's displeasure over the obstruction.

As Baum and Eckstein approached Personnel they saw Danny Romano waiting in the open doorway. His usually optimistic expression had been replaced by a somber look, and he was shifting his dry briar between the fingers of one hand.

"Benni. Eytan. Come in here for a moment."

He went into the office and held the door. Baum and Eckstein exchanged a quizzical look and followed him. Yudit was on her feet, gathering her purse. She glanced up at

Eckstein and then touched him on the sleeve as she went out.

"Take your time, Yudit," Romano called after her. "At least half an hour."

"What's going on?" Eckstein asked.

Romano went to his desk. He turned and sat back on the edge of it, his posture slumping. He studied his pipe for a moment. When he looked up, he saw Benni and Eytan staring expectantly. Their victorious smiles from the morning's briefing were quickly fading.

"*Nu?*" Baum barked. "I've got work to do, Danny."

Romano sighed.

"Traffic just received a coded cable from the consulate in New York. No one knows yet but me. Sylvia told me first, so I could tell both of *you* first."

Baum and Eckstein were still staring blankly. Romano went on with the hard part.

"Zvika Pearlman is dead."

Eckstein expelled a sharp grunt, as if he'd been punched in the kidneys. He turned away and started to move to a chair. Then he stopped. A rod of fire was coursing up his leg and he could not bend it. He spun back on it, like a roast on a spit, and faced Romano once more.

"Say it again," he whispered.

"Zvi Pearlman. He was killed in Manhattan."

Benni Baum stood stock-still, expressing nothing. He slowly reached into his pocket, removed two cigarettes, lit them both and handed one to Eckstein without looking at him. Then he folded his fingers together, as if in prayer, and placed them over his belt buckle.

"More," Baum said.

Romano began to chew his pipe stem.

"There isn't much. Apparently it was a traffic accident, but until the security people are positive they wanted us to have it in code."

Eckstein's head was throbbing. He leaned back stiffly against a desk and braced himself with his hands.

"Does Lisa know, Danny?" he whispered.

"She was in New York with him. He was studying at NYU. The kids are there too. He was completely retired, you know."

"Yes," said Benni. "We know."

Eckstein inhaled deeply on the cigarette and then expelled the smoke with a rasping cough. He pulled the butt from his lips with a shaking hand and dropped it on the floor.

Harry Webber. He had known the man by that name for so many years that Zvika Pearlman seemed like someone else altogether. Yet they were the same man. Harry. Zvika.

Eytan had lost comrades before, but mostly in uniform, when they were all gung-ho paratroopers who stood up in a firefight and charged with the fury of impetuous youth. Yet in Special Operations, death was an infrequent and impacting event. In particular, Zvika Pearlman had seemed to be blessed with a special kind of light, a joyful, optimistic flexibility which seemed unbreachable by such banal concepts as mortality.

Harry Webber. They had been through so much together. Eckstein had first met him in their initial stages of indoctrination. Pearlman was recruited rather late in life. As a green soldier in the regular infantry, he had survived a horrific trial by fire, having been surrounded in a bunker on the Golan Heights by a mass of Syrian troops in the first week of the Yom Kippur War. Perhaps the fact that Pearlman still smiled easily after that trauma was the trait that had initially attracted his recruiters.

Eckstein searched in his memory for the shards of his friend's life. He remembered that Zvika had been born in Vienna, had lived there until he was a teenager, and been sent to Israel by his aging survivor-parents who saw no future for their only son in a European land which still barely tolerated its Jews. And while Zvika had certainly become a typical kibbutznik, he could, at the drop of a hat, return to the personage of a middle-class Austrian, replete with the coarse mannerisms and tortured *Hochdeutsch* of a typical Viennese. It was most certainly this inexorcisable birthright that gave Zvika Pearlman the schizophrenic ability to become Harry Webber, a jolly yet banal individual who mostly resembled a cabaret master of ceremonies circa postwar Vienna.

And it was this Harry Webber with whom Eytan and Benni had shared many a complex mission. It was this Harry Webber who had always functioned with a smile, ready with a joke under the most pressing situations, performing his tasks without fail, improvising and pulling a last trick from his hat with joyful relish. It was this Harry Webber whom each and every team member had loved without reservation.

Harry's "truck gambit" at Bogenhausen had been his final professional act. He had slipped away from Munich with aplomb, and in the after-action dissections he had escaped blame. But the Bogenhausen Fiasco had acted as a catalyst for Harry, and he gracefully retired. His kibbutz near Ashkelon owed him a year abroad, and he took his wife Lisa and their two young girls and headed out for a sabbatical in the United States.

Eckstein wanted to ask Danny for more details, but when he thought of Lisa and the children he could not find his voice.

Benni spoke for both of them.

"An accident," he said. "They're sure."

"Almost one hundred percent," said Danny. "He was loading the trunk of his car for a trip. A taxi rammed into him. Manhattan police say the driver's in the hospital, in shock. Guy's an Armenian and barely speaks English."

"Fucking New York drivers," Baum spat.

"Nearly as bad as Jerusalemites," said Romano without humor.

Eckstein pushed himself upright. He felt very unsteady and kept one hand on the desk top. He turned to Benni, who faced him with a sad, unwavering gaze. Both men needed to say something, perhaps a profound word, or a prayer. But it was far beyond that.

"Benni," Eytan whispered. "I need . . . I have to get some air."

"I'm not your boss, Eytan."

"He has no boss today," said Romano. "Go."

Eytan and Benni continued looking at each other.

"I can reach Rainer," said Baum. "And Peter, and Francie."

"I'll tell Ettie," said Eckstein.

"You still have to go to Wingate today, Eytan," Benni warned him. "Remember, check the time with Training."

"I'll be there."

"Good."

They looked at each other for another moment.

"Zvika Pearlman," Benni finally said. "*Zichrono le'vracha.* Blessed be his memory."

"Harry Webber," said Eckstein, and he limped out of the room.

———

Ettie Denziger lived in the heart of Tel Aviv. That is to say, whenever she was in the country, that was where she resided. Her apartment was a third-floor walk-up, located on a shady side street not far east of the intersection of Sokolov and Dizengoff, only four long blocks from the beach. Dizengoff Street was probably one of the most socially precocious avenues in the Middle East, two kilometers lined with bustling outdoor cafés before which a constant parade of pretty Israelis and Europeans peacocked for each other. But it was neither the swinging nightlife nor the lure of the Mediterranean that had attracted Ettie to Tel Aviv. Quite simply, it was the only city in Israel where she felt comfortably anonymous, safe harbor in a sea of communities where everyone was at least distantly related, acquainted or recognizable from recurring encounters.

Ettie's apartment did not appear to be inhabited on only a part-time basis. It had a large, well-furnished salon that extended into a cozy lace-curtained bedroom, which could be closed off by a pair of delicately paned white sliding doors. The close end of the salon led to an eat-in kitchen. The refrigerator and gas oven were at least twenty years old, but they functioned, and although the coats of cream-colored paint on the high cabinets were past counting, everything was spotless. The single bath was rather cramped, yet it provided the necessities, and the European-style bathtub spray hose could be hung up securely for a stand-up shower.

To a careful eye, perhaps one unusually familiar with the local textile industry, it would be quickly clear that most of Ettie's accoutrements were not of Israeli origin. Pillows, tablecloths, knickknacks, and even much of the dishware came from various European countries. The books and magazines were mostly in English, German, and French, and as most Israelis were multilingual, this did not seem of particular interest, except that an examination of their jackets would have revealed that they were purchased in their countries of origin.

The only real clue to the nature of Ettie's profession was her collection of artwork. There were no photographs or posters on the walls, only original framed pieces in oil, watercolor, or charcoal. The subjects were European cities and landscapes, some nearly photorealistic and others bordering on barely discernible impressionism. Here a snowy park in London, there a fog-enshrouded *Tour Eiffel*. A blinding white beach in Lisbon, striped with multicolored fishing barks. A quiet borough in Munich.

They were all unsigned, and they were all original Denzigers.

The final evidence of Ettie's vocation was a small brass table on slim legs and rolling casters. The table had a mirrored top, and it reflected the labels of Courvoisier, Dewar's, Harvey's and Weinbrand bottles which it supported. For an Israeli home, it was a highly unusual collection.

Ettie sat in a large cushioned armchair, a small glass of iced Stolichnaya in one hand, her bare feet curled up beneath her. She had been back in Israel for over a month now. The days were warm, and even after a few long walks on the beach her legs beneath the short blue cutoffs were smoothly tanned. She wore a large white T-shirt with the sleeves rolled to her shoulders, her blonde hair lay curled in a long tail around her neck, and she stared blankly at the far wall through wide, shining blue eyes that looked as though they might have seen too much too soon.

Eytan's call had shocked her. She had quit smoking, again, but his voice and his somber news had nearly driven her into the street to buy a pack. Instead, she had settled for the vodka. It was not having much of an effect.

Harry Webber.

Ettie had wanted to forget Bogenhausen, and up until now she had done an admirable job of it.

Her assignment in *Operation Flute* had included remaining in place after the hit. She was to maintain her cover, observe the repercussions, even gather intelligence, if possible, regarding the local investigations. With the catastrophic death of the innocent Mohammed Najiz, none of Ettie's superiors would have been unduly shocked had she bolted. Yet she maintained her cool and carried out her assignment. When she was finally recalled to Tel Aviv, it was probably this exhibition of pure professionalism which had protected her from the otherwise indiscriminate wrath of Itzik Ben-Zion.

Unlike most of the other team members, Ettie did not find her career stanched or spoiled by Bogenhausen. Even more so than successful men in the field, within the Israeli intelligence community talented female agents were treated like princesses at court, accorded more loyalty and respect than they might find in any other walk of life. As women, they could gain access to places which no man might approach, put the most suspicious individuals off their guards, could utilize instincts and intuitions which remained out of reach to their male compatriots. Even within the top echelons of Mossad and AMAN, their identities were jealously guarded. For the past two years, Ettie had not had to set foot in Headquarters. She was briefed and debriefed in private.

She had managed to place Bogenhausen somewhere in the recesses of her mind. She had been on three long deep-cover operations since then, and the distance helped. Yet it did not take much to snap her back to that sad winter in Munich. 'Harry Webber' was dead. She wanted to forget Munich, but she could never forget Zvika Pearlman, nor any of her other comrades in arms. Most of all, she could never forget Eytan Eckstein.

Eytan. He would be arriving soon. Ettie Denziger's real name was Tamar Shoshani, and she had been trying to reacquaint herself with that sound, the way people said it, the occasional surprise as an old schoolmate addressed her in the street. Now Eytan would come, and he would call her Ettie, and that whole cycle of suppressed emotions would begin all over again.

In any other line of work, had they been co-workers in almost any other government or civilian facility, Tamar Shoshani and Eytan Eckstein would most certainly have wound up as husband and wife. While it is certainly true that opposites often attract, there are millions of couples whose unions support the reverse case, and Eytan and Tamar were very much alike. Their coloring was the same, their temperament, their German background. They had cynical senses of humor and the ability to remain functional under immense pressure. The magnetism had been immediately apparent to both of them, but in the Israeli intelligence community there existed a superstrict regulation whose premise could not be breached. Field agents, no matter the circumstances, were forbidden to have relations with each other. Agents were encouraged to socialize with support staff, even "marry into the family," as it were, as this relieved much of the pressures of secrecy at home. But field agents? Together? Never. It invited operational strain, obfuscation of an objective, even dangerous vulnerability to hostage-taking and the like.

Eytan and Tamar knew the rules and had worked very hard to keep their distance. They only had one option—to retire from AMAN and be free to marry—but at the time neither of them was prepared for that leap. Only once, during a mission in North Africa, had they slept together. It remained their most closely guarded secret. Not long afterward, during one of Tamar's routine polygraph exams, her needle had jumped at the questioner's mention of Eytan Eckstein. Tamar told Benni Baum that if they pressed her on this subject they might have to fire her, so the questions were reworked and the test administered again, without mention of her team leader.

While Eytan lay in traction at Assaf HaRofe, more than once Tamar had been tempted to quit her current mission, return to Israel and join him forever, no matter the professional repercussions. But she stalled, and by the time she made her preparatory inquiries Simona was firmly entrenched, and it was too late.

The sharp buzz of the doorbell startled her. She stayed in her chair and said, "*Kaness.*"

Eytan entered the apartment. He looked much *unlike* Tony Eckhardt, without his European clothes and pale winter skin. He was dressed in casual local style, shirttails outside his light slacks, sneakers, his face tanned and his hair already going even blonder with the springtime sun.

More than that, his eyes had lost some of that hardened stare which field agents acquire after so many months of constant strategic calculations.

He closed the door with his back, leaned against it, looked at her.

"Hello, Ettie."

There it was, his voice, her cover name, just as she'd expected.

"Hello, Tony." The name seemed strange to her as it left her lips, here in Tel Aviv. But those were the two people who had worked together, shared secrets, had a private world that even their superiors were unaware of. Tony and Ettie.

Eckstein had decided that he would never touch her again, no kisses on the cheeks and perhaps not even a handshake. But Harry's death made the degree of that platonic extreme seem disrespectful of the man's memory. If nothing else, the death of a comrade should be observed by the coming together of his survivors.

Eckstein started forward. Ettie immediately saw the limp; she could not help but notice. It drove her to her feet and she walked to him and they embraced for a long time, rocking slowly together without speaking, like a pair of vines twisting in the wind.

Finally they sat down, at opposite ends of the sofa. Ettie wiped an eye with a knuckle and pointed at the bar tray. Eytan said, "Yes, anything. But not too much," and she rose to get him a glass.

"So, was it an accident?" Ever the professional, Ettie asked the correct question first as she rejoined Eckstein in the salon.

"Yes." He took the glass and gulped. The ride from Jerusalem had seemed endless, the stretch through the Valley of Ayelon particularly stifling. The cool gin and tonic was a blessing.

"What does Itzik say?" Ettie asked.

"Don't know. I left right after Danny told me and Benni."

"Which Danny?"

"Romano. But you know Itzik. If he likes you and you die of cancer within ten years after retirement, he'll still swear the Bulgarians did it. But if he doesn't like you, he'll say you smoked too damn much and you deserved to croak."

Ettie showed a small smile, but she could not laugh. Eytan's tone revealed deeper bitterness and pain than she had ever seen him express. "How are you?" she asked.

"I am as you see me." He smiled. "Rushing to retirement yet somehow unretirable." He pointed to his head, indicating an adjustment problem. "But forget about me. How are *you?* You look wonderful."

"Thank you."

There was a moment of embarrassed silence, while each of them knew that they were seeing the other again, without clothes, in the dark bedroom of an obscure hotel in Morocco.

Ettie got up and turned on the radio, not bothering to tune in a desirable station. It was just a field agent's habit, which somehow pleased Eckstein to witness, and he smiled at her.

"Harry was one of my most favorite people on this earth." Ettie sighed as she poured a bit more vodka.

"Lots of us will say that over the next few days."

"And mean it."

"Yes. And mean it."

"Can we go to the funeral?" Ettie wondered.

"I can go. I don't know about you, Ettie."

She brooded for a moment. "I guess I'll visit later."

Being successful in The Game had many small but cruel prices. At times, you could not even mourn properly.

"Oh, Harry." Eytan sighed and let his head fall back on the couch. "Zvika."

"What else did he use?" Ettie tried to remember.

Eckstein suddenly began to laugh. "Once, for a week he actually tried to use *Adolf*. Do you remember that? Benni finally made him drop it because we cracked up every time we talked to him."

Ettie laughed also, and for the next hour they talked about Harry Webber in all his forms and guises, his brilliance and his humor. They mourned him as friends have been mourning since the dawn of memory, recalling every experience, assembling the images and melancholies, tucking them away after blessing them with silent nods.

At 2:15, Eckstein rose stiffly from the couch.

"I actually have something to do today," he said wryly. "Itzik's sending me for some retraining."

"Good," Ettie said.

"I think it's just physical therapy, but it's better than sitting around."

Ettie stopped him before he reached the door. She held his sleeve and reached up, kissing him lightly on the cheek. Eckstein looked at her.

"Will you come to visit us?" he asked.

"I'd like to meet Simona."

"She knows about us, though," Eckstein warned.

Ettie was surprised at the degree to which she suddenly felt betrayed. If Eytan's wife knew about her, about *them*, it meant that their secret bond had lost its importance to Eytan.

"Nothing to know," she said, feeling stupid and emotional as she put her hands to her sides.

"Oh yes there is," Eytan said and he looked directly into her eyes. "For me, at least."

Vulnerability was not a trait which Ettie had often witnessed in Eytan, and it immediately punctured her jealous reflex.

"Me too," she said, and then she looked at the floor.

They both realized, in that long moment, that it did not matter if they touched or did not, if they came together or kept their distance. Ettie and Tony, Tamar and Eytan, were as intertwined as memory and regret. Eytan reached out and touched her cheek.

"*Litraot*. See you again." He smiled and left.

Ettie closed the door, and for a very long time she stood alone in her salon, touching the cool white wood.

———

The Wingate Institute for Physical Culture was located on the seashore between Tel Aviv and Haifa, just a few kilometers south of the resort town of Netanya. It was an easy drive along the coastal road from Tel Aviv and Eckstein made it with time to spare. Quite unconsciously, he had exceeded the speed limit during the entire half-hour drive. His eyes, hands and feet motor-visually piloted the Fiat, but his mind raced along a hundred paths to other places.

He thought too much about Ettie Denziger, each bit of her, the physical and the spiritual, the professional soldier and woman. Alone in the car he felt safe to explore his feelings, could admit that he loved her, even muttered the confession aloud. For so long he had managed to deny her a place in his emotional memory, and the sudden view of the depths of his feelings shocked him, brought a surge of confusion, some remorse and a great deal of guilt, which caused the image of Simona to rise as well. Exploring his love for his wife, he realized an equal passion, although different. He adored Simona, but Ettie was his closest comrade in arms, and even without the sex it was an unbreachable bond that carried a sting of betrayal with regard to his marriage.

The day had already been too long, filled with tensions, then rending crisis. Harry's death and the visit with Ettie filled Eckstein's brain with images and fantasies, and packed the empty car with ghostly passengers.

Eckstein pushed the gas pedal to the floor, racing to a destination where he could escape the car and its unwelcome opportunity for contemplation.

He reached the main gates of the Institute with a sigh of relief. He drove into the civilian compound, a maze of narrow streets and high cedars, modern dormitories, lecture halls and expansive sport courts. The civilian section was a large facility, used for training Olympic athletes, team coaches and even high school gym teachers. It was easy to get lost among the curving roads and pathways, and Eckstein skirted the facility, driving down a long circular road that eventually led him to the barbed-wire fences of the military section of the Institute.

Here the colorful civilian buildings gave way to squat, unimaginative barracks and hangars. Closer to the beach than the civilian section, the slate walkways here were blown over with sand and there were no carefully pruned hedges or fussy flowered vines.

Eckstein parked the car outside the main gate of the base. He got out and was immediately slapped with a blast of humid wind from the Mediterranean. He shook out his stiff leg, rolled his shoulders, did not bother to lock the car and walked toward the base.

The guardpost was manned by a tough-looking kid from the Givati Brigade, his bright purple beret tucked into the epaulet of a dress uniform. The soldier was wearing a battle harness and carried a loaded Galil slung from his neck. He looked carefully at Eckstein's military ID card, grunted, and swung the gate aside.

Eckstein knew the facility well. He had trained here as a Paratrooper, and later again as an AMAN recruit. He smiled as he limped along the walkways, for a part of his youth returned with the distant pops of gunfire from the pistol ranges; the thin smell of sweat and salt air; the cadences of small groups of elite troops who jogged after their P.E. instructors, wearing shorts, T-shirts, work hats and sneakers and bearing that dumb, happy muscled look of as yet unsoiled idealism.

He reached a long, low cement building and entered one of four wooden doors. The first thing he noticed was a large white sign posted on the rear wall. It said, No Smoking Anywhere on This Facility—By Order of Colonel Maimon. The next thing he noticed was a young, bespectacled second lieutenant, who sat at his desk directly beneath the sign. He was writing in a file. And smoking.

Eckstein couldn't help himself. He laughed.

The lieutenant looked up. "What's funny?" he asked.

Eckstein pointed at the cigarette. "Your quaking fear of your commander."

The young officer shrugged, pleased with his own chutzpah. "He's off base today. What do you need?"

"I'm Eytan Eckstein." He showed the young man his identity card. Had he still been active in the field, he would have used a cover name and appropriate papers, but it was hardly necessary anymore.

"So?" The lieutenant was in no mood for guessing games.

"So, I'm supposed to start some sort of retraining today."

"Where you from?"

"Queens Commando."

The lieutenant's eyes widened and he cocked his head in a gesture of respect. That always seemed to happen whenever you mentioned *Queens,* mainly because everyone knew it was some secret section of AMAN but no one really had any idea

135

what the hell it was all about. The lieutenant flipped through a stack of cabled orders.

"Yeah, here it is. Eckstein." He picked up a telephone and called someone. The IDF telephone system was as bad as its civilian counterpart. The recipient of the call was probably meters away, but the officer still had to shout. The lieutenant hung up. "He'll be here in a minute," he said and returned to his work.

Eckstein waited. After a minute, a shadow filled the door frame and he turned.

"Eckstein?" A low, clear voice came from the throat of a very large young man. The white blaze of the sun cast his form in silhouette.

"That's me."

The figure extended a hand, which Eytan took. The grip was powerful, the hand calloused and engulfing.

"I'm Boaz. Let's go."

Eckstein followed the man out of the room. In the bright afternoon sun, his appearance was foreboding, to say the least. He had the triangular trunk of a weightlifter, the bulging muscles pressed against a blue tank top that said Sports Instructor across the back. He wore plain fatigue pants that seemed ready to burst at the seams from the press of his thigh muscles, yet he moved quickly and lightly in a pair of black leather Reeboks.

He did not look much like a physical therapist.

"Where to?" Eckstein asked.

Boaz stopped. When he turned, Eckstein saw a visage to match the form. The young man was about twenty-five; his enormous neck supported a square-jawed face topped by short, thick, sun-singed hair. The lips and nose were wide and Slavic, the flat grey eyes clear and without life. Boaz looked like a Russian nightmare from a Fleming novel, except that he quickly smiled.

"To get you a uniform," he said. "Didn't they tell you? I'm *Krav-Maga*."

"Oh. Of course. Let's go," said Eckstein, and they continued to walk.

That sonofabitch Itzik Ben-Zion. He and Heinz had probably had a good long laugh together after cabling his orders to Wingate. *Krav-Maga*. Contact-Combat. Eckstein had just begun to walk again, and they were sending him off for some hand-to-hand. *Okay,* he thought, *no matter the outcome, I'll smile at them and say it was fucking* wonderful.

Boaz led Eckstein into his office, a large cool room decorated with diplomas, karate trophies and the various tools of the trade—dummy pistols, wooden truncheons, knives and boxing gloves. Given Boaz's size, it did not surprise Eckstein to see piles of half-empty cookie boxes, milk cartons and juice bottles.

"Drop your pants," said Boaz. "Let me see the leg."

"You know about it?" Eckstein asked as he unzipped his trousers.

"I was told." Boaz squatted to the floor and looked at Eytan's knee and thigh. He fingered the scars, ignoring a grunt that came from above as he squeezed the thigh muscle. He looked up.

"Bullets?"

"Three."

"Caliber?"

"Nine-millimeter, Scorpion 68."

"Not serious," Boaz said in typical Israeli fashion.

"What's serious?" Eckstein asked. "Tank shells?"

Boaz laughed. "Come on," he said. "I've got a guy with one arm. After a year here he can already take me." He leaned across his desk and rummaged for something in a cardboard carton.

"I can take you too," said Eckstein. "That's why they invented the .44 Magnum."

Boaz came up with a pair of soiled fatigues and handed them to Eckstein. Then he lifted up his gym shirt and pointed to an ugly, puckered pink scar to the left of his huge navel. "Forty-five," he said and let the shirt fall.

Eckstein's eyes glowed briefly, but he did not react verbally. Neither man asked the other where he had acquired his mementos.

When Eytan was dressed in an IDF shirt, baggy fatigue trousers and his own sneakers, they walked out to the training area. It was a sprawling lot of sand, interspersed with the strange devices of an obstacle course. There was a tall cement wall, ditches, barbed wire, climbing ropes, horizontal ladders and the like. In the center of the course was a large expanse for calisthenics.

As they approached, Boaz took measure of his new private student.

"Had *Krav-Maga* before?"

"The standard course."

Eckstein was trailing behind the giant, looking at his huge back. The sand made it hard going, but the warmth was comfortable.

"When?"

"Few years back."

"Remember anything?"

"I think I remember a lot . . ." Eckstein's sentence was cut short as Boaz suddenly stopped, turned, grabbed the front of Eckstein's shirt and twisted violently, hurling him over a cocked hip as his legs snapped up into the air and he slammed down into the sand.

The impact sent the air rushing from his lungs. He lay there for an eternity, his head jerking skyward until he finally caught a breath. Then he lay back in the sand and tried to recall the simple act of inhalation. Boaz stood over him, hands on hips, obscuring the sunlight.

"You don't remember how to fall," he said.

He reached down and grabbed Eytan's shirt again, pulling him erect one-handed in a single swift motion.

"I thought I fell rather gracefully," Eytan managed. "Considering the circumstances."

Boaz did not smile. "We're going to start all over." His humor had quickly faded. There would be no more games. "Now, we'll do the whole theory later, but to review quickly: *Krav-Maga* is a physical science, *not* a martial art. We will begin with all the basic stances, elementary moves. However, and most importantly, I want you to reacquire your reflexes, Eytan. Understood?"

Eckstein nodded. He realized that it was going to be painful. Boaz was unconcerned with Eytan's handicap, and perhaps that was exactly the kind of therapy he needed.

"You will be slow at first," Boaz continued. "But soon, for your own good, you will begin to defeat my attempts."

The youth was true to his word. For two hours, without a break, he reviewed the basic stances of *Krav-Maga*. They were strange, as Eytan remembered, seemingly unnatural, yet typically practical as in all IDF methods.

With your upper body, you held much like a boxer, with raised fists blocking your face and elbows close to the body. With your legs, you stood in a stance resembling classical Japanese karate: one foot forward, one back, slightly pigeon-toed, feet prepared to strike.

The stances were excruciating for Eckstein, and he sweated a liter of water and salt and ground his teeth. And as promised, Boaz constantly surprised him, without warning or remorse. At least twenty times during the lesson, the Contact-Combat expert lunged at his student and violently hurled him to the sand, until, toward the end, Eckstein began to sense the attacks, and once even managed to escape his fate.

For the most part, it was an afternoon of intense thirst and repeated suffering.

Eckstein welcomed his punishment with a certain masochistic delight.

4

London

AMAR KAMIL'S SLUMBER had not been disturbed by the howls of the wind or the pounding of the rain. While certainly at any other time and place the insistent drumming would have roused him from the deepest sleep, today the tapping at the windows, like the soft fingernails of a gardenful of children, was not a factor in his reveille. Nor was it the vibrations of the trains as they pulled into Victoria Station, or the low honk of taxi horns, or the click of walking-cane tips on cement outside his room at the Danforth. For although it was only 7:00 A.M. of a Friday morning, Amar had already been awake for two hours.

It was like this when he was mission-oriented. It had been like this for three days. Suddenly his worst professional obstacle—the desire to languish in bed until late morning—would disappear without a residue of dark-circled eyes or early sluggishness. It was as if Kamil, when not actually in any real physical danger, accumulated a horde of reflex and energy. And then, when motivated by duty, he released his fuel to feed his body and mind for the duration of the action. All at once he needed no more than five hours of sleep, and could function on three. He was totally alert, and even while sleeping he floated near the surface, his body prepared to wake and act at opportunity's bidding.

In Russia—*Petach Tikva*—Rina had often teased him about his laziness, wondering aloud how such a sleepy dog could possibly be of use to the State. He wished that she could see him now. And then he was instantly glad that she would never see him like this.

He sat in a large armchair; it was soft and bloated in the seat and back, upholstered in a teal blue and puckered around navy buttons. He wore a black silk robe, something acquired once in Red China, with an embroidered dragon of yellow and green and red weave striking across his shoulder blades. In his lap lay the parts of a recently stripped and cleaned Makarov 9mm pistol He no longer liked the weapon, for its origin was a dead giveaway, but it was all the Russians had at the time in the diplomatic pouch. He would change it for a European tool at the earliest convenience. The pieces lay there like the black bones of a reptile carcass.

He looked at the window, past the white lace curtains, through the thin sheafs of water sliding down the glass like white wine being turned before a tasting. He watched the roofs across Ebury Street, the white-trimmed stones and mottled awnings of Belgravia being sprayed with water, reminding him with some pleasure of frequent steam cleanings he had once applied to the engine of a black BMW. With all of his travels, Kamil had come to identify major cities by a single feature. Moscow was bone-brittle cold. New York was nose-choking dirt. London was rain. He wondered if, due to its constant washing, the city might not be the cleanest on the face of the earth. Naturally, as with all major capitals, there were corners of litter and trash, but he decided that if you got down here on your hands and knees with a camel brush and a brass pan, you would not gather a handful of dust.

Dust.

Bethlehem was dust.

He moved the pieces of the Makarov into one hand, opened his robe and stood up, leaving the black silk shroud draped over the chair. Wearing only his black underpants, he stepped onto the dark mahogany floor and knelt down, laying the parts of the pistol out in a row on the spotless oiled wood. Then he stepped back and began his exercises.

Sambo, the Russian hand-to-hand combat method used by the KGB, was a technique culled from a number of Oriental martial arts. It most closely resembled jujitsu, combining short thrusted blows and lightning throws, while dispensing with all of the meditations and philosophies inherent in the Eastern arts. The Russians were very practical about such things. "If you are looking for an ascetic way of life," the KGB instructors always said, "then become a priest. This is combat."

Amar lowered himself into the standard sambo stance, one foot forward, knees bent, hands held raised and open like hatchet blades. With his right foot, he began his forward kicks: blinding thrusts that snapped from the knee and nearly cracked the air like whips. Yet after each one, he returned the bare foot to the floor without a sound.

He counted in his head: from one to ten in French, eleven to twenty in German, twenty-one to thirty in English, thirty-one to forty in Italian and forty-one to fifty in Hebrew. Having finished the right foot, he repeated the exercise with his left. He was not even breathing hard when he rewarded himself by approaching the stripped Makarov and assembling one part of it—the bolt spring into the barrel. Then he stepped back again, remembering another Makarov, the first one he had ever seen, as he began his side kicks. . . .

The burning winds of the *Khamsin* were sweeping wildly down Shari Bet Lechem as Amar strode toward the house of Abu Kaddoumi, the woodworker. The soles of his worn sandals slapped the dusty stones and he reached up and pulled the wrap of his filthy *kaffieh* nearly up over his eyes as bits of stinging sand flew toward him like desert hailstones.

Amar welcomed the *Khamsin,* for it gave him an excuse to cover his face, to spend a day unrecognized, free from the abuse of his classmates. His shame was so deep that he wished he had the courage to slice off his own nose, to slash his lips, to grind his flesh to paste and forever be free of the features that were so much like his father's.

His father. The war had only ended three weeks ago, and already the Jews were offering the elder Kamil a seat in the new military government in Bet Lechem. Nightmare of nightmares, his father had decided to accept.

Farouk Abu-Amar Kamil. As Amar heard the name of his father ringing in his brain he pulled his *kaffieh* away for a moment, turned his head and spat into the wind.

Farouk Abu-Amar Kamil. Philosopher, teacher, intellectual, all the things to make a man's family proud—except for the fact that he was also a pacifist. The elder Kamil unabashedly held forth that the Israelis could not be defeated in war, and that peaceful coexistence was the only way. Farouk Kamil was a righteous man, and the derisive "Jew lover" epithets that came his way did not faze him. But Farouk had children, and his children had to go to school. They paid for their father's political philosophies with bloody noses and torn schoolbooks. Being the eldest, Amar suffered the most.

It was July 1967. The Jews had just turned the Arab

world on its head in six horrible days of thundering blitzkrieg. Bethlehem, like most of the West Bank, had surrendered without firing a shot. Farouk Kamil had all but expressed relief. For now, at last, the pipe dreams were over and true peace could come.

Farouk Abu-Amar Kamil.

Traitor.

Amar turned down a side street and banged open the door to Abu Kaddoumi's shop. The woodworker looked up from his lathe, beginning to smile until he saw the look in his godson's eyes.

"I cannot stand it any more!" Amar exploded as he pulled his *kaffieh* off his head. His nose was still bleeding slightly from the fistfight he had just endured in the school courtyard. He wiped it with his fingers.

"Shhh, Amar." Kaddoumi rose from his bench, the elderly man moving slowly to pour some tea for his favorite apprentice. "What happened?"

"What always happens!" Amar shouted, then he stopped himself. He thought he might cry. He slowed his breathing. "What *always* happens, Baba."

Amar called Kaddoumi *father,* for he had long felt closer to the old man than he did to his own flesh and blood. Kaddoumi and Amar's father had once been the greatest of friends, but now they would no longer even exchange a simple greeting. Abu Kaddoumi had been a militant Palestinian since 1929.

"They won't accept me into the Wolves," said Amar.

"You tried again?" Kaddoumi offered Amar a glass of the black tea, but the boy shook his head fiercely.

"I try it every day."

"Perhaps you should wait. The war is still fresh, the young patriots still angry."

"How long can I wait, Baba? How long must I wait while

they call my father an *Issrayelee* and they call me a Son of a Jew?"

"You are only fourteen, Amar."

Amar began to pace inside the small shop. The fresh smell of lathed olive wood usually calmed him, but he was marching to the rhythm of a decision.

"Baba, I must have the rest of my pay. I am leaving this place."

"Amar, my son, let us talk."

"I am going, Baba. No one can stop me. I cannot live here. You know it too."

Kaddoumi sighed and put down his porcelain cup. Amar was right. As long as his father lived, and perhaps long afterward, the boy would be a pariah among his own people. Pulling at his grey beard, Kaddoumi removed a small iron strongbox from the base of a Christ statue and gave Amar the pay that he had kept for him as a savings account.

"What will you do?" Kaddoumi asked, afraid to hear the answer.

"Whatever it takes to change my life. To prove that I am not my father's son."

Kaddoumi knew that only an extreme act could provide Amar with such relief, yet he did not question further.

"Go with Allah," he said as he embraced the boy.

"I will not forget you," said Amar as he clutched the money and quickly left.

For days, Amar had planned his next moves. If his final bid to join the Wolves of Resistance failed, there were two actions which would break this grip of dishonor and punish his father until the old man went to his grave.

Amar had one younger brother and five sisters. Their father loved his daughters, for they reminded him of his long-departed wife. But to an Arab, only the sons really mattered. Farouk Abu-Amar Kamil was constantly at war with his eldest, Amar, but his ten-year-old boy, Jaja, was a supple, charming, loving child who understood nothing of politics. Farouk adored Jaja and heaped attention upon him, his pride and joy.

Amar took his money and bought the pistol from an old Christian Arab in Bet Jalah. It was a Russian Makarov, a souvenir from the man's service with the British Army in Berlin during World War II. Amar had often admired the weapon, and the Christian, who owned the lumberyard where Amar bought wood for Kaddoumi's shop, had even let him shoot it once.

Afterward, Amar's humiliation propelled him onward like a schooner in a hurricane. He walked back into town, the Makarov tucked under his shirt. He had already chosen the spot. Night was coming on, the city cooling as the stones surrendered the July heat. The winds of the *Khamsin* were beginning to die with the sun.

The Café Al Quds was on Paul VI Street, tucked up into a corner of the town center. Already the Israeli officers had begun to ignore their curfew orders and frequent the local shops and restaurants. Amar was sure that he would find a target at the Al Quds.

Sure enough, a lone Israeli lieutenant was seated outside at one of the rickety tables. He was drinking an orange juice and reading a Hebrew paper. He had one of those short Israeli submachine guns lying across his lap. No other Jews were in evidence—only the local Arabs who stared at the conqueror as they passed, and the café waiter who served him with a disgustingly subservient grin.

Amar walked straight up to the officer and stopped across the table. As the soldier looked up, Amar drew the pistol and shot him twice in the chest. The officer flew backward onto the stones. Someone began to scream; a man yelled to Amar to stop in the name of *Allah*.

"I am Amar Kamil, the son of the traitor, Farouk Abu-Amar Kamil," he shouted as he still held the pistol extended. "Tell the Wolves of Resistance that they are the children of whores!"

He walked away, shouts echoing from behind, and then he turned a corner and began to run. He was at his own house within ten minutes, where he found his little brother, Jaja, playing on the stone floor with a train of wooden camels. His sisters were nowhere to be seen, and he knew that his father would be in the city, cavorting with the Jews.

Amar's breath was coming in rasps. He could barely speak. He looked down at his younger brother. Despite their father's overt favoritism, Amar loved Jaja as much as Farouk did. He reached out a hand.

"Come, Jaja."

"Where are we going?" The little boy looked up with his pale eyes. Both Kamil brothers had the unusual green eyes of remote Circassian blood. In fact, had they not been four years apart they would have looked like twins.

"For a long walk," said Amar.

Jaja sprang to his feet, excited by the adventure. "Will I need anything?"

"Nothing," said Amar. "Quickly now."

They took no food, only a camel bag of water. Hand in hand, they walked west from the city, then into the Judean desert. They took some nourishment from Bedouins, and when Jaja could walk no farther, Amar carried him on his back—down toward Jericho, across the slim river and finally into Jordan.

Amar's wandering had begun.

Jordan. The stinking refugee camps, the hatred of Hussein's Bedouin troops, who made the Jews look like pacifists by comparison. There were bitter humiliations. Amar Kamil, like so many of the intelligent Palestinian youths, followed one idol of liberation after another, only to watch his hero's words unfold into lies, to see the generals of the Liberation of Palestine retreat from every field of battle while hideously proclaiming ridiculous victories.

He had hoped that Lebanon would prove to be different, and it *was* in a sense. There the Palestinians had numbers, power. Yet once again they squandered it in internecine quarrels. They fought ferociously against their brother Arabs, Moslem and Christian alike, while in the south the Israelis went on building, farming, giving battle when necessary. Arafat, Habash, Hadad—they were all politicians, their military efforts tentative and ineffectual. And as the years dragged on, Amar Kamil came to realize that if he subscribed to the tactics and rhetoric of his brothers, he would be doomed to wander on the fringes of his homeland forever. Like Moses, allowed to look and long, but never to enter.

The October War had been Amar's Revelation Day. He had served as a captain with the Palestinian Liberation Army, alongside the Syrians. But even with the element of total surprise on their side, after a few days of glory they had been routed along with everyone else. It was then and there, in that cold and bitter winter in Damascus, that Amar Kamil became his own man.

No more words. No more promises.

Action and Silence. They became Kamil's watchwords, his codes. For nearly ten years his small group of dedicated soldiers became the most feared group of guerrillas in the Western world.

To his credit, Amar Kamil never fell into that stereotypical category of the Master Terrorists. He was a brave man, clever, intellectual, yet he did not dilute his cause or his professionalism with that self-appointed, overly romantic image so often assumed by many of his compatriots.

He had no particular affinity for fast cars or fast women,

and he had not acquired luxurious tastes as a result of having Palestinian coffers opened at his bidding. To Kamil, abusing the wealth that was available to him would have been a dilution of his mandate. Many of the other terror chiefs of Europe and the Middle East had come to be addicted to their high life-styles. Kamil, on the other hand, was a student of the world's most effective intelligence apparatuses. He had noted, and tried to teach same to his ranks, that good operatives only assumed the trappings of the wealthy when that became necessary in order to convincingly play a given role. Otherwise, as far as Kamil was concerned, a soldier could just as well drive a Volkswagen Beetle and live in a tenement. For these beliefs, he had become somewhat unpopular outside of his own network.

For in fact, as Amar Kamil was painfully aware, many of his fellow Palestinian freedom fighters had long ago given up hope of achieving their given aim—the creation of a Palestinian state in place of the Zionist entity. These men had come to be addicted to the life of the Terror Master, whereby terror became the end rather than the means. He also believed, and rightly so, that the subversion of the cause also made a man an easy target. For if he became more enamored of being a terror chief than of achieving his objective, he would begin to be careless. And where the Israelis were concerned, your first mistake was almost inevitably your last.

And still, despite his righteousness, Munich had nearly been the end of him. That very close call was pure evidence that his network was blown, his security nonexistent. The Russians had pulled him out of it, and he was grateful for that. Yet he harbored no illusions as to their motives.

Munich had been the catalyst for the third major turning point in Kamil's life. He had gone to sleep in Moscow, entrenched himself within the KGB system, absorbed every tidbit of their most useful indoctrination and the training in *Petach Tikva*.

Moscow had their plans for 'Yossi Yerushalmi,' and Kamil indulged them with apparent enthusiasm. But in his heart and soul, he remained a man of silence, of action, and when he awoke he knew that he would pursue his own agenda. The Russians could not control him, like some Doberman on a leash.

And he could not forget Munich. . . .

Something stirred from across the room. Amar had finished his exercises and assembled the pistol. Only his head moved, slowly, scanning. With the help of the grey morning light, his eyes selected details of the Danforth's decor.

The room was tasteful, intimate as the chambers of obscure pensions can be. The wallpaper was cream with a thin grey stripe, the molded wood trims a spotless white. The small desk, side tables and chairs were not new, but they were dustless, oiled, preserved as if a finicky spinster inhabited each chamber when unoccupied by a paying guest.

The large brass bed was the grandest feature, its wide shiny finials throwing high shadows on the far wall beneath an oil painting of the Bristol seashore. The small lamps on the side tables had soft rose shades. The black telephone looked as though it had been there since 1940.

Beneath the bed's white wool coverlet a figure rolled momentarily, like a dolphin's back breaking the surface of the sea. Then it was still again.

Kamil turned back to the window. He examined his own reflection where it wavered like a fading memory against a fresh current of rivulets. Even after so much time, his second face was still strange to him. In place of the wavy red-blond hair, he tried to recall the mahogany curls of his former self. He mentally reacquired the thick sharp hook of his nose, drew long dark brows over the yellowish wisps which now arched above his eyes. He conjured up his once-proud moustache; he could almost feel the coarse ends again where they

151

had once tickled the corners of his mouth. But even with that repainted image, the old Amar Kamil was not quite there.

Almost imperceptibly, he shook his head in wonder, for he thought that as strange as his new face still was to him, it should have been an utter shock to Leila. His wife had not seen him in nearly two years, yet she had accepted his return and his changed appearance as could only a true daughter of the Revolution. Naturally, at first she had had her doubts. Yet not once had she exhibited a reaction more emotional than scientific curiosity. She had felt his face, touched his ears. Then she had made him strip, and only when she had closely examined those parts of him which only a wife could identify in utter darkness had she finally smiled with satisfaction.

He was terribly proud of Leila. There were no others like her. Only Leila could have accepted a husband's total disappearance, the thin thread of a promise to return. Only Leila could take him back in an instant, not question his metamorphosis, make love to him as if he'd been merely away on business, and now be lost in sleep while knowing how soon he would again be gone. It was terribly brave. And terribly sad.

Amar's encounter with this emotion was not his first signal that he was changing, getting older. He had recently experienced a twinge of a feeling which as a soldier he had always managed to shelve—remorse. Granted that none of this was directed toward the victims of his terror activities. They were combatants in a new kind of warfare where you needn't carry a weapon to be considered the enemy. Rather, his feelings emerged with regard to Rina and Katya. His other "wife." His only child.

Of course, Rina had been an agent. She was neither dupe nor victim. The KGB had many of them. They left the Soviet Union as refuseniks, with prearranged target countries. They were at the very least half-Jews; the cover demanded authenticity. In Rina's case, she had settled in Israel for the required period and, having absorbed sufficient language and cultural knowledge, she had become "disenchanted" with her new home and made a new start in America. Not long after, she had left her Brooklyn apartment for a vacation in Europe, returning to Moscow to spend the rest of her career helping train agents who were targeted for Tel Aviv.

Yes, Rina was a dedicated Party member. But she was also human, a warm, giving woman who had pretended for so long to be his loving wife. Kamil had also played his role well, and even though they had never verbalized the depth of the emotional predicament, the couple realized the painful truth of the adage, You become what you pretend to be.

And what of Katya? Of course she would be provided for, would want for nothing material, educational, social or at least *socialistic*. But who would be her father? Who would carry her when Rina was tired? What pair of coarse hands would be there to tuck her in at night? Would she long for a second, lower voice to read her stories and comfort her when she dreamed bad dreams?

Stalingrad, the Gulag, Afghanistan. There were already too many Russian children who had for their fathers fading photographs in black wood frames.

For all of his wanderings, sufferings, fanatical and violent dedication, Amar Kamil had managed to suppress most of his racial hatred for the foreigners who occupied his home. But the irony did not escape him, that his only child was half Palestinian Arab and half Russian Jew.

"Are you praying for sunshine, Amar? If so, you should be on your knees and facing in the other direction."

The voice startled him. For a moment his fingers stiffened around the Makarov. Then he settled quickly and calmed, gathering his black robe and slipping into the sleeves, turning to Leila with an ironic smile.

She lay there in the bed, on her back, her shoulders propped against a pile of white down pillows that were puffed against the brass headboard like sheep gathered under a sheltering olive tree. Her magnificent curly black hair fell around her face and over the linens, reaching almost to her elbows. Even in the gloomy light, her dark eyes glistened brightly, and her lips against her olive skin looked almost as though she had sneaked a touch of ruby gloss, though she never wore makeup. The soft wool coverlet was pulled up over her breasts, but the inviting position of her legs was so clearly defined beneath the cloth that it brought a swelling to Kamil's throat.

Wild. There was no other way to define her. It was the word that came to Kamil's mind whenever he faced his wife, or thought of her.

In actuality, the word *wife* was merely a technical term, an ironic curtsy to their hasty betrothal in Lebanon five years before. They had been married in deference to her father's strict Moslem beliefs, but both of them knew then that their relationship would never take precedence over Amar's career.

While he worked, they would never live together or have children. Their couplings were occasional, carefully planned, elaborately disguised as the chance encounters of strangers, so that no opposition would deign her as more meaningful to Kamil than any other paramour.

Leila moved about, living off a network fund, but never a true part of the Movement. She would check in to various telephone numbers for a coded instruction to rendezvous. When Amar went to ground after Munich, she ensconced herself in Paris and got on with her life, although she continued to believe in his survival, and she never missed her monthly call.

And here they were, together in London. If only for a weekend.

"Actually, I was hoping that it would continue," said Amar, referring to the inclement weather.

"So that you can stay here with me all day?"

"So that other people will stay inside. So that the traffic will stay light."

"Bastard."

"Let's not talk about it, Leila." Such open and careless discussion of his objectives made Kamil uncomfortable. His mission had hardly begun.

"If anyone is following you, my darling, tracking you already," Leila offered with a trace of appetite for danger, "then you'll be dead by lunchtime at any rate. So it hardly matters."

"How I hate sentimental women." Amar laughed and turned, putting the pistol on the chair. "I must dress."

"So soon?" Leila pouted, pushing the hair away from her face and edging down on the bed just a bit. "It's still early."

"I can't miss the opportunity," he said.

"For what?" She knew that she should not ask, but she was just being naughty.

"For tea and scones."

Leila ignored his parry and reached out with slender strong fingers.

"Kiss me once, then. Before you shave."

A trap. Amar smiled. A kiss for Leila inevitably ended in a two-hour struggle beneath the sheets. He approached her, determined not to surrender. He took the hand and held it away from his body, leaned to her and touched her lips. She lifted her chin and trapped his mouth with her own, then reached for his free hand and placed it over her left breast. She pushed up to him with her shoulder.

He managed to extract himself. Leila's eyes were already wide, her breath quickened with a few seconds' passion.

"You are a devil," Amar said.

"And you worship Satan." Leila was still holding on to his robe. He took her hand away and kissed it as he left the bedside.

"Yes," he said. "Sometimes I do." He walked around the foot of the bed to a small closet. He began to select some clothing, and in the process he made to remove his robe in preparation for shaving and showering. Leila sat up in the bed on her elbows.

"Amar, it's been so long." For the first time in three days, her voice had a pleading quality. "And it will be so long again. I know you. I can tell."

He did not bother to lie. "Yes," he said.

"Then don't deny me." Now her demand grew harder. "I deserve that much of you. God knows you haven't been celibate for all this time."

He had not told her about Rina, and certainly not of Katya. What would be the point? But then she was right; he had given all of himself to his cause and much of himself to another woman. What could he give to Leila but as much of his physical self as he could manage? He pulled a pair of blue jeans off a hanger, clearing the pockets of unnecessary items. He just did not have enough time. He decided to turn her off by igniting a minor conflict.

"And I suppose you have been a nun all this time?"

"When I fucked someone," her answer came quickly, "I thought only of you. They were awful. I would gladly have used a cucumber instead had it not been so cold."

Kamil had to laugh. Leila was so plain, so out there, up front. She was half Palestinian and half Italian, an explosive combination to say the least. He often thought that her normal blood temperature must run well over a hundred degrees Fahrenheit.

"You needn't be quite so honest," he said as he selected

156

a plaid flannel shirt and an Israeli *Dubon*—an IDF-issue winter field jacket.

"Amar." Leila's voice purred from the bed. Kamil tried to ignore her. She called him again. *"Amar."*

He turned to say something. His voice stuck in his throat.

The coverlet was pushed aside. Leila lay there, her upper body propped on the pile of pillows, her back arched. Her brown skin shone in the dusky light like oiled olive wood, her wide breasts pressed between her upper arms and the nearly black nipples erect. One of her legs lay straight out, the other knee raised and angled to the side. She was touching herself with both hands, inviting him; her dark eyes filled with liquid and she looked directly at him as she bit down on her lower lip.

She was a powerful electromagnet. And he was merely the dust of iron filings. He dropped the robe and came to her, up onto the bed and then plunging down like a divining rod finding a secret pool. She moaned loudly, a sound like pleasure, pain, and fear in one, and she gripped his buttocks hard and drove her nails into his flesh until he cried out.

"Give me bruises to remember you by," Leila gasped.

Amar obeyed.

Serge Samal was experiencing a dull ache which had not disturbed him in years. Homesickness.

He did not quite understand it. He had been born in Europe, Paris to be precise, and even as a teenager had traveled extensively whenever studies and finances permitted. Serge spoke five different languages with near-native fluency, and he had the chameleonlike ability to assume the natural gestures and inflections of the surrounding natives. He could quickly feel at ease in the most cosmopolitan and chauvinistic of capitals—Bonn, Rome, Geneva, Vienna, London. So it made no sense that he should suddenly long for the provincial ways and means of Tel Aviv.

But there it was, a powerful urge for a cold Maccabee and a greasy *schwarma,* to be consumed satisfactorily only by the eastern shores of the Mediterranean.

His immigration to Israel, like that of many European Jews, had been intended at first as only a visit. But then he had stayed on, discovering the cliché of a melting pot where he could exercise his language skills at will yet feel a comfort incomparable to that of other stops along his wandering path. Serge had not even really thought of himself as a Jew until long after his arrival in Tel Aviv. He looked decidedly Scandinavian and had been raised without the pervasive self-doubt and moral examination common to his Diasporan brethren. Then suddenly one morning he had awakened in the filthy fatigues of a Golani Brigade recruit, and he realized that he was as Semitic as one could ever hope to be.

However, his travels were interrupted only by the first two years of his military service, for he soon found himself volunteering for duties in AMAN. The wanderings, albeit under assignment for Special Operations, recommenced with glee, tempered with purpose.

Israel, he had always known, was really too small a place for his Odyssean appetite. Serge needed to move, to drive the endless autostradas, to cross over borders and converse with strangers, to board an aircraft and arrive in a strange new land with the surge of adventure in his veins.

So what the hell was this sentimental ache in his chest?

Maybe it was simply fatigue. After all, he'd been working pretty hard of late. He had not slept for thirty-six hours. Or maybe it was Talia. She was well into her seventh month, and the serious considerations brought on by imminent fatherhood had begun to weigh on him considerably. It was still very early, but he was sure that he did not want his own child to be raised as an unidentifiable expatriate. And the thought of having a son or daughter who would speak like an English boarding school brat was certainly repugnant.

It was his age. Yes, that was it. He was getting on, only in his early thirties yet prematurely edging toward that emotionalism of old men who gravitated toward their graves in the Holy Land.

Maybe it was the weather. Late spring, and the London skies spewed water like February in the Golan. In Tel Aviv, the beaches would already be crowded tomorrow. The Israeli schoolgirls would already be turning their summer almond. By the seashore the *pa'kok, pa'kok* of paddle balls would echo off the high towers of the hotels, vendors would be hawking their lemon popsicles, aggressive young men on leave from the army would be seducing women tourists with their unabashedly horrible English.

Oh, to put on shorts and a T-shirt, sit out on Dizengoff drinking a cup of *afooch* and read some trashy paper like *Olam Hazeh*.

Work was getting to him. That was part of it. The embassy staff inevitably commiserated, comparing notes, places of birth, chattering about their kibbutzim or their army units, how they missed Jerusalem or friends or families in the Galilee. Someone always wished he were diving in Eilat or hiking in the Negev, rather than working a security detail in Westminster. It rubbed off after a while.

Yet Serge was grateful for the job. After Bogenhausen he had wondered if he would ever work again, except as a taxi driver. Ben-Zion had nearly had his ass, but he was smart enough to resign from the army quickly. The General Security Services had been pleased to have him. They were a tough, somewhat more primitive outfit than the other intelligence arms. The fact that he and Eytan had shot the wrong Arab did not seem to disturb his new bosses to any great degree.

Eytan. He wondered what kind of shit Eckstein was enduring. He missed him. He missed all of them—Eytan, Peter, Ettie, Francie, Benni Baum.

Harry Webber.

Maybe that was part of it too.

When an army buddy died, your life could suddenly be brought into close focus. Serge was satisfied with the GSS conclusions that 'Harry's' death was an accident, but that did not obviate the fact that Zvika had met his end eight thousand kilometers from home, in a filthy city full of strangers, squashed between a taxi bumper and his own beat-up Ford. The *there but for the grace of God* thoughts had sobered him for the last two weeks and resulted in some serious re-examinations.

Where was he going with his own life? He was past thirty, time for some considered assessments. He was about to start a family, and as a result of his own experiences he was surprising himself with the rather mature conclusion that children needed an anchor, that they would be better off with physical roots and the attendant security. He had been moving so hard and so fast for so long and what did he have to show for it? An album of adventures, a few languages, a permanent scar on his waist from the butt of a Beretta.

A bump in the road suddenly snapped him from his reverie, and he asked himself a more immediate question: *Where the hell am I going right* now?

He looked up and saw the passing windows of the Hyde Park Barracks, reflecting the bright-red side of his double-decker bus. The upper deck's fuselage was covered by a long white-and-blue ad, and Serge read the reversed message in the barracks glass—It's Quicker By Us—the guarantee of an express courier service.

The bus was still on Knightsbridge, moving west, and either Serge had not been daydreaming for very long or the traffic was already heavy. It was just after noon; the rain was letting up and the atmosphere actually rather humid. But still the pedestrians outside were bundled up as if for January. Londoners were mistrustful of the weather, and rightfully so, but they could manage to look cold even on the cusp of summer. Serge reckoned that if he had worked as a London umbrella salesman instead of an Israeli security officer he would already be a wealthy man.

Serge looked across the aisle and out of the far windows at the greeneries of Hyde Park. The weather was not conducive to picnicking, yet he could see two riders on Rotten Row, sitting erect on their wet steeds and cantering along in their slickers. The British were truly a strange people; the cliché that they preferred their pets to fellow humans seemed to be accurate, at least superficially. Their values were difficult to discern, their emotions hidden by layers of proper manners and swollen snobbery.

He rubbed his itching eyes. He had had a nightful and a bellyful of the British. The Foreign Office had summoned the Israeli ambassador to Whitehall for "extraordinary consultations," a phrase applied to a calling on the carpet. The Brits were expressing disapproval over Israel's heavy-handed policy with regard to the Palestinians in the West Bank. This of course seemed blatantly absurd to the Israelis, considering the intense anti-terror war being waged by the British against the IRA. Even more contradictory was the memory, still fresh, of England's recent invasion of the Falklands, where the Brits had sacrificed hundreds of killed and wounded over a few sparse, unstrategic islands occupied primarily by sheep.

However, the absurd diplomatic game had to be played out. Serge's security detail was out all night, checking the routes of travel, arranging decoys and escorts for the ambassador, and finally appearing at Whitehall only to have their members forced to wait outside in the rain while Scotland

Yard and MI5 Security took over the detail with thinly disguised disdain for the "Jewish gorillas."

They're still pissed off 'cause we threw them out of Palestine, Serge had decided.

The work with *Shabak*—The GSS—was important, but it did not compare to those exciting years with Special Operations. Serge knew that he would never again experience comparable adventures, tensions, danger or camaraderie. He liked his present co-workers, but no one would ever be a partner or a friend the way Eytan Eckstein was. 'Rainer Luckmann' and 'Tony Eckhardt' had been a perfect match, a yin and yang of field operatives. Maybe their failure at Bogenhausen had been a signal that the relationship should dissolve. They cared too much for each other, and that would probably have proved fatal in the long run.

Yet Serge truly missed the friendship, and had found no substitute. Perhaps, if he did decide to chuck it all, he would talk Eytan into joining him in the private sector. The idea of working again with his old partner brought a smile to his lips and another pang to his heart.

He reached into the pocket of his leather flight jacket for a pack of Rothmans. He felt the butt of his holstered pistol as he searched for his lighter. The Brits did not like the idea of foreign security personnel walking around London with firearms, but no sane *Shabak* man would leave the embassy unarmed. It was the same with the Egyptians, Syrians and Jordanians as well. A city full of small, private armies.

"Ay now. Yeh can't smoke 'at thing in 'ere, lad."

Just about to light up, Serge turned in his seat. An old woman with rotten teeth and a motheaten woolen cap was shaking a finger at him. He smiled and replaced the cigarette in the pack.

"No. Of course not, madam." His English was near native, accent and all.

"They's a good lad."

Serge blew out a sigh. Well, he would take the edge off his longing some other way. Because he had worked all night long he was out even earlier than usual for a Friday. Coming straight from the embassy after the Whitehall detail, he could have taken the Circle Underground Line from Westminster all the way out to Paddington, then switched to the Metropolitan Line until Westbourne Park and walked straight over to North Kensington. Instead, he had decided on the bus lines. The 103 would take him to Notting Hill and Kensington Park roads. From there, rain or no, he planned a leisurely walk through the market on Portobello Road.

Of late, he had been spending more and more time in the market. Many of the raggedy stalls were proprietored by Middle Easterners, and if you just squinted a little and indulged your nose, you could imagine yourself in the Tel Aviv flea market on a Friday before Shabbat. He would buy some Turkish coffee, a packet of *helld,* some houmous and tchina, fresh pita loaves. Then he would walk home, bringing Talia some fresh flowers, and later Avi and Dvora would come over and he and Avi would smoke and drink some arak and play *Sheshbesh*.

If Rainer Luckmann can't go to Tel Aviv, Serge decided, *Then we'll bring Tel Aviv to Rainer Luckmann.*

The bus stopped again on Kensington Gore, between the huge round dome of the Royal Albert Hall and the Albert Memorial that stood back inside Hyde Park. Serge looked out at the peaked monolith while the driver on the lower deck sold someone a London Explorer ticket, said "Good travelin' to you, sir," and the vehicle moved on. Serge heard the sound of footsteps ascending the narrow stairs behind him, then the scuff of a misplaced foot, a loud thunk and the ringing of small change as it spilled all over the floor and went rolling down the aisle like the poker chips of an irate loser.

"Koos och tak!" A furious voice spat the Arabic curse

which alludes to the private parts of one's sister. *"Koos em ek!"* Now the victim had included someone's mother in the roster of the damned.

Serge turned his head, nearly laughing aloud, because the expressions of frustration spewed forth in an Israeli accent and the originator was down on his hands and knees hunting for his lost funds.

Serge stuck his head out into the aisle. There was a young man on the floor. His face was obscured as he bent to his task, but he was wearing blue jeans rolled at the cuff, tan canvas sneakers clearly marked with the Commando trademark, and an IDF *Dubon* field jacket. It was the traveling kit of many Israelis abroad, and it made them readily identifiable to their own countrymen, if to no one else. Serge felt a wash of pleasure as he grinned from ear to ear.

"Efshar lazor l'echa?" He offered his help in Hebrew, almost as a reflex.

The man raised his head, somewhat shocked to hear his native tongue. He was probably unaware that he had uttered his exasperations aloud. He was handsome in a rather kibbutznik, strong-jawed way, with bright eyes and curly redblond hair. He smiled in return.

"Toda." He thanked his benefactor. "And you can look for my brain down here as well."

Serge gladly bent to his task and in a minute both men were sitting together in a window seat, somewhat breathless from their exertion.

"Thanks for the help," the other Israeli continued in Hebrew as he stuffed his change back into the pocket of his jacket. "Did I yell?"

"Loud enough," Serge laughed. "But I'm sure only I understood."

"Don't be so certain," the man said as he looked around at the other passengers. In typical British fashion, none of the others on the deck had intruded on the encounter with more than a brief glance. "Half the city seems to be Arab."

"Or Israeli," said Serge.

"Yeah. Lots of us, too."

"The eternal wanderers." Serge was thinking of himself in particular.

"You know," said the man as he wiped some rain from his face with a sleeve of the olive *Dubon,* "I think it's a racial defect. I get sick to death of our puny country until I think I'll go crazy. Then I explode, got to travel. I get outside and after two days I'm homesick."

"Homesick, huh?" Serge revealed nothing of his own feeling on the subject.

"Like a kid at *Bahkoum.*"

Serge nodded. The reference to the IDF Induction Center was something to which every Israeli could relate.

"Yossi Yerushalmi." Amar Kamil extended a damp hand.

"Serge Samal," Serge responded in kind. He looked at his compatriot for a long moment. Something about him was familiar, the face, the curved scar beneath the right eye. But he could not place him.

"You just a tourist?" Kamil asked. "Or can you help me get where I want to go?"

"I might be able to help," said Serge. He stopped himself from staring.

Kamil removed a slip of paper from his pocket. He showed it to Serge. In Hebrew script were the words "Aunt Yudit. Hazelwood 33, Kensal Town."

"You're in the right direction," said Serge. "You've got time yet. I'll coach you."

"Thanks." Kamil recovered the paper.

"Relatives?" Serge asked.

"Like all of us. They're everywhere."

"I don't have any here," said Serge. "Except my wife."

"What do you do?" Kamil asked.

"Embassy."

"Ahh," Kamil raised his eyebrows. One could assume that a young, well-built Israeli such as Serge was not an agricultural attaché. "I almost took one of those jobs, but three years in the regular army was enough bullshit for me."

"Where'd you serve?" Serge asked.

Now Kamil had to be clever. He had already decided on the answer to this inevitable question—with Israelis it was as common as asking after a hometown. He had concluded that a bold response would be the best, and a careful selection would deflect further inquiry.

"Intelligence," said Kamil.

"Really?"

"Yeah, just field observer stuff mainly. But you know, 'Ask me no questions . . .'"

"And I'll tell you no lies," Serge finished the phrase.

"*Biddyook,*" said Kamil.

The conversation went on for a quarter of an hour. Kamil was so well prepared that he never faltered. After all, he had lived in a replica of Petach Tikva for a whole year, where every detail was duplicated to perfection. His Hebrew was flawless, save for a trace of an accent which was common to Israelis born in Eastern Europe. He was unabashedly aggressive in asking Serge for details of *his* life in Tel Aviv, and at one point he even invented a certain café by the seashore which did not exist, and he exhibited some suspicion when Serge embarrassingly confessed that he had never heard of it.

"Well, I'm away quite a lot," said Serge.

"I guess you are," said Kamil.

They rode in silence for a while, finally reaching the end of Kensington Church and approaching Notting Hill Gate.

"Well, it was good to talk to someone from home," Kamil said after a bit.

"For me too," said Serge.

"What do I do now?"

"We'll get off here, and you'll switch to a bus on Pembridge."

"*Yoffi.*" Kamil paused, allowing the next thoughts to seem spontaneous. "You live near here?"

"North a bit. But first I'm going to Portobello Market."

"What is that?"

"Kind of like the *Shuk Hapishpishim* in Tel Aviv. I pick up my 'goodies' there. You know, houmous, pita."

"Aha!" Kamil pointed a finger at Serge as if he'd caught him in a deception. "Maybe a little homesick yourself?"

Serge laughed. He had enjoyed the encounter fully, a taste of home to dull his ache, as if God had sent a temporary relief messenger. "Maybe a little," he admitted.

"Hey." Kamil turned to him. "How about a drink? Not one of their disgusting warm beers, we'll find a good cup of *botz* somewhere." His look was imploring, as if a taste of the dark Turkish brew would fix them both up as would a pint of Guinness do a local. "Can we get some around here? You in a hurry?"

Yossi Yerushalmi's expression was so childishly hopeful that Serge could hardly resist. He looked at his watch.

"Okay. Yeah, I know a place."

Kamil clapped his hands together and rubbed them gleefully.

"*Al ha'kefak,*" he said.

They left the bus together at Notting Hill. The rain was fairly heavy again, and Kamil put up the hood of his *Dubon,* pulling the upper edge forward with his fingers to keep the water off his face. Serge pulled a much-battered baseball cap from his rear pocket. It had the bright white *NY* of the New York Yankees embroidered on the front. Serge was no baseball fan, he simply liked the style and practicality of the American design. Kamil also liked the cap. It had made the tracking of Serge Samal an easy task.

Kamil followed Serge as the Israeli moved quickly along Kensington Park Road. *"Ya Allah, ayzeh mahbool!"* Kamil commented on the rain as he trotted along.

"Yeah. It's really coming down now," Serge called over his shoulder. He had to raise his voice considerably due to the pounding of the water on the sidewalks and the swishing of the wheels of the black taxis and minicabs. "Maybe a walk wasn't the best idea."

"Oh, come on," Kamil yelled. "One hot cup and you'll feel different."

"Yeah." Serge pointed ahead. "North Kensington's up that way. Lots of rich Arabs. Their kiosks start up here in Notting Hill."

They were running parallel to Portobello and the market, and the surrounding area was congested with tall brick apartment buildings, delivery vans in the road and the battered used cars of immigrant laborers. Yet the surge of weather was already driving pedestrians indoors to wait it out.

Serge suddenly turned left on Blenheim Crescent. The bustle died almost instantly. There were lower buildings, a quieter street, the awnings of shops and cafés.

Kamil had to act now; he did not know how soon they might arrive at a crowded eatery. He spotted a tiny storefront. The glass door had a large Camel cigarette ad on display and the windows were stacked high with grocery cartons. He stopped.

"Hey!" Kamil called out.

Serge halted his trot and turned.

"Cigarettes!" Kamil jerked a thumb at the store and bounded down the three cement steps.

A bell jingled on the door as he entered the gloomy space. The shop was very small, the piles of goods making it look

like a basement warehouse rather than a neighborhood grocery. Boxes of diapers, laundry soap and toilet paper formed
a single narrow aisle straight back to the cashier. There was
a slab of scuffed wood on a peeling formica bar that looked
like a relic from a burned-out pub and served as the cash
counter. On the top was an ancient register next to a wire
basket of candies. The proprietor was an Indian, complete
with a navy wool turban. Behind him the wall was lined with
shelves bulging with cigarettes, tobacco, cheap pipes and
condoms.

The proprietor looked up at Kamil, watching his customer
shake the droplets off his jacket onto the cement floor. "*Welcome*," he smiled. "Is it very, very bad?"

Kamil only managed a half smile. "Bad enough," he said
as he opened the zipper of his *Dubon* halfway and shook his
hood back over his shoulders. His heart was pounding against
his shirt, his breath coming very fast now and not from his
trot in the rain. His hands were slick and he wiped them on
his jeans at the back of his thighs where the water had not
reached the denim.

Serge popped in through the entrance. He closed the door
and said, "*Yo*," shaking himself off and pulling the baseball
cap from his head. He snapped it against his leg a few times,
smoothed back his hair with a hand and replaced the cap.

Kamil looked up at him and smiled, shaking his head at
the weather. Serge looked around the store, then he walked
toward the counter, passing Kamil as he perused the cigarette
rack.

"What's your brand?" Serge asked without turning
around.

"Camels," said Kamil and he reached inside his jacket
for the Makarov.

The bulk of the silencer stuck for a moment in his belt,
but he freed it with brute force. The device was an unusual

type, being rather small and held against the snout of the pistol with a spring-loaded extension to the trigger guard. It would not quiet the weapon fully, but the report would be sufficiently muffled and the pounding rain was on Kamil's side.

Serge's head began to turn, his mouth opening to say something.

Kamil placed his free left hand on Serge's back and shoved with all his strength as he clicked off the safety of the Makarov with his right thumb.

Serge's body responded with its years of training and instinct. He caught himself with a forearm against the countertop, not even stopping to assess the situation, knowing that he could never be fast enough in this position but snapping his right hand up under his jacket as he groped for his Beretta and turned.

He was right. He was not fast enough.

Kamil reached out with the Makarov and shot him once above the right eye.

Serge's head snapped over his left shoulder as if he'd been struck with a baseball bat. His hat disappeared along with a spray of liquid and bone, his back slammed against the countertop and he slumped down onto the floor. There was no accompanying clatter. The Beretta had not cleared its holster.

Kamil looked down. There was no need to check for signs of life. He stood there for a moment, his nostrils flaring like a bull's.

"That was for Jamayel," he whispered.

He raised his head. The Makarov was still there at the end of his extended arm, and to the right of the barrel the Indian proprietor was standing behind the counter with his eyes closed. His brown hands were clasped together, his beard twitching as he prayed. The right side of his tan wool shirt was spotted with blood.

"The money, please," said Kamil.

The Indian did not seem to hear.

"The *money,*" Kamil said, a bit louder.

The Indian suddenly snapped from his stupor. His trembling fingers snatched at the register handle and the drawer bounced open with a resounding clang. The fingers gathered all of the pound notes quickly, and for some reason the proprietor began to sort them in order of value, which he probably did out of daily courtesy for his bank teller.

Kamil proffered his hand and took the bills. He stuffed them in his pocket.

He did not want to shoot the store owner. He did not want to very, very much. But his mission had only just begun and he knew full well that if he did not act, a perfect description of him would be faxing its way across all of Europe in a matter of hours. And then, all of his training, his work, his new face would be for naught.

He had once trained with an Irish terrorist, whose favorite expression was now ringing in his ears: *"Leave one witness . . . and make sure it's you."*

He slowed his own breathing, lowering his voice to a calm, even tone.

"Prayer is an admirable thing," said Kamil.

The Indian looked up. His eyes were glistening. "Pardon me?" he managed.

"I respect a man of God."

The proprietor immediately closed his eyes again, folded his fingers and began to implore his deity.

Kamil extended the Makarov, shot the man in the heart and was out of the store before the body hit the floor.

5

Jerusalem

Two Days Later

EYTAN'S BLACK FIAT PANDA climbed a long stretch of highway that rose between the rocky peaks and towering pines of Shar Hagai, its carburetor taking deep breaths of the chilled morning air, its engine seeming to hum with pleasure at the prospect of leaving sultry Tel Aviv for the purer atmosphere of Jerusalem's mountains. As the incline steepened, Eytan clutched and jammed the gearshift from fourth to third, pushing the gas pedal hard to the floor as if a lapse of speed might threaten his rare euphoric mood.

He reached over and rolled down the passenger window to fill the car with the nostril-burning scent of fir needles. Then he lit a cigarette, turned up the radio so that Shlomo Artzi fairly deafened him, and he pounded on the steering wheel with his open palms. A searing jolt shot through his hands and he jerked them away from the wheel. Then he laughed and quickly recovered, this time using only his fingertips to keep his smarting wounds from the plastic.

His hands were bloody, his back ached, and his leg throbbed, but it did not matter. For after five grueling, humiliating *Krav-Maga* lessons, this morning at Wingate Eytan had finally bested Boaz.

It was a perfect way to begin his thirty-third birthday.

For over two weeks now Boaz had been teaching Eytan a single technique—unarmed defense against an armed opponent. Successful execution of the exercise required blinding speed and total psychological commitment, and in most other martial art disciplines it would not even have been introduced to a student before his basic defensive moves were perfected. However, as with all Israeli military techniques, practicality overruled patience, formality and aesthetics. More important, Boaz was sure that if Eytan could successfully disarm him it would be a terrific confidence-builder.

The basic precept of *Krav-Maga* was simple—no two brains could act and react simultaneously. There was always a lapse, albeit in milliseconds, between the offensive move and the defensive countermove. Therefore, if you were being threatened with a loaded weapon, you could disarm your aggressor before his brain commanded an accurate pull of the trigger.

However, success demanded days of painful drill.

They began with Boaz's favorite reflex exercise, standing barefoot in T-shirts and fatigue pants, face-to-face one meter apart on a stretch of beach near the obstacle course. Boaz held his massive arms forward, calloused palms together, fingers pointed at Eytan's chest. Eytan held his own hands at his sides, touching the seams of his trousers with his fingertips.

Eytan's assignment was simply to strike Boaz's hands with one of his own before the instructor jerked the target out of range. At first Boaz allowed his student to make contact a few times. Then, as Eytan swung again, the *Krav-Maga* expert snapped his clasped hands out of the way and Eckstein spun half around with the momentum of his failed attempt.

"You missed," said Boaz.

"I know."

"Punishment."

"Pardon?"

"Hold your hands out, together, like mine."

Eytan obeyed, and Boaz cocked his right arm back and slapped the side of Eytan's hands with a blow that made his eyes water.

"Failure has a price," said the instructor as Eckstein exhaled through the residual sting. "This is not a parlor game."

Eytan missed on the next nine attempts, and the outsides of his hands were soon meat-red from punishment slaps and the sweat rolled over his lips. On the tenth try, again he failed as Boaz simply dropped his arms toward the sand. Eckstein extended his trembling hands for punishment, but this time he witnessed a blinding flash of atomic light as Boaz smacked him hard across the face, sending him to the ground in a skull-banging stupor.

"Up," said the instructor. Eytan stayed down, babbling curses at Itzik Ben-Zion's mother and sisters and Captain Heinz's firstborn, if ever there should occur such a genetic catastrophe. Boaz shook his head. "And what do you think the results will be when you face a pistol?"

Eytan licked his lip, searching for blood. "I don't intend to ever face one again."

"And I don't intend to crash when I fly, but I always fasten my seatbelt."

Eytan struggled to his feet. A squad of Naval Commandos came by, thrashing through the chest-high surf in full battle dress, reminding Eytan of a Woody Allen film in which the primary action was juxtaposed with an absurd background activity.

"Stop thinking," Boaz ordered.

After two more jaw-quaking slaps and a straight-fingered

blow to the solar plexus, Eytan finally hit Boaz's hands. The instructor grinned.

"Free hit," he said. Eytan reached back and smacked him as hard as he could across the granite slab of his face. The grin never left, but the blow did twist Boaz's head around.

Eytan eventually graduated to a dummy pistol. Boaz threatened him with the black rubber .45, and Eytan, beginning from a rest position, would attempt to snap out his left hand, catch the barrel between his thumb and fingers, deflect the weapon as he sidestepped and punch Boaz in the face with his free fist. The follow-through was trying to twist the weapon from Boaz's grip and turn it on him before the beast threw him to the ground.

Finally, they used a live Browning FN loaded with blanks. They both wore goggles and earplugs, but no other protective gear. Eytan failed miserably for two full sessions. Most often Boaz would "shoot" him before he got his hand near the pistol. Later, Eytan managed to deflect the barrel's searing flame and nearly land his blow, yet Boaz would recover the weapon, step back and "execute" him with a pitiless sneer. On those mornings Eytan died a hundred times before breakfast.

"I told you. Stop thinking," Boaz said in an incongruously gentle tone as Eytan lay in the sand, half deaf from the gunfire, smarting all over with powder burns. "When you see the pistol, grovel if you have to. Distract me with tears. Beg for your life, and in the middle of the sentence, take me with *fury*."

Eytan kept trying, but nothing seemed to work.

On the morning of his thirty-third birthday, Eytan trudged behind Boaz to the beach. His head was low with gloom, his movements desultory as he dragged his goggles onto his face and jammed in his earplugs. Boaz loaded the pistol with the hateful blanks, took up his position, and pointed it at Eytan's chest.

"Forget it," said Eytan in a whisper. He put his hands on his hips and toed the sand, looking at his feet.

"What?"

"I want to stop. I'll never do it."

"Come on, Eytan," Boaz coaxed him like an older brother whose sibling no longer wants to play.

"Look," said Eckstein, raising his eyes sheepishly, "I really don't care about all this. And fuck my C.O., I'll just tell him . . ."

He snapped out with his left and caught the FN perfectly in the V of his hand, pushing the barrel to the right, stepping in as he drove forward with his right fist and connected with Boaz's nose. The instructor's head snapped back as Eytan quickly grabbed the pistol with both hands and twisted as hard as he could, pulling it out of Boaz's grasp as he jumped back, ignoring his buckling knee as he fell to the ground, rolled, came up and got off a shot at Boaz's torso. Then, as the pistol's action had to be worked manually with blanks in the chamber, he cocked the slide again, took aim and fired once more at Boaz's chest as the giant came at him.

Eytan thought he was going to die, but Boaz just picked him up and hugged him, swinging him around and around and crying, "*Kol hakavod! Kol hakavod!*" until they both fell to the sand laughing.

They went for a swim and had a huge breakfast in the Wingate mess hall. . . .

An angry car horn blared and Eytan woke from his victorious reminiscence, realizing that he was smiling like an idiot and had driven the last ten kilometers without really seeing the road. He swung quickly into the right lane and allowed a baby-blue Mercedes taxi right-of-way; then he regained the left lane, downshifted and floored the gas pedal. He had his reflexes back, and he felt like a pianist who had lost his touch for a very long time, but had just sat down and flawlessly played the "Minute Waltz" in fifty seconds.

He was already past Motza and the road became very steep and it twisted around to the right and then back again every few hundred meters. Jerusalem's face of pink-veined granite, glowing with the wash of the early sun, teased him as it appeared and disappeared with each careen around another mountain curve.

Things were going to be different now. Eytan could feel it, knew it in his heart. Nothing had really changed for him in Special Operations—he was still only an Interviewer and might well be until the end of his tenure. But *he* was changing. For two weeks he had been working with Boaz and returning to H.Q. battered, bruised, and demoralized, yet saying only that it was going fine. He would rather die than admit defeat to Itzik Ben-Zion, and he had summoned reserves of stubborn determination that he had not needed since he was a paratroop recruit. Today, when he reached H.Q., he would not declare his victory. But he knew that Boaz would file a glowing report.

Things would be better now with Simona as well. Eytan's black moods had begun to wear on even his wife's patient and resilient personality. He would not wonder if their failure to conceive had been directly connected to his frayed nerves and depressive state. Now all that would change. He felt an energy and a suffusion of power that would extend into every corner of his world, and whatever he imagined for himself would be within his reach.

He burst forth into the big intersection at Weizmann and Yirmiahu. God, but Jerusalem was the most beautiful place on earth. The sun made the building stones glow bone white behind the reds and blues and yellows of the women's clothing, the sharp greens of soldiers' uniforms as they hurried across the roads for the Central Bus Station. The birds in the trees lining the Convention Center were still ecstatic with morning, and even the most impatient, horn-stabbing drivers could not break Eckstein's mood.

He was tempted to speed to Hadassah Hospital, find his wife, spin her around and crush a bouquet of roses between them. It was a lovely fantasy, yet he was already running late and had to pick up his files and get over to the Industrial Center. His celebration with Simona would have to wait till evening. It would be doubly joyous. He would have his birthday dinner, and she would have a new husband. She had told him that she was planning something extra-special, and that he should not be late.

He should have driven the back way through Romema, but he felt this morning as if he owned the city, and he wanted to march through its soul. So he drove straight down Yaffa Road, for once not giving a damn about the traffic, singing along with the radio, as proud as a king returning from conquests abroad.

He nearly bounded into the entrance hallway of Special Operations. Shlomo Bornshtein looked up from the paperwork on his desk and fixed Eytan with an uncharacteristically serious stare.

"*Boker tov,* Tony," he said. "ID, please."

Eckstein happily produced the laminated card. Apparently his recent lecture to Shlomo about access regulations had had an effect.

"Thank you," said Shlomo. "Password."

"What?" Eckstein leaned forward, thinking he had misheard.

"Password," Shlomo repeated without changing expression.

Eckstein laughed. "What are you, kidding? No need to exaggerate."

"There's a perimeter alert on today."

"On your life?" Eckstein laughed again, sure that Bornshtein was pulling his leg. "We're in Jerusalem, not Metulla."

"Password," said Shlomo.

Eckstein shrugged, refusing to allow Bornshtein's mood to foul his own. He had to think hard for a moment.

"Eskimo Limon." He snapped his fingers as he came up with the answer.

Shlomo looked up at the TV camera, said, "It's Tony," and the door clicked.

Eckstein entered the chamber and before anyone could speak to him he said, "Tony Eckhardt, I've got a briefcase, a sandwich for lunch, and I am armed *and* dangerous."

He expected the usual snappy retort from the intercom, yet the secondary door just buzzed, and he went in.

Eytan still could not exactly fly up the stairs, especially with Boaz having abused his body as of late, but he actually took them two at a time. Moshiko was sitting at his desk on Two, though he was not reading. His hands were folded on his desk top, his face set.

"Morning, Bavaria," said the young man.

"To you, too," said Eytan and he made to walk by.

"ID," said Moshiko, putting up a hand.

Eytan sighed and showed Moshiko the pass. "Want the password, too?"

Moshiko shook his head and waved Eytan through.

Ben-Zion must have announced salary cuts, Eytan said to himself as he walked along the corridor. There seemed to be something strange floating around the building, almost like a vapor. Eytan tried to pinpoint the change, then, hearing his own sneakers slapping the tiles, he knew. It was very, very quiet.

He stopped at the canteen and looked in. The counter girl was wiping a table, picking up empty tea glasses. Only one table was occupied, and the five young people conversing in low whispers were all of Benni Baum's Research Staff. They turned their heads and fell silent as Eckstein appeared in the doorway.

"Morning." Eckstein maintained his bright tone. "What's the occasion?" Benni Baum rarely allowed his people to take their breaks simultaneously.

Yablokovsky the computer whiz fidgeted with his spectacles. "Morning, Eytan. Benni left a message for you. Go right up to Itzik's office."

"Okay." Eckstein continued on down the hallway. *It can only be good,* he said to himself, fighting to maintain his mood. *Haven't made a mistake or opened my mouth in two weeks. Haven't even* mentioned *a closed file, not even to Benni. It can only be something good.*

Yet all of the signals indicated the negative. He tried whistling as he walked, covering his limp very well now; still he felt like a man who has been summoned to pick up his wife after minor surgery, only to discover that the nurses are turning their heads away and the doctors wearing expressions of guilty regret.

No one was in Personnel. He dropped off his briefcase and began to walk faster. The climb to the third floor was painful; the guard waved him through quickly and Eckstein stopped outside Itzik Ben-Zion's door and took a moment to collect himself. Deep muffled voices came from inside.

Eytan opened the door and went in. The talk quickly cooled to a silence. He looked around.

It was his first time in Ben-Zion's office since the move to Jerusalem, and the space was imposing. It was very large, more than half the size of the conference room. Itzik's desk, a giant mahogany holdover from the British Mandate, sat catercorner at the southeast end near the windows, its surface covered with files and operation orders. Against the close wall was a long couch, a coffee table and some hard-backed chairs.

The Israeli Army did not give out medals; rather, a career officer's successes were marked by plaques and statuettes given by his troops or commanders. In one corner a glass table overflowed with such standing shields and trophies, looking like a chess table for giants. One wall was covered with more such wood and brass awards, imprinted with obscure compliments such as, With Recognition—from the Chief of the General Staff. There were also framed photographs of Ben-Zion with every major politician since Golda Meir's time, and a few photos with nameless, serious-faced men and women. The rest of the wall space was covered with huge maps, all mounted on cork and peppered with color-coded pins and little pennants.

There was not a single bookshelf in the office. The Colonel did not read history. He made it.

Ben-Zion himself was sitting on the edge of his desk, his long legs touching the floor. He sipped coffee and stared at Eckstein. Benni Baum was also in the room, along with Danny Romano, the matronly Sylvia from Ciphers and Intercepts, and a man named Uri Badash whom Eytan recognized as a Shabak officer. Heinz was also there, and Eytan immediately expected him to jump up and try to shoulder him back out the door. But the malevolent captain just sat quietly in a chair. The oscillators on the window panes hummed. Jerusalem shimmered outside.

The way they were all looking at him made Eytan's heart begin to race. Alarms began to sound in his head; he felt his sore palms going slick and trembly. Benni walked to him quickly and put an arm over his shoulders, leading him to the couch.

"Sit, Eytan," said Benni.

"Is it Simona?" Eytan whispered quickly, bracing himself for the horrible reply. He could not bear to have such news broken this way, but he had to know, now, and he squeezed his eyes shut and listened as Benni gripped his arm and said, very sharply, "No. No, it is not your wife."

Eytan sat down, instantly relieved yet still massively fearful. Benni sat down next to him, very close.

"Tell him, for God's sake," said Heinz, snapping up from his chair.

"Shut up," Romano spat at the obnoxious officer.

"Uri." Ben-Zion's deep voice reverberated as he addressed the GSS man. "Brief us again, please."

The dark-skinned, muscular Shabak agent focused on Eckstein, who stared up at him like a prisoner awaiting sentence.

"On Friday night," Uri began, "London police discovered the body of Serge Samal in a small kiosk in Kensington. He had been shot once in the head at point-blank range, along with the proprieter, who was shot in the heart. The cash register was empty. No witnesses, and the lab reports aren't in yet."

Eytan continued to stare at the GSS man. He did not even blink. He couldn't move.

"I am sorry," said Uri as he dropped his official tone and looked down at his feet. "I understand he was your friend."

Eytan's mouth moved, barely releasing a sound.

"What did he say?" Heinz demanded in an exasperated tone.

"He said," Benni Baum repeated for Heinz, " 'Practically my brother,' and if you say one more word in this meeting I am going to throw you right through that fucking window."

"Cool down, Baum," Ben-Zion rumbled. Then he wagged a finger at his mad-eyed aide. "Heinz," he warned him as a master warns his guard dog.

Something as cold and as large and as undigestible as an iced bowling ball was sitting in Eytan's esophagus. He struggled to control his breathing, to quell the rising rage, but it all came rushing back to him as if *he* were expiring and viewing his entire life in those last moments before the fire dies: Serge Samal racing across an open expanse of training ground, firing his pistol, diving behind cover, reloading, rolling, coming up and running again, his hair swept back by the wind over his sunburned face, smiling, always smiling, almost laughing with the exertion of the game. . . . Serge Samal plopping himself down on the sand at Herzaliya amid a trio of surprised girls, then quickly capturing one for a date and all at once he was smiling again, under a wedding *chupa,* gripping Talia's hand as Eytan held one of the canopy poles and grinned right along with his partner. . . . Serge Samal's head popping up from the surface of the dark cold waters in the port of Marseilles, climbing aboard the yacht, doffing his mask and his regulator, not even looking back as a ball of light rose from a PLO-chartered freighter on the far side of the quay and a thunderous report echoed across the water. And then, oh yes, he actually unzipped his wetsuit to reveal a white tuxedo shirt and cheap black bowtie, grinning his captivating grin as the tension-filled team members rolled on the deck planks. . . .

"Again," Eytan said softly as he continued to stare at Uri.

"What?"

"Tell it again, please."

The GSS man relaxed a bit, relieved that Eckstein had not burst into tears. He lit a cigarette and retold the gory details, sparse as they were.

But Eytan hardly heard a word. It was all still coming back, like a terrible tune that one cannot erase from the mind's musical memory. He had almost forgotten about Zvi Pearlman—not the man himself, no, never—but the whys and wherefores of his death in New York. After all, there was nature, and fate, and not every bad thing that happened to a soldier could be blamed on his profession. But now it all shattered again, the reasoning and the acceptance, it was exploding into his mind like a huge gong being hammered by a steel mallet that only a blind man cannot see and a deaf man cannot hear.

"Amar Kamil," Eytan said.

No one reacted. It was as if they were all ice figurines. Eytan looked over and realized that Sylvia was sitting in one corner of the room on a hard chair. She was staring out the window and chain-smoking filterless Nobless, coughing intermittently in a grinding rasp and pulling the cloth of her purple shift away from her froglike body. She was a brilliant old woman, exceptionally kind, with a shock of bushy white hair and a face that would frighten a child. Eytan wondered what she was doing in the meeting, then he realized that Ben-Zion had probably called her in case someone needed a motherly shoulder. That was Itzik's idea of comfort.

"Amar Kamil." Eytan repeated the name again, a bit louder, pronouncing it slowly and carefully. "Are you all deaf?"

"We heard you, Eytan," said Danny Romano, who stood leaning against the windowsill, moving his pipe stem to alternate corners of his mouth.

Heinz groaned in disgust, and Benni shot him a look. The young captain turned away, folding his arms and muttering to himself.

"Okay, Eytan," Benni said as he squeezed Eckstein's arm. "We're not ready for conclusions yet."

"Eckstein," Itzik Ben-Zion's tone warned him. "I called you in here because of your relationship with Samal. The investigation will be conducted by Uri and his Shabak people, with our records for support and that is all. Now—"

"It's a horse!" Eytan yelled it so loudly that everyone in the room flinched. He rose to his feet in one quick jackknife of his body and he clapped his hands together and shook them at the ceiling, raising his eyes and praying to God in a trembling voice dripping with disdain. "*Elohim,* help them. It's a horse! Can't they see that it's a horse?" Everyone stared at him as if he had gone completely mad. Uri actually took a step forward in case he might have to restrain Eytan. "It's big and it's brown, it has four legs and a long tail." Eytan gestured wildly. "It has big eyes and pointy ears, and it's even wearing a fucking saddle! God, help them see it's a horse!"

He smacked himself in the forehead and laughed, once, an ugly, mirthless sound. He looked around, more calmly now, returning the shocked stares of his co-workers. He put his hands to his hips and dropped his voice to a controlled, yet still fiery tone.

"People, I'm not crazy. But *you* are if you can't see this. Two of my men have been killed within thirty days of each other—"

"They are not your men," Itzik interrupted.

"Two of my *former* men," Eytan continued without pause, "have died violently within the month. Two men, in the same business, with the same histories, the same enemies. God, a fucking street policeman could figure it out."

"You are not here to draw conclusions, Eckstein," said Itzik again.

"*Someone* has to," Eckstein snapped, and Ben-Zion rose from his desk top like a gathering hurricane.

"Let the man talk," said Uri, holding out a hand like a traffic cop.

"Are you working with me or against me on this, Badash?" Ben-Zion demanded.

"I'm working for my government," the GSS man said, implying that the Colonel's self-serving reputation was well known even outside of AMAN. "Let him talk."

Ben-Zion said nothing. Eytan removed a cigarette from his pocket. His hands were shaking. Benni lit it for him.

"Two men." Eytan blew out the smoke and began to pace, wincing with his leg. "Zvika gets it and okay, it's a traffic accident. Fine, we all bought that. Me too, I swear I did. These things do happen. But Serge?" His voice nearly cracked as he said his friend's name, yet he held on. "Serge? A robbery victim? Are we completely out of our minds? He's so good the rest of us are always *jealous,* so fast he can knock you down while you're still thinking about it. His gun hand has its own eye, I swear it." Eytan caught himself speaking of his old partner in the present tense, and he stopped.

"It is very suspicious," Sylvia croaked through a cloud of smoke.

"Thank you." Eytan bowed to her grandly. "A brave and intelligent woman."

"And what the hell does this have to do with *Flute?*" Ben-Zion demanded. One of the telephones on his desk began to ring. Instead of answering it, the Colonel simply yelled at the top of his lungs. "Ariella! I said no calls!" It stopped ringing.

"Amar Kamil is a prime suspect," Eytan said simply.

"Nonsense. Kamil is a dead issue."

"Show me the corpse," Eytan challenged.

"This is simply an obsession with you, Eckstein," Ben-Zion flared. "And I will not tolerate emotionalism."

"Fine," said Eytan. "I'm emotional. Yes. Colonel Ben-Porat was emotional, too, before the Yom Kippur War, and nobody listened to him and we lost three thousand men and he wound up in the *Beit Meshoogaeem.*" He used the diminutive for an insane asylum.

"And that's where you'll be," said Heinz, feeling safer now to join the challenge against Eckstein.

"I'm in Russia," said Eytan, looking up once again at the ceiling. "God help me, I'm in Russia."

"I thought the Kamil file was closed," said Uri quizzically. "For all the branches."

"Then. Let's. Open. It," Eytan said slowly as if addressing a nursery school. "For God's sake, people, let's face reality. Our mothers aren't virgins anymore."

"This meeting is over." Itzik suddenly moved behind his desk, sat down and began to shuffle some papers. Everyone stared at him, but no one budged. He looked up. "I am sorry, Mr. Eckstein. It's a hard thing to take, I know. But this is too absurd."

"Why absurd?" Danny Romano spoke up, angering Ben-Zion further, who pounded once on his desk top, making his papers bounce and an empty tea glass topple.

"Because! The idea of a dead terrorist coming to life again just to take vengeance on one of our old teams? It's ridiculous!" He suddenly got up again, which indicated to all that he was failing to convince himself. "And how the hell does this ghost have all of the team members' identities?" Itzik waited, for the question was a good one and no one responded. "Answer me." He shot each one of them a stare. "Are you telling me we've been penetrated?"

"That's not impossible," said Sylvia.

"It's probably him," said Eckstein sarcastically as he jerked a thumb at Heinz. "He tries to veto every good idea we ever have."

Heinz flushed bright red under his white-blond roots. He clenched his fists and stepped forward with a growl, but Danny grabbed him by the sleeve.

"Wait. Stop." Benni stepped into the center of the room, holding up his hands like a referee at a wrestling match. "Let's think for a minute. Really. Calmly." Baum's tone quickly quenched the dangerous ego fires that were sparking up in the office. He was a master, knowing just when to shut up, and when to speak his piece. He and Eckstein had discussed the Kamil problem before, quietly, like puzzle masters laboring over an old crossword. He turned to Eckstein. "Okay, Eytan. It's an excellent question. How would a *supposedly* resurfaced Kamil know who the individuals are?"

They all waited while Eytan lit a fresh cigarette with the stub of his first. His heart was still hammering and his armpits were soaked, but he knew now that he had been so right when he told himself that morning that he was changing. Yes, he was undergoing a metamorphosis, yet he had been wrong about the results. He was not becoming something better, opening up, finding a new path. He was not the caterpillar becoming a butterfly. Rather, he was crawling back into his cocoon, changing back into his old self, recovering his operational thinking, donning his old familiar cloak. His voice, though sharp with strategy, sounded weary.

"Okay. Listen," he said as if addressing troops under his command. "Acquiring my team's identities is not really that difficult." He looked over at the Shabak agent. "Uri, you're probably not cleared for this."

"He's not," said Ben-Zion without even knowing what Eytan was about to say.

"But you will be, I'm sure," Eytan continued, "So just follow along." He started to pace again. "Rainer, I mean Serge, and I are trying to get Kamil in Munich, but we shoot the wrong man." He had to stop for a moment and breathe. He had never, ever said that out loud. "We shoot Mohammed Najiz instead. The Munich Police conduct a six-month investigation. Six months of files, photos, reports, and all that *Papierkrieg* that we all do." He used a German expression—paper war. "Since they actually have my man Peter in prison—"

"In prison?" Uri asked innocently.

"Yes, in prison. Don't you remember the scandal?"

"Oh, yes." Uri put his hands in his pockets, feeling lousy that he had probed a wound. "Sorry."

"Since they have Peter Hauser," Eytan continued, "they've got a pile of photos of him—left, right, full face, the works. Now, Ettie Denziger stayed on, but let's say because of her proximity to the takedown in Bogenhausen, her neighbors have been canvassed. So, full witness descriptions of her." He continued to pace. He could tell by the silence in the room that he was doing well, but like a tennis pro he had to suppress all thoughts of the score and just play. "Now, Zvi Pearlman had a brief but very significant encounter with the Bogenhausen cops and an ambulance driver. Full descriptions of him. Francie was stopped at a roadblock outside the city. They let her go, but they were photographing everyone that day. Benni." Eytan turned to Baum. "You rented an office at the trade fair for two weeks. Do you deny that you are a memorable figure?"

"No denial." Baum smiled like a teacher watching his best student give lecture.

"And finally, Serge and I also rented a flat for those weeks. And Munich airport guards got a long hard look at both of us and our Brit passports at Kentworth Air." He stopped talking and looked up. He was standing in front of Uri Badash.

"So?" the Shabak man prompted.

"So, routine police work. A good artist, and they have our faces. Standard rundown on abandoned vehicles and flats, and they've got phony names and a paper trail, plus fingerprints wherever we might have neglected them. They've got a file as thick as my arm is long. Routine, plodding surveillance and they pick us up again."

"Who?" Heinz scoffed. "The West Germans?"

"No, Heinz. Not the West Germans," said Eckstein patiently.

"Run it out for us," said Romano.

"Fine." Eytan turned to the head of Ciphers. "Sylvia? Would you say that the West Germans are penetrated by the East Germans?"

"Like Swiss cheese," the old matron croaked. "Ever since Gehlen rebuilt the organization."

"And if the East Germans are puppets, then who is the puppet master?" Eytan asked like a rabbi performing responsive reading.

"Mother Russia, God bless her," said Sylvia again.

"And despite the persistent rumors of an impending wave of decency descending on the CCCP—" Eytan searched for the word. "What's the working title?"

"*Glasnost,*" Baum snorted.

"Ah, yes," Eytan said sarcastically. "*Glasnost.* Despite this supposed reform effort, who is still financing the training of the PFLP, IRA, SWAPO, ad nauseum?"

"But I thought the KGB was pulling back on terror support," said Badash.

"Directly, yes," said Eytan. "But they're still training, still aiding by proxy. The East Germans, Romanians, and Bulgarians are still the muscle in the field."

"No one knows which way the hammer and sickle will fall," Romano added.

"So again, Moscow writes the checks," said Sylvia.

Eytan lifted his hands. He was finished. He moved to the couch and sat, waiting.

"*Nu?*" Ben-Zion was truly annoyed after this virtuoso performance.

"So, Itzik," Eytan concluded, "if, and I'll grant you the *if,* Kamil is still alive, he could have been sitting on a beach somewhere for a year, studying the goddamn file."

No one was speaking. Uri Badash was rubbing his dark face. He was a handsome man, looking rather like an Egyptian film star. "It is possible," he said. "It's certainly somewhere to begin."

"It is patently absurd," said Itzik, resuming his annoyed vocal posture. "Some phoenix rising from the ashes to even the score. *Stahm shtuyot.*"

Eytan's color began to rise again. "Tell me, Itzik. Do you think we own the copyright on vengeance?"

"It's blatant paranoia," Ben-Zion stormed. "Why Kamil? Because you want it to be so? What about our other targets, Eckstein?" He pointed at a large green iron safe that sat in the corner behind his desk. "What about a hundred other operations that could just as easily have enraged a hundred other men? Why couldn't it be one of *their* survivors out for Israeli blood?"

"Because, Itzik." Eytan fought to control himself, knowing that it was no good; with Itzik he had lost before he began. "Because Zvika Pearlman and Serge Samal only worked *together* on one project. One. *Operation Flute*."

Nothing infuriated Itzik Ben-Zion more than being successfully challenged in front of his subordinates. Nothing. He looked at his watch.

"All right," he snapped. "Enough. This is over. Dismissed to all tasks."

Danny and Sylvia glanced at each other, took their cues, and left quietly, while Heinz stood by and waited. Being the commander's aide, he loved the fact that no matter who got thrown out of the office, he always remained.

"Eckstein," Ben-Zion ordered. "You will write up a full history on Samal for Uri and the GSS. Samal was theirs, and it's now their jurisdiction. I want it quickly and I want it in minute detail, and then I want it passed through the departmental censor and reworked. So you'd better get moving."

The Colonel sat down and picked up a telephone, but he stopped dialing when he saw that Eckstein and Baum had not yet moved. He fixed them with a threatening glare.

They left the office.

———

"Eytan. Stop." Baum was amazed to find himself actually chasing Eckstein down the stairwell from Three to Two. The crippled captain was gripping the steel handrail, stomping down with his bad leg and hurling himself along three steps at a time. Baum's lumbering girth made the cement vibrate as he tried to keep up. "We can't get anywhere this way."

"We?" Eckstein spat without turning. He reached the landing and went marching along the corridor. Some people in the hallway turned to look at him as he shot his right hand out and pushed into the men's room, surprising Baum, who had to stop short like a cartoon character. Baum followed inside.

Eytan went into a stall, opened his fly and began to urinate into a toilet. He could hear Baum pacing the tile floor.

"Yes, Eytan. We. You think because I don't shout and wave my arms like you I'm not on your side? Someone has to play the rational one."

"Oh," Eckstein snorted as he zipped up and turned the toilet faucet. Water trickled into the bowl. Someday this country was going to hire one decent plumber. "So you think I'm nuts, too."

"I think you're reacting. You have to stop. Think. Plan."

Eytan shouldered past Benni and went to the sink. He did not look in the mirror. He splashed his face with water and wiped it on his sleeves, one after the other. Then he stalked out into the hallway again.

He was stopped short by Pnina from Cover. She was waiting for him and she blocked his way, gripped both of his shoulders and looked into his twisted face with liquid brown eyes.

"I'm so sorry," she said. "I'm sorry about Tiger." Pnina always used agents' cover names.

Eytan calmed a bit. He could be furious at Itzik, Benni, and everyone and everything, but not Pnina. She meant what she said. He put a hand to her red hair and said, "Thank you." Then he pressed on.

"Okay. That's enough." Benni grabbed Eytan's bicep in

a vise grip. "We're going to talk." He dragged him toward his office and pounded the door open. Baum's staff members sat at their terminals. They looked up as the door banged against the wall.

"Everybody out," Baum's voice boomed. "Breaktime."

The young researchers pushed to their feet and moved toward the door. "I'm swimming in coffee already," one of the girls muttered.

"We just had a break," said Yablokovsky.

"Have another," Baum ordered.

As Horse passed Eckstein, he looked over the top of his spectacles and shook his head with empathetic sadness.

"Look, I agree that something may be happening here," said Baum when they were alone.

"Congratulations." Eytan's tone was petulant.

"I don't care how mad you are, you're not goading me into a fight."

Eytan stopped himself from retorting further. "Sorry."

"I'm not saying I agree with you," Benni continued. "Yes, this may be Kamil, or one of his old cell. Also, it may not be. Do you agree?"

Eytan said nothing.

"Eckstein, do you agree that it may *not* be?"

"Yes, all right." Eytan sighed and looked out the window. "It may not be. I probably wouldn't be so adamant about it if that sonofabitch upstairs would give just a millimeter on this."

"Itzik has his reasons."

Eckstein turned, hearing something in Baum's voice. "What reasons?"

"Trust me. Itzik Ben-Zion has a history in these kinds of things, layers upon layers that you aren't even aware of. You have to lead him into this, not push him. He has to be manipulated."

"What reasons?" Eytan asked again.

Baum remained evasive. "It doesn't matter. The simple fact is that unless you have something better than a hunch, he won't listen to you, and every time you say *Flute,* it'll be like a red flag to a bull."

Eytan stifled his curiosity and lit another cigarette. He was almost out. What a joke. And just yesterday he had promised himself he would quit tomorrow. Well, here it was, tomorrow, and all he could think of was the next pack.

"It is Kamil, Benni," Eytan said quietly. "I know it."

"How? What makes you so sure?"

"Benni, you know me. I'm a skeptic, not one for astrology or extrasensory stuff or any of that bullshit. But I know this, like a twin knows when his brother's in trouble. Like a mother knows when her son's been killed in a war. I know this."

Benni threw up his hands. There was no arguing with a reborn mystic.

"I want to see George Mahsoud," said Eytan.

"In al deenak." Benni smacked himself on the great plane of his forehead. George Mahsoud was the only member of Amar Kamil's cell ever to have been captured alive by the Israelis. He had been tried, convicted of terrorism and murder, and had been sitting in a maximum security prison in Atlit for over a year. Mahsoud was doing twenty-five years to life. He had been questioned by every intelligence expert in the country, offered plea bargains, threatened, subjected to psychological tricks and tortures. Yet he had never uttered a single helpful bit of information.

"You *are* crazy," Baum said. "Everyone's had their hands on him. He'll never talk. You think he'll like your face so he'll confide in you? You going to bring him flowers?"

Eytan would not be discouraged. "He knows the truth. He knows what really happened to Kamil after Bogenhausen. He's the only one who can support my theory."

"It's ridiculous."

"You're beginning to sound like your boss."

Benni actually blushed. He would not have Eytan think that he was afraid for his job. On the other hand, plotting against the C.O.'s orders was not a healthy way to run an intelligence branch.

"Benni, I'll make a deal with you," said Eytan. "A calm, rational, unemotional agreement."

Baum examined his former team leader. "Show me your cards."

"We're going to call Ettie Denziger. We're going to tell her what happened. Do you respect her opinion?"

"Yes," Benni said with a suspicious tone.

"If Ettie agrees with my 'hunch,' as you put it, you're going to contact Atlit and arrange for me to see the prisoner. If she says I'm way off the mark, I'll drop the whole thing and sit down and write that stupid obituary."

"What about your interviews today?" Baum asked, groping feebly for a way to save Eytan from snowballing down this icy precipice.

"You'll tell Romano I went home sick. He'll understand."

Baum waited, thinking. Then he said, "Okay, let's call her," and he moved toward one of his telephones.

"Not here," Eytan said. "The voice logger."

Benni stopped. "Where then?"

"Let's take a walk." Eytan opened the door, motioning for Benni to leave first. Baum sighed and shook his great bald head.

"I must be nuts, too."

They walked down the corridor. Eytan seemed calmer now, though he was barely covering his boiling emotions. As they passed the cafeteria, Benni stuck his head inside and yelled at his staff members. "Back to work. You've had enough coffee for a whole week."

They found a pay telephone across the compound near the Central Court Building. The booth was the typical open-air type, just a metal rain guard covering the old rotary-style instrument. Eytan's hands were still shaking as he dropped a token into the slot and dialed Ettie's number in Tel Aviv. Benni leaned against the booth and smoked, looking up at the SpecOps building, wondering if Ben-Zion was standing there staring at his insubordinate subordinates.

"Ettie? It's Tony in Jerusalem," Eytan said. "Call me back at 02–53211." He hung up and the phone rang almost immediately.

The line was not a secure one, so it took Eytan a little while to relay the horrid news in coded hints that only Ettie would comprehend. She groaned and stopped speaking when she understood that Serge Samal was dead. Eytan waited while she collected herself, then apologized for having to do it this way. Then he tried to explain the next part, without unfairly tipping the scales in his own favor.

"Listen, Ettie. We have a little dispute going on here. A slight disagreement. Hans-Dieter is here with me. I contend that this event is the result of an old bank check that we thought had cleared, but apparently has bounced. I say this bad check is back now. Hans disagrees with me, as does everyone else. Be objective. Just tell him what you think."

Eytan handed the phone over to Benni, who took it the same way he took the phone from his wife whenever she made him chat with his mother-in-law. He listened for a while. Then he said good-bye and hung up.

"What did she say?" Eytan asked.

"She said," Baum frowned, "and I quote, 'It sounds like it may be long and silver colored, with lots of finger holes and a place to put your lips.'"

Eytan nodded, yet no hint of a victorious expression crossed his lips.

"It's a flute," he said.

———

For a maximum-security prison, the facility at Atlit was not very impressive. It could not compare, at least physically, to an institution like Ramla, with its parapeted walls, massive guard towers and machine-gun posts. Atlit was not a civilian prison, so its name never appeared in the newspapers. It was rather small, and its one hundred prisoners never rioted or demanded better conditions. They did not bang their cups on the mess tables, clatter their bars or perform hunger strikes. Or at least if they did engage in any of those stereotypical antics of incarceration, no one ever heard about it.

The facility was fairly new, having been constructed just after the war in Lebanon. All of the prisoners were high-ranking terrorists. In fact, the words *maximum security* were more apropos to Atlit than to any other prison in Israel. Civilian prisons could not, by definition of a citizen's rights, be designed in such a way as to violate an inmate's basic living requirements or endanger his welfare. He had to have light, exercise and hope. However, Atlit was not a civilian prison.

It consisted of a single square building, with meter-thick walls of concrete over a steel skeleton and steel floors. There were no windows. There was no exercise yard. Surrounding the walls on all sides were thirty meters of flat-brushed earth peppered with antipersonnel mines. Surrounding the mine fields was a seven-meter-high electrified fence, topped with razor concertina. You accessed the single entrance by virtue of a steel bridge above the mine fields.

As a final touch, in case a prisoner dreamed too enthusiastically of freedom, the location of the facility was its most discouraging trait. For the ancient coastal port of Atlit, with its picturesque Crusader Castle and breathtaking view of the

Mediterranean, was also home to the secret training base of the IDF Naval Commandos. The *Shayettet,* as the Israeli SEALs were called, had a reputation as the toughest troops in the Israeli order of battle. They had absolutely no connection with the prison facility, but if by some miracle you managed to escape from it, you would be like a rabbit hopping into a pack of wolves.

It took Eckstein nearly four hours to reach the prison. Atlit was just south of Haifa, normally a two-hour ride from Jerusalem. However, a Subaru had gone under a tank trailer on the coast road and Eckstein had been stuck there for an eternity. Left alone with his rage and his grief, he had nearly abandoned his car. When the traffic finally cleared, he immediately picked up some hitchhiking soldiers, just to have their banter drown the horrible voices in his head.

Now it was already evening, and he had waited another two hours outside the prison while his clearances were processed and the prisoner was prepared. There was a small canteen truck at the gate, and he finally bought an egg sandwich, ate half and threw the rest away. He wished he had a shot of whiskey instead of the lukewarm grapefruit juice that nearly caused him to regurgitate.

He was impatient with the waiting, yet not angered by it. He understood that you never allowed a visitor immediate access, no matter his rank or position. If an escape plot were afoot, few conspirators could wait coolly without breaking and running.

Someone finally called Eckstein's name and he climbed up the steel stairway and crossed the bridge, surrendering his pistol and stopping to have his ID examined and his photograph taken.

He descended into a submarine chamber like the one at Headquarters, answered the usual questions and signed the official request cable from Baum, allowing him to visit George

Mahsoud. The secondary door clicked and Eckstein was met on the other side by a huge Druze sergeant wearing pressed fatigues and a black handlebar moustache as wide as a cantaloupe slice.

"Come," said the giant, and Eckstein followed him along a lime-colored corridor that was so brightly lit it was almost painful to the eyes. Eckstein realized that in Atlit, there were no days or nights, storms or seasons. The warden was the Lord, the lightswitch and thermostat his rod and staff.

"Have you seen Mahsoud before?" the sergeant asked in his burry, accented Hebrew.

"At a distance."

"Do you know how many times he's been interrogated?"

"I'm not here to interrogate him."

"One hundred and twenty-two times. Do you know how many officers have worked on him?"

"You'll tell me, I think."

"Twenty-seven. Colonels, majors, Mossadnikim. Even a brigadier general." Clearly the sergeant did not have much faith in Eytan's powers of persuasion. He stopped outside a small steel door. "Want to look at him first?"

"Okay."

They entered a small space, completely dark, with raised wooden benches like a sauna. Eckstein did not sit. He stared at a smoky glass pane the size of an art poster. He could hear the Druze breathing heavily beside him.

From the other side of the pane, George Mahsoud stared back at him.

Eytan had, of course, seen Mahsoud many times before. But always it was in Europe, under surveillance, and he was not prepared for this diminished version of the man. For if you could like a member of the opposition, a terrorist who would blow you out of the sky and then eat cordon bleu for dinner, Eytan had liked George. By the man's gait, his tone in intercepted conversations, his simple and elegant manner of dress, George evidenced an idealistic sense of purpose, a certain professionalism, tempered with irony.

Almost immediately after Bogenhausen, Kamil's cell had scattered. Mahsoud's trail was quickly picked up. He was pressured with carefully planned, exposed surveillances, until he began to run. And when he finally reached the Cote d'Azur in near panic, the girl was sent in. She lured him aboard a yacht, and that was that.

He looked so much smaller now, sitting on a hard wooden bench against the wall of the interrogation room, wearing a light blue shirt, matching baggy trousers, and soft woolen plaid slippers. His moustache drooped and his tan had faded. His black hair had gone much greyer around the ears. There was no light left in the sharp black eyes.

George kept looking at the two-way mirror, his hands folded in his lap. His expression said, *I'm here. You're there. Let's get on with it.*

"Let me in," Eckstein said.

The sergeant led him out into the corridor again. Then he pulled a baton from his belt, unlocked the interrogation room, and waved Eytan inside.

Mahsoud was looking down at the floor.

"Do you have to be here?" Eytan asked the sergeant.

"Yes."

"How about watching through there?" Eytan pointed at the two-way glass.

The sergeant looked at Mahsoud, as if taking measure of the prisoner. He had already frisked him. Twice.

"Okay." He left the two men alone.

Eytan stood in the center of the room, feeling awkward. After all, a man's dignity was a precious thing. It was hard to see it taken away from anyone. He had to remind himself of his purpose.

"Want a cigarette?" Eytan offered.

George did not respond. He did not even look up. Eytan lit one for himself. The sound of the match exploding echoed off the walls of the empty room.

All at once, his heart felt so heavy, his hopes worthless. He knew exactly what he was going to get from this man. What could he offer him? Freedom? Some kind of deal? What had not been done that he, The Great Eckstein, could bring into the picture? He had driven all this way for nothing, fueled by the rage of impotence.

He sat down next to George on the bench.

"Listen, George." He tried to sound almost apologetic. "My name is Eckhardt. I'm no one important. I just want to ask a couple of simple questions. One question really. Okay?"

George said nothing. He examined his knees.

"I'm just a low-level staffer. Really. Practically just a clerk, a historian for the Ministry of Defense." It sounded so ridiculous as it came out of his mouth that Eytan wanted to bolt from the room. He was grateful that George did not laugh. He suddenly wondered if Mahsoud understood him at all. Then he remembered that the Palestinian was from a village near Bethlehem and spoke dead-fluent Hebrew.

"Maybe I can help you," Eckstein lied. "Maybe if you help me with this one thing, your cooperation will do something good for you."

George said nothing.

"Okay." Eckstein rose from his seat. He moved in front of Mahsoud, with his back to the two-way mirror, as if shielding George's face from view in order to offer some privacy. "It's like this. I'll tell you straight. You knew Amar Kamil better than anyone else. Everything about him. No one knows what really happened to him, no one but maybe you. Some of the people who worked on the Kamil case have been killed recently. Just tell me this one thing, George, and we'll leave you alone. Is Kamil dead or alive?"

For the first time, George raised his head and looked at

Eytan. His eyes narrowed ever so slightly, the deep lines at the corners gathering like the folded wings of a hawk. Yet he did not smile. It was almost an empathic expression, the look of a doctor regarding a terminally ill patient. And he did not speak.

Eytan allowed a full minute to pass. Then he surrendered. He turned to walk from the room, but what he heard stopped him dead cold in his tracks and a shocking chill coursed up the length of his spine.

"Yitgadal, Ve-yitkadash, Shmei Rabah."

George was quietly reciting *Kaddish*. The Hebrew Prayer for the Dead.

———

Eytan sped the whole way back to Jerusalem. He stopped only once to gas up and he did not play the radio. He smoked one cigarette after another and he kept all of the windows open, for he felt that he might fall asleep at the wheel. He knew that he should stop and call Simona, but something told him that he could salvage a piece of the day and it would not be too late as long as she was still awake when he got home. He would tell her everything and she would understand. She always did.

The night was black as a moonless desert sky can be, and the highway from Tel Aviv to Jerusalem accursed for its lack of illumination. Eytan had emptied himself of memories. Everything that he had ever done with or shared with or seen of Serge Samal had been played over and over until the film finally burned out and there was nothing left but a void that left his face flat and expressionless.

Around midnight he climbed the long flights to the apartment, his leg burning, the aches and sores of his body coming back full force. He let himself in, wearing a contrite expression, but the house was dead still.

A single light burned in the salon. The coffee table was

covered with plates smeared with chocolate residue. Plastic cups wore lipstick smears and the dregs of juice and champagne, and the ashtrays were filled with cold butts. The stereo power light was still on, glowing like a tired red eye in one darkened corner of the room. One of the wooden end tables near the television was piled with soft-looking, multicolored wrapped gifts. Turning toward the kitchen, he could see a plastic-covered, ravaged dark hulk shining in the dim light on the slate counter. His cake.

There was a white piece of paper on the seat of Eytan's black rocker. He picked it up, squinting at Simona's round script.

"Happy birthday. We had your party without you. The surprise was that you never showed up."

Eytan dropped the paper on the floor. He sat down in the rocker and his pistol banged against the slats. He put his hands in his hair and his elbows on his knees, and he began to rock. And then he began to cry. He cried hard, harder than he had in a long, long time, maybe since he'd been a recruit some fifteen years before. Maybe harder than he had ever cried in his whole life.

6

Europe

Thirteen Hours Later

THE BLACK LOCOMOTIVE at Aachen Station snorted white plumes of steam into the night, waiting like an angry bull at a winter rodeo. It lay low and hulking at the eastern end of the dark platform, its sharp snout pointed toward Bonn, emitting deep rasps from its iron lungs while scurrying German workmen coupled its vertebrae of sleepers and diners together in a fruitless effort to remain on schedule. The fancy FrenchRail electric from Brussels had barely survived the border crossing, succumbing to a final rebellion of capacitors and transformers as it limped—silent, dark and dejected—into its first German stop. So the six-hundred-odd passengers would continue their journey to Vienna the old-fashioned way, amid the clatter of pocked iron wheels and the mournful wails of a steam whistle.

Amar Kamil did not mind the switch at all. Nor the delay. He was a patient man of the Levant, and he viewed the worship of modern accoutrements with a cynical eye.

He stood on the damp concrete platform and cleaned a new pair of gold-rimmed spectacles, watching the other passengers as they hurried in and out of the washrooms and rushed to buy beers and sandwiches from a squad of gleeful pushcart vendors who had magically appeared on the scene. They were all underdressed. It was already summer and no one had anticipated a two-hour, fresh-air wait at a North German station in the middle of the night. They stamped their feet and hugged themselves, dragging their valises around and looking like refugees awaiting one last chance at freedom.

The doors to the German train opened and the stampede ensued. Amar stood by and watched, his hands in the pockets of a long olive trench, his retouched red-blond hair glistening with the droplets of a fine drizzle. In a minute, the platform was nearly abandoned. Amar looked around. No one but the vendors remained, and as the huge iron wheels began to turn he picked up his small suitcase and jogged toward the first car.

"Vite, vite, mon ami!" A remaining Parisian ticket conductor reached out for Amar's valise, and he tossed it up and swung aboard. The small Frenchman shook his head at Amar, squeezed past him and hopped down onto the platform, running for a moment with the momentum and then suddenly turning away, as if pitying the poor souls who were continuing on into Deutschland.

The single-aisle cars were packed to overflowing, and already there were bursts of loud protests from those who had paid for seats or pull-out sleepers and found themselves with barely room to stand. Yet Amar was not concerned for his comfort.

He slowly made his way back along the entire length of the train. He examined the eyes of all the adults whom he passed, and he stopped occasionally to take measure of those who followed along. Whenever they found a resting place, or overtook him, he continued on.

He was supposed to have boarded the FrenchRail electric at Brussels. Instead, he had flown to Rotterdam, then Dusseldorf, and driven to Aachen, abandoning the rental car at the station. In a training environment, Kamil was as punctilious as a teacher's pet. In the field, it was his neck and he wrote his own timetable.

He reached the last car of the train, a plush mahogany-veneered *coche* of first-class private compartments. No one stood in the narrow carpeted aisle along the left side of the car. He marched quickly now to the last compartment, checked the number on the door, and without knocking he jerked back on the handle and slid it open.

Major Vladimir Kozov of Department VIII, of the First Chief Directorate—*Komitet Gosudarstvennoy Bezopashnosty*—sat alone in the richly adorned compartment. The fold-down bed was still in its cocoon, and the major was nestled against the far corner of the cobalt-blue upholstery as if he'd been punished by a schoolmaster. He was a big-shouldered man, the major, with a wide Slavic face and short, stubbly, greying blond hair over a big bony skull. Kozov had long ago been transferred over from the GRU, yet like most field-grade officers of large military intelligence organizations he could not shed the posture or complexion that made him look uncomfortable in civilian clothes.

Kamil nearly laughed, for Kozov was wearing those silly Slavic tweeds that made the Soviet advisors in Lebanon stick out like nudists at a black-tie party. At the moment, his collar was open and his clothes in sweaty disarray, attesting to the fact that Kamil's late appearance had had a neural impact.

Kozov looked startled for a moment; then he tossed his copy of *Paris Match* onto the sofa and threw up his hands in thanks.

"Oh! L'enfant terrible!"

Kamil did not smile. He put a finger to his lips and slid

the door closed behind him. He put his suitcase down and looked around. There was one large window at the far wall, and outside the distant countryside lights danced with the rhythmic vibrations of the clacking wheels of the train. Above the secured bed was a luggage rack with a guardrail, holding Kozov's single soft valise. There was a small mirror across from the bed above a low cabinet containing a washbasin covered by a fold-down counter. Kamil put one hand in his coat pocket and then snapped open the closet door nearest to the entrance. Empty. Then he crossed the compartment and opened the washstand cabinet, latching it again after a brief inspection. He kicked the foot of the sofa and then moved his free hand along the walls, not so much a tactile inspection as a way of focusing his thoughts on all eventualities. Then he turned to leave.

"*Où est-ce que tu vas?*" Kozov asked with a hint of annoyance.

"To get acquainted with our neighbors."

"We have no neighbors," said Kozov. "We are the last compartment and I rented the adjoining one as well. And it cost me 200 Sterling in cash to do it, so . . . *s'il vous plaît.*" He motioned for Amar to sit.

Kamil stood for a moment, thinking. Then he locked the door and moved to the sofa. He sat at the opposite end from Kozov, back to the wooden corner wall. He removed his hand from his coat and placed a Walther 7.65-millimeter PPK on the upholstery next to his leg.

Kozov glanced at the pistol and shifted in his seat. "You seem to have lost some faith, Aswan," he continued in French.

"I had a professor in a foreign land who taught me that faith is only for the clergy."

Kozov nodded, recognizing his own words. "Perhaps he omitted some exceptions."

"Well, let's see," said Amar, like a law student searching

for a precedent. "In 1975, Carlos's most trusted aide, Michel Mourkabal, arrived at the operative's Paris flat on Rue Toullier with three 'friends' in tow. These friends . . ."

"Were agents of the French DST and Carlos had to shoot his way out of it, yes." Kozov finished the lesson with a sigh. "Point taken."

The Russian reached into the pocket of his tweed coat, keeping his movements slow and deliberate. He removed a box of Balkan Sobranies and lit one of the black cigarettes, spewing a cloud of thick, acrid smoke.

Kamil smiled. "My dear major. How cliché."

Kozov shrugged. "Perhaps. Cliché may be annoying, but it is not dangerous. You were supposed to board in Brussels."

"Yes, but predictability—"

"Is death," Kozov said. "Yes, yes. May we go on?" If he heard his own words thrown up to him again he feared he might scream. He wanted to conduct the briefing and be rid of the Palestinian. Kamil was decidedly different out here than he had been in Moscow. The difference was not a welcome guest.

Amar was also anxious to continue. He had waited a very long time for this moment, and he had done so patiently, knowing that his new masters had something in store for him which they would reveal at their discretion. His feelings for Kozov were at once resentful and thankful, rather like the way the French viewed the Americans. After all, it had been all too clear in Munich that the Western intelligence services were snapping at his heels. Then suddenly, like some grand deus ex machina, Vladimir Kozov had appeared to snatch him from the fire, effectively wiping Amar Kamil from the face of the earth, to be reborn as someone else.

Amar harbored no illusions as to the motive. It was clear that his training was focused on enabling him to carry out an elimination on Israeli soil. However, as with all such operations of Department VIII, his target would not be revealed to him until the last possible moment. He assumed that it would be someone important, perhaps another Palestinian, most probably a West Bank leader who had strayed from the Russian agenda. He accepted that. He would simply add the individual to his own private list.

It was payback time.

Kozov, despite the unnerving feeling that he was sharing a cage with an asp, edged closer to Kamil. He leaned his elbows on his knees and rubbed his wide jaw with a set of meaty fingers. He switched to English.

"Let us begin with your face."

"My face?" Amar looked a bit startled. His own English emerged in the flat tones he had practiced once a week in the American Training Facility.

"Your face. Did you think that we simply allowed our surgeons aesthetic license? Feel the scar."

Amar reached up and touched the short, curved crevice below his right eye. Yes, he had always wondered how the KGB would tolerate such a careless slip of the scalpel. But then he had grown to like the slightly piratical look. He tilted his head and saw his own wavering reflection in the big window on the far wall. Rain was striking the pane, driving back in horizontal streams with the wind. Amar loved trains. They were incredibly mysterious and romantic.

"On a daily basis," Kozov continued, "the Israeli Cabinet is briefed by IDF staff officers from General Headquarters. Unless there is an immediate military crisis, most of these officers are from Planning, Logistics and Intelligence. Do you follow me so far, Amar?"

"Yes," Amar said slowly. Already he sensed that his guesses had been way off the mark. He could feel a growing constriction in his bowels, such as one might feel upon the impending smuggling of a weapon aboard an international air carrier.

"Now," Kozov went on, warming to the pleasure of the

certain shock he was about to administer. "One of these strategic defense advisors is quite a talented young man, though I must say that in typical Israeli fashion he has attained his rank at too young an age. His name is Major Rami Carrera. Would you like to see a picture of him?"

Kamil said nothing. He could feel his heart against the starched cloth of his shirt. His silk regimental tie suddenly felt like a noose.

Kozov reached into his breast pocket and came up with a small rectangle of black plastic. It looked like a single sheet of Polaroid film. The major held it out in front of Kamil and jerked on the tab, peeling the covering away.

Amar swallowed his gasp. The face that looked out at him was his own. The hair was slightly longer, more curled and unkempt, and sunglasses were perched on the crown of the head. The skin was very tan, but the scar was plainly there. It was obviously a surveillance photo, for the head was framed by a background of café umbrellas and animated human forms, and the eyes looked at something else to the left of the lens. Part of the rumpled uniform—with single metal oak leaves on the epaulets and a pair of silver parachute wings over the chest—could be seen below the face. Yet most startling was the broad, carefree, flashing smile. Amar thought instantly that he would have to cultivate that smile, and simultaneously with that thought came the piercing blow which might well be felt by a debutante as she appears for her ball, only to see another girl wearing the exact same gown.

Amar reached out and slowly took the photograph from Kozov. Even as he did so it began to darken. As he watched, it turned coal black until nothing was left but a flat ebony surface.

"Unfixed," said Kozov as he recovered the picture and pocketed it. The major took his Sobranies from his other pocket and offered the box to Kamil. Amar waved them away and Kozov snorted a short laugh.

"No. I know these are not your brand. At the bottom of the box you will find Carrera's curriculum vitae. All you need. You see?" He pushed the pile of cigarettes aside and lifted one corner of the foil to reveal a white sheet covered with minuscule Cyrillic print. "You'll need a lupe to magnify it. Buy one. Schneider is the best."

Amar was only half hearing Kozov's drone. He felt a coldness in his chest. So that was why Rainer Luckmann had stared at him so intently on the London bus, obviously thinking that he knew "Yossi Yerushalmi" from somewhere. At the time, Amar had attributed this to a fluke. In fact, Luckmann *did* know him, had probably seen his face in newspapers, or on television, perhaps even served with Rami Carrera at some point. *Allah* in heaven, he had come very, very close to being blown right then and there. He tasted the bile that welled up along with a surge of anger, as he could see that Kozov was enjoying the surprise. Until this moment the major had told Amar nothing. On the other hand, Kozov had simply been following procedure. He could not possibly have known that Amar's own private efforts would again bring him so soon into contact with Israeli intelligence operatives.

He fought the anger and calmed his racing heart. He had to hear the rest of it. All of it.

"Nice-looking fellow." Amar managed a small smile as he took the Sobranies, closed the pack, and put it into the inside pocket of his suit coat. "Do go on."

"Yes," said Kozov, somewhat disappointed that Kamil had not had a more emotional reaction to his surprise. "So. Your target." The major once again reached into his suit pocket, reminding Amar of a burly cabaret magician. He took out a small notebook and a pen, wrote something on a leaf of paper, tore it off and handed it to Kamil.

Amar took the paper and looked at it. He blinked. He held it closer and looked at it again. The name of the Prime

Minister of Israel jumped up at him from the white scrap. He held it out for Kozov to take back. It fluttered in his fingers.

"Bist du verrückt?" Amar switched to German and his voice was hoarse. Images of the hateful little Israeli politician popped into his brain, but the idea that they wanted to kill him had to be a joke, a ruse, a test of Amar's sincerity.

"Nein. Ich bin nicht verrückt." Kozov attested calmly to his mental health as he recovered the paper. He went to the washbasin, lifted the cover, took out his cigarette lighter and incinerated the evidence. He walked back to Kamil and stood over him, barely whispering now. "First, I will describe how it will go. Then we will discuss the politics of it. *Klingt das gut?"*

Amar stared up at the mad Russian.

"On the fourth of September—I believe it is the last day of your holiday, Ramadan—this man will address a swearing-in of elite troops at the Western Wall in Jerusalem."

Amar listened, yet he felt as if his brain were splitting, dividing itself into two distinct halves. One belonged to Kamil, Aswan, Gregor, the Palestinian hero who could bring salvation to his people. The other belonged to Amar, the intellectual, the planner who always managed to escape the labyrinth. No one had ever attempted to assassinate an Israeli head of state. No one. It would be like entering a bees' nest in an attempt to crush the queen.

"Now, Major Carrera sees this man every single day. The security people are so used to his presence that he has free rein of the Knesset. He can even approach your target and speak freely without prescheduling. Even the Israelis do not view this as, how do they say, *chutzpah*. Are you following, Aswan?"

Amar just stared at the major's chest, watching his beefy hands crisscross in blurry gesticulations.

"On the morning of the fourth, Major Carrera will not show up for work. He will be abducted by some of George Habash's people and disposed of. The PFLP operatives will, of course, be handled by a Department VIII control." Kozov stopped to light another Sobranie from a spare pack. Then, unthinking, he mumbled, "These people cannot be trusted to do anything right by themselves."

Amar raised his eyes. Kozov went slightly pale, yet there was no use in trying to apologize. He cleared his throat.

"That evening, just before the ceremony, you will surface in Carrera's place. Quite simply, you will execute the target with a pistol and promptly surrender."

The major paused, waiting for a signal to continue on. However, Amar Kamil began to laugh. It started as a low snort from his nostrils, and then he threw himself back against the sofa and gave in to it, letting the waves roll over him as he slapped his leg and tears came to his eyes. Finally, when he was done, he loosened his tie and opened his eyes. The KGB major was once again perched next to him on the seat, studying him like a concerned psychiatrist.

"I am so pleased that you are amused."

"I am sorry, Comrade Major," Amar managed as he recovered. "But just imagine that I will order you to jump under this train, and expect you to take me seriously."

"You will not be killed, Aswan."

"Oh, no, of course not. They'll give me flowers and make me Miss Israel."

"The Israelis have no death penalty."

"They'll change the law!" Amar jumped to his feet and began to pace, growing furious with the realization that these Russians were dead serious and he was expected to play the pawn in a game for the very highest of stakes.

"You will not be killed, Aswan. You will behave as an Israeli officer gone mad. After the assassination, you will not even speak, except to mumble incoherently. We have worked this out at Yasenevo, over and over again. Do you think this is off the cuff? Years of research, my friend."

Kamil stopped pacing and stood before the picture window. He watched the tall black shapes of telephone poles as they flashed by. The clatter of the wheels was like a headache that would not diminish.

"They will hospitalize you, pure and simple. You must retain your discipline and silence for six months. At that time, a Spetsnatz team posing as terrorists will take an American aircraft. They will demand the release of only forty Palestinians from Israeli prisons. And they will include in their demand the release of the 'demented' Carrera. In less than a year you will be back in Moscow, teaching at the Institute."

Amar said nothing. He realized that he was gripping something hard, and he looked down to see the PPK clutched in his hand. Moscow. He actually wished he were back there now. He thought of Rina. Katya. He had never expected to see them again. As for Leila, he knew now that she was gone from his life forever. He had been given the face of a top Israeli cabinet advisor. Where could he go that he could not be tracked? The wastelands of Libya? That garbage scow called Yemen?

"It is a politically catastrophic idea," he whispered.

"Come, Aswan," Kozov said in a gentler tone. "Sit, and I will explain the politics of it all."

Amar moved woodenly to the sofa again and sat down. He looked at Kozov, debating whether to hear him out or shoot him in his slabby Slavic face.

"Aswan, what is your greatest dream?" Kozov waited. "No? You do not remember? Then I will refresh your memory. I will tell you as you have told me. You wish to return, someday, to Bethlehem. A Bethlehem in the hands of its righteous sons, correct?"

Truth. Amar's dream, perhaps the fantasy that fueled

214

him, was to return to his hometown as a hero. It would again be a Palestinian city, and in a perfect world he would be her *Muktar,* and all the sins of his father would be wiped away.

"Well, if this man lives, your dream is dead," Kozov said simply. "You think that he is a radical hard-liner, like Begin was? Well, Begin bedded down with Sadat. And now, *this* man is about to wed with Arafat."

Suddenly Amar was alert again, listening, no longer indulging his own self-pity.

"Yes," Kozov went on. "We have a copy of the plan, courtesy of a certain American State Department official in Vienna. The plan calls for an international peace conference, West Bank elections, rapid autonomy and then a relinquishing of certain sections of Judea and Samaria to Arafat's proxies. Yes, Aswan, Arafat is going to sell out in exchange for eventually returning home to live out his treacherous life as prime minister of a new Palestinian state. But no Palestinian will return home to Haifa, nor to Jaffa. And Bethlehem, my dear friend, will remain on the *Israeli* side of the lines."

Seeing Kamil's look of stunned disbelief, Kozov finished off his story.

"Yes, it is true. Now, I will not insult you by pretending a selfless Soviet heart for the Palestinian cause. Your act will deal these holier-than-thou Israelis a crushing blow. Our own disinformation will spread word of an attempted coup by Israeli hard-liners. This will, of course, cause a total collapse of their coalition government and destroy the plan for this bastard state. We will then move quickly to have the Syrians and the Iraqis initiate one final military putsch, which they can only do with our support and mediation, given how much they despise one another. However, Assad and Hussein will not be able to resist the opportunity. The Israelis will be floundering, and we will be back in the game."

Kozov waited for some sort of verbal reaction. It did not come, as Amar simply stared at him.

"Would you like to go home, Aswan?"

"I would like to kill you."

Kozov swallowed hard. "You may shoot the messenger," he said. "But the message will still be there." He realized just how dangerous was this encounter. He had seen Kamil perform in hand-to-hand classes. The Arab did not even need the pistol. Kozov had no idea if Kamil was buying the lie. The major had to believe that their past relationship would carry him through it. The plan, of course, was much, much simpler. There was no pending agreement between that maniacal little Jew and Yasir Arafat. That was just a story to feed Kamil's rage and warped sense of idealistic nationalism. It was much, much simpler.

Kamil would kill the PM, and Kamil himself would die immediately. The dead Kamil would be revealed as a Syrian agent, and the Israeli Tiger would turn immediately on her nemesis across the Golan. Damascus had been all too cold to her Russian godmother of late. How warm she would become when Moscow stepped in to save her ass once again. Afghanistan was lost, Iran a wild mare, a volcano was building throughout the East Bloc. The Politburo was becoming increasingly pathetic, but at least the First Chief Directorate understood that Moscow had to get back into the Middle East with a flourish.

Even if Kamil's attempt failed, KGB would still blow him to the Mossad as a Syrian-sponsored operative. Hopefully, with the same results. Moscow could not really lose with this one. No matter what happened to Kamil.

And yet, seeing Kamil's eyes ablaze, Kozov was not sure that he would survive this briefing at all. He was getting old for a field officer. Nearly fifty. After this, he swore that he would retire to a modest *dacha* and spend the rest of his life fishing on the Black Sea.

"Aswan," Kozov resumed in a careful, soothing tone. *"Ich will, das Sie—"*

"Shut up, please, Major." Amar switched back to English. "I have to think."

Kozov sat dead still as Kamil rose and began to pace again. The Arab reached out once and grabbed a wall as the train bucked over a bad stretch of track. The whistle blew somewhere out ahead, like a tug horn in a treacherous inlet.

Amar knew a trap when he saw one. Kozov and his masters had manipulated him. These Russians with their chess, always playing chess! It surpassed sex in their national psyche, and they layered their political moves with plots and counterplots so you never saw the true objective until your king lay bleeding on its side. Amar was smart, too, yet in an instinctive, animal way. He could not beat Kozov at the Russian game. Yet he could refuse to play by the KGB's rules.

With this accursed face of his there was nowhere to hide, for Dershinsky Square could have photos and faxes of him flying to the capitals of Europe within minutes of Kozov's order. In addition, it did not escape him that Rina and Katya were at Moscow's mercy. Oh, they had run that well! Giving him a woman who exuded selfless love and then *instructing* him to conceive a child with her. And did they really know how he felt about his Russian family? Of course they knew—they had listened to their every word, every whisper. Most probably they had recorded their lovemaking with pornographic glee.

The question was, Could he do it? All of it? Could he fulfill his personal pledge to avenge Jamayel, then carry out Moscow's order and still get out of it alive? Had the Westerners called him the Houdini of Terror for nothing? He was stronger now than he had ever been. Faster, armed with more languages and skills.

Amar had resources, safe deposits and old networks. He had telephone numbers in his head and the names of men who would bow to him and obey his orders implicitly.

The final objective, even without any benefits to Moscow,

did sound sweet. He could strike a massive blow for Palestinian nationalism. He could slash at the heart of Israeli arrogance and derail Arafat's cowardly capitulation.

He knew that his chances of survival were slim indeed. He was no amateur and certainly no fool. *The KGB will allow me to live about as long as Oswald lived after the JFK assassination,* he thought with some irony. And that ridiculous plan to free him from an Israeli mental ward? He also knew that the Russian commando-cum-terrorists could hijack Air Force One and the Israelis would still never surrender a man who had assassinated their prime minister.

He made his decision. He would do it. However, he would carry it out in his own way, using his own methods without aid from a single Russian network. *And,* Amar pledged to himself since he knew full well that his own death was highly probable, *I shall take Tony Eckhardt and the rest of his comrades along with me.*

"The fourth of September?" Amar asked for confirmation in a strong, decisive tone.

"Yes, my comrade. The fourth." Kozov's voice was bright with pleasure. He reached into his coat pocket and took out a blue plastic wallet of the type issued by international banks when selling travelers' checks. He handed Kamil the wallet like a game-show host giving away prizes. "Ten thousand U.S., in American Express checks. Unsigned. In twenties, fifties, and hundreds." He did not want Kamil to think that this was some sort of cheap payoff. "Just for additional expenses."

"I shall be there." Kamil took the checks.

"Excellent." Major Kozov was rather amazed at himself. He had done it, much to his own surprise. Unfortunately, he had orders to broach one additional, sensitive subject. Damn Moscow! How he wished he could just leave well enough alone.

"Aswan, there is one more thing I must ask you." Kozov lit up another Sobranie. He coughed briefly and glanced up at Kamil, who suddenly looked extremely impatient as he leaned against the washbasin. At least the Arab had put the pistol away. He was staring out the window. The train was slowing considerably as they neared the outskirts of Bonn. "I must ask why you killed the Israeli GSS man in London."

It was actually only a guess, for Moscow was not positive about it. The signals pointed to Kamil, however, and Kozov had been instructed to probe. He hoped that Kamil would deny it successfully, but the Arab's eyes flashed for a moment and that gave him away.

Amar said nothing.

Kozov sighed. "I, we, are very upset about this, my friend."

"It is of no concern to you," Amar barely whispered.

"You must cease this, whatever it may be, at once."

"It is of no concern to you!" Amar yelled and he turned on Kozov, his fists clenching.

"Now, now, you must hear me, my comrade." Kozov put his hands up, trying to make calming, pacifying gestures. His voice came out in a stutter and he felt the sweat prickling over his scalp. Goddamn them, why did he have to do this? But he had his orders and he could not decide which would be worse, Kamil's rage or the wrath of Colonel Stepnin. "Now, *I* know why you are doing this thing and believe me, I understand it. But you must stop it. It will endanger the plan."

"It will not," said Amar in a half growl.

"Yes, Aswan. It will."

"No, Major. You are not *always* correct. Moscow does not have all the answers." Amar spat it out. "As I said, I shall be there on the fourth. However, I shall also conduct this secondary operation as I see fit. If you are not a fool, you will see that this will also alter the character of Israeli invincibility in the eyes of the Western agencies. In addition, it will draw the focus of Mossad, AMAN and GSS. They will never suspect a totally unrelated target."

Amar's eyes glowed with barely controlled rage, frightening Kozov further. The major tried to appease.

"Yes, I see that. And I personally agree. However, I have been instructed to inform you that if there is dissent on this matter, I am to personally escort you to Vienna and witness you boarding an aircraft bound for Tel Aviv."

Amar raised his eyebrows. He laughed. A single sound. "Really?"

"Yes." Kozov swallowed.

"*Aufstehen!*" Amar snapped.

"What?"

Kamil reached down and grabbed Kozov by his tie. He yanked the Russian to his feet and pulled his blanched face close to his own.

"Aswan . . . ," Kozov croaked.

"Give me your belt," Amar ordered.

"What?"

"Your belt. Now."

Images of his own bloated body hanging in the compartment doorway made Kozov nearly foul himself, yet he managed to unbuckle his belt and pull it through the loops.

"Thank you, Major," Amar said. He took the belt and released Kozov, who fell back on the sofa, clutching his throat where the tie had nearly choked him.

Kamil walked over to his small suitcase and lifted it by the handle. He looped the belt around the leather case and buckled it as tightly as he could. He hefted the case and walked to the door.

"What . . . What are you doing?" Kozov managed.

"I prefer that my underwear not be scattered over the

entire German countryside. *Dasvedanya,* Major. Perhaps we shall meet again. But let us not count on it."

Kamil went out of the compartment and slid the door home with a bang that made Kozov jump.

Then the major understood. He sprang up from the sofa and put his quaking hands to the latches of the big picture window. He threw his weight against the locks and all at once it slid up into the frame, letting a scream of wind and rain come tumbling into the car. He grabbed the sill with his hands and thrust his head outside and looked back at the rear of the train. The clatter of the wheels deafened him.

Kamil's suitcase went hurtling off into the night from the rear platform of the car. And then, like some horrible ghost with its cape madly whipping behind, Kamil launched himself from the train and floated for a second in midair. His feet together, his arms clamped against his head, he disappeared below the embankment like the end of a nightmare.

Kozov pulled himself into the car. He closed the window, turned and fell against it with his back, breathing like he had sprinted a full kilometer. He had no doubts that Kamil would survive the jump, probably without a scratch. As for the mission, Kozov had done all he could. If he had played Kamil correctly, and he believed he had, the Arab was in a vortex that had only one funnel, and a single destination.

At the moment, Kozov realized that he did not, personally, nor as a KGB major, give a shit. He was alive. He made to walk to the door, then had to grab his waistband as his trousers began to slip. Holding himself that way, he jerked the door open and stuck his head out.

"Porter!" He yelled at a uniformed German who was just going forward through the coupling door. The man turned.

"Ja, mein Herr?"

"Get me a bottle of schnapps."

"Something to eat?"

"*Nein. Schnell!*"

"*Jawohl.*"

Kozov half fell back into the compartment. He swayed to the sofa, crashed onto his back, and lay there for a long time, holding his chest.

7

Munich

EYTAN ARRIVED ON THE EARLY MORNING Lufthansa flight from Rome. The wheels of the DC–9 banged down onto the runway with a screeching sloppiness uncharacteristic of German captains, and the former Stuka pilot apologized profusely over the intercom. He joked that there must have been an earthquake occurring in Munich, for the ground had suddenly jumped up and struck his airplane. Some of the passengers laughed and applauded. They were the ones who had been frightened the most.

The airplane crawled toward its gate, and in typical native fashion the passengers actually followed instructions and remained seated. In the last half hour, Eckstein had gone to the restroom, stripped to the waist, shaved, washed his torso and changed into a white short-sleeved shirt, slim striped tie and navy summer sportcoat. However, the clothes were already sticking to his skin as he sat in an aisle seat near the

223

forward exit, gripping the metal armrests and hoping that he would not bolt like a rabbit when the steward hauled on the hatch.

He glanced out the window. An El Al 707 was parked at some distance from its gate, like a lonely orphan forbidden to join the play at recess. It was flanked by Bundeswehr armored cars and grey-uniformed, machine-gun-toting guards, waiting for the Jews to show themselves.

Security.

Eckstein's choice of a German air carrier was superficially outrageous, for if alerted, the cabin crew would have had two hours in which to examine their passengers and pinpoint him for the authorities. Yet even if Itzik Ben-Zion was already aware of Eytan's unauthorized trip, the Colonel would assume that even Eckstein was not crazy enough to be flying around on the national carrier of a country in which he was still wanted for murder. Which was precisely why Eytan had made the selection. It was operationally correct—he knew that because the sweat rolled down over his rib cage.

In any case, it was highly unlikely that anyone had yet realized that he had left Israel. He had returned to work and feigned utter emotional sobriety for two full days. With his plans simmering in his mind, he was even able to effect a mood of calmed resignation as he worked up his report for GSS. It was quite a tome, and he handed it over to Yudit for typing, then informed Danny Romano and Benni Baum that he was taking Simona to Eilat for a few days. He said he had to salvage the shards of his ruined birthday party.

To Simona, he played the penitent husband. He brought her flowers, kissed her often, and apologized for having to attend a cryptology conference in Tiberias.

At Serge Samal's funeral, which took all of half an hour and was held at the military cemetery at Mount Herzl, Eytan held Talia's hand and played the brooding commanding officer with award-winning stoicism. He suppressed the powerful urge to scream out at the top of his lungs, and he was only able to do so because he knew what he had in mind.

Someone had to stop Amar Kamil from killing the rest of his team.

"Wiedersehen. Auf Wiedersehen."

The stewardess had begun her litany, bobbing her blonde head at the departing passengers like one of those annoying little dolls on the dashboards of cheap cars. Eytan's soft suitcase had just fit into the overhead, and he jumped up, dragged it out and joined the ordered line.

He started quickly down the hydraulic transfer tunnel, shaking out his knee as the tune popped into his mind again: "Walk Don't Run." He welcomed it like an old school chum one cannot shake, then he joined the rhythm and slowed his pace, letting the air-conditioning relieve his feverish skin.

This was the most dangerous leg of his air journey. If he survived passport control he would have a chance. The most effective weapons of his trade had never been his Beretta, explosives, or ammunition. Rather, they were his papers—forged passports, driver's licenses, bank cards. But he had none of those now, for they were as jealously guarded by the Documentation Center as were the weapons by the Armory. Everything ever issued to him had been recovered while he was still in hospital.

He was traveling on a simple, legal Israeli passport. He had not set foot on German soil as Eytan Eckstein since he was six years old, and he realized that traveling without a cover was as unnatural to him as spelunking would be to a claustrophobic.

A line of proud-postured, patient passengers led back from the control desk that had *Deutsche* boldly displayed above it. Eckstein joined the shorter line before a sign that said *Ausländer*.

Once he had so relished arriving and working in Germany. Along with Benni Baum, who was a child "graduate" of Dachau, he had enjoyed the self-congratulatory arrogance of returning to the fallen Reich in order to carry out Tel Aviv's missions. Yet now he was alone, without his team, any kind of backup or the support of his government. He felt like he was wearing a yellow star.

"Willkommen in München, Herr Eckshtein." The girl was pretty, petite and dark. Almost Israeli looking.

"I'm sorry. I don't speak German," Eckstein said as he smiled and tried not to look at the stern-faced customs officials on the other side of the desks. He put his bag up on the table and pulled a folded copy of *Ma-ariv* from the side pocket, clamping it under his arm and letting the big red Hebrew headlines flash. He hoped that reverse discrimination was still alive in Germany.

"Of course." The girl smiled as she pecked at a keyboard. "Where are you coming from, please?"

"Rome, by way of Tel Aviv."

"Your purpose?"

"Business."

"For how long, please?"

"A week maybe."

"And where will you stay?"

"I don't know. Any suggestions?"

"Anything to declare?" The girl just continued her litany.

"Just myself."

She smacked his passport with a metal stamper and grinned broadly. "There is a tourist help desk on the main floor. *Willkommen und auf Wiedersehen.*"

"Thank you."

He was in. He took his bag and walked. He played the tune again in his head and tried very hard not to think about the last time he had been at Munich International. He was ready to bet his life that Kentworth Air had lost its operating license for German airspace.

There was a small *Wechselstube* window for rapid currency exchanges just next to a row of rental car desks vying for customers. Eckstein changed one hundred U.S. dollars for deutsche marks and went straight to Hertz, where he used a Bank Leumi VISA card and rented a red Opel Kadett compact wagon.

The car was delivered to him outside of the terminal. He threw his bag into the rear seat and drove almost to the last *Ausgang* sign at the airport outskirts. Then he cut back and parked it in a long-term lot. He took the bag, left the newspaper, locked the car and dropped the keys to the pavement, toeing them behind a wheel. He had no intention of using the Opel again. He had created his first dead lead.

He took the bus into town.

———

Munich was not the same city, although only a year and a half had passed. The images frozen in Eckstein's memory were of snow-slickened streets under a purple-grey Bavarian sky, the sidewalk cafés empty of tourists and the *Münchner*s shrouded in wool and leather, bent under the assaults of winter. Now it was midsummer and the city was bright, flowery and festive, full of playful foreigners who gave joy to their German hosts as they swilled thousands of *Maas* tankards of beer and happily surrendered their dollars and pounds and francs to this Bavarian Disneyland.

Eckstein's first feeling was nearly disappointment, for he wished to be greeted with a proper gloom to match his mood of frustration and vilification. Yet as he passed over the Isar and saw the hundreds of nudists frolicking on its stony banks, he knew that he would always be schizophrenic when it came to the land of his birth. He hated Germany, and he loved it.

When he had worked as a team leader here, there had

227

been occasional lulls in operations. Sometimes you simply had to wait for the next event, a move by the opposition, and you could visit the endless museums, take in a play or a concert, and even indulge your lust if you did so with care and anonymity.

But this time, Munich was like an old battlefield upon which some very bad things had transpired. It was a place you never wanted to visit again until you were too old to feel the pain, yet you suddenly realized that you'd dropped a precious family heirloom in the bloody earth and you had to go back and root it out.

Munich was the only place for him to begin again. If Amar Kamil was operational, there was one man in Munich who might know about it. This time it would be all business. No time to enjoy the city, the weather or the people. Eytan had planned every step in his head, and he would move so quickly that he would arrive and be gone like the *Föhn*—the dry wind from the Alps that gave everyone a brief, irritating headache and then disappeared in a wash of welcome rain.

He got off the bus outside the *Hauptbahnhof* and walked into the massive station, making one quick weaving pass through the thousands of travelers awaiting their trains. As he pushed through the throng, never looking behind him, he began to do something he had not done in a long, long time. He began to pray.

"Let it be there, God. Please. Just let it still be there."

When you began training with AMAN, you were in awe of your instructors, expecting them to know everything and teach you every trick of the trade. But as you went along, you realized that your bosses were just humans. They learned from their mistakes and rarely made them twice, yet someone was always inventing a new, potentially fatal error.

Once in Argentina a nervous young Mossad agent had

forgotten his cover name because it was not inexorably linked to his subconscious. That never happened again, as all the services revamped their cover policies, making sure that agents' noms de guerre were organic and unforgettable. In Poland, an AMAN operative had once been completely strip-searched, revealing underwear manufactured in Ashkelon. Now, the closets of all Israeli agents were full of foreign-made clothes, devoid of even a cotton fiber that had been grown east of Cyprus.

These things were basic, yet the additional nuances were picked up along the way.

Zvi Pearlman had been an encyclopedia of such survival tips, sort of a professional guardian angel to Eytan's Team. 'Harry Webber' had always warned Eytan about the fallibility of Headquarters. They could make mistakes, and you had to have your own secrets, your own reserves in case everything came apart on you. You had to have an insurance policy. Eytan hoped his policy was still in effect.

"Let it still be there."

He walked out of the station and into the *Bahnhofplatz*. Crowds of tourists swarmed around him, chattering like conventioneers in Babel. At the corner of Schutzenstrasse, Schlammers was still there. Now, if only they had not renovated.

He walked straight for the café and pushed inside, past the crowded tables, his guts constricting as his suitcase banged against his knee. He went into the men's room and waited for a customer to finish his business and leave the corner stall.

Eytan stepped in, locked the door and held his breath. The window looked the same. Maybe the frame was freshly painted, but the walls were still cracked and crumbly. He put his hands under the sill and felt along the slight separation between the wood and the lower wall.

His fingers stopped. He gripped, then pulled, and the

laminated Deutschesbank card, along with the small key taped to it, popped out. He looked at it and then held it to his chest, raising his eyes to the ceiling and saying a silent *Todah*.

The Deutschesbank branch was just to the left of the Stachus. Eytan ignored the clusters of pretty girls perched around the huge fountain, and he did not hear the music of a brass quartet that encouraged the beer drinkers in the Karls-platz. He marched into the bank and went straight back to the officers' desks, holding out the customer card as he greeted a tall, slim German in a grey summer suit.

"*Morgen,*" Eytan said in a clipped, businesslike tone. "*Ich würde gern mein Schliessfach sehen, bitte.*"

"*Ein Moment, bitte, Herr Eckhardt.*" The officer took the card. He went to the file drawers and returned with a pained expression. "I am afraid the payments on your safe deposit are in arrears, sir."

"Yes, but my box is still intact, I expect."

"*Natürlich.*" The young officer snapped even more erect, as if offended by the suggestion that Deutschesbank might violate its own regulations.

"*Wie viel?*" Eckstein opened his wallet.

"Eighty marks, I'm afraid."

Eckstein paid the sum without hesitation and he was led down a curved stairwell to a guarded vault. The young officer opened a small vestibule and offered Eytan a seat at a wooden desk. Then he returned with the steel box and left the room.

It was there. All of it. Five thousand marks in a sealed envelope, which Eytan divided and placed in three of his pockets. The brown paper package was untouched as well. He felt the familiar L shape of the Beretta inside, yet he did not open it. He put the package into a side pocket of his jacket. The final packet was the most important, for he could not go on stalking around Munich as an Israeli national.

Nearly two years before, Eytan had taken all of his German papers—passport, driver's license, military ID card—and paid 1,500 U.S. dollars to have them duplicated by an underground forger in Hamburg. The artist could not, of course, reproduce the infrared markings on the passport pages, but for everyday use and for *leaving* Germany, the document would suffice.

He stripped the packet, putting the smaller documents into his wallet and the German passport in the inside breast pocket of his jacket. He reached into his pants pocket and drew out a handful of pfennig coins, dropped them into the box and locked it. When he moved the heavy little safe, the coins made a sufficiently mysterious rattle. He wanted Deutschesbank to think he was making deposits rather than withdrawals.

He rang the buzzer to recall the young bank officer.

Back in the sunshine and the cacophony of the Karlsplatz, Eckstein felt considerably refreshed and optimistic. He did not hesitate, knowing exactly where he was going, with hardly a limp in his gait as he strode back the way he had come, into the *Hauptbahnhof* and through the pressing crowd. He took no evasive action, for if he were being "curiosity tailed"—as was sometimes the case when West German BND randomly selected an interesting foreigner—any movements that pegged him as a professional would cause his watchers to stick to him like bees on halva. He had no teammates to perform diversions for his sake, so he would save his best gambits for later.

He exited the station, walked straight up Seidlstrasse to the corner of Marsplatzstrasse. The medium-size, economy-class hotel called the Württemberger Hof was still at Number 5. At this time of the year there was hardly a room to be had in Munich, but the hotel had not earned its nickname

Wursthaus for nothing. German businessmen frequently rented the rooms for one purpose only, and as their liaisons with their secretaries or girlfriends only lasted for an hour or so at lunchtime, a room could be had for the night if you knew what you were doing.

Eckstein maneuvered his bag through the front door into a cool, darkened lobby. The reception desk was to the left; a few padded chairs sat out on the dark maroon carpet around low glass tables. There was a small newsstand across the lobby, three stairs leading up to a coffee shop, a bank of elevators further on, and finally, another exit at the far end. Fine.

Three Japanese businessmen sat bobbing their heads at one another around one of the tables. Behind the main desk, a very large, bald Bavarian looked uncomfortable in a green uniform coat that hadn't fit him for years. That was good. Eckstein could be bold and bawdy with this man. He walked up to the desk and grinned.

"Guten Tag. Ist heute nicht ein schöner Tag?"

"Guten Tag, mein Herr." The clerk's expression was already apologetic. *"Ja, ein schöner Tag, aber . . ."*

Eckstein passed quickly from the weather to business, knowing full well what the answer would be. *"Haben Sie ein Einzelzimmer?"*

"I am very sorry." The fat man placed his hands together, begging forgiveness. "We have no singles. Nor doubles. We have nothing."

"Ja. Natürlich," said Eckstein without a hint of annoyance. He opened his wallet, looked around conspiratorially, and stuffed a fifty-mark note into the surprised clerk's hands. "You know, I just need it for the night," he whispered. "I'll be out by morning." He pointed to an empty chair in the lobby. "I'll just be over there. Let me know when someone's finished fucking."

He winked and walked away, leaving the stunned German staring after him. He carried his bag to the newsstand, bought a pack of Rothmans and a copy of the *Süddeutsche Zeitung,* and took up his position. Within a quarter of an hour he had a room on the third floor.

He stayed in the room for less than ten minutes, hardly noticing the decor as he showered, washed his hair, and scrubbed off the nervous sweat from his travels. He realized that he had to get some fuel, soon, for he had been too edgy to eat on his flight. He dressed again in the same clothes, tie and all, left his suitcase on the bed and went shopping.

He walked back to the Stachus and through the arches of the Karlstor. The pedestrian way on Neuhauser was jammed with summer visitors. Musicians in *Lederhosen* oompahed for pfennig, and swarms of hungry *Münchners* and tourists laughed through the great swigs of "liquid bread." To Eckstein, it was just backdrop.

In an apothecary he first bought a sewing kit. In a camping store, he acquired a short stainless-steel knife with a clip-on holster, and a black nylon knapsack. He found a German franchise of the American Gap and he nearly had to wrestle with a couple of pretty college students to get at a pair of black Levi's.

Finally, he held his breath as he paid 280 marks for a black leather Alpine jacket. It had metal crossbuckles and a rich green lining, a stiff standing collar and it closed across the chest like a suit of armor. He suppressed the realization that it would only be usable on perhaps ten winter evenings in Jerusalem, and he would probably be too embarrassed to wear it there anyway.

At last, hauling a massive shopping bag that made his bad leg wobble, he bought a summer straw hat. He stopped, sweating like a sheepdog in Florida, at a small beer garden. With the hat plopped on the back of his head, he stood and ate a greasy *Weisswurst,* and he swore he could hear his stomach acids devouring it as he drowned the sound with a *Reichelbräu* in a glass tankard.

Now there was still something Eckstein needed, and he had no idea where to get it and no time for research. He waited for a short while, examining the crowd, until three young men drew abreast of him. They wore leather jackets, various pins and jewels in freshly acquired wounds, and their hair was violently spiked and colored. Eckstein stepped forward and boldly asked for advice.

He found the shop on the far side of the Promenade Platz, just north of the Frauenkirche. An odd assortment of students and harmless-looking punks were gathered near the descending stairwell.

There were ten chairs in the shop, and business was brisk, but Eckstein's timing was lucky as one of the barbers snapped his filthy cover cloth and freed a young man who had just been shorn nearly to the skull. The boy stood up, looked in the mirror, rubbed his bristling scalp and said, *"Ja! Das ist sehr schön!"* His two friends laughed and pushed him as he tipped the barber.

Eckstein felt like a zebra at the Vienna Riding Academy, and certainly the clientele, who were all at least ten years his junior, did nothing to ease his discomfort. The girls giggled and the young men made unsubtle remarks, the word *Gross-vater* repeated more than once. Eytan just smiled and made his way to the free chair.

The barber was past forty himself, yet he was dressed in accordance with the current fad, wearing black leather trousers and a torn sweatshirt. If his clientele had been aliens he would have rented a spacesuit.

"Entschuldigen Sie, mein Herr." The barber stood away from the chair, shrugging and slightly embarrassed. "But I don't think I can help you." He clearly did not wish to be caught giving a regular haircut.

"Oh, I'm sure you can," said Eckstein as he took the seat. "I want it short and punk, please."

The barber remained frozen. "Pardon?"

"Yes." Eckstein continued to smile. He leaned forward and stuffed his shopping bag under the mirrored counter. "You see, for ten years my wife has been asking me to change my style. 'For God's sake, Johann,' she says. 'I'm sick of that boring haircut. You want me to dress sexy?' she says, 'So I dress sexy. You want me to wear high heels, so I wear them.' " He was imitating his *wife's* voice, a low, sexy, Bavarian drawl.

The barber had begun to smile, understanding his growing role in the conspiracy.

"So, *I* say," Eckstein pounded the armrest, "let's give her what she wants!"

"*Ja!*" A girl with high blue spikes on her head blurted from one of the chairs. "Give her what she wants!"

"*Ja!*" A young man joined in. "*Gib es ihr!*" His friends growled with the double entendre.

"So?" Eckstein said.

"So?" The barber picked up a pair of electric shears as he closed in with a laugh. "Short and punk?"

"And blond."

"You are already fairly blond."

"Blonder," said Eckstein, and he closed his eyes and settled in for the ride.

———

He walked back into the Württemberger Hof with his straw hat pulled low over his head, and he went straight into an elevator and up to his room. He locked and bolted the door, checked the closets and bathroom out of habit. Then he stripped out of his clothes and emptied all of his pockets, arranging his documents on the brown coverlet of the bed.

He dumped the contents of his shopping bag and opened the new Alpine jacket, laying it out on the floor like a freshly hunted carcass for the skinning. With the short steel knife, he slit open the green lining, fifteen centimeters near the zipper at the bottom left flap of the jacket. He took his Israeli passport, identity card, driver's license and his only shekel notes, sealed them in a hotel envelope and slipped them into the lining. He double-stitched the wound with green thread from the sewing kit.

He pulled a black T-shirt from his suitcase and cut three gashes in it across the chest. He also removed a pair of black Adidas sneakers and a pair of metal-framed Ray Bans.

Five minutes later he stood before the tall mirror on the bathroom door.

His reflection was ominous, black from sneakers to jeans to jacket. His spiked blond hair stood out against his Jerusalem tan, and with the sunglasses on he reminded himself of a character from a Mel Gibson film, the name of which he could not remember.

His marks and his German passport and papers found homes in the various pockets of his new costume. His straw hat, denuded wallet and newspapers were closed in a plastic laundry bag which he stuffed under the bed. He estimated that no one would clean under there for at least a week.

He emptied his suitcase, refolded his meager wardrobe, and filled the knapsack. There was enough of him in there to switch identities back—if he could find some hair dye at the appropriate juncture. The empty case fit nicely into a lonely corner of the single closet.

Finally, he tore open the brown parcel from his deposit box. The paper was stained, as the Beretta had been wrapped in a sock dampened with gun oil, then stuffed into a black waistband holster. One full magazine was in the pistol, and another was nestled alongside the holster.

Eytan checked the action, stripped the weapon, wiped everything down with a dry washcloth and clipped the full holster inside his jeans on the right hip. He had, of course, traveled unarmed. Now he felt fully dressed.

He lit up a Rothman and sat down on the bed. He dialed an outside number that had never left his head. A woman answered.

"Guten Tag."

"Guten Tag. Would you take a message please?"

"Who is this?"

"Have Thomas call me at this number." He recited the digits from the phone. "Room 316. I will wait only five minutes. Do you have it?"

"Yes. Who is this?"

"Do it. Now." He hung up.

He had not yet finished the cigarette when the phone rang. Eckstein answered with *"Wie geht's?"*

"Who is this?" The voice was so familiar to Eytan, so full of veiled suspicion.

"Hello, Thomas. This is an old friend from the East. Can you meet me today?"

"I don't know anyone from the East. Who is this?"

"Hans-Dieter sends his regards," Eckstein said. Now there was dead silence on the line. "Can you meet me today?"

"I . . . I am rather busy."

"Four P.M. at the Pagoda on Leopold. I'll find you."

"I don't know."

"Be there."

Eckstein hung up. He finished his cigarette and stabbed it out. He had just exposed himself. The clock was running.

He shouldered the backpack and looked around the room. 'Harry Webber' would not have been pleased with such a cursory inspection. But then Harry was dead, and 'Peter' would have said that speed was more important now.

Yes. Speed.

Eytan left the hotel by the side exit off the elevators. If

anyone saw him, they certainly made no connection between the tough-looking punk and the businessman who had checked in.

He caught a taxi to the *Viktualienmarkt,* a giant series of food stalls that reminded him of Machane Yehuda in Jerusalem. At the south end of the market there was a rundown alley filled with motor repair shops and used cars. Eckstein walked along until he saw what he wanted—an old BMW 650. Thankfully, the motorcycle had no sidecar.

A mechanic was under a Volkswagen Beetle. Eckstein toed his exposed workshoe and bent down.

"Grüss Gott."

"Ja," said the mechanic without looking out from his repair job.

"How much for the bike?"

"Not for sale."

"Is it yours?"

"Yes."

"Six hundred marks," Eckstein said.

The wrench work stopped and the grease-stained boy wriggled out from under the car. "It's too late today," said the boy. "All the paperwork."

"Are you insured?"

"Yes."

"I'll rent it," said Eckstein.

The boy rubbed his jaw, thinking he understood now. "For how long?"

"Forever."

The boy thought for a moment. He looked around. "How much did you say?"

"Six hundred." Eckstein produced the cash.

The boy produced the keys.

———

He almost had an accident in Schwabing. He had not ridden a motorcycle in three years, and besides the unfamiliarity, the strange pressure on his legs produced a new kind of pain in his knee. But his aggression spurred his progress and he roared onward, enjoying the warm wind in his face and the weird feeling over his freshly cut hair.

He found the row of low apartments on Victor Sheffel without difficulty—you memorized potential safe houses like important phone numbers. He paid an old woman 200 marks for a second-floor flat facing the street in a crumbling red-brick house that was home to transient actors from the KEKK Theater. The woman was slightly alarmed by his threatening appearance. However, his money looked quite safe.

At 3:30, with the keys to the flat in his pocket, he rode off to his meeting with Thomas. The motorcycle was out-rageously obvious, and no experienced agent would have used it. Which was precisely why he had chosen it.

———

Thomas Skorzeny did not remotely resemble his namesake, neither in appearance nor in character.

Otto "Scarface" Skorzeny had been a *Standartenführer* of the SS, notoriously known as Hitler's Commando and leader of over a hundred daring raids against the Allies during World War II, including the glider-borne rescue of Mussolini from a mountaintop fortress in Italy. At the end of the war, Otto Skorzeny had been captured by the Allies, then pre-dictably escaped and fled Germany. Hardly the apologist, he had gone on to run operations for Odessa, the infamous evasion and escape organization dedicated to aiding former members of the SS.

Thomas was not even distantly related to the colonel. In fact, Thomas was an orphan who had been raised by the widow of another officer, who had himself been killed in action while serving under 'Scarface.' When the poor widow passed on, Thomas was left with a single possession—the right to adopt any history and identity that pleased him. His childhood having been filled with glorified stories of the

Oberkommando der Wehrmacht, he changed his last name and ever since had continued to claim that he was a surviving nephew of a famous war hero.

Unlike his idol, Thomas's service in the West German army was desultory and unexceptional. When he mustered out, he found himself working as a postal clerk in Munich, filling his long days with fantasies about exotic places and exciting adventures.

The Red Army Faction was a perfect breeding ground for such lonely, unfocused youth, and although Thomas really had no political convictions, he joined this extremist offshoot of the Bader-Meinhoff Gang as a way to find some self-definition. It was soon discovered that he was really not a man of action, but he did have a certain penchant for facts and figures, and that was how he became the RAF paymaster for all of Bavaria.

For the Western intelligence agencies, penetration of the RAF was no simple matter. The terrorists were cellular, secretive, suspicious and extremely violent. British, French and American agents had been kneecapped or killed trying to make the plunge. The BND had had some success, but the West Germans jealously guarded the fruits of their penetration labors. The Israelis always tried to first turn a member of the opposition before risking an operative's neck, and that was how they found Thomas Skorzeny and "convinced" him to play a double game.

It was Benni Baum's brainstorm, and it resulted from a freak of happenstance.

In the early sixties, former Nazi scientists were helping the Egyptians build strategic rockets for use against Tel Aviv. At the time, Baum was a young Mossad field agent, and it was his idea to approach the infamous Scarface Skorzeny in his hideout in Spain. Using his Hans-Dieter Schmidt cover for the first time, the German-born Baum presented himself at the gates of Skorzeny's villa. Benni was supposed to use a "false flag" approach, introducing himself as a NATO Intelligence officer. Yet even as a young agent Baum often bent the rules and followed his instincts. He came right out and claimed that he was an Israeli intelligence officer, and that he needed Skorzeny's help.

The colonel respected nothing if not reckless courage and audacity, and he listened intently as Schmidt pleaded his case, explaining that only Skorzeny could stave off the oncoming slaughter which would result from Nasser's Nazi rocket program. Baum and his bosses already knew that Skorzeny's only serious disagreement with Hitler had been over the extermination of the Jews, and after a series of meetings with the bold young Israeli agent, he had agreed to have the Germans (some of whom had already begun to suffer mysteriously fatal accidents) withdrawn from Cairo.

Baum kept a keepsake of his adventure with Skorzeny— a photograph of the two of them conversing on the colonel's sunny veranda.

Turning Thomas was therefore a simple matter of blackmail. It was known through the BND that Thomas bragged of his relation to the now-deceased Scarface. Benni Baum simply set up a meet, showed Thomas the photograph and made a modest pronouncement: "Otto Skorzeny was, as you can see, a friend of Israeli Intelligence," Baum had stated almost apologetically. "You claim to be his nephew. We would like to avoid informing your RAF comrades that *both* of you cooperated with the Jews." Having made that statement, Baum had then pointed out another passing photographer who was recording the meeting for "posterity."

Thomas had no choice. He could not now claim to his pro-Palestinian comrades that he had been lying about his "uncle" all along, nor could he refute the incontrovertible photographic evidence that his hero was a closet Zionist, and that he himself was no better. Thereafter, Thomas was a ball on Mossad's tether. When Benni later transferred to AMAN, Thomas "transferred" as well. He was never trusted, but he was often used.

Eytan had parked the BMW on a side street off Leopold-strasse, and now he leaned against a lamppost two doors down from the Pagoda. He did not bother to obscure himself, as his punk costume would make him unrecognizable to anyone who had known him previously. He watched the sidewalk action in front of the cafés. The scene was like a giant version of Dizengoff, with literally hundreds of multicolored tables occupied by tourists and locals soaking up the sun, perusing the passing parade, inhaling both an inexhaustible flow of beer and an endless supply of noxious fumes from the slow-moving street traffic.

Thomas arrived in a taxi. He also was wearing his ever-present, short-waisted motorcycle jacket, but it looked rather silly over the starched blue shirt and dark clip-on tie that were apparently the uniform of a postal officer. As Eytan watched, Thomas tore the tie off and stuffed it into a pocket. He had not changed much. He still had that wavy blond hair crowning a perfectly complected, tanning-salon face. His brown moustache drooped in duet with his posture, and the tired blue eyes darted nervously over the tables before him.

Thomas did not recognize anyone, so he took an empty seat and turned it to face the street, drumming his fingers on the metal tabletop and craning his head for a waitress.

Eytan took a minute and scanned for Thomas's watchers. He vectored his eyes away from the German's position, across the boulevard, into the compartments of parked cars, along the sidewalk and the storefronts. There were no obvious tails—at least no one invited to attend by Thomas himself.

Eytan pushed through the crowd, approaching from the

rear. He pulled out a chair and sat down at the small round table as Thomas turned to stare at him. The German squinted, showing no sign of recognition.

"*Wie geht's, mein Freund?*" Eytan grinned and lifted the mirrored sunglasses from his eyes for a brief moment. Then he dropped them down again.

Thomas's cheeks blanched, the ever-present tan suddenly turning to a Siberian grey. His mouth opened and his eyes bulged, and he started to stand.

Eytan's left hand shot out and grabbed a leather sleeve. "*Setz dich, setz dich,*" he said soothingly, though his grip implied a warning. "I just got here."

Thomas slowly sank back into his chair. His mouth was still agape, working like a decked fish. Eytan quickly extracted his Rothmans and offered them up. The German looked at the pack, rolled his eyes at the sky and took one of the filters with a trembling hand. Eytan lit up for both of them. Thomas chewed his filter and continued to stare.

"*Du bist ein Wahnsinniger, Eckhardt.*" Thomas shook his head.

"*Ja, ich weiss.*"

"*Wirklich. Ein Wahnsinniger.*"

Eytan smiled and shrugged. It was okay to have the opposition think you were *nuts*. Insanity suggested danger, and danger demanded caution.

"You are still a wanted man in this country," Thomas said as if Eytan might have forgotten.

"Please," Eytan smiled. "Let's not announce it."

"*Meine Herren?*" A pair of bulging brown breasts above a frothy white blouse came into view. The waitress smiled and asked for their order.

"Beer, please," said Eckstein. "Two tankards."

"*Sofort.*" The waitress left.

Skorzeny's eyes darted around, scanning the other tables.

He shifted in his seat. "This is not healthy for me," he said.

"I know," said Eytan with sympathy. He reached into a jacket pocket and took out a prepared wad of one thousand marks. "Allow me to contribute to your sense of well-being." He slid the cash over to the edge of the table and then held it down near Thomas's leg.

Skorzeny had taken so many payoffs that just by glancing at the roll he could guess its value. He took it and then he groaned, realizing that if Eckhardt had a photographer working he had just opened himself up to another hundred years of blackmail.

The beer arrived. Eytan picked up his tankard, clanged it against Thomas's and took a long swallow. He wiped his mouth and smiled again.

Skorzeny pouted. "So what is this, Eckhardt? Old home week?"

"What do you mean?"

"Oh, please." Thomas slapped the table and his beer slopped over his tankard. He picked it up and drank for a long moment without stopping. He swiped the foam from his moustache. "No games, okay? Let's just do it and I'll go. You're not here for the weather. What do you want to know?"

"Whatever *you* know," said Eytan carefully.

"Okay," said Skorzeny with resigned annoyance. "I'll play." He leaned in closer and smoked hard, already a little more relaxed with the beer. "He's here. Or he was, yesterday."

"He is?" Eytan felt his blood quicken. This could not be the *he* that he wanted it to be, so he tried to remain smooth and calm as the Mediterranean in July.

"Yes. He is. He contacted Horst straight away, just like he used to. He said he was active again, but he refused a meet. He's never done that before."

"What did Horst do?"

"He assumed your old friend didn't want to show his

face for a reason. But the RAF owes the man some favors, and he called them in."

"What favors?"

"Foreign passport and airline tickets." Thomas snorted with disdain. "Horst and some of the boys actually had a party last night, sans guest of honor. They celebrated as if Carlos himself had risen from the dead."

"Ummm." Eytan did not speak for a while. His heart was racing and the blood pounded in his ears. He could not believe that he might be so lucky, yet there was absolutely no way that Thomas could have improvised all of this. He just wasn't that tactically brilliant. "Tell me, Thomas," Eytan said matter-of-factly, "just for the record, to whom are we referring?"

"Oh, for God's sake!" Thomas reacted like a spoiled child, then he assumed an expression of supreme impatience. "Okay, we are speaking of Gregor, all right? Is that clear enough?"

"Quite clear," said Eytan as his foot began to tap the pavement. *Gregor* was the RAF's code name for Amar Kamil.

"And I suppose you're all in town for the second round," said Thomas.

"All of us," Eytan lied.

"Schmidt too?"

"Schmidt too."

"*Wunderbar*. I did miss him so." Skorzeny's sarcasm oozed as he finished another long pull of the beer. He put the tankard down and looked at Eckstein. "I heard you were all shot up, Eckhardt."

"I got better."

"Humph." Thomas began to brood. He stubbed out his cigarette and held his hand out for another. Eytan lit one for him. "What else do you want?"

"Is there more?" Eytan raised a brow.

"Yes, but goddammit you know how this is for me! I

could be finished by this. Finished!" Tears actually welled up in the German's eyes. He looked up at the sun as if taking one last gaze at the heavens.

Eckstein slipped him an additional three hundred marks.

Thomas pocketed the money and then began to speak quickly. It was a low, mournful tone, like the confession of a doomed man.

"I was at that party last night. Horst was drunk and bragging. He has a contact at Munich Police headquarters. They got a copy of the latest files on the Najiz case. You do remember Mohammed, don't you?"

"I remember Mohammed." Eytan suppressed his anger and listened.

"They dead-dropped the file to Gregor. I don't know where. It had updates on the whereabouts of all the murder suspects, including yourself. Gregor recontacted Horst and asked for some more details. He refers to all of your comrades by code names. 'Venus' is someone named Denziger. 'Saturn' is someone named Hauser. I think you might be 'Mars.' "

Eytan felt an icy stickiness under his arms. Hearing Ettie's and Peter's cover names on a hit list made his spine stiffen like an electrocuted limb. "Is that all?" he managed.

"That's all I heard."

"Are you sure?"

"I'm sure, goddammit!" Thomas was rapidly draining of courage. Consorting in a public restaurant with a wanted murderer was clearly unhinging him.

"Okay, okay." Eytan tried to soothe the nervous German. "Just one more question. Tell me about the plane ticket."

"*Tickets*. Plural," said Thomas. "One to London, and one to Cyprus. And I don't think he's picked them up yet."

"Then he's still here."

"Or not."

"Or not." Eytan took out some cash and paid the bill,

leaving it under his tankard. Conversationally, as if he had all the support of his service and was clearly unworried, he posed his final question. "So tell me, Thomas," he asked. "Why the vendetta?"

For the first time Skorzeny seemed to forget his own predicament, and he actually looked at Eytan with some pity. "I don't know, Eckhardt. I don't know. But I suggest that you just go on home and pay up on your life insurance."

Eytan took off his sunglasses and stared at the German, who finally broke eye contact and began to examine his fingernails. Eckstein took out a pen and wrote something on his beer coaster. He pushed it over to Skorzeny.

"That's where I'll be. You contact me with anything further. *Verstehen Sie?*" He rose from the table and waited for an answer.

Thomas looked up with a weak smile. *"Jawohl, mein Kommandant.* And fuck you very much."

Eytan returned the smile, for he did not want to leave Thomas with a completely evil taste from their encounter. Then he walked away.

Eytan did not go far. He worked his way through the crowd along Leopold and then stepped behind a bus shelter. He peered back through the smoked glass and watched Thomas drain his tankard and get up. The German walked south along the sidewalk, teetering a bit with the beer and adrenaline. Then he performed as expected, entering the first available telephone booth, and Eytan, knowing he could never get close enough to eavesdrop, went back to his BMW.

Thomas did not really want to turn Tony Eckhardt over to Kamil, but he valued his own life more than a clear conscience. No matter what he did, Eckhardt would not kill him. You had to have committed serious acts of murder to get yourself on an Israeli execution list. Kamil, however, would have no

such moral hesitations. That was why the Arabs would probably win this war in the end, and Thomas preferred to side
with the winners.

He called a contact number in Untermezing, and the deep,
flat voice that answered set his knees to quaking. He gave
the location of Mars's flat and hung up. Then he threw the
beer coaster into the street.

He caught a cab back to the Central Post Office, claimed
he was feeling quite ill, and walked to the car park and his
waiting Volkswagen. He did not go home, nor call his girlfriend. He started driving immediately to Switzerland. With
the wad of cash from Eckhardt, and twice as much from
Kamil, he would be able to take a long, quiet, prudent
vacation.

———

Eytan rode the big BMW for half an hour. The skies began
to darken, but he did not really care that it might rain. He
headed for Neuhausen and chose quiet streets and small alleyways. He did not want to have to focus on traffic. He had
to concentrate.

His strategic thinking was coming back, yet too slowly,
like tennis talent long abandoned by a disillusioned athlete.
His head pounded with the variations.

It certainly was likely that Skorzeny was tripling on him,
working him and reporting back to Kamil. On the other
hand, Thomas might not be relaying all of it to Kamil—just
enough to save his own neck. Or he might be too frightened
to recontact the terrorist at all, but that was unlikely. Such
fear would work in reverse.

Then there was the possibility that Skorzeny had bluffed
the entire Gregor story, knowing what 'Eckhardt' would want
to hear and giving it to him. Yet he had never demonstrated
a talent for tradecraft, and the facts themselves—especially
the parts about Hauser and Denziger—were too accurate.

That led Eytan to the option that Skorzeny had been turned by the BND, or the Munich Police. He could well be setting Eytan up for the authorities. But then why had they waited and not grabbed Eytan at the Pagoda?

Eytan pulled into a small one-way off Wendl-Dietrich and abruptly stopped the bike. He got off and watched the mouth of the street. No vehicle slowed at the turn, and in fact no car entered the little alley for a good five minutes. And then it was just a very old lady squeezed down behind the wheel of a burbling yellow Fiat.

He smoked another cigarette and gathered his mental reflexes once more as a light drizzle began to spatter the sizzling Rothman. He decided that he was trying to evade the obvious. He had to follow his instincts and pursue the simplistic. To the best of his knowledge, Skorzeny had, through Horst or otherwise, made contact with Kamil. Skorzeny would, being essentially a coward, recontact Kamil if possible and give over the address of Eytan's safe house.

That was what Eytan wanted. He had to act with that as truth.

Now he had to move, and move quickly. He suddenly felt a surge of panic, like a starving fisherman whose catch is slipping off the line. Skorzeny was unwittingly setting Kamil up for *him,* yet he had few operational options. He could contact AMAN, call the duty officer at the embassy. But if Kamil did not show, then his operation was blown before it got started. Eytan had to lay the ambush first, yet he harbored no illusions that he could take Kamil without backup. His professionalism was still the master of his ego.

He finished the cigarette, reached into his pocket and counted his remaining cash.

———

He found the motorcycle gang in front of an old warehouse in Moosach. He knew where they would gather, like every

New Yorker knows that Hell's Angels hang out in the East Village.

The street was a cul-de-sac of steel loading docks and repair bays for heavy equipment. The warehouse at the end featured an old garage with a big flip-up door on steel lift chains. In front of the door was a perfect row of motorcycles—Triumphs, BMWs and Suzukis—noses out and all leaning together like thoroughbreds taking the last turn into the finish. A girl in a black leather jumpsuit was throwing a plastic tarp over two of the bikes. She did not look up as Eckstein stopped his machine next to her, and he could not see her face behind the tumble of red hair that fell over it as she worked.

"Where's the mechanic?" he asked as he killed the engine and pushed the BMW onto its double stand.

The girl tossed her hair toward the big door, which was partly raised, and Eckstein could see pairs of black boots stamping around on the concrete inside. He walked through the bikes, ducked under the door and adjusted his vision to the dark interior.

The walls of the concrete cave were covered with posters of outrageous motorcycles and picture calendars of half-naked women. Black pegboards held lengths of wire, drive chains, tire tubes and greasy metric tools. The floor was strewn with spare parts and stained with oil, brake fluid and water. Along the far wall were three iron army beds made up with dirty sleeping bags. A squat grey icebox sat in one corner, and on top of it a boom box blared Billy Idol. Next to the fridge on the floor, an extensive set of slimy barbells was piled like freshly dropped Pickup Stix.

There were four men and one woman in the garage. They all wore leather pants, jackboots, and except for the woman they were all stripped to the waist and showed heavily muscled, glistening torsos. The girl might as well have been half bare, for she wore a black singlet that barely contained her breasts. All of the heads were close-cropped and stiffly spiked. By comparison, the bikers made Eytan feel like he was wearing a dinner jacket.

Somehow this crew had acquired a stainless-steel morgue table. It glistened under the greenish fluorescent light. The patient was a purple Honda, lying on its side at the mercy of its physicians, who poked it and banged it and argued over the cure.

They stopped working and looked up at Eckstein. One of them walked over and killed the cassette player.

"Who the fuck are you?" The largest gang member—two meters of hairy muscle, broken teeth and a gold ring in his left nipple—was holding a spanner in a filthy paw.

"A client." Eckstein advanced across the floor and focused on the prone Honda.

The gang members, as if choreographed by Michael Jackson, moved from the table and formed a horseshoe between him and the table. He stopped and looked up at them.

"We don't do repairs for strangers," another one said. He was the smallest of the group, so his hair and his voice were the loudest.

"I don't want anything repaired," said Eckstein. He felt the hairs prickle at his neck as the girl from outside stepped into the garage. The door came down with a clank of chains.

"Then say what you want, *Arschloch*." The big one growled at Eckstein as he put the spanner at port arms across his chest. He had seen *The Wild One* once too often.

"I want something *dis*-repaired."

The gang members looked at each other. The other girl, short and dark with a stream of sweat running down between her breasts, lit up a cigarette and blew smoke in Eckstein's direction, though it failed to reach his face. "What is it?" she demanded.

"Something," said Eckstein.

"*Raus,*" said one of the other men as he jerked a thumb at the door.

"Five hundred marks," said Eckstein.

No one said anything for a moment. Then the big one growled, "Do we look like Jews, you cheap bastard?"

It was then that Eckstein saw the swastika on his huge forearm. It was not tattooed; rather it looked like it had been etched with a blade. He nearly laughed. *Perfect,* he thought as he released his most dangerous grin. It was the smile of a madman who fails to recognize danger.

"Actually," he said, "you look stupid, but capable."

Six pairs of eyes widened.

"Seven hundred, then," Eckstein added.

"Let's take his money, break his legs and burn his bike," snapped the redheaded girl.

The big leader sneered, nodded, and took a step forward.

Eytan's Alpine jacket was already open. His right hand darted inside, the Beretta jumped out, he cocked it with his left and instantly the barrel was just a centimeter away from the big man's forehead.

All movement ceased. No one shuffled a boot; the giant's mouth went silently slack. Eytan could not even detect breathing as he stared directly over the sights of the Beretta and into the leader's bulging eyes.

"Eight hundred is my final offer."

After a moment, the giant snorted. And then he began to laugh. He threw his head back and his torso shook, but he made no careless motions with the spanner as his comrades joined his mirth. This was the kind of business they understood.

Eytan smiled, yet the pistol stayed trained throughout the entire transaction.

———

He waited across the street from the safe house for two hours. There was a concrete stairwell leading down from the sidewalk to a basement exit, just thirty meters along the quiet block. He had backed the BMW down the stairs and now stood on a step with only his eyes above the lip, watching the front door of the small building where he'd rented the second-floor flat. The evening cooled and turned to night, and it rained on and off as he pulled his collar close and squinted.

His "backup team" had their instructions, and he had no doubt that they would perform, for he had guaranteed a bonus. Besides, to the gang members it was like getting paid to have an orgy.

They had let themselves up with Eytan's keys, hauling a shopping bag full of food and beer, supplied by their "client." Their orders: Disarm and disable anyone who knocks at the door to the flat.

At 8:10, a dark blue Ford Fiesta came cruising down the street. It passed Eytan's lair and stopped just beyond the flat. Eytan watched, holding his breath, as three men got out of the car. He inched his way up the stairwell and crouched like a cat as he unzipped his jacket.

Yet instinct kept him from moving further. The three men wore long, light-colored trenches, and they were hatless. Something in their determined gaits began to register in Eytan's subconscious as they pushed open the front door to the building and went inside. Then the grill of a green-and-white Audi appeared at the far end of the street, slowly nosing its way along like a hound sniffing for game.

Police. And the three men were Munich detectives.

As Eytan's conclusion registered a series of loud crashes echoed from inside the second-story flat. Shadows jumped across the lighted room as if a gorilla were loose in a furniture shop, and then the front window splintered and one of the detectives flew through the glass, back first, with his arms and legs thrashing. He crashed down into a row of hedges, came up, staggered, and held his head with both hands as he sank to his knees.

A flurry of shouts echoed into the street as Eckstein jumped onto his BMW, kicked the starter and launched up the stairway, nearly skidding it over on the sidewalk but he banged down onto the street and rode the wrong way out as a siren hee-hawed somewhere behind.

Kamil had bested him. He knew that for certain. Eytan had used a motorcycle gang as backup. Kamil had simply called the Munich Police.

But from where? From the city? No. He was long gone. He might have used a car phone, or a distant booth. Or he had had someone else do it at just the right moment.

And where was Kamil going now? He had two tickets. One to London. One to Cyprus. But if Eytan was right, Kamil had just *come* from London.

And Mike Dagan was in Cyprus.

Eytan hammered the handlebars with his fist and yelled into the rain that pounded his eyes and face. He slammed the brakes and skidded into a U-turn that sent cars swerving and honking out on Franz-Joseph Strasse.

He put his nose to the speedometer and headed back toward the airport, racing against his own stupidity.

8

Cyprus

FOR THE FIRST TIME IN A LONG TIME, Mike Dagan was a happy man.

In truth, Dagan was not one who surrendered quickly to melancholy, but it had taken him months to emerge from the psychological black hole of half a year in a German prison cell. Not that the stiff-spined BKA, BfV or BND agents had tortured him or, in fact, had treated him with anything less than professional respect. For despite his tight-lipped indifference, they certainly knew who his employers were. It was just that a man who is accustomed to racing around Europe in all sorts of high-powered machines does not take well to lengthy confinement—whether it be a five-star hotel room or a five-square-meter cell.

On the road to Munich Airport, 'Peter Hauser' had given the Bulgarian KGB stringers a good thrashing with his Audi. Fortunately for him, the men had survived their rather serious injuries. The Germans, unable to conclusively tie Peter to the Mohammed Najiz murder, had instead convicted him of reckless driving, resisting arrest and carrying an unlicensed firearm. He had been given a two-year sentence, yet it was quickly commuted to six months when a faceless Israeli police liaison suggested to his counterpart at the *Bundeskriminalamt* that a confirmed story about a West German engineering firm selling chemical weapons technology to Libya was chomping at the bit to go to press.

Dagan had been quietly repatriated to Israel, where the first order of the day was an obligatory ass-chewing by Itzik Ben-Zion, followed quickly by the Colonel's firm, congratulatory handshake before Mike could tell him to go straight to hell. Ben-Zion then handed him a check for double the amount of his retroactive pay, which was customary whenever an operative was missing in action, a prisoner of war or had served time in a foreign detention center.

Immediately thereafter, Mike's AMAN comrades threw him a rousing party, for he had honored the unit and shown exceptional bravery beyond the call. In any other nation's service, there would have been a medal to be briefly caressed and then sealed in the Commanding Officer's safe. But in the IDF there were only three awards for valor, and to get one you had to single-handedly destroy an enemy tank battalion while dragging your wounded comrades to safety.

It didn't matter. Mike did not want a medal. He wanted to eat something other than *Wurst* and *Sauerbraten*, get laid without keeping an eye on the door and breathe fresh air.

In Larnaca, he had all the food, women and oxygen he could handle.

The assignment was gorgeous, the stuff of an agent's fantasies, and if Mike had not transferred to Mossad he would never have come close to something like this. AMAN's idea of a choice assignment was clerking the desk of a whorehouse in Port Said while counting the Russian sailors who made the headboards bang. However, the civilians at Mossad had more cosmopolitan imaginations. Mike had not quit AMAN in search of this luxury—he had done so because his old team was history and he did not want to work for Ben-Zion another long minute without them. In fact, he would have retired from The Game altogether had an uncle not talked him into an easy stint with the civilians.

Cyprus was perfect. It was as close to being at home as he could get. The light seemed like overflow from the Israeli sun, the buildings of the same dusty stone, the hills covered in the same bleached shrubbery. A steady diet of *souvlaki* and Coke easily replaced *shishlik* (his cover forbade *falafel* and *houmous*, though they were certainly available), and if you were playing a resident convincingly you had to consume your share of ouzo and arak. When you squeezed your inner ear, the jabber of Greek could even sound like Hebrew.

Mike hailed from a family of Orthodox American Jews, and in Israel he wore a knitted *kipa* on his head and adhered to the rabbinical statutes. However, religious Israeli agents were under a *hatara*—an exceptional order—to forswear kosher food and religious observance while on foreign soil. It was one of those dichotomies that gave Mike his wry smile. You could be condemned for driving on Shabbat, but you could kill for your country on Yom Kippur.

The most amusing order in reference to his present assignment was regarding women. The Cypriot beaches were full of available specimens, many of them Jewish or even Israeli girls on holiday. Yet Mike was instructed to liaise only with non-Jewish foreigners—French, German, British, Italian—and he utilized his American charm and sandy-haired good looks to do so with frequent, martyred surrender. He called it the "T.P." order—*Trafe* (non-kosher) Pussy.

Mike Dagan was working in the port of Larnaca under

the cover of Mitch Angler, an expatriate American who owned and operated a one-man water taxi and land transport firm called Still Waters Ltd. He was thirtyish, diminutive, boyish and friendly, his off-hour hobbies running toward women and amateur photography. He traveled frequently across the length and breadth of the Greek side of the island, had many friends and acquaintances both Cypriot and foreign, and he was free and generous with the extra monies that came from a trust fund inherited from his wealthy and estranged California family.

The Cypriots were adept at dealing with foreign invaders, and 'Mitch' was able to conduct all of his business in English, which was a relief to those occasionally subjected to his tortured Greek. In typical American fashion, when unable to make himself understood, he simply pronounced his errors louder. Yet he was well-liked in Larnaca, and on Athens Street near the port everyone knew him as The Yank.

'Mitch's' place of business and residence was a two-room, single-story stone structure at the foot of one of the long wooden piers that extended into the shallow, azure-blue harbor. Rows of bobbing, white-hulled boats stretched away from his Still Waters headquarters like winding strands of pearl necklaces. The piers themselves were covered with greasy coils of hemp, rolled and bleached sail canvas, shiny petrol cans and clumps of multicolored nylon tubs overflowing with weighted fishnets. The local boat owners were not wealthy, but their mechanical improvisations kept the fleet afloat. The Mediterranean sun acted as a nasty-natured paint peeler, so the captains and crews of vessels from skiffs to charter yachts were constantly repainting their wooden crafts. Fiberglass hulls, which 'Mitch' referred to as Tupperware, were not affordable to Cypriot skippers. Predominantly, the most available and inexpensive marine paints were in bright blues and reds, and together with the snowy hulls, the shimmering hues made the Larnaca port look like a recreational flotilla of the French navy.

'Mitch' owned two fast wooden boats that resembled large Boston whalers with stand-up wooden bridges and steel poles for canvas sun covers. He rented them to qualified tour guides, business firms, or dive operators. If the client "interested" him, he would captain the boats himself.

But he was not on Larnaca to bolster the Israeli economy through sea trade. One-hundred-and-eighty-meter ferries made daily runs to and from Beirut or Juneih, depending upon where the artillery shells were raining most heavily on any given day. Palestinians from the PLO and all of its factions, Amal fighters, Hezbollah fanatics and Arab intelligence agents from Lebanon, Syria and Iraq all used the ferry like a commuter express from the war zone. 'Mitch' tried to photograph all of them without prejudice.

His assignment was fairly simplistic, as he was not expected to identify specific targets unless ordered to do so. The small side window of his sleeping quarters at Still Waters looked out over the embarkation pier of the Lebanese ferry at a range of one hundred and fifty meters. His double fishnet curtains made it virtually impossible to detect the monster lens of a Nikon 1200-millimeter mounted there, and the lens was prefocused at the exact spot where the big boats always dropped their gangways and the passengers, conveniently enough, single-filed on or off.

The beauty of the set-up was that Mike did not have to mysteriously retire to his bedroom every time the ferry came in. The camera was motor driven, refitted with nylon gears for silence, and remote activated from up to one hundred meters. Mike kept the trigger device, which looked like a whistle-finder key chain, in his pocket at all times. He could be lying outside in a deck chair, sipping ouzo with a client, and photograph every ferry passenger as he cheerily twirled his keys around his suntanned fingers.

'Mitch' was known for his amateur photography, frequently clicking away at the vessels of local friends and presenting them with oversize, full-color portraits as gifts. But for the "ferry study" he used only black and white. Headquarters preferred it for its flexibility. At night he used 3200-ASA Kodak recording film, which was quite sufficient as the target quay was lit by a string of bare bulbs on an outdoor wire.

He never printed his black-and-white studies. While his office was conspicuously covered with piles of color prints of weathered fisherman's maws, rows of painted prows, and portraits of local beauties, not a single black-and-white photo was in evidence. Those rolls were developed at night, the negatives washed, dried and clipped. Once a week he would take them into Nicosia, along with his bank deposits, insurance forms and tax payments, where they were dead-dropped for a contact he never saw. If he was to receive special instructions—for example, to concentrate on a particular vessel—they arrived in his mailbox in a code contained in one of the frequent, annoying, bitter letters from his "mother" in Santa Barbara.

It was a fabulous life—exotic, sun-filled, sexy—with a touch of danger yet low risk compared to his former assignments. He was instructed to socialize, be a "party animal," and keep his ears open, and as he obeyed these orders his water and taxi business flourished. He could not, of course, keep the profits, but he was allowed to turn them around and expense them as long as he kept impeccable books and a receipt for every wine-induced belch. Yes, it was the stuff of an agent's dreams. If he hadn't paid for it with half a year in prison, he might have actually felt guilty about it.

This morning, although it was not yet eight o'clock, Mike Dagan was running late. He had to drive all the way to Nicosia, conduct a full day of business and be back in time for a dinner date with a French girl named Gabrielle, whose striking flaxen hair, green eyes and lithe tennis-player's body promised more than a culmination of *loukoumades* and *Emva Cream*. Nicosia was only fifty kilometers away, but all of it was uphill and the banks were only open until noon. In addition to the juggling of funds, he had to make a couple of insurance payments and, most important, deposit his drop at precisely the predetermined time.

Finally, he had promised Niko Stavrapolous, the owner of the Helenica Bar and Grill on Zenon Kitios Street, a landscape portrait from the precipice of the Stavrovouni Monastery. Niko did not believe that 'Mitch' could—by using a tripod and sweeping his lens step-by-step across the spectacular view—create a giant panorama which would grace the entire wall behind his bar. The monastery was well off the fast route to the capital, yet Mike was determined to accomplish the shot as well as all of his missions of the day.

He had been up half the night developing six rolls of film. With a renewed rocket and artillery duel between the Moslems and Christians in Beirut, the ferry traffic that week had been lucrative for the Cypriot captains. The Larnaca customs officers were renowned for their flexible integrity, and it was anyone's guess just how many tons of Palestinian arms and ammunition had found berths aboard the ferries. Mike had photographs of all the movements. It would be up to the analysts in Tel Aviv to decipher the meaning of the images.

Mike shaved and showered quickly, pulled on a T-shirt, jeans and a pair of Nikes as he gulped a cup of Maxwell House instant. He donned an American leather flight jacket and swung the strap of a leather mail satchel over his head. His desk was covered with forms and papers, and having no time to sort it all out, he stuffed most of it into the satchel, along with a collapsible tripod and one of his Nikon F–3s.

He grabbed four rolls of Fujicolor because he wanted the blues and greens to stand out. Then he hurried outside and locked his wooden door with a big padlock.

His copper mailbox was nearly overflowing from the previous day, but rather than sift through it he simply stuffed that pile into his pouch as well. The evening telegram from Eytan at Munich International Airport went along for the ride, unnoticed.

Mike chose his trusted Vespa for the long drive, which might have surprised his friends of the past. He also owned a Suzuki, but when you wanted to get where you were going without mechanical shenanigans you used the Italian workhorse. He popped the white, half-bowl scooter helmet onto his head, gunned the engine and heeled the kickstand up as he rode off the pier toward town. Theona Meltis, the fisherman's daughter, yelled "*Yia-soo, Mitch!*" as he passed her, and he yelled "*Sto kalo!*" right back at her.

The beachfront off Athens Street was already peppered with the heartiest Larnacans as Mike sped by, the cool morning air whipping at the flaps of his open jacket. Out of habitual tradecraft, he checked his rearview and then cut sharply to the right through an alley, left onto Zinonos Kitieos, and right again onto Ermou, which would take him north and then west again toward Pyrga and the mountains.

For Mike, driving was a sort of meditation, the only time when he was completely at rest. It was as if the act of employing his reflexes allowed the intellect to engage, a fact he had discovered as a sixteen-year-old. Surely it was this sole manner in which to attain peace that had moved him to love motorcycles, cars, fast boats, and even airplanes. The faster he went, the more challenging the course, the better he felt.

He was out on the open road and completely out of the city when he attained his state of grace. The sun from the east was blinding even behind his Ray Bans, and the smells of Cyprus blossoms and donkey dung washed through his system, a refreshing break from the sting of sea salt in his nostrils.

The drone of the Vespa's motor brought on sense memories of other engines, cars and places, and these brought images of the past—the faces of Eytan Eckstein, Serge Samal, Tamar Shoshani. This was not unusual, for hardly a day passed that he did not think of them. He missed them all, for even though his solo assignment was a choice piece of fruit, there would never again be the blood bond attachment of working deadly missions with a team. In a way, it was better now, for he knew that love was a dangerous thing in this business. It was love of his comrades that had driven his spontaneous deeds in Munich—not duty, honor or country.

Serge was dead. He had read about it in a British paper, and he had mourned in silence and alone. No one would come to hug him for the loss of his friend; there was no one with whom to commiserate. Surprisingly, he actually felt worse for Eytan, for he knew that the crippled captain and Serge had been like Siamese twins. Tamar would also have taken it badly, wherever she was. He wondered if she was still out there somewhere playing Ettie Denziger, the wandering painter who packed a Beretta.

He had seen Benni Baum at AMAN H.Q. in Tel Aviv, before they moved Special Operations to Jerusalem. Baum seemed unstoppable, yet Mike knew that the old man was an emotional "Picture of Dorian Gray." His outward appearance never changed, but somewhere in a closet Baum's heart shriveled and wept with each soldier's death. Francie, Mike knew from his uncle in Mossad, was working in Cairo for AMAN under a flimsy attaché cover. Francie would also have taken Serge's death very hard. Everyone knew that she'd had a serious crush on him. His passing would not end that emotion—only turn it to an empty longing.

Mike of course wondered about Serge's death in professional terms, but he assumed that the mystery would be well investigated. A connection to Amar Kamil never crossed his mind, for he had gladly accepted the conclusions that the terrorist was dead. He did not even know about Zvi Pearlman, for 'Harry Webber's' death had not made a single newspaper outside of the *New York Post*. He imagined Zvika off studying at NYU, probably raising a ruckus in every class he took.

Traffic on the ascending highway was very light this morning, and suddenly Mike thought he had missed the turnoff to Pyrga. To the southwest he could see the commanding peak of Stavrovouni, from which he would soon shoot a panorama that would make Niko's arak curdle. Then the turnoff appeared almost immediately, and Mike leaned into it as the tires scrabbled across loose stone. In his reverie and reminiscence, he had not noticed the lime-colored Volkswagen minibus that had loosely tailed him all the way from Larnaca.

He rode through the center of the little village, with its neatly ordered olive groves planted there as if to remind the wayward Israeli of his roots. He was almost to the Nicosia–Limassol highway when he turned left along the old road, then left again for the climb up to Stavrovouni. Now the fun would begin. The peak towered above him, the bone-white cap of the monastery's bell tower swinging first left and then right as the road began to curve around deep cuts in the mountain range. Far below to the southeast, the bowl of Kolpos Larnacas Bay reminded him of a view of the Mediterranean from the Carmel. Soon the winding curves turned to hairpins, and Mike shook his head at the British colonial snobbery that forced him to drive on the left over a crumbling asphalt track that dropped off into hundreds of meters of abyss and sharp rock piles below. There was no guardrail, and he could not hug the mountainside.

The memories of *Operation Flute* and his old team had dampened his mood, so Mike turned to thoughts of Gabrielle. He had approached her on the beach, quite sure that she was "secure," for his selection was random and spontaneous. He never dated girls who made the first move—standard professional policy. They had since then met only once for lunch, yet now Mike sensed that tonight might be the night. He tried to imagine her, to bring her face into view, her body. He pictured her hand in his own, evening, walking back to Still Waters from the city, both of them flushed after dancing at the Golden Bay. Now she was inside his small salon, her bright eyes shining as she moved the glass of wine from her soft lips and kissed him. The simple white blouse was slipping from her tanned shoulders, a long leg curling up around his waist—and he shifted over on the seat of the Vespa as something, an instinct, the sound of another, louder engine made him jerk his head around as the blunt nose of a VW minibus bore down on his bumper.

He swerved hard to the right, across the narrow road and into the shoulder, yelling "Fuck!" in his native American, but sure that he could recover if he hugged the mountainside and let the idiot rush by. But instantly the panic welled as he felt the monster come with him, its lime-green snout crawling onto him, now careening into his left leg, smashing it into his own machine as the roar engulfed him and he was flipping head over heels, the scream of metal against stone and his own leather rending against the tearing claws of the cliffside as his head banged and the world went black.

He opened his eyes. He was on his back and the sky above was white-blue, painful to look at as a dark, salty curtain ran across his vision and he blinked it away. He could not move his legs.

But he was alive. He would survive.

He looked down. He could see only one of his feet, the

white Nike pointing at the sky. He did not know where his left leg was, but he felt that he might be lying on it, curled or broken beneath him. His left elbow lay on something hard, but the hand seemed to dangle in midair. He was at the very edge of oblivion.

He twisted his head to the right and blinked the liquid away again. The Vespa was nowhere in sight. Only a wheel lay on the gravelly roadbed, slowly spinning on its metal hub.

He looked down toward his foot again. An engine was idling, coming from a sickly green VW bus parked some distance away. It was very hard to focus, but he could see a figure walking slowly toward him, shimmering with the sun and the blood in his own eyes.

The figure stopped above him. He could not bring the face into focus, but he felt some relief as the man bent and hands reached out, surely to help him. Then the pain came, searing, flashing, rumbling over his body like molten lava as the man took Mike's leather satchel and tore it from his body and his head banged back onto the pavement.

When the agony returned to a dull roar, Mike opened his eyes again to see his envelopes flying from a pair of hands, like cards from a croupier. The shuffling stopped. Something tore. A moment of silence while the man flicked his eyes over a flimsy telegram paper. And then, of all things, a voice hissed at it, in German:

"I'll make you crazy in your cage, Mr. Eckhardt. How does it feel to be hunted?"

Eckhardt? German? Then Mike knew for sure that he was dreaming. Oh yes, a horror of a nightmare it had to be, for "your past coming back to haunt you" could not possibly be this literal. And besides, *he* was not Eckhardt, had never been Eckhardt. But no, the voice was not talking to *him* at all. It was talking to that fluttering piece of paper, the paper that now went into a ball and sailed into the wind.

Now the face was bending; it was coming into focus. Curly blondish hair, a sharp jaw, a scar. His heart began to hammer, for the eyes were slits of recognizable rage, familiar only because he had felt his own eyes narrow so at the culmination of very bad deeds. *Now* the voice was speaking to him. English.

"This is for Jamayel," it whispered.

"Who the hell is Jamayel?" Mike tried to say, but no sound would come. And then he heard the sharp scrape of leather on stone and the kick slammed into him and the wind was rushing over his body as he squeezed his eyes and began to say the *Shm'a Yisrael,* faster now, faster.

He wondered if he would finish the prayer before he hit. . . .

———

Despite the growing heat of midday, the man who walked into police headquarters on Arkhiepiskopou Makariou III Street in Larnaca looked as relaxed and refreshed as a diplomat with an umbrella of immunity and an air-conditioned limousine. He was tall and trim, his wavy red-blond hair freshly cut; horn-rimmed Wayfarer sunglasses perched above a sharp, straight nose and a relaxed, pensive mouth set into a strong jaw. He wore a single-breasted, cream-colored linen suit over a white cotton shirt and medium blue, pinstriped tie. The cuffed trousers broke over a pair of chocolate Churchill loafers.

The man's face was untanned, as if he spent much time on the Continent, but his skin had the ruddy glow of an athlete. His left hand rested easily in a trouser pocket, while the other hand lay partially open in front of his body, the elbow resting on his right hip, a ribbon of smoke rising from a white cigarette held between thumb and forefingers.

Amar Kamil walked gracefully up the wide stone slabs of the entranceway, sidestepping as nimbly as Gene Kelly while a pair of Cypriot Tourist Police in heavy blue kit and caps manhandled a manacled burglar down and out into a waiting van.

He resumed his ascent and leveled off before the main desk, a wooden affair topped with paperwork, an old rotating fan and a small silver hotel bell that seemed to indicate that the local police could not be expected to be vigilant at all times. The desk was high and wide like an oversized bar, and the young corporal manning it must have been perched on a tall stool as he looked down at Kamil like a Kafkaesque bureaucrat.

"*Khérete,*" said Kamil as he approached the bench.

"Good day, sir," the corporal replied in English. The foreigner's guttural pronunciation precluded his being British, but he was certainly not a Cypriot.

"I would like to speak to the officer in charge, please." Kamil got right to business in a Mediterranean-accented English that again furrowed the corporal's brow.

"The officer in charge?"

"Your captain."

"I am in . . . He is eating lunch."

"I would join him," said Kamil as he reached into his breast pocket and produced a small rectangular booklet. He held it out over the desk top, close to the corporal's face, and he flipped it open with his fingers. Then he snapped it shut and put it back inside his jacket.

The corporal stared at him for a moment, weighing the unfamiliar document with the gold Semitic print on its dark blue cover against the peril of interrupting Captain Dimitris Lordos's repast. He raised a finger, begging patience, picked up an old black telephone and dialed three numbers.

A chatter of Greek, an apologetic shrug into the handset, an embarrassed smile at Kamil, and the corporal said, "He is coming."

A full minute passed while Kamil stood and smoked,

then the wooden door to the reception foyer banged open and Dimitris Lordos barreled through.

He seemed as wide as he was short, with a glistening bald bullet head and a black steel-wool moustache, the fringes of which glistened with drops of ouzo. A carpet of black curls poked from the open collar of a blue shirt stained with sweat, but the captain retained formality by keeping his navy, short-waisted jacket in place.

"Lordos!" The captain boomed his own name as he stomped up onto some kind of wooden platform behind the desk and slammed his porcine palms onto the countertop, making the papers flutter, the corporal wince and the hotel bell tinkle.

Kamil did not move. Then, slowly, he reached up and carefully removed his sunglasses, folding them with one hand as he gave the captain both barrels of his ice-green stare. The captain's posture sagged a bit, some of the wind out of his sails.

"Yerushalmi," said Kamil. "Yossi Yerushalmi."

"Sas parakaloh."

Kamil produced the passport again, holding it close so that Lordos would have to reach for it, and setting his mouth hard with impatience so that the captain would be disinclined to request further proof of identity. Lordos perused the document and returned it.

"How may I help you?"

"May we speak privately?"

"I am at my dinner hour. Have a seat for—"

"It cannot wait, Captain. Perhaps your superior officer is available."

Lordos raised his palms in exasperated surrender. He swiped the droplets from his moustache. "Come."

The captain banged through the doorway again, and Kamil walked around the desk, following slowly enough so that the policeman would have to wait for him.

He emerged into a large open floor that exhibited most

269

of the features common to urban police stations worldwide. It was as if there existed somewhere a Detectives' Old Testament, in which was commanded under the Genesis chapter, "And Thy Squad Room shall appear thusly."

Rows of scarred wooden desks lined the walls like church pews, converging on a large steel-framed window on the far side whose glass was permanently grayed from years of tobacco smoke. Two large metal standing fans kept hundreds of flimsy papers dancing on the desk tops and in ancient typewriter platens, for it would be some time before the Cypriots surrendered to the computer age. Midcentury, black cradle telephones jangled in a variety of discordant voices. The room had the mandatory inverted-bottle watercooler, a pathetic jungle of neglected plants and a collection of pegboards holding unread notices yellowed by age and weather.

The police officers, uniformed and plainclothes, were all male. They wore heavy blue kits with white Sam Brown belts and Webleys, or they sported cheap synthetic suits over bulging shoulder rigs. To a man, they sat in their wooden chairs with feet propped on desk corners or wastebaskets, and not a single one of them wore a bullet-proof vest, as if stating quite clearly that their union rules forbade gunplay of any kind.

In typical Mediterranean fashion, this center of southern Cypriot criminal investigations had all the urgency of a rural post office. The only females present were a couple of mini-skirted hookers seated on a wooden bench. They were surrounded by five officers, and from the chatter of the men and the warble of the girls' laughter Kamil knew that the discussion was not centered on moral responsibility. The room smelled like lamb meat, goat cheese, olives and cheap tobacco.

Kamil stopped just inside the doorway, where he perused the room slowly and took a long drag from his cigarette. He made certain that Lordos had also stopped and had turned to look at him as he allowed a small smile of amusement to cross his lips.

"This way, please," the captain called out through the clatter of telephones and typewriters as he held open a peeling green door at the left side of the room and gestured for Kamil to enter.

The captain's office was large enough, with a wide stone floor partially covered by a frayed Persian carpet. Yet it was somehow claustrophobic, probably owing to the high transom slits instead of normal glass windows. Kamil decided that it had once been a lavatory.

Lordos moved, quickly for his muscled girth, behind a black desk covered with bound police reports and framed photos of each of his six sisters and brothers, wife and eight children. A large plate of half-eaten *bourekia* filled with meat, cheese and brains lay before him. A tall etched glass held a milky, swirling liquid.

"Please." The captain gestured at a chair as he tumbled into his own slat-backed, caster-mounted relic.

Kamil closed the door with his fingertips. He walked over and stood before the desk.

"Captain, I am the Chief of Security to the Israeli embassy in Nicosia. I am here to request your assistance in a rather delicate matter of state."

Lordos reached into a drawer and set another glass on the desk top. He poured some more of the milky liquid and handed the glass to Kamil. Then he clicked his own against Kamil's and took a ferocious gulp. Kamil, debating whether his next move would put him on friendly or subservient terms, decided to sip the liquid. It was fiery and distinctly licorice. He put the glass down.

"My office is rather concerned about the welfare of an Israeli national who resides in Larnaca."

Lordos looked up at Kamil, showing no expression at all.

He did not even blink. Kamil decided to sit, and he pulled up a wooden chair and perched lightly at its edge so that his face was close over the desk top.

"This gentleman," Kamil continued, "performs certain tasks for our embassy. He acts, shall we say, as a delivery man. He maintains, under my instruction and given the rather large Arab population in your city, a rather obscure profile."

Lordos continued to watch Kamil, yet he still exhibited no obvious interest, though he did begin to pull at the crust of one of his stuffed pies.

"This same gentleman," Kamil pressed on, "was scheduled to appear at our offices in Nicosia this morning at nine sharp. He has not responded to telephone calls since yesterday. Nor did he respond to my personal appearance at his residence less than one hour ago."

With that Lordos finally showed a spark of interest, for the Israeli official was suggesting foul play of an order somewhat more significant than the barroom homicides committed on occasion by drunken seamen. Lordos came up with a pack of local filterless, and he leaned back and began to smoke.

"What is this man's name, please?"

"Dagan," said Kamil. "Mike Dagan."

Lordos stared at Kamil, and then he shrugged as indifferently as he could manage. "I do not know this man." The captain began to tuck in his soiled shirt, signaling that the meeting was about to be over.

Amar realized then that this was going to be far more difficult than he had imagined. Irony of ironies, the Cypriots had once been blatantly pro-Israeli. As little as fifteen years before, such a scenario would have caused a scramble akin to that should a head of state be threatened. However, Arab money had managed to supersede local sympathies to such a degree that most Cypriots were now openly pro-Palestinian.

Having just murdered Dagan himself, Amar had entered

the police headquarters knowing that he was walking a tight-rope. However, the outrageous and the unexpected were his specialties, and besides his political and personal motives, it was this blood-pounding risk that produced such high-wire tactics and drove him to perform these gambits, the way a parachutist returns again and again to the wind-thrashed door of an airplane.

Yet here his boldest move was being threatened by a policeman's unexpected response—Lordos clearly could not give a damn for these arrogant Jews! Amar had to do something quick to hook this lazy, disinterested fish.

He stood up.

"Sir, this may seem to you a trivial matter. However, I assure you that our concern involves matters that could impact on your station."

Lordos gave him a look that said either "I don't understand your English" or "Go ahead, smartass. Impress me."

"If I might phone my embassy, they may allow me to share this information."

Lordos shrugged and gestured at the phone. While Kamil dialed 02–445195 in Nicosia, the captain recommenced his meal in earnest.

An embassy secretary answered, and Kamil began the conversation in his fluent Hebrew, asking simple questions about a passport renewal. Then he altered his tone and began to berate her over the ridiculous reception hours at the embassy, which allowed him to build to a controlled fury, until he was shouting into the telephone. Finally, he slammed the receiver down and collected himself.

He could feel Lordos staring at him, and the chatter from the other side of the wall had receded to the whisper of eavesdroppers.

"I apologize," said Kamil. "It required some convincing of the Consular General."

Lordos's mouth was open, his moustache flaked with *bourekia* crusts.

"All right, Captain. It's like this." Kamil began again, and he leaned in conspiratorially. The captain offered him a cigarette, which he ignored. "This information is highly classified by our intelligence services. However, this *is* your jurisdiction, and we have no choice."

Lordos sipped his ouzo and kept his gaze riveted on Kamil.

"We believe that Mike Dagan may be the victim of an attempt on his life. We believe this, because there is a certain individual abroad whose trail has gone cold for us."

"What indi . . . Who is this man?"

"He is a renowned German terrorist, formerly a member of the Bader-Meinhoff Gang, now a killer for the Red Army Faction."

"And he may be in my country?" Lordos asked as liquid dripped from his wiry handlebar.

"Yes."

"Who is this man?"

"His name," Kamil whispered as he leaned even closer, "is Adolf Shtarker." Amar's invention of a name was a good one, memorable. "I am sure that you have heard of him. But he is traveling under an alias, as a Mr. Tony Eckhardt. We know that his mission is to kill Mike Dagan."

Lordos stood up. He finished tucking in his shirt as he began to pace. A German terrorist. A famous one? He had never heard of him, but this could be good. Yes. The courts would surely let him go, not wanting a tribe of leftist thugs blowing up Cypriot airplanes to get him back. But the *capture*. That would be a sizable feather in Lordos' cap.

Amar saw the shift in attitude as clearly as a flashbulb in a broom closet, and he knew that he was nearly home free.

"But this Mr. Dagan of yours," said Lordos as he paced. "I must know more." He wanted it now, badly. Amar could see it.

Kamil stood up. He waited, looking at his fingertips as if deciding something.

"All right, Captain. I can see that you are a man of discretion and I can trust you."

Lordos stopped pacing, proud of himself as he tricked the Israeli out of some pernicious intelligence secret.

"Mike Dagan was working under a cover name. I cannot, in good conscience, reveal that name. However, I can tell you that he owns a transport firm down at the pier. It is called Still Waters."

"Petrakis!" Lordos screamed out to one of his subordinates, forgetting completely that he was supposed to be discreet. A small man crashed through the door as if propelled by the suction of his captain's voice. "Who owns Still Waters Ltd.?" he demanded in rapid-fire Greek.

"I . . . I don't know." The little man trembled.

"You don't know? The harbor is your beat, you fool!"

"The Yank," a voice called from the squad room.

"Oh, yes!" Petrakis cried as if saved from the gallows. "Mitch, the American. The photographer boy."

"Ahngler," someone else called. "Meetch Ahngler."

"Get me a car!" Lordos yelled. "And find Constantinou, Tavelas and Nikitas!"

All at once the captain was so bent on speed that Kamil realized he would not have much time to assure the idiot's success.

"And Captain," Amar said quickly as Lordos pulled a Browning from his drawer and checked the action, "we also believe that Dagan was stopping somewhere en route to Nicosia today. He may have gone to meet a contact near the Stavrovouni."

"Where?" Lordos asked as he holstered his pistol and set his cap at an angle onto his slick bald pate.

"The monastery. It should be checked, perhaps."

"Petrakis!" Lordos called out again to the little officer, who had just left to get the car.

"Yes?" the responding voice echoed.

"Call Pyrga and have them check all the routes around Stavrovouni."

"Yes, Captain."

Lordos was already at the door. Then he turned and looked at Kamil, who stood in the middle of the office, slightly dumbfounded by his results.

"The German's name again?" Lordos asked. "The name he is using?"

"Eckhardt. Tony Eckhardt."

Lordos threw his shoulders back. "If he is here, I will find him."

"I know you will."

"Thank you for the tip."

"Thank *you*."

"I will keep you informed. *Sta kaló.*"

"*Shalom.*"

And Amar was alone in the office. He waited for a moment for the rumble of feet to recede from the squad room, while he slowly shook his head and smiled.

Then he walked out.

———

Kamil was at Larnaca airport in less than ten minutes. He did not, of course, have a limousine, and he had parked the VW minibus way up on Vmikhailidhi, so he grabbed a taxi.

Within an hour, he was about to board a plane for Cairo. But before he did so, he stopped at a public telephone and placed a long-distance call to Tunis.

Speaking in French, he identified himself as Mr. Theodore

Klatch, and made an unusual request to the station manager at Radio Al-Quds.

"*S'il vous plaît,* I have a favorite Christmas song which I would like to have broadcast over the next three days' breakfast programs. . . ."

9

Cairo

That Evening

EYTAN THOUGHT THAT HE MIGHT FAINT.

He stood in the middle of Heliopolis Airport, looking down at the dusty tile floor. He lifted his hands and saw that the fingers trembled. He had not eaten anything since morning, and the lack of sucrose in his blood made his body sway above his throbbing knee and aching feet. He raised his head slowly, found a support column, and took three careful paces to the right until he could reach out and brace himself against the cool stone.

For a moment he was engulfed by a swarm of tourists as they flowed around him like trout passing a rock in midstream, chattering and trotting after someone who yelled, "Thees way, thees way pleeze." The cacophony subsided, leaving him to take measured gulps of the tepid Egyptian air.

He wanted desperately to doff his ridiculous Alpine jacket, but he was afraid that the effort would leave him flat out on the airport floor. His black, razor-sliced T-shirt was soaked through with sweat, and he knew that his spiked hair was now matted to his skull like a bad toupee.

He had arrived in Cairo without an Egyptian visa, so it had taken over an hour until he was finally allowed to pay the twenty-three U.S. dollars required of West German citizens for such spontaneous admissions. On top of that, local regulations had forced him to exchange an additional $150 into Egyptian pounds. Thanks to the Cypriot police, he was now traveling without his knapsack or a change of clothes, and he was left with only his motorcycle jacket, his documents, the wad of Egyptian notes and a few odd dollars and deutsche marks.

He did not really care. He knew he was at the end of the line.

A small boy walked by pushing a dust bin and a broom. Eytan called out weakly to him in English, "Hey, kid." He tried to smile. "Come here."

The boy approached with a wide, unselfconscious grin, his eyes aglitter with the knowledge of impending profit. Eytan slipped his trembling hand into the sticky pocket of his jeans and produced some coins.

"Bring me something sweet to drink, my friend. Quickly now."

"Yes, meester!" The boy ran off somewhere while Eytan rubbed his pounding temples with one hand. Almost immediately a bottle of orange liquid appeared in front of his face. He stared at it as two small hands popped the cap, then he drank it down in one long swallow. "Again," he said as he reached once more into his pocket. The boy took off without waiting, and this time Eytan gave him a whole pound as he finished the second drink, more slowly now.

"Thank you."

"*Ahfwan,*" said the boy. He took the empties and his money and he sprang away.

Eytan felt a little better. He was able to stand without

support. His hand was wet from the sweaty bottles and he rubbed his face with the cold liquid. His vision cleared, but he blinked hard twice at the figure that appeared before him.

An Egyptian in a baggy black cotton suit was standing ten meters away. The man wore a checkered *kaffieh* on his head, smoked a cigarette and was perusing the arrivals hall as he held up a small white rectangle. Printed on the cardboard was a name in bold marker: Mr. Eckhardt.

Except for a small, ironic smile, Eytan hardly reacted. It was as if he had been shot in a gunfight, knew that he had died, and now nothing that appeared or transpired could possibly shock him.

"Hey," Eytan called out to the man. "Over here." He reached up beneath the right side of his jacket and hooked a thumb in his belt. It was silly, really, for he had dumped his pistol and his German blade in a sewage drain outside Munich Airport before flying to Larnaca. But it made him feel better to keep one hand out of sight.

The Egyptian turned and walked toward him. He had a narrow, open face and he wore bifocals, as if he spent a lot of waiting time reading. He smiled a wide, toothy smile and asked, "Are *you* Mr. Eckhardt?" as if he had already approached a hundred others, with disappointing results.

"I might be."

The man stopped and frowned. "Are you not sure?" The last word came out in two syllables with its thick, accented vowels: shoo-reh?

"I will give you two pounds to see the leather of your belt," said Eytan.

Without thinking, the Egyptian opened his jacket with both hands and examined his own waist, wondering why this crazy foreigner would be interested in his attire.

Eytan, satisfied that the man was unarmed, handed him the notes.

"Shukran." The man grinned again. "I have a letter for you."

"Of course," said Eytan, his tone exhibiting tired surrender. Feeling like a pathetic old man dancing to the whims of a young fashion model, he reached out and took the small envelope. Inside was a folded piece of paper. He opened it to see one sentence in neatly scripted English.

"Would you care to join me at the Nile Hilton for negotiations?"

It was signed, "Saladin."

Eytan nearly laughed. Saladin had been one of the most ruthless of Arab sultans, a hero to the Moslems for his wars against the Crusaders. He had once invited all of his enemies to his Cairo palace for peace talks. Once inside his gates, he had them all slaughtered.

He almost destroyed the note out of habit. He put it in his jeans pocket instead.

"I have been waiting many hours for you," said the Egyptian, hinting openly at his expected *bahksheesh*.

"I am sure. I hope you were well paid."

"I was paid."

"I don't suppose you actually saw the man, did you?"

"The letter and the instructions and the money were all offered by one of the counter boys here, Mr. Eckhardt."

"Naturally. Do you have further instructions?"

"Only to take you wherever you wish."

"To the Nile Hilton perhaps?"

"Only if you wish."

"Naturally."

Eytan looked around the arrivals hall. It was fairly empty now. There appeared to be a lag between flights. The terminal looked rather like Ben Gurion at Tel Aviv. Eytan wished he was there instead of here. No one seemed to be watching them.

"Do you have a car?" Eytan asked.

"My taxi, of course."

"Of course."

"Where would you like to go, sir?"

"I want to go to Dokki."

"Oh. It is very far."

"Yes, I know."

"Across the Nile." The Egyptian said it as if there were no bridges and he would have to swim it with Eytan on his back.

"I know."

"It will be expensive."

"Let's go."

They walked out of the terminal into the main entrance drive, where taxis, *servees* cars, and buses all blared at one another, yet no one seemed to move. It was as if in order to shift gears, Egyptian drivers had to honk the horn rather than put in the clutch. The Egyptian led Eytan along the sidewalk toward a black-and-white Peugeot, which was actually up on the curb—all four wheels of it.

"You have no baggage, Mr. Eckhardt?"

"Not anymore."

Some sort of uniformed security guard was leaning against the Peugeot, looking bored and smoking a cigarette.

"You will have to pay for the parking, I am afraid," said the Egyptian driver.

Eytan looked more closely at the guard. He was a Cairo policeman.

"How much is it?"

The policeman said, "Ten pounds," without so much as a sideward glance. He took Eytan's money, tipped his cap, and walked off.

"Very discreet," said Eytan as he got into the battered taxi.

In a few minutes they were on Shari Ramses, heading

toward Cairo. It was only a twenty-five kilometer drive, but with Egyptian drivers and road conditions, Eytan knew it might take an hour.

"Do you mind if I smoke?" the Egyptian asked as he turned in his seat. He had to raise up a bit as Eytan had fairly collapsed in the rear.

"Not if you'll share," said Eytan. He took a Gauloises from the driver and leaned forward for the light. Then he slumped back again and let the hot breeze from outside dry his slick scalp. He still did not have the strength to wrestle with his jacket.

"Normally, when I have my 'Special' sign out," said the Egyptian, "the trip is eight pound." He left the s off the plural. "And, because I can really take four people, each further person has to pay three more."

"Cut to the chase," said Eytan.

"I beg of your pardon?"

"How much?"

"Twenty-five."

"Fine." Then he said, "I just want to rest a bit."

The driver took the hint and stopped talking. Eytan put his head back on the cracked leather. The sun was setting rapidly. He glanced out the window at the barren wastes of Cairo's outskirts, at the burdened donkeys and their masters who passed the hulks of abandoned car wrecks, making a mockery of the twentieth century. Just as the Palestinian farmers did on the West Bank.

He closed his eyes. There was nothing new for him here. He had been in Cairo many times.

Before Sadat had come to Jerusalem in '77, Israeli agents-in-training had learned all of their tradecraft in the streets of Tel Aviv, Jerusalem and Hebron. If you were going on a mission to an Arab land, you practiced in Israel and then jumped into the fray.

However, the peace treaty had opened up Cairo to the

young teams of agents who needed to learn the Arab ropes. Eytan's first visit had been exciting; the second, pure business. By the time he had helped train a fifth group of operatives there, he no longer liked the Egyptian capital, with its hordes of beggars, impossible transit system and the eyes of a million hungry children.

Today, he hated it.

For a moment, he felt his throat constrict and liquid rise in his eyes. Then he swallowed the despicable self-pity and snorted at his own stupidity. Was it really less than seventy-two hours ago that he'd departed for Munich, electrified by the egotistical conviction that he could ensnare Amar Kamil? Within two days his plan had been turned upside down. Now it seemed that the whole world was after *him*.

He had just spent the entire day in a sweltering Cypriot police cell. . . .

He arrived in Larnaca from Munich and literally hit the ground running, hoping that he was wrong about Kamil, that the Arab was decoying him, that he was not really going after Mike Dagan. And even when he jumped from a taxi at the foot of Still Waters Ltd., and was immediately arrested by that bull of a Cypriot cop, he still held on to the prayer that he was not too late.

But when they booked him in Larnaca for murder, he did not even have to ask who the victim was supposed to be. His screams of denial and remorse only made the fat captain smile.

They stripped him of his belongings, manacled his hands and feet, and threw him into an empty concrete cell in the dank cellars below Larnaca police headquarters. It was more like an animal cage than a detention cell, and there was actually straw on the piss-stained floor. Three armed guards were posted, yet the event became a circus as every cop in town—and not a few of their wives and children—came by to view the murderer.

Lordos came down to begin his interrogation and he was increasingly angered by Eytan's constant attempts to reverse the procedure.

"Who are you?" the captain demanded.

"What happened to Mike?" Eytan shot back.

"What is your name?"

"You have my passport. What happened to my friend?"

"Your 'friend'? You killed him."

"I killed him? *I* did it? You *let* him be killed, you idiot!"

"Your name is Eckhardt. But your real name is Shtarker. Are you not a member of the Red Army Fraction?"

"*Faction,* you fool. And who told you such nonsense?"

It went on for hours. Eytan argued with Lordos, using all of his wits to counter the supposed evidence, finally able to piece together what had happened. He waited until he thought Lordos was on the verge of self-doubt. Then he played his ace.

"All right, Captain. I will admit this much."

"Yes?" Lordos was fairly drooling now. He made Eytan wait while he had a tape recorder brought down to the cell. "Go on." Ten men were gathered outside Eytan's bars. All of them, including Eytan, were exhausted and dripping with sweat.

"Mike Dagan was an Israeli intelligence agent," Eytan said.

"Good!" Lordos clapped his beefy hands together. "Now we advance!"

"Bring me my jacket," Eytan said.

"What?"

"Bring it, if you are not a coward as well as a fool."

The captain had no choice. Eytan's leather Alpine was brought down, and following his instructions the lining was

285

slit open. Lordos sat there with his minion, staring dumbly at the blue passport with the embossed Israeli Ministry of the Interior emblem. For a long moment, the sweltering dungeon was dead silent.

"So, as you can see," Eytan began softly, "I am an Israeli national. So I can hardly be a notorious German terrorist, you goddamn idiots!"

"Then why do you have a German passport also?" Lordos boomed, fighting to maintain a lost position as he stood and banged on the bars.

"Because I am a dual national."

"Then why is it a different name?"

"Because it is common for Israelis to change their original names into Hebrew." It was truth, although not in Eytan's particular case.

"Then who is Mr. Yerushalmi?"

"*He* is your terrorist."

"Nonsense. He is the Chief of Security at the Israeli embassy in Nicosia."

"Oh, really?" Eytan's voice oozed sarcasm. "Then why don't you *call* the embassy and speak to him?"

Once again Lordos was trapped—he had to pick up the glove. He went up to his office and returned after ten minutes, looking quite the worse for wear. Eytan almost had to feel sorry for the man. After all, he himself was apparently not much brighter than Lordos.

"He wasn't there, was he?" Eytan asked quietly.

"They have never heard of him." Lordos's answer was barely audible.

"Okay, Captain." Eytan took a breath. "Please let me out of here now."

Lordos considered it for a moment. Then he dismissed the rest of his officers. They were reluctant to leave, not wanting to miss the last chapter of the drama.

"Get back to work!"

They rushed upstairs. Lordos spoke quietly to Eytan.

"It is not so simple. You are my only suspect."

Eytan grasped the bars, and his chains rattled against them. He tried to stay calm.

"Captain, believe me, I understand your position. We have, all of us, been duped. However, if you do not release me, I will make it known to your national newspaper that you held an Israeli official in your cell while you allowed a terrorist and murderer to escape your grasp."

Lordos pulled at his moustache for a while as Eytan held his breath. Then the captain decided that he had had enough for one day.

"You will have to post substantial bail," said the captain.

"All right."

"And you will have to return here for—How is it said?—depositions, perhaps."

"Cross my heart."

"Petrakis!" Lordos bellowed. "The keys."

They kept Eytan's knapsack, saying the contents would have to be examined by their laboratory. And the bail posting was painful. Eytan asked for a full description of 'Yerushalmi' and a follow-up on his movements, but Lordos declined on all counts. He had to release the Israeli, but he did not have to help him.

Still fuming with the rage of humiliation and impotence, Eytan went to Larnaca Airport. He examined the daily flight schedule and noted that only three planes had departed that day—to Morocco, Athens and Cairo. He washed up, calmed himself, pasted a smile and a concerned look on his face, and at every counter inquired as to whether his "cousin," Mr. Yerushalmi, had boarded the daily flight. He had to find him, he maintained. The man's mother had suffered a severe heart attack.

He was almost certain that the answer would come at Egyptair—and so it did. For Francie Koln was in Cairo, and she was probably the next "planet" on Kamil's list. He waited for two hours for the next flight—unable to eat, drink or think. . . .

Eytan opened his eyes. The taxi had stopped, but by the looks of the buildings and the angle of the disappearing sun they were only in Abbasiya. The driver was out of the car and was poking his *kaffieh*-swaddled face into the open left passenger window, like some genie from a poor man's Arabian fable.

"Why are we stopping?" Eytan asked.

"It is *Feteer*," the Egyptian said as if Eytan should know.

"What?"

"Ramadan has begun, my friend. It is our greatest holiday, the fourth of our five Pillars of Faith."

"Oh, yes," Eytan said. No sense interrupting. The man was going to finish his little speech.

"We fast from dawn until sunset, to gather strength against the evil spirits."

Only the Arabs fast in order to gather *strength,* Eytan mused in silence.

"When the sun sets," the Egyptian continued, "we must have the *Feteer*—a good meal and something to drink."

"I am in a great hurry." Eytan's tone was stern, but he tried not to lose his temper. He no longer harbored great illusions about being able to save Francie. It seemed he was always too late, and Kamil had a full day's jump on him. Still, for his own sanity if nothing else, he had to try. "I can't take an hour now for a feast."

The Egyptian frowned like an offended child. "I must have something, my friend. And to be truthful, you look as though you should take something as well."

The man was right. Eytan needed some fuel. He could barely think for the pounding in his temples.

"Can we take it along?"

The Egyptian raised an eyebrow. "It is not proper." Then he banged an open palm on the door sill and smiled. "But we shall do it. What would you like?"

"Up to you."

"I shall get us *kebab* in pita, *baklawa* and a cola. Okay?"

"Fine." It actually sounded terrific. "But please—quickly."

The Egyptian looked at his foreigner with some pity.

"I shall be quick. But you must learn, my friend, that during Ramadan you must bend to the winds of our faith. With Ramadan we are most stubborn, most determined. We feed our hunger with righteousness."

"I am learning."

The Egyptian nodded and waited.

"Oh." Eytan reached into his pocket. "How much?"

"Ten pounds should be enough."

Eytan handed over the notes.

"*Mumtaaz*. Excellent," said the Egyptian as he walked away.

"*Hah-rah-mee*. Thief," Eytan muttered under his breath.

In ten minutes they were back on the road. Eytan had finished the sandwich and was licking honey-soaked flakes of the *baklawa* from his fingers. He could feel his strength returning, and he sat up on the rear seat and drank his Coke from an old-fashioned glass bottle.

"Cut over to Saleh Salem," he instructed the driver. "Ramses and Said will be crazy now."

The Egyptian obeyed, turning down Shari Masna el-Tarabish to get over to Saleh Salem. They would avoid most of the central congestion by skirting the city.

"You have been here before, my friend?"

"Once or twice."

"You will miss the sights."

Eytan suppressed his laughter. To him, Cairo was just another sweltering urban slum. The continual migrations to the city had overwhelmed all of the services. Housing shortages were becoming critical, the buses were packed to overflowing, traffic paralyzed most of the city, sewage poured into the streets from unrepaired pipes. Everything in Cairo was muddy and discolored to a grey-brown paste from smog and dust.

By taking Saleh Salem you could delay your entrance and just stare at the passing mess, like you did from the FDR Drive in New York, or the Ayalon Highway in Tel Aviv.

"You can stay on it all the way to El-Roda," Eytan said. "Then cut north through the island up el-Manial."

"You have an excellent memory," said the Egyptian.

"Yes."

When they reached El-Roda Island it was already growing dark. Eytan could see the lights of the restaurant on top of the Cairo Tower on Gezira.

"Take a left and cross the El-Gama'a."

Eytan's orienteering abilities had left the Egyptian slightly sullen, for he was unable to play shepherd to such a knowledgeable *kchah-wag-ah*. They crossed the bridge to the plush neighborhoods of Dokki, but Eytan did not even notice the beautiful feluccas that passed beneath him, their towering triangular sails tipping in the winds above the shimmering Nile. When they arrived at the first intersection on the other side of the river, he told the driver to stop.

"Can you wait for me?" he asked the Egyptian.

"I can always wait."

"I don't know how long it will take."

"Only Allah knows."

Eytan paid for the ride and gave the Egyptian another ten pounds as a deposit. He left the cab and began to limp quickly north, parallel to the Nile, until he came to Ibn al-Malek. When he reached the corner he could already see the squat stone structure of the Israeli embassy. The flags on the roof were still flying, yet he felt none of the relief of impending sanctuary. The drive and entranceway were peppered with Egyptian security troops toting Kalachnikovs.

Israeli embassies were the same all over the world—fortified castles disguised by local architectural facades, the government employees protected by a moat of edgy Shabak security officers, always waiting for the next letter bomb, car bomb or assassination attempt. The Cairo version was even worse than most, because the present Egyptian government felt doubly responsible for the lives of its marginally welcome Israeli diplomats. Every Palestinian and Moslem fundamentalist group in Egypt wanted a shot at Mubarak's guests—and not a few wanted a shot at Mubarak himself.

Two uniformed Egyptians stopped Eytan twenty meters from the front steps. Without speaking, he showed them his Israeli passport.

"The visit hours are closed," one of the officers said in broken English.

"I am not a visitor." Eytan offered no more. One of the Egyptians took him by the arm and led him to the front entrance, which was a tall pair of mahogany doors set into the sandstone face of the building. The Egyptian spoke English into a walkie-talkie as he kept Eytan from mounting the stairs.

"Mr. Motti. There is an *Iss-ra-aylee* out here."

"What does he want, Ali?" a voice crackled back.

"I want to see Francie Koln," Eytan said. He half expected to hear the order, "Arrest that man!" or a mournful, "You're too late. She's dead."

The Egyptian repeated Eytan's request as best he could. "He wants to see Nancy Cohen."

"*Francie Koln*," Eytan shouted before the Arab released the microphone key.

There was no further response from the walkie-talkie.

After a minute one of the big doors cracked open and a head emerged. It was balding, very suntanned and wore pilot's sunglasses despite the descent of evening.

Eytan broke free and hobbled up the steps. The Egyptian charged after him. Eytan switched quickly into Hebrew before he could be dragged away.

"I have to see Francie Koln!" he shouted. His heart was pounding now, for he had regained some hope that she might still be alive. Had she been murdered, the reactions would have been decidedly different.

"And who the hell are you?" the Israeli security officer asked.

"I'm Dorothy and you're the fucking Wizard of Oz. Now let me in, *b'chayechah,* before we have an international incident out here."

The door slammed shut with a resounding echo. After a moment, two young men emerged from a side entrance. They were typical *kabahtim*—Shabak security officers—not long out of the army, muscular, rock-faced. They walked up to Eytan and looked him over. One of them opened his jacket and frisked him—front, back, arms, crotch and legs.

"Clean," one Shabaknik said.

"Come," said the other, then, "Thanks, Ali," to the Egyptian, who looked extremely pleased with himself.

They led Eytan to a steel door off to one side. Within, he entered the standard submarine chamber common to all Israeli embassies. The guards waited while a steel drawer opened and Eytan dropped his Israeli passport into it. It slammed shut, and after another minute the secondary door buzzed and the two men escorted him into the embassy.

He found himself in a large, arched reception hall. The building had probably once been a pasha's palace. Although reception hours were over, many of the government workers were still at their tasks. As they passed through the area, some of them stopped to stare at the blond stranger in punk getup.

Motti, the Chief of Security, came into the expansive room. He put his hands on his hips and looked Eytan over without removing his own sunglasses. He wore them to frustrate recognition, for he was a juicy target in Cairo.

"All right," the conversation recommenced in Hebrew. "What's the problem?"

"I have to see Francie Koln."

"We have no such person here."

"Of course not, but I have to see her anyway."

"I am afraid we can't help you, *Adoni*. Are you lost?"

"I'm not an ex-husband or a jealous lover. Get yourself a second secretary and a notepad and let's talk."

The chief looked Eytan over. The costume was weird, to say the least. However, the man was clearly not a simple tourist in distress. He seemed to know the drill.

"Didi," he gestured to one of the guards. "Take him upstairs to room 101 and wait for me."

The two *kabahtim* escorted Eytan up a long stone stairway. He looked at the face of every female employee who passed by, hoping to spot Francie, but the strangers just returned his frank gaze with disdainful expressions.

Room 101 was simply an empty office with a desk, some steel chairs and a telephone. The chief returned with another young man in tow. By his age, modest suit and expression of enthusiasm, Eytan could see that he was not of the rank assigned to tasks of any import.

Eytan sat down in a chair, wanting very badly to appear composed and rational. He looked up at the four men.

"How about a cigarette?"

Motti produced a pack of Time. Eytan took one and lit up, as did everyone else in the room.

"Okay, let's hear it," said the officer as he examined his ravaged cigarette box.

"Fine, but can we keep the guests to a minimum?" Eytan asked.

The chief looked at Eytan, then at his two men. He cocked his head, and they left him with the second secretary and the interviewee. They knew their chief could handle himself.

Eytan smoked for a moment, considering how much he should say—*could* say.

"All right. First of all, Francie Koln is in danger of being killed." He put up a hand. "No, don't say it. You've never heard of her. Fine. But if you *have* heard of her, and she's in the embassy, don't let her leave."

The second secretary began to write furiously in a notepad.

"And if she's not in the embassy, find her and put a team on her, round-the-clock. No, better than that, ship her home. Tonight."

The chief just smoked his own cigarette and stared at Eytan. He put one foot up on an empty chair.

"Okay, *Chaver*. Who are you?"

"You have my passport."

"All right, Mr. 'Eckstein.' Once again, who are you?"

Eytan knew what the question meant. "It doesn't matter," he said. "Just do it, for God's sake, and we'll play policeman later!"

Motti watched his charge for another thirty seconds, while Eytan returned his stare without blinking.

"Didi!" the chief called out, and one of his officers appeared almost immediately. Motti took the second secretary's notepad, scribbled something on it, tore off the sheet and handed it to his man. Didi left quickly.

Eytan headed off the impending interrogation.

"Look, I can't give you the details. I want to, but I can't." He felt stupid playing the compartmentalization game, but old habits died hard. He knew it didn't really matter—his career was over. He could have dictated his whole damned biography, but he just gave over enough to keep it all going.

"I served in the 35th Brigade, Battalion 202. My brigade commander was Moofaz. My serial number is 2141013."

"And then . . . ?" the chief asked.

"And then, I transferred to 'other duties.' You want to land us both in Ramla Prison?"

Motti was fairly sure he was dealing with a professional now, but his own code of conduct demanded extreme caution.

"You want to play some more Jewish geography?" Eytan asked without malice. "We'll probably wind up related."

Motti actually smiled and the second secretary laughed.

"So, that's all?" the chief asked. "You're worried about this Francie Koln?"

Eytan considered his next move. If Francie was still alive, then she would probably be safe very soon. The Shabaknik had to act on the tip. That was his job. Eytan knew that his own run was over. They might hold him over for questioning, delay his departure for home. And in the meantime, Amar Kamil was out there, and who knew where he would go next?

"There is one more thing," said Eytan.

"What is it?" Motti asked.

"It's a big thing." Eytan took a deep breath. "It's information about Amar Kamil."

The chief put his foot back on the floor and placed his hands on his hips. Eytan could see the ripple of skepticism as it crossed the man's eyes. "Amar Kamil the terrorist?"

"Yes," Eytan said.

"Amar Kamil is dead, from all the reports."

"He is not dead."

Motti and the second secretary exchanged looks.

"Amar Kamil is *not* dead?"

From the new tone that had crept into the chief's voice,

Eytan knew that he had lost his credibility. Both men were now observing him like some scientific experiment gone awry.

"He is very much alive," Eytan pressed on.

"And I suppose *you* know where he is."

"Yes. He is here, at the Nile Hilton."

Even as Eytan said it, Kamil's brilliance washed over him like a shock wave from a nuclear blast. Yes, he knew for certain that the Hilton was *exactly* where Kamil would be. Why? Because it was too, too simple to be believed by any sane professional. Kamil knew that Eytan would be found mad by anyone whose aid he attempted to enlist. What could the Israeli claim? That the terrorist had left him a note, inviting him to dinner?!

"So," the chief was growing angry now, "Amar Kamil is staying at the Nile Hilton, is he?"

"And Abu Nidal is at the Sheraton, I hear." The second secretary spoke his first words of the encounter. "And Arafat is singing at the Gezira Club tonight."

"All right," Eytan spat. "To hell with both of you. Just let me see Francie. Let me see her face, see that she's alive. Then you can put me in a straightjacket and ship me to Tel Hashomer."

The chief jabbed a finger at Eytan's face. "You *are* behaving like a madman. I don't know who the hell you are, and you're not going to see Francie Koln or anyone else until you calm down and I've checked you out." He turned and called out into the hallway again. "Didi!"

The young officer came back into the room. "Entertain this gentleman while we go over to Communications," Motti ordered.

The chief motioned for the sneering second secretary to accompany him. They left the room and closed the door while Didi stood over Eytan and looked at him.

Eytan knew exactly what was going to happen now. He

envisioned the telexes and flash messages, the orders that would soon have him immobilized. But he could no longer be sure that Francie would be protected, and he was damn sure that Kamil had not yet done his worst.

He looked up at the young *kabaht,* and he smiled.

"Where you from, Didi?"

The officer did not answer immediately.

"I'm a Jerusalemite myself," said Eytan.

"Me too." The ice thawed a bit.

"Really? I'm in Talpiot Mizrach." Eytan grinned.

"My folks are in Gilo." Didi returned a small smile.

"Didi," Eytan said as he rubbed his right knee, "I have to stand up. I've got a bad leg, from *Shalom HaGalil.*"

The mention of the war in Lebanon caused Didi to offer a helping hand to a wounded comrade, which Eytan accepted gratefully as he said:

"Sorry, Didi. . . ."

The Chief of Security came marching back out of Communications, the second secretary barely able to keep up. In his hand, Motti clutched a flimsy telex sheet. He had begun to send out a coded query to both Mossad and AMAN headquarters in Tel Aviv, asking for information on an Israeli citizen named Eytan Eckstein, with passport number and general description delineated. Yet even as he dictated the communiqué, he saw the Red Flag Message from the office of a Colonel Itzik Ben-Zion posted on the Flash Board. It was an order to worldwide embassy personnel to detain one Eytan Eckstein at all costs—being an IDF officer Absent WithOut Leave.

The chief slammed open the door to room 101. Didi sat on the floor against one wall, holding his head and groaning, blood from his nose running over his chin and into his lap.

Eckstein was gone. . . .

"You are going to have to move very quickly now. Very quickly."

Eytan was hunkered down in the back of the Peugeot, finally stripping off the jacket he had adored in Munich, and now despised in Cairo.

"Yes, Mr. Eckhardt. Quickly."

The Egyptian had waited for him as promised. He was driving as fast as traffic would allow, south on Shari el-Giza, a block west of the Nile. They had already passed the zoological gardens, which took up most of Dokki.

"What is your name, my friend?" Eytan finally asked. He was sorry now for the disdainful way in which he'd treated the Egyptian all evening. He realized that at the moment, an Egyptian Arab was his only ally, and that included Eytan's fellow countrymen.

"My name is Fahmi."

"Pleased to meet you, Fahmi," Eytan said as the driver swerved to avoid a donkey cart and Eytan's head banged against the door handle.

"The pleasure is mine, Mr. Eckhardt." There was true joy in his voice, for hospitality was the greatest trait of the Egyptians.

"Don't miss the El-Giza Bridge, Fahmi," Eytan instructed. "You must drive across it very fast, and then through El-Roda again and quickly into the city. When you get across the water turn south, okay?"

"Yes, sir." Fahmi must have reached the intersection at that moment, for the car careened hard to the left and he yelled, "*Koos em-uk!*" at someone as horns blared and tires squealed all around them. The rear door on Eytan's side actually opened with the centrifugal drag, and he reached out and slammed it shut.

He raised himself in the seat a bit and looked around.

No one seemed to be following them, at least no one but a thousand cars, taxis, buses and donkey carts.

"Fahmi, you must do two things for me now. Maybe three."

"What should I do, Mr. Eckhardt?"

"You will take me to someone you know, perhaps someone in Old Cairo. Not too far inside, for we will have to go north again after that."

"Who will it be that I know?"

"Someone who will give me a change of clothes. A shirt and trousers."

There was silence from the front seat. It was clear what Fahmi was thinking.

"Mr. Eckhardt," the Egyptian said after a long moment, "I do not want trouble with the police."

"I am not a criminal, Fahmi. I swear by Allah. But I am in danger and I must change these clothes."

Silence again. Then, "I know someone in Old Cairo."

"Good. Now one more thing, Fahmi."

"Yes?"

"I want you to get me a *shabriyeh*."

The image of the wickedly curved Bedouin blade made Fahmi gasp. "*I'mil ma'ruf* please, meester. It is too much."

"Don't worry, Fahmi. I will not harm anyone."

"Then why do you want a *shabriyeh*?" Fahmi was not a fool. You didn't use such a knife for cutting carrots.

"I promised it to someone."

"To be shhooor."

"Look, Fahmi." Eytan began to bargain as they came across El-Roda and were about to cross the narrow waterway between the island the eastern city. "I'll give you all the money I have left."

The driver smiled. Eytan could see gold fillings in the

rearview mirror. "Forgive me, my friend, but perhaps you only have a few piasters left."

"I have two hundred pounds. When you are done with me, it is yours."

Two hundred pounds was more than Fahmi would make in the next two weeks.

"Fi amani'llah." Fahmi wished the foreigner God's protection as he turned south toward Old Cairo. . . .

———

Eytan had to wait patiently while Fahmi's cousin finished ironing a short-sleeved, yellow cotton shirt. He wanted to scream at the man, "I'll take it wrinkled, goddammit!" yet he just stood there massaging his aching knee.

He certainly had no illusions left about taking Amar Kamil down alone, but he did not much care anymore. He was functioning on a soldier's momentum, the same poison that made men stand up in a firefight, yell "Follow me!" and charge.

He knew that the terrorist's list of "planets" was growing shorter with each killing, and he felt that Kamil was probably saving him for last, like an exorbitant dessert at the end of a fat meal. But if Eytan was lucky, the terrorist might go for him at this juncture, and Eytan preferred to die than witness the demise of any more of his friends.

Fahmi's cousin took a last mouthful of water from a large jug, and he sprayed it slowly through his teeth over the shirt as he passed a huge iron full of smoking coals back and forth over the cloth.

The man stepped back and lifted the shirt, examining his work. He smiled through a wide gap in his teeth. *"Khud!"* he said proudly, and Eytan took the shirt. He was already wearing a pair of the man's baggy tan trousers and the hot cloth stung as he slipped it on. The Arab immediately picked up the Alpine jacket that had been offered in exchange. He pushed his *kaffieh* aside and began to smell the leather.

They were in a cool stone basement of a slum in Old Cairo. Fahmi came down the steps holding a kerosene lantern in one hand and a bundle of wrapped cloth in the other. He set the lantern down and walked over to Eytan. He opened the cloth slowly, and there lay the *shabriyeh*. Its handle was inlaid with jewels, the curved scabbard of hammered silver plate. Eytan lifted the knife and withdrew a nine-inch steel blade that glittered under the dancing yellow flame.

"Let's go," he said as he tucked the knife into his belt.

Eytan had Fahmi pull the car over just north of the Egyptian Museum. The hotel was just a short walk along the Nile. The evening had cooled considerably, like desert evenings everywhere, and the Peugeot's engine ticked as the metal condensed.

Eytan sat for a minute and watched the passing crowds. In this district they were mostly wealthy foreigners. The men wore summer suits, and many of the women wore gowns. He felt an inexplicable disdain for their wealthy indifference. After all, he was of the Levant himself, and more like an Egyptian than these cavorting peacocks. He reached over the seat and handed Fahmi the two hundred pounds.

"*Shukran,* Mr. Eckhardt. Do you want me to wait?"

"No, Fahmi. I am going to the Hilton. There may be danger there and I don't want you involved."

With what he was about to do, Eytan realized that Fahmi might be the last man to know him, the last soul to share his last day before he died. He did not know how he would find Kamil, for if Thomas Skorzeny had been right then he would have no idea what the man looked like now. But if he could manage to locate 'Mr. Yerushalmi,' he would do his very best to kill him, even if it was right there in the lobby in full view of the world. He was just as sure that Kamil would probably disarm him of his newly acquired knife and slice him to ribbons with it.

"Fahmi, you have been a good friend."

"You paid me well, Mr. Eckhardt." The Arab had turned in his seat. His eyes watered.

"No, a good friend." Eytan got out of the car and leaned in the front window. He took Fahmi's hand. *"Ma'asalaama."* He said farewell in Arabic.

"U'a! Be careful!" Fahmi called after him. *"Kattar allah kherak!"*

Eytan walked straight for the hotel. He did not pause, or hesitate, nor did he bother to check for tails or watchers. His leg hurt like hell but he ignored it. He could feel the cold hilt of the *shabriyeh* against his belly beneath his untucked shirt. He crossed the great circular drive, where the big cars of diplomats and wealthy Europeans cruised in and out like ocean liners in a brightly lit harbor. Bellhops in ridiculous uniforms whistled and called to taxi drivers, and the local camel shepherd had a woman in a blue cocktail dress giggling as her date photographed her on top of a huge, slobbering ship of the desert.

He neared the steps. They loomed before him like the ladder to a gallows. His heart was hammering a paradiddle in his chest as he lifted his aching leg onto the first stair.

Both of his elbows were suddenly locked in a crushing grip. He turned his head to see three Egyptian plainclothes policemen. One of them flashed a badge while quick hands moved over Eytan's body. He felt the *shabriyeh* being jerked from his belt.

"Please, Mr. Eckstein," a low Arabic accent rumbled, "just come along."

He did not resist. The detectives escorted him across the drive. A large black car sat there with its rear door open, like a panther waiting to swallow him. He was pushed inside and the door slammed.

The Chief of Security from the embassy sat in the rear

seat. Two of his men perched on fold-out stools in the large cabin.

"I think it is time for you to go home, Mr. Eckstein," said Motti.

The car began to move.

On the steps of the Hilton, Amar Kamil stood casually conversing with a pair of striking Danish women. They tittered as he entertained them with a concocted story about life in the African Congo, replete with British accent and the amusing snobbery of a colonialist.

Yet all the while, as he smoked a Dunhill and smiled at the women, his eyes were watching the lightning-quick capture and removal of 'Mars.'

He smiled, dropped his cigarette, and crushed it out on the rich carpet of the stairway.

———

Eytan arrived at Ben Gurion International Airport at one o'clock in the morning. He had flown unescorted aboard the El Al 707, although the Cairo embassy Chief of Security had told one of the aircraft's armed guards to keep a close eye on him.

He sat in his seat while most of the passengers hurried to the exit, anxious to see their friends and families and tell of their visits to an Arab land. Eytan was not avoiding the crush; he simply found himself unable to get up. His body rebelled against the inevitable, until a stewardess finally offered to help him and he managed to disembark with a declining shake of his head.

He walked to passport control as if trudging through a swamp, his legs heavy, his arms like carcasses at his side. Except for his flight, there was no other arrival, and the lines moved quickly.

The customs clerk asked him for his passport, which had been returned to him, but he did not have his reserve officer's travel document, so he had to fill out a form. It took him a long time.

He passed through the control desks and into the baggage claim hall. He stood there for a minute, wondering what to do, where he should go.

The problem was solved for him.

A team of GSS men approached, four gorillas in jeans and summer blazers. One of them showed an ID and cocked his head, indicating that Eytan should follow along. They surrounded him as they would a head of state, leading him past the tourist information desks and the restrooms, past the groups of excited Israelis who were claiming their bags and wondering if they would get caught with their smuggled cameras and VCRs. They skipped the declaration section of customs and went past a uniformed guard, through a side exit, and suddenly they were outside on the sidewalk.

Heinz was standing there. He was in full uniform, his bars and boots polished, his black beret folded beneath an epaulet, his white-blond hair nearly fluorescent, his hands on his hips and his dead eyes glittering.

He stepped forward and made his pronouncement with undisguised pleasure.

"Captain Eytan Eckstein . . . You are under arrest."

Part 2

RAMADAN

10

Jerusalem

Before Dawn

"YOU ARE A SOLDIER, ECKSTEIN!"

Colonel Itzik Ben-Zion's voice banged off the walls of his office like a medicine ball fired from a cannon.

"A soldier!"

He pounded on his desk top and the pencils and papers bounced as he marched around it like a boa constrictor closing on a rat.

"You're *not* some goddamn Mossad executive in a French-cut suit, running around Europe whenever you damn well please. You are a soldier, and you will follow orders, and if you *can't* follow orders then you will be subject to the same disciplines of any pathetic private in this fucking army. Is that *clear*?"

Eytan sat in a metal chair in the middle of the room like a murder suspect at a police interrogation. They had been at it for over an hour. Or rather, Ben-Zion had been at it, for most of the hearing consisted of Itzik's ranting, interspersed with Eytan's attempts to explain himself.

Eytan was long past tired. His body felt like a molten, burning liquid that should have been poured into a sewer. His eyes stung and his stomach churned, and his leg made him wish they had opted for amputation.

Yet Ben-Zion's dressing-down, replete with exaggerations, insults and threats, was far more painful than Eytan's physical condition. And even more excruciating was the fact that Benni Baum stood there the entire time—saying absolutely nothing.

"I asked you a question, Eckstein." Itzik was looming over him now, arms folded across his chest, bending at the waist and sticking his nose in Eytan's face.

"What was the question?" Eytan asked groggily.

"Do you correctly understand your position in this unit?"

"Yes."

"Do you understand your duties and obligations as an army officer?"

"Yes."

"Do you realize that I could send you down to Prison Six for *half a year,* for being AWOL?"

"Yes."

"Good." The Colonel backed away and leaned against his desk. It was well past 3:00 A.M., and outside, Jerusalem was as quiet as a sleepy Scottish sea town. The Special Operations building was also in repose, except for the remote clacking of the telex machines from Communications on Floor Two. "Then I assume you also understand my displeasure."

"Not really," Eytan said simply. "Actually, it seems out of proportion."

"Koos eema shelcha!" Ben-Zion stamped up onto his feet and began to pace again, but this time he turned on Benni, who sat passively on the couch along one wall. "Baum, this is all your fault."

"Mine?" Baum placed a hand over his chest.

"Yes. Yours." Itzik stared at Baum as he jabbed a finger in Eckstein's direction. "This man is insubordinate, conniving and unrepentant."

Baum suppressed a laugh. "I was his field commander, Itzik, not his father."

"I'll take the blame." Danny Romano stood over near the windows, one foot up on a chair, clicking his teeth on his cold pipe stem. "If that's what you're looking for."

"Don't get smart with me, Romano." Itzik warned him. "You're all *this* close to transfers." He put a thumb and finger together to show just how close they were.

"You can't transfer me," Uri Badash said. The Shabak agent was leaning against a corner wall, smoking. "I don't work for you."

The Colonel looked over at the GSS man as if seeing him for the first time. "Remind me, Badash. What are you doing here?"

"You asked for a GSS team to pick him up at the airport," said Uri, and he shrugged as if the idea was absurdly melodramatic. "If you don't want to have eggs, then don't keep a live hen." It was a nasty double entendre, as in Hebrew the word for eggs also meant *balls*. Ben Zion ignored him.

"He's going to penetrate now." Eytan's voice was soft, quiet, drained of tone.

"Don't start that again, Eckstein," the Colonel snapped.

"All right," said Eytan, "but he is."

"*Ya Allah,*" Heinz groaned from where he sat near Itzik's desk. He adjusted the beret under his epaulet and shook his head. He was so pleased to be wearing a uniform.

"Ariella." Ben-Zion turned to his secretary. She was a plain-looking girl with mousy brown hair and freckles, and she looked like she'd been woken from a pleasant postcoital sleep. "You can type up the report and go home." The girl nodded and rose from her chair. Eckstein had repeated his story three times, and she had enough notes for a novella. She left the room.

"Come on, Itzik," Eytan sighed. "It's only logical." With his fingers he made a smoking motion to Baum, who threw him a pack of Time and a plastic lighter. The room already swirled with a ribbony haze like the rings of Saturn.

"Logic?" Itzik sneered. "Logic?" His tone began to rise again. "You go running off like an overemotional schoolboy and you're selling me logic?"

"Forget about me for a minute and look at the facts."

"Believe me, I'd love to forget about you. However, the fact is, that Kamil—if this *is* Kamil—may be a fanatic, but he is certainly not suicidal."

For a moment Eytan allowed himself the luxury of a small success. All right, he had failed miserably in his attempt to ambush the terrorist. But at least Itzik was no longer deriding the claim that Kamil had resurfaced. If nothing else, Eytan's venture had brought the truth to light, and perhaps Ben-Zion would finally take some action.

In fact, Itzik was much more firmly convinced now of enemy activity than he let on. He had listened to Eytan's story, then made him repeat it twice. The Colonel was an ambitious career-builder first and foremost, and that cover-your-ass mentality forced him to swallow some distasteful theories. At the very least, events of the past three days surely indicated a vengeance play against Eckstein's old team. Most of Itzik's present anger stemmed from the fact that the captain might be right, rather than from his unauthorized mission to Europe.

On the other hand, Itzik truly did not believe that the killer or killers would attempt to penetrate Israel proper. Terrorists tried that nonsense across the borders every week, but they were mostly drugged-up, half-assed Palestinian kids from Lebanon. The professionals rarely attempted to get inside. They preferred the soft targets in Europe: airliners, restaurants, synagogues.

Based on that history, Itzik had already begun to take action to protect his interests abroad. He had done so upon hearing of Mike Dagan's death in Cyprus the day before. He revealed his moves now, just for the record.

"However, Mr. Eckstein," Itzik announced, "despite the fact that you may think me a bull-headed incompetent, I did not attain this post through *proteksia*." He used the slang for *connections*. "Francie Koln is now under round-the-clock guard. Three of our people are already in Cyprus, using covers as Israeli detectives. An additional team is in Cairo, working out of the embassy." He watched Eytan's reaction, which gave him some arrogant pleasure. "Does that meet with your approval?"

Eytan nodded. "Thank you." At least Francie was safe. For the time being.

"Don't thank me. We're not doing it for you."

There was a knock on the door. Heinz rose and strutted to it, his combat boots slapping the tiles. A sergeant from Communications peeked in and handed the captain a telex sheet. The door closed.

Heinz took a while to read the cable, enjoying being the focus of everyone's attention.

"*Nu?*" Itzik demanded.

"It's from the Cairo embassy," said Heinz. He began to recite the stilted decryption:

BEGIN MESSAGE. LOCAL POLICE REPORT INDIVIDUAL USING ISRAELI PASSPORT BOARDED EGYPTAIR FLIGHT 771 FOR NAIROBI AT 0145 HOURS. MANIFEST RECORDS SHOW PASSENGER'S NAME AS YOSSI YERUSHALMI. END MESSAGE.

For a moment there was silence in the room. Then Itzik rose from the edge of his desk.

"Well, Eckstein? Isn't that the correct name?"

"Yes, but. . . ." Eytan furrowed his brow.

"Yes? So what's the problem?"

"The destination," said Eckstein. He lifted a hand to scratch his head and then his own incredible stink washed over him. No wonder he was sitting alone in the middle of the room.

"What about it?" Itzik demanded.

"Nairobi, Eytan," Danny Romano coaxed. "Come on, who's in Nairobi?"

"No one." Eytan shrugged. It didn't fit. None of his teammates, in fact, no one he knew at all was in Kenya.

"Oh, shit." Benni Baum finally said something. "Johann."

"Who the hell is Johann?" Heinz asked, mimicking his boss's impatient tone.

Benni got up from the couch and began to rub his hands. "It doesn't make real sense, though." He looked around at the eyes that were fixed on him. "He's a free-lancer. One of my own. A German. He's just a Watcher, works for me sometimes." The image of Johann wearing his feathered hat and constantly petting his German shepherd floated before Baum's eyes.

"So?" Itzik tried to pry it out of the burly major.

"He was on *Flute* in Munich, but only for an hour. No one saw him. Not even the Team."

"I've never met him," said Eytan as if lauding the major's professionalism.

"He has a daughter, I think," said Baum as he pulled his lip. "I seem to remember she lives in Africa. A paleontologist. Johann spends time with her occasionally. But it's too farfetched."

"Heinz!" Itzik clapped his hands together and his aide

nearly clicked his heels. "Call Cairo on a scrambler and get that team to Kenya right away. Baum will give you this Johann's full name and description."

"I shouldn't do that," Benni began.

"Wait, Itzik," said Eytan.

But the Colonel was already on a roll. He was smelling blood and he was going to snatch this 'Yerushalmi' fellow, whoever he was.

"Uri," Itzik boomed, forgetting that the GSS man was not one of his troops. "Contact your people at Nairobi embassy and get someone to the airport immediately."

"Excuse me, *sir,*" said the Shabak agent. "But I already *have* a boss."

"Are you going to quibble with me?" Ben-Zion had risen to his full height and was beginning to wave his arms.

"Itzik." Eytan was shaking his head. "Wait a minute. Please . . ."

The Colonel seemed not to hear. He strode to the door, opened it, and caught Heinz with his voice as the captain bounded down the stairwell. "And call the Civilians." He meant the Mossad. "They have the best contacts with the Africans. Get me the duty officer on the phone."

He slammed the door and turned back to the room. He was like a tank commander now, exposed in the turret, headed for battle and glory.

"Itzik, will you wait one minute?" Danny Romano said. "Something's not right here." He was gesturing at the faces of Baum and Eckstein.

"What's not 'right'?" Itzik snapped.

"Stop racing," said Baum.

"What's not right? You want this man or don't you?"

"No," Eytan said. He was shaking off his fatigue, trying to reason. It had taken him a minute, but now he knew. "It's a ruse," he said, rising painfully to his feet.

"What?" The Colonel's face folded into an ugly grimace.

"It's a feint, Itzik. A decoy move."

"A *what?*" Ben-Zion actually kicked a chair. "Are you out of your mind?"

"You're wasting your men," Eytan said, forgetting his own very precarious position. He should have simply acquiesced, allowed Ben-Zion to run it out, let him fall on his face. But his problem was that he cared too much. "This is typical of him, Itzik, I'm telling you."

"*You* are telling *me*, Eckstein? What are *you* telling *me?!*" The Colonel advanced on his battered captain, dwarfing him.

"It's a feint to the south, Itzik!" Eytan began to shout back in defense. "It's a typical ploy for him. He never boarded that plane."

"Baum." Itzik turned on the major. "This man is hallucinating."

Benni just shrugged, which made Eytan even more desperately furious.

"He is coming straight for Tel Aviv, Colonel," Eytan shouted. He shot a finger at the commander. "Straight for your balls. And you're playing right into his hands again, just like a fool."

"A *what?*" Itzik's windows rattled.

"I know this man better than you, better than anyone in this room." Eytan's bloodshot eyes were bulging. "And if you'd listened to me last week, Mike Dagan would still be alive!"

There. He had said it. An icy silence engulfed the office. No one moved. Finally, Itzik walked behind his desk and sat down. He folded his hands together and placed them on the desk top.

"Ariella!" he shouted. No one spoke while Itzik and Eytan stared at each other like two cats before a brawl. The secretary came back into the room clutching a notepad, as she always did. "Sit," Itzik ordered. She sat. "Take this for the record." She poised her pencil.

314

Heinz, having heard the shouting match, had reappeared in the room. A vulture smelling a fresh kill.

"Captain Eckstein." Itzik's tone changed to one of imposed calm, though his anger had not left his face. "The word *chutzpah* was invented for officers such as yourself. As of this moment, you face summary court-martial for unauthorized leave. Verdict? Guilty. Sentence? Three months suspension at half pay. Forfeiture of all vacation time until further notice. Disallowance of all related expense chits."

The Colonel knew his men's personal records by rote. He knew how to hit them and where. He knew about Eytan's financial problems, his apartment and his wife's longing for a holiday with her husband. He knew too much.

For want of a gavel, he slammed a palm onto his desk top.

"Dismissed."

Eytan could not move. He was stunned. His hands opened and closed. He wanted them around Itzik Ben-Zion's throat.

"Get the hell out of my office!" Ben-Zion roared.

Eytan took a step forward, but Heinz was there quickly. He took Eytan's arm and pulled him out the door.

Colonel Ben-Zion was alone. His officers had left and he had finally released his exhausted secretary. He sat behind his desk and looked through the large windows as the Jerusalem night began to go violet, and the chatter of the starlings only aggravated his brooding.

He should have gone home as well, but Tzahala was a long drive off and a nap on the sticky vinyl of his office couch seemed more appealing than the image of his sad wife in her frumpy nightdress. She had been so beautiful once, Shula, yet now the light was gone from her baggy eyes and a thin whine had replaced the throaty voice that had lured him so long ago.

It was like that with so many of the career officers' wives.

The men were strapping, handsome, youthful, middle-aged warriors in crisp uniforms. And you were shocked to see their women, heavy with their days and nights of longing, filling their emptiness with food, all but widows except that their absent husbands still lived.

He reached down into a desk drawer and removed a glass and a rarely touched bottle of brandy. He poured a few centimeters and drained it neat. And then he poured some more.

He did not like the way he felt about Eytan Eckstein, for Itzik was not a stupid man and he knew that his anger was misplaced and unfair. He also knew where it came from, but he could not help himself.

Feldenhammer. . . .

It returned to him every day now, and every night. He lived with it like a crippled limb, or the loss of a child. . . .

It was the summer of 1973, and Itzik was a young officer, on loan to Mossad from the army for *Project Quest*. The horror of the Munich Massacre was still fresh in the minds of his countrymen, and Itzik was proud to be one of the team leaders chosen for a dangerous mission approved by Golda Meir herself.

Vengeance assassination was, at the time, an untried tool of the Israeli intelligence community. The Israeli justice system did not even have a death penalty, and that reluctance to kill the enemy was only set aside on the field of battle.

Yet the massacre of her athletes at the Olympic Games had pushed Meir over the edge, and she ordered the assembly of *Project Quest*. One by one, the architects of the Munich terror were executed, by bullet, bomb and booby trap. They were felled in the alleys, fields and waterways of Europe by righteous, idealistic young agents like Itzik Ben-Zion.

Yet unlike his comrades, Itzik was not sobered by the

bloody chase. The killing did not quench his vengeful thirst, nor stir an inkling of remorse. Ali Yassin Abdallah, the ultraterrorist, the mastermind of Munich, was still at large and Itzik was not only determined that it be his team that made the hit, but that he himself be one of the heroic shooters to do the deed.

And then, Feldenhammer, the tiny town in Norway where it all went wrong. It was Itzik who incorrectly identified the innocent waiter named Samir Amkari as the terrorist Yassin Abdallah, and it was Itzik who arrogantly insisted that his target analysis was irrefutable, and it was Itzik who led his team into committing a murder that blew *Quest* wide open.

Just a few seconds of Itzik's misplaced gunfire, and all at once the righteous chase was reversed: the hunters became the hunted. Having allowed the heat of pursuit to cloud their judgment, the *Quest* team members suddenly found themselves in a remote Scandinavian village. There was no urban populace with which to blend, no massive, sprawling city into whose slums and alleyways they could fade. The Norwegian security forces flooded the flat, uncrowded highways, and within three days all of the field operatives were awaiting trial in Norwegian prisons.

Except for Itzik. Somehow, he managed to slip through the net.

Back in Israel, the embarrassing revelations of roving Jewish hit teams caused a spectacular uproar. Yet upon his return, Itzik was unrepentant. He had done his job and done it well, and who the hell cared about one lousy Arab waiter when his team and the others had shown the world that Jewish blood was no longer a cheap commodity?

Even as a junior officer, Itzik was damn sure of himself and loathe to admit even the remote possibility of an error, unless it could be proved to him. He had *not* made a mistake.

He had correctly identified Ali Yassin Abdallah, the "Blue Knight." But then his team had been *set up* to kill the wrong man, as Samir Amkari was inserted into the picture at the last minute before the kill. Yes, his professional judgment was sound, his instincts correct. There had been no error— only clever enemy action.

Itzik's superiors did not have much time in which to dispute his claim. In October, the Yom Kippur war erupted, dwarfing the significance of the Feldenhammer Fiasco. Many of Itzik's peers perished in the all-out struggle for Israel's survival, and most of his superiors were forced into retirement for failing to predict the cataclysm which nearly destroyed the Jewish State.

Itzik Ben-Zion had been on assignment in Europe for almost a year, his hands awash in blood, yet clean of blame for Yom Kippur. His career was catapulted forward . . .

Now, Itzik was well on his way to becoming the Commander of AMAN, and someday perhaps, the Chief of Staff. In his mind, Feldenhammer had been relegated to a footnote in an officer's tactical education, part of the adventures of a young man.

And then, out of nowhere, it happened. Captain Eytan Eckstein, one of his best young team leaders, a veteran of *five* perfectly executed anti-terror missions, suddenly mirrored Itzik's historical blunder with that cataclysmic murder in Bogenhausen. How could it have happened again? How? Hadn't Itzik warned his agents time and again to be careful, to be absolutely certain? Hadn't he ordered them to withdraw if there was even the slightest doubt?

Perhaps if Eckstein had also been self-righteous, bullheaded, refusing to take the blame for the Bogenhausen Fiasco, Itzik could have stomached him. But the captain's pathetic acceptance of responsibility left the Colonel's heart cold and pitiless. As commander of Special Operations, Itzik was ultimately responsible for Eckstein's screwup, and the captain's admission that the murder of Mohammed Najiz was anything but an act of God brought every one of Itzik's fears and insecurities thundering to the surface.

Only a handful of AMAN officers were aware of Itzik's past, and they were forbidden by regulations to reveal it. But the arched eyebrows and whispers of "Feldenhammer" in the hallways certainly did nothing to allay his suspicions.

Now, no matter how much he denied it, it seemed that another head had regenerated itself on the Medusa of Arab terrorism. Like the ghost of the Blue Knight himself, Amar Kamil—or another like him—was on the move, and Itzik's empire could crumble.

Every time Itzik saw Eytan Eckstein, he was reminded of his fragile self.

A shattering crash made Itzik jump in his chair. He looked down, realizing that the brandy glass had slipped from his fingers. The jagged shards glittered in the dawn light that was washing the hard tile floor, and he saw the yellow liquid oozing away, like the lifeblood of his career.

The Shabak security teams were already out in force at Ben-Gurion Airport when the morning El Al flight arrived from Athens. Despite Itzik Ben-Zion's apparent disdain for Eytan Eckstein's "fantasies," the Colonel had reminded Uri Badash, before dismissing him from his office, that internal security was really the responsibility of the General Security Services. Badash did not need to be prodded. With three Israeli operatives now dead, and the theories of an AMAN captain—who seemed perfectly sane to him—ringing in his ears, Uri had already ordered an upgraded security alert at all ports of entry.

But Amar Kamil barely attracted a nod.

He appeared quite rested, almost jaunty considering that he had been flying all night after first doubling back to Greece. His face and arms were lightly tanned, though you could not tell that the color came from a bottle. He wore a blazing white polo shirt, navy baseball cap, sunglasses, blue jeans, and Topsider boat shoes, and he carried a two-suiter and a golf bag, of all things. You had to really be a fanatic to want to play that scruffy course at Ceasaria.

He not only looked the brash American, he sounded it too, careful to not be overly loquacious, yet responding through a bright smile and armed with plenty of "Yups" and "Nopes." He was quite secure in his cover, having used it once to gain access to a TWA baggage repository in Frankfurt. The results of said penetration were still making worldwide headlines.

The choice of the passport was a good one, as Americans were not required to obtain a visa prior to visiting the Holy Land. Upon ordering the document from Horst in Munich, Amar had taken care to specify that the name be decidedly Jewish.

He breezed through passport control, unquestioned by even one of the steely-eyed security agents who stared past him, examining the faces of those travelers who "fit the profile." The GSS men seemed rather jumpy, and the Arab behind him in line was all but strip-searched right there in the terminal.

An attractive female control clerk took his passport, examined it briefly, and stamped it with a metal plunger.

She looked up, compared the photo with his handsome features, and smiled as only the young can smile at that hour.

"Welcome to Israel, Mr. Goldstein," she said warmly.

"Thank you," said Kamil. "It's good to be home."

II

Ramallah

7:00 A.M.

YUSSUF HASSAN WAS NOT REALLY A TERRORIST.

He knew nothing of sabotage and had never fired a weapon. He could not land-navigate or fight with a commando knife. He had never run through the flaming obstacle course near Sidon while gleeful instructors fired Russian rounds at his feet. He could not tell Semtex from Silly Putty, an F–16 from a MIG–23, and he had never attended a seminar at Sanprobal.

In point of fact, even as a boy Yussuf had not participated in anti-Zionist demonstrations. He had never thrown so much as a glass marble at Israeli troops, nor climbed a telephone pole to drape Arafat's flag under the levantine stars. Even on the walls of a distant well house, he had never dared to scribble *Ilyawm Al-Quds, Ghadan Falasteen.*

Yussuf Hassan was first, last, and eternally a musician. As far as acts of terror, his only crimes along those lines

321

would have been the occasional alarming of his neighbor's sheep when he would forget himself and practice his oboe past the midnight hour.

Yussuf lived alone in a small stone house on Sabah Street, at the edge of a huge grove of olive trees. He was a slim, bespectacled, hunched fellow, whose love for music had superseded all attraction to materialism, politics or women. Or perhaps, due to Yussuf's own recognition of his physical detriments, he had found in his beloved instrument an excuse for his social ineptitudes.

For the most part, Yussuf played his oboe in a local classical quartet. Given that the indigenous inhabitants of Ramallah had little appreciation for Stravinsky, the audiences were usually Europeans who soothed their consciences by working in the refugee camps under the auspices of the United Nations Relief and Works Agency. He was not paid for these concerts, though he did manage to gather a few shekels teaching the children of the more cosmopolitan parents in the city. He taught the boys clarinet. To most Palestinian children, the oboe sounded like a dying goat.

Most of Yussuf's money, which had afforded him the opportunity to study music in Amman, came from a small stipend in an East Jerusalem bank. It had been deposited there regularly for nearly ten years, and the young man had almost forgotten why he received it.

Besides his oboe, Yussuf's only apparent obsession was his radio. Had he been fortunate enough to have friends or family, they might have noticed that his bulky, incongruous, portable Aiwa radio-tape only received attention from the hours of seven to eight each morning. No matter what, Yussuf never failed to hear the breakfast broadcast from Radio Al-Quds in Tunis. He did not like the fanatical rantings of the PFLP announcers and could barely stand the whining Arabic ouds and thumping tambours. Yet his addiction to the show seemed borderline religious. On the very few occasions when he had known that he might miss the program—an overnight performance in Hebron, a trip to hear the London Philharmonic in Amman—he had laboriously taped down the Aiwa's record button and carefully affixed a Shabbat light timer that he had bought from a religious Jew in Jerusalem.

On those rare days Yussuf was as nervous as a camel in a snowstorm. Like an obsessive-compulsive worrying over a gas range, he would recheck his mechanical improvisation over and over before leaving his house. However, his fear was justified, for if he missed the program just once on the wrong day, his stipend, his livelihood, and his music would be gone forever. Not to mention his life.

Yussuf was the classic Sleeper—although he would not have recognized that term. He did not know who paid him, nor the full scope of his mission, and for his Master he existed only to perform a single act.

He sat at a small table in the kitchen corner of his salon. Unlike most of his neighbors' homes, his modest two-room house had Western-style furniture, although the chairs, table, dresser and bed were scuffed leftovers donated by his UN admirers. He rejected the notion that to be a true Arab, you had to consume your meals while seated cross-legged on a pile of worn pillows, picking at your bowl with your fingers like a prisoner of war.

He sipped his tea and reread a program from a recent performance of the Israeli Philharmonic. He had not attended the concert himself but had obtained the copy in the same way he came by his furniture. He would have loved to hear Zubin Mehta perform his magic, yet he dared not be seen mingling with the Jews in a grand public forum.

He was trying to keep his tie out of his *khubz* and *zibda* when he suddenly froze, his hot glass lifted halfway to his mouth, his wide eyes fixed on a spot of sun on the far wall.

He had long trained his ears to relegate the annoying utterances of Radio Al-Quds to subliminal background noise, while leaving one small part of his brain alert to that single snippet of music which might set him free from his vigilance. Now, like a messiah whose appearance he never really expected, it was there in the room, and he did not believe it. Slowly, he lowered the glass of tea to the table, not even feeling his scorched fingertips. He dropped the slice of bread to the plate, and he focused his hearing as he turned his head toward the Aiwa.

A large group of men, handsome tenors and basses and baritones he imagined them, perhaps the Yale Glee Club, were singing *We three kings of Orient are.* . . . He blinked at the machine and hardly realized that he was rising to his feet, reaching up to remove his steel-rimmed glasses, cleaning the lenses with his skinny black tie as if his eyes rather than his ears deceived him.

When the music ended, there was a long moment of silence. Yussuf began to think that he had imagined it, that he was actually still in bed and dreaming, until the announcer opened his microphone.

"That was an early holiday greeting from Mr. Theodore Klatch," the voice said in Arabic. "Apparently he likes to begin his Christmas well in advance."

Immediately the station cut to a Pepsi advertisement, the jingle incongruous in its Tunisian accents. That was it. It was over. The song, and a Christmas greeting.

It was mid-August.

Like a farmer wading through a swamp, Yussuf walked slowly to the radio, reached out and switched it off. Then he turned and walked across the room, feet nearly dragging on the worn carpet, to his old black telephone.

He was not hypnotized or brainwashed. He was simply shocked by the wash of relief and the rising heat of fear that clashed in his brain like cold rain striking a blacksmith's forge. His hands appeared before his face like disembodied limbs as they reached for the telephone, and the number popped from his brain as clearly as if it were blinking on the stone wall in orange neon.

He dialed, sure that it would not work. After so many years, it was impossible. The line would be dead, or the number changed. Or, if it did actually ring through, the party would have long since departed.

"Sabaah alkhayr." A deep voice answered almost immediately with a morning greeting.

Yussuf could barely get it out. He felt that he should chat first, maybe establish that he had the right person on the other end. But his instructions were clear, the phrases burned into him like the brand on a Bedouin lamb.

"This is Yussuf," he croaked. Then he cleared his throat. *Allah*, he did not want to have to repeat himself. "I just want to wish you a Merry Christmas, in case I'll be out of town."

There was no response, just silence coursing down the wire. Yussuf hung up.

He began to move more quickly now. He could almost taste his freedom, and he started to fantasize as he hurried through the house. No longer would he be chained to his breakfast table, no longer would he be afraid of fatigue, cold with dread that he might oversleep. Tonight, when he returned, he would smash the hateful Aiwa. So, he would miss a few evening BBC concerts. He would buy another radio-tape. A clean, new, innocent, virgin one.

Beneath the sink in the kitchen nook there was a white metal cabinet. He opened it and behind the battered pots he found a hammer and a stone chisel wrapped in a moldy towel. He took them to his bedroom, and with his meager muscles he hauled on his rickety French closet until it came away from the far corner wall. He pushed it aside with his shoulders, then remembered the front door, ran to lock it and returned.

His hands were shaking as he bent to his task, chipping at the loose cement that held the jagged stone in place. It seemed like an hour until he was finally able to dislodge the rock, and though the morning was cool, the sweat ran through his eyes and dripped off the end of his nose. His glasses were fogged into uselessness, and he folded them into the soggy pocket of his white shirt.

He lifted the long cloth package from the dank hole, and he jumped back as a huge spider ran between his legs. The package fell, clanging dully on the stone floor.

He lifted it again, unwrapping the dusty cloth.

Inside was a short, wide iron tube. One end was splayed, like the bell of his beloved oboe. The middle was encircled with polished wood, also like some alien musical instrument. However, the other end was threaded, two short turns, unlike any woodwind he had ever seen. He did not know what it was, and he did not care.

He replaced the stone and the closet, and he brushed up the chips and the dust. Then, from inside the French doors he removed his precious oboe case and laid it on the bed.

There were many times when he had wanted a new case, for his instrument lay too loosely inside the purple velvet trenches. But the case had been a gift, delivered anonymously long ago, with a note that said he should not divest himself of it. Now, as he extracted the bottom half of his oboe and replaced it with the strange tube, he knew why. The ugly iron pipe lay there as if returning to its womb.

He closed the case and locked it with a small key. Then he laid the homeless bottom half of his instrument on his pillow and draped it with his frayed coverlet.

He left the house quickly, hurrying to catch the bus to

Bethlehem. He felt like he was carrying a cobra, and he wanted to be rid of it before it bit him.

———

Unlike Yussuf Hassan, Tawfik el-Aziz was not a stranger to iron hardware.

His tiny workshop on Wadi el Jadid Street in Hebron looked like the aftermath of an explosion in a toilet factory. Everywhere you looked there were piles of jagged copper tubing, ceramic sink parts, steel faucet handles, and broken bath tiles. The smoke-blackened stone walls were punctured by rows of square-sided cement nails, upon which hung scores of elastic pipe-joint tape, rubber drain stoppers, and greasy plastic washers from wedding-ring to horse-collar sizes.

The workshop had no real windows—just a trio of vent holes made high on the walls with a pickax. Above the steel workbench in the center of the single room, a pair of bare electric bulbs hung under aluminum reflectors, providing harsh yellow projections like the generator lights of a combat field surgery. The air stank of burned acetylene.

When you were inside Tawfik's shop, you could hardly tell day from night, and that was just as well for Tawfik. Being a highly demanded plumber, he was always in his shop by 5:00 A.M., and after his daily house calls, he returned to prepare the next day's replacement parts, often working until midnight. He did not keep a clock in the shop—he needed no reminder that he spent three-quarters of his life soldering, bending and shaping the venues that would carry someone else's shit into the gutters of Hebron. His wife made certain to repeatedly apprise him of his absences. However, she never complained when he handed over his weekly pay.

Tawfik was a bear of a man, his gleaming muscles evidence of years of hammering and hauling. To his friends and neighbors, he could hardly have been regarded as a political animal. He wore heavy boots, work pants and flannel shirts, not even bothering to sport the checkered *kaffieh*s that were the minimal costume of Arab nationalists. In public, he never expressed his militant, anti-Zionist viewpoint. However, at home he made sure that his four young sons knew precisely where he stood as far as the Jews were concerned. The effort paid off, and he was supremely proud when they would come home battered and bruised from rioting against the occupation troops.

Tawfik el-Aziz was his own man, an independent owner of a thriving business, answering to no employer and bound by no schedule. The only constraint in his life, the single undefiable rule, was that he had to be in his shop, every morning, from 7:00 A.M. until 8:15. During that time he could listen to any radio program that pleased him. However, he had to keep the telephone line clear.

He happened to be standing next to it when it rang. Otherwise, he would have had to charge through a thicket of PVC pipes and plastic toilet seats to get to it. He expected the voice of Nabila Um-Khalef, for the old lady kept complaining about a drain that was perfectly functional, if she would just stop mixing *mooz* cakes in the sink.

Unlike Yussuf Hassan—whose name he did not know and whose voice was not familiar—Tawfik was not alarmed by the signal which activated him. As a boy, he had been a brigade runner for the Jordanian Legion. Later, he had begun the initiation into a local cell of the PLO. Yet before he completed the rituals, a senior officer had approached him, suggesting that he could serve The Cause much better by withdrawing from the Resistance. Tawfik was a simple man, but he realized quickly that as a deep-cover "agent," he could go about his business, bound to perform only one or two crucial, patriotic tasks.

The package had been delivered nearly ten years ago. Except for the annoying morning schedule that he was forced to maintain, he would have forgotten about it completely.

He looked at the receiver in his grease-stained hand, then he hung it back on the wall cradle. "Christmas." The voice had said, "Christmas." Well, that was it then. All he had to hear. He clapped his hands together. It was going to be a beautiful, exciting day.

There was a large metal bin at the back of the shop, something like a restaurant's outdoor garbage trolley. It was full to the brim with copper and plastic tubing, which made Tawfik curse. Yet he moved quickly to his task.

It took him almost half an hour to empty the bin. Finally, he had to climb inside to get to the package. The heavy black plastic wrap was covered with drip stains and sour mold, but when he peeled it away the object inside was still sealed in a length of unscathed truck-tire tube. He pulled it off and examined the hidden treasure.

It was a length of black iron pipe, about forty millimeters at the mouth and just over half a meter long. Part of the back end was covered in polished wood. Below the tube, there were two handles, their grips of the same umber wood as the rear of the piece. One handle was smooth and without mechanical additions. The other grip was more like that of a pistol, complete with trigger, guard, and a thumb catch for cocking.

Tawfik was not afraid of the obviously lethal device. He would have been much more alarmed had he found the body of an oboe.

He rewrapped the device and climbed out of the bin, nearly falling on the precarious pile of tubing. He went over to his worktable and pulled his tool box from underneath. Then he lifted out the metal top tray, emptied the lower contents of the box into a burlap sack, and laid the tire-tube package into the bottom of the box. The tray went back in, and he locked the metal catches and left the shop.

Um-Khalef's sink would have to wait.

He hopped into his battered blue VW van, putting the

tool box on the passenger seat floor. As he began to drive north toward Bethlehem, he realized that he had forgotten to make the prescribed telephone call.

"*Ya Ahabal,*" he cursed himself. Well, it was all right. The number was as clear to him as his own birth date.

He began to look for a public telephone.

———

In Jericho, Mustaffa Zuabi lowered himself slowly to the ground. He was wearing a long, gray-and-black striped *jallabieh,* yet he did not lift it away from his knees, for the sharp stones of the Jordan valley had finally begun to discomfort his tired old flesh. With his sandaled feet beneath him, his aching coccyx settled over his heels, he lowered his white *kaffieh*-swathed head and stretched his arms out toward the east, the tip of his regal nose nearly touching the dry earth.

He was not praying. He had done that already. Mustaffa was checking the new seedlings in his watermelon patch.

He turned his face and peered along the arteries of fragile vines that wandered over the coarse earth. Water. More water. There was never enough of it.

Grunting, he placed a hand on one folded knee and levered his body upright. He turned slowly around to the west, and at last he managed a smile. On that side of his small property, the watermelons multiplied like African locusts, growing into long, fat, hard green balloons, which at this stage of his life he could barely lift.

The western grove flourished because the earth there was rich with the spillover from Wadi Kelt, a snaking ravine that cut down to Jericho from the Jerusalem hills and was always sputtering with chilled fresh water. On the other hand, the eastern grove might as well have been in Saudi Arabia. It had to be watered by hand. And it showed.

That was the difference between the Power of *Allah* and the pathetic tribulations of Man.

All right, so he would never be wealthy, the owner of a

sprawling plantation, a *muktar* respected for his business acumen or ability to employ the town's *fellaheen*. He was lucky to have been born in Jericho, an oasis that had flourished for eight thousand years, never subject to destructive droughts, always enviably green.

If they ever managed to be rid of the Jews, it would once again be Eden.

But that would have to be left to the younger men. Mustaffa had fought in '48, and again in '67, yet he was too old for the battlefield now. However, he was not embittered by defeat, for he saw the Israeli presence as temporary, a flea on the massive oxen's rump of Levantine history. The Arab nation possessed a secret weapon unfathomed by any of the Western cultures—*patience*.

All right, so his battles were over. Yet the war was still on, and Mustaffa still had one act to play out. He had waited for it for nearly ten years, and if he lived, he could wait another ten.

He lifted his face and squinted up at Qarantel, the arching monastery at the top of the jagged mountain just south of his home. When the sun was high enough in the east, the stone abutments above the monastery's windows would begin to throw shadows on the metal window bars. As with every morning, when that happened Mustaffa could begin his daily watermelon sales.

"Father!" A voice called from behind, the direction of his house. Sandaled feet padded over the furrowed earth. "Father!"

"*Dir b'alak*. Watch the seedlings," said Mustaffa without turning. Then he mentally shook his weary head.

It was one of his three sons—*Jamil,* by the sound of the voice. When he had chosen the name for the infant, almost eighteen years ago, he could not have imagined that *beautiful* would become the only positive adjective of which his youngest would be worthy. Jamil was handsome all right, striking as a Hashemite king. He was also quite stupid. As a matter of fact, all three of Mustaffa's sons were stupid, a realization which pained the old man much more than his arthritic bones or his fusing spine.

His daughters, however, all six of them, were terribly bright. They all excelled in school, and three of them were well on their way to university degrees, a pursuit which Mustaffa would certainly have forbidden had his sons not been so pathetically hopeless. The boys could barely tell a watermelon from a pomegranate.

I did not pray enough, thought Mustaffa. *I must have offended Allah.*

"What is it?" He spun on Jamil. The boy's beautiful eyes glowed with excitement, his perfect eyebrows arched together like a Druse moustache.

"The telephone rang!"

Mustaffa took a step back. This was truly an event, for none of the Zuabi's friends or relatives had a telephone, and Mustaffa only kept the instrument because he had been told to do so. Except for the occasional wrong number, it almost never quivered in its cradle. Someone else paid the meager bills.

"Are you sure?"

"Yes, Father."

Due to the range of Jamil's IQ, which was somewhat below the level of the Dead Sea, Mustaffa was afraid to ask the next question. But he pressed on.

"Did you answer it, Jamil?"

"Yes, I did, Father!" The boy was now hopping from one foot to the other.

Mustaffa reached out his hands and gripped his son's shoulders to steady him.

"And . . . ?" Mustaffa encouraged the boy, afraid that he might soon forget what had been said.

"A man spoke to me, Father. A Palestinian, this time, I think." The last telephone event had occurred almost a month before. It had been a Jew from the phone company checking the lines.

"What did he say, Jamil?"

"He said . . ." The boy knitted his brows, enjoying the rare paternal attention. "He said, 'Tell the man of the house that I send him good wishes for an early Christmas.'"

Mustaffa stared at his son, not quite believing him.

"Christmas, Jamil? The man said *Christmas?*"

"Yes, Father."

"Did he say anything else?"

"No, Father."

"Are you sure?"

"Yes, Father."

Then Mustaffa did something he had not done since Jamil was a toddler. He reached up and kissed him on the cheek. Then he patted the soft skin.

"You are a good boy, Jamil."

His son was shocked. Tears came to his eyes, almost as if he'd been slapped. A blinding smile overcame his lips.

"Thank you, Father!"

"Yes, Jamil. Now, run and bring me my trowel."

"Your trowel?"

"Quickly!"

Jamil turned and ran toward the house. In a moment he returned with the short tool in one upraised hand, his brothers Abed and Fuad following close behind.

Mustaffa took the tool. He looked at his three sons. Actually, they were all handsome. The combined intelligence of a loaf of pita.

"My sons," Mustaffa said as kindly as he could manage. "There was no telephone call. Do you understand?"

The boys looked at him blankly. They slowly shook their heads, like the fools in an Egyptian comic film.

"You must *pretend* that there was no telephone call. Do you understand me now?"

There was a bit more light in their eyes. They nodded.

"Now, go back in the house, and don't come out until I call for you."

The boys just stood there.

"Go!"

They spun around and ran.

Mustaffa turned back toward the western grove. There were only three trees on his property, gnarled ancient olives. He walked to the first, stepped past it, and then backed up until his painful spine touched the coarse bark.

The other two trees stood about fifty meters away, ten meters apart on a perpendicular line to the first. Mustaffa stretched out his left arm and splayed the fingers of his hand until the tip of his thumb met one tree, and the long nail of his little finger met the other. Then he lowered his middle finger until it pointed to one of his shiny melons. He fixed his eyes on that green orb and began to walk toward it, taking strides as long as his body would allow.

Conquerors could come and go, children were born and soldiers died, but a man's hands and legs remained the same, *Allah Issalmak*.

He counted thirty paces and quickly knelt to the earth, this time ignoring his knees and feeling no pain in his spine.

He dug furiously for a long time, perhaps an hour, and when he was done the top of a long metal crate lay exposed at the bottom of a hole half a meter deep. The surface of the green strongbox had long been encrusted with mineral deposits and rust from years of exposure to the grove's watery roots, but the integrity of the steel appeared intact.

Mustaffa did not expect to be able to lift it from the hole. Instead, he stretched himself out prone at the lip of the fresh crater and scraped with the trowel until the entire lid was unobstructed. Then he used the blade of the tool and pried it open.

There were three long packages in the box. Each one was a many-layered wrapping of the kind of thick clear plastic that the Jews used in their tomato farms. Inside each wrapping there were two olive-green tubes. Of each pair, one of the tubes was simple, like a policeman's truncheon half an arm in length. The other tube was more meaningful, as at one end was an ugly steel head the size of a brass *finjon*. Each head looked like two green cones joined at the mouths, with one point melding with the tube, while the other exposed tip was covered with a flattened protective cap.

Mustaffa rose painfully from the hole. He began to tramp through his grove, selecting three of his largest melons. With his curved *shabriyeh* he freed them from their vines and rolled them over to the open crater.

He hauled the melons into a row, side by side. Then he sheathed the *shabriyeh*, reached inside his robes to the pocket of his pantaloons and came up with a Swiss army knife. He needed a scalpel now, rather than a machete.

He cut the ends off the watermelons, making careful zigzag incisions so that he could later replace the rinds. Then, like a maniacal abortionist, he sliced into the fruits, scooping out long holes with his hands until the ground was littered with pulpy red entrails and his arms were covered in wet black seeds.

A few more slices, some more scooping, some careful pushing and maneuvering, and all three plastic cocoons were hidden inside the melons. Finally, Mustaffa pushed the left-over red meats into the metal box, closed it, and refilled the hole with the fresh piles of earth. He stamped it all down and pulled on some vines until the scar was covered with leafy sinews.

He sat down. His thirst was raging, his *kaffieh* soaked

through, and he took some time to catch his breath. At last, he managed to cry out.

"Jamil."

The boy must have been watching from a window, for he came sprinting from the house. When he reached his father the old man looked up and whispered.

"Mayy baarida."

Jamil sprung back to the house for a jug of cold water. When the old man had finished it, he said, "Bring your brothers."

Jamil sprinted again, this time reappearing with Abed and Fuad.

"Help me up," Mustaffa said to his waiting sons.

They pulled him to his feet, and like an emperor's tailors, they brushed him off and smoothed his robes, cleaned his soiled arms, and brought him a fresh *kaffieh*.

"Today, we will begin to sell in Bethlehem," Mustaffa announced as he straightened his *Jallabieh* and lifted his head high.

"But Father," said Jamil, "we always start in Beit Sachur."

"Bethlehem," said Mustaffa, and as he began to stride toward their Ford pickup, he turned and pointed at the trio of nestled fruits.

"Place those three melons at the bottom of the pile on the truck."

The boys sprang to the melons, heavier now than any such prizes they had ever grown. They lifted them up and staggered after their father, who was striding as he had not done in twenty years, his robes flowing behind him.

He lifted a finger of caution.

"And if you *sell* them," he warned, "I will sell *you*."

12

Jerusalem

That Evening

EYTAN'S PARACHUTE WAS NOT GOING TO OPEN.

Everything was wrong. None of the rapid-fire sequential events that made for a successful deployment were going to occur. That was already too clear. He was stretched out prone, belly to the earth in the frog position with the wind slapping at his coverall, splaying his cheeks across his skull, trying to snap his limbs. He watched his hands out in front of his face, the black leather gloves vibrating in the slipstream.

The pilot chute, a strange, mustard-colored piece of nylon, fluttered and ballooned like a crushed mushroom out in front of his goggles where it definitely did not belong. What the hell was it doing out there? The little chute should already have been high above his head, yanking the deployment bag and the main canopy and then all the guts and risers from his backpack. But the horrible thing just stayed there, flapping like a weighted pennant, while all around him the horizon of green-and-brown earth rose quickly to engulf him like deadly, algae-coated quicksand.

He had never, ever had a main malfunction. And even as his bowels constricted and his breath went hard and raspy he believed with his blind parachutist's faith that it would straighten itself out.

Suddenly the pilot chute snapped above and away, yet even as he heard the familiar rending of the grommet cords and the whip of his pack flaps, Eytan knew it was no good. His descent was not slowed in the least, for instead of the popping of an opening canopy came the thunder of a twisted streamer being hammered by the wind.

The reports of heavy gunfire began to reach him from below, a steady bang that infuriated him and made him want to cry. Couldn't they see that he was going to die anyway? Did they have to try to blow him from the sky with tank cannon?

He tried to stay calm. There was only one chance left and he had to execute the procedure perfectly. But when he looked down to find the red cutaway handle he saw that he was wearing a chest reserve chute, and the ground was rushing toward his boots. Too close! He was already much too close!

He grabbed the reserve handle, turned his head and pulled so hard that he felt the muscles tearing in his shoulder. The reserve chute exploded from his chest, rushing past his eyes as the risers flew across his face and cut his cheeks like a band saw through butter. His goggles flew off and the sound of the big guns was slamming into his ears now as he felt the reserve begin to save him. He jerked his eyes open, and they widened in horror as he saw that he was already passing the blurred tops of the pine trees.

It was too late, and he screamed.

———

Simona was crying. In the hard blue moonlight that slanted through the window, Eytan could see her curled up at the edge of the bed, her arms covering her face.

He looked down. He was sitting upright on the sweat-soaked sheet, the only sounds his wife's whimpers, his own sobbing breath and the blood pounding in his ears. On his lap was a crumpled pillow. A piece of its cloth case was torn away. He looked at his right hand. A ball of the white cotton was clutched in his fist.

He put a hand to his clammy forehead and he squeezed the temples, trying to emerge from the horrid tunnel of his nocturnal subconscious. What day was this? He tried to remember. Yet it was not day, it was nighttime. The night of which day?

Fragments of his free-fall nightmare still jabbed at him from that other world, so he accepted with some relief that his cold fear was merely the product of a dream. Then he began to wonder if, to hope even, that all of his discomfort might be patently unreal. Had he really been in Munich again? In Cyprus? In Cairo? Maybe his confrontation with Ben-Zion and his court-martial and suspension were also merely milliseconds of lucid dream production?

He lay back onto the sheet, cold with his own evaporating sweat. He reached out to the night table and brought the luminous face of his watch close to his eyes. Seven o'clock. It was dark outside. It was seven o'clock at night.

Then he remembered. And he groaned.

Only his death-by-parachute was a dream. The rest of it was as real as the white plaster ceiling above him, and the absurd voice of *Alf* the puppet-alien that filtered through the window from a neighbor's TV set. He realized with a degree of disgust that he had been sleeping since morning—hibernating from the winter of reality.

He had arrived home at dawn, cursing Itzik Ben-Zion,

cursing the Service and cursing Benni Baum for failing to back him up in his hour of need. Major Benni Baum, Eytan's commander and idol, a legend of military brains and brawn, had shattered the IDF's sacrosanct rule: "You never leave a wounded man in the field." Eytan could not soon forgive him for that.

On top of it all, Eytan had braced himself for the onslaught of Simona's justifiable ire. Yet that did not materialize.

He had expected to find her asleep in their bed, but she emerged from the bathroom, pale and shaky, and she threw her arms around his neck and babbled with happiness. Immersed as he was in his own grief and fatigue, Eytan did not at first comprehend why she expressed such joy over an episode of nausea.

"I'm vomiting, Eytan!" she cried. "Do you know why I'm vomiting?"

The news of Simona's pregnancy flooded their reunion with joy, superseding Eytan's exhaustion and relegating his professional troubles almost to the mundane. They embraced and kissed and they danced on the big veranda as the sun rose over the Judean hills. Eytan ate some breakfast and Simona laughed as she scrunched her nose at the smells and sight of food, and Eytan decided that he would not discolor their happiness by revealing details of his latest disasters.

Simona wanted to know what had happened, where he'd been, but he simply promised his wife that he was giving up the *Flute* case forever and planning a new, bold future. He actually had no idea of what the hell he was going to do, but he plastered over his self-doubt with a broad smile. Inwardly, he decided to just hope for the best and guard his home and his family until this whole Kamil thing had blown over.

His fatigue returned full force within the hour. He made Simona promise to take the day off, lock up the house, and not leave for anyone or anything. Then he fell into an abyss

of warrior's sleep. Apparently, sometime during the afternoon, Simona had joined him.

Her back was warm beneath the sheet that covered her,
and it shivered with a quiet sob. Eytan did not understand
why she recoiled when he reached out to stroke her.

"You're crying," he said, assuming that she was already
subject to the emotionalism of hormonal assault.

She sniffed and wiped her nose with a knuckle. "You hit
me."

"What?"

She pushed her hair back from her ear and turned her
head. Her eyes were filled with liquid and she touched her
sore nose.

"You hit me." She looked at him as if he'd struck her
for becoming pregnant.

Then he realized what had happened. He had yanked on
the "reserve handle" of his parachute rig and had probably
smashed her with the back of his fist.

"Ya Allah, motek sheli!" He reached out and cupped her
face, kissing her eyes and whispering, "I'm so sorry, Mona.
I was dreaming."

Simona blinked. Then she smiled and curled an arm
around his neck, kissing him and yelping once as her tender
nose pressed against his cheek.

A hard bang made Eytan jerk his head back. He sat
straight up and Simona started, putting her hands up to her
face in fright. "What is it?"

"Shh!" Eytan's heart was racing again. The "artillery"
from the landing zone in his dream. It was a violent pounding
on their front door from the floor below. Slam! It came again,
the big wooden door rattling against its jamb.

He rolled from the bed and landed on the cold tile floor,
crouching as he focused his hearing. He squatted there for a
moment on the balls of his bare feet, then he reached out

slowly and slid open the night-table drawer. He found the steel of his Browning and lifted the pistol into his hand.

Slam! He quickly found his underpants and slipped into them, for he knew that he could not do battle with his naked balls swinging exposed. The rest happened instinctively, and he moved swiftly and quietly despite a knee as stiff as a rigored corpse. He cocked the pistol and then let the snout of the barrel emerge first, clearing the bedroom door, then the upstairs landing, then the curved, darkened stairway down to the salon.

All right, he thought, *so it's going to end right here, right now. He is here. No ambush, no stealth, no surprise. Goddamn them all, no one believed him.* Kamil was at his front door— simple as that. But the bastard would not get Simona, or their baby.

Slam! The front door shook with a hammering fist from the hallway. Eytan had the advantage. It was pitch-dark inside the house, and the hallway was fiercely lit. He backed up next to the door, pistol in his right hand. He reached out with his left and turned the key hard, clockwise, leaving only the flip handle between himself and the final encounter.

He stepped back and gripped the Browning two-handed. For a moment nothing happened. Then the door handle dropped and the slab of wood swung into the room.

Eytan lunged into the opening and jammed the pistol between Benni Baum's eyes.

Neither of the men moved. Eytan's breath was coming in ragged gasps. Baum just stood still, looking calmly over the iron sights, until Eytan finally lowered the pistol toward the floor.

"I thought you might be sleeping," said Baum.

Eytan could not yet speak. The adrenaline in his veins kept his arms locked and stiff as birch branches. Benni reached out slowly and laid a palm over the slide of the Browning, slipping a thumb between the cocked hammer and the firing pin.

"Did you really think that I would leave you 'in the field'?" Benni asked with some hurt in his tone.

Eytan stared at the major, feeling suddenly ashamed. Beyond Benni's shoulder, up on the next landing of the hall stairs, he saw the alarmed visage of a white-haired old lady peering from her apartment doorway. He forced a weak smile and found his voice.

"It's all right, Mrs. Dubinsky," he said. "I thought it was a burglar."

The old woman returned a skeptical nod, yet she retreated and closed the door.

Eytan backed into his apartment and Baum followed, his hand still on the pistol as he closed the door with his foot. Eytan said, "It's okay," and as Baum released his grip Eytan managed to release the magazine into his left hand. He pushed the slide back and Benni caught the ejecting round in midair.

Baum found the light switch, bathing the salon in a harsh yellow glow. He could see how frightened Eckstein had been, for the captain's skin was slick with sweat and his limbs shivered despite the warm evening air. He did not bother to apologize.

"You look like you're ready for battle," Benni said.

Eytan slowly shook his head. He backed up and sat down on the coffee table, knocking over an empty glass. He put his arms on his knees and dangled the pistol between his legs.

"I almost killed you."

Baum shrugged. "Unintentionally, I would hope." Eytan did not respond to the humor. "So," said Benni. "What's the answer?"

"To what?" Eytan looked confused.

"Are you ready for battle?"

"Am *I* ready?" His tone was somewhat accusatory.

"I would think, after all these years," said Baum, "that you realized that my silence in that fool's office was not the result of some newly acquired shyness."

"Then what was it?"

"Strategy, of course."

"I see," said Eytan. He rose from the table. "Benni, I'm tired."

"So am I. You just slept too much."

"I have other considerations now," said Eytan.

"I'm pregnant, Benni." Simona's voice surprised Baum. She was standing at the top of the staircase, looking sexy in a white silk robe, her black hair wild around her face. She must have been quite frightened by the episode, but she could not help smiling as she relayed her news.

"Mazal tov!" Baum slapped his palms together and danced a little jig. *"Kol hakavod!* It's about time. I thought I'd never be a godfather!"

Eytan could not help smiling. "Pretty presumptuous of you, Baum."

"I'm an arrogant bastard," Benni said. "It's wonderful. Quick, darling." He pointed at Simona. "Some wine. We have to drink *L'Chaim.*"

Simona obeyed gladly, bounding down the stairs and into the kitchen. Benni looked at Eytan. "It's all the more reason," he said.

"For what?"

"You can't quit now."

"I've pretty much been fired, Benni."

"Not by me."

Simona appeared with a bottle and three glasses.

"Darling," said Baum as he took the bottle and began to peel the seal. "Eytan is involved in a crucial case. With your permission, he must carry it through. It cannot succeed without him."

Baum did not wait for a response. He began to fill the glasses.

"You don't need me," said Eytan.

"That's a lie," Baum said to Simona, not even looking at Eytan. "Simona, this is so important, so vital, that I need your approval to work here with Eytan. Outside the office, in absolute security."

Eytan did not know what Baum had in mind, but he found himself unable to resist his own obsession. And Simona, knowing that Eytan's need to serve was the essence of his being, found herself compelled to give her assent.

The two men waited while she looked from one to the other. She sighed.

"Well, as usual, I have no idea what it's about. But if it's important, I have to say yes, Eytan." She turned to Baum. "The rest is up to my husband, Benni."

More than halfway home now, Baum turned on his captain. "If you can say no to this, then let's see you do it." He was actually grinning at Eytan, like a devil making a pitch for a soul. Eckstein smiled weakly in return.

"Okay, major. For the last time. I volunteer."

"Good!" Baum boomed. "But wait." He put out a hand to stop Eytan from raising the wine to his lips. "We'll need more glasses." He strode to the apartment door, pulled it open, put two fingers into his mouth and made a single shriek as loud as a police whistle. While Simona and Eytan watched, Benni stepped back and held the door like a butler at a soiree.

After a moment, footsteps began to quicken up the three flights of stairs. First into the apartment was Yablokovsky, the tall, bespectacled computer whiz from Research and Investigation. Yablo was dressed in a T-shirt, shorts and sandals, and he carried a hard black plastic case in one hand and had a heavy gym bag slung from one shoulder. He looked at

Simona and then shyly turned his gaze away, saying, *"Erev tov,"* to Eytan as he set his equipment on the floor.

"The windows," Benni said to Yablo, and the young man moved quickly to lower the slat blinds throughout the large salon. As he did so, he kept stealing glances at the mussed blond spikes on Eytan's head that had replaced his normal haircut.

Horse appeared next, breathing heavily as he hauled in two file cases that looked to weigh as much as he did. He sat down on one of the cases and wiped his bald head with a handkerchief, not bothering to greet anyone in the room.

Sylvia, the old matron from Ciphers, had to stop in the doorway and steady herself. She was smoking a cigarette and she croaked, "We can build fighter planes but we can't make a goddamn decent elevator."

Danny Romano pushed past her, grinning over his pipe stem. He was carrying only a light briefcase, and he winked at Simona as he stepped inside.

Eytan thought that his eyes could not open wider, yet they bulged considerably at the appearance of Uri Badash, the Shabak agent. The convening of a renegade AMAN operation was risky enough, but involving other agencies seemed like borderline treason. Badash saw Eytan's look and just shrugged, jerking a thumb at Baum as if the major had somehow blackmailed him into participating.

A man whom Eytan did not know appeared in the doorway. He was tall and broad-shouldered, somewhat stout yet powerful-looking. He wore a black golf shirt, tan chinos and white Nikes. He was around forty, with a tousle of curly brown hair that crawled over his collar. Despite the hour, he wore large pilot's sunglasses, though they could hardly have concealed his features. He hesitated in the doorway, until Baum said, in English, "Come in, Arthur. Come in," as he waved him inside.

Finally, Danny Romano's secretary appeared. Yudit

looked somewhat nervous, probably more so at the idea of entering Eytan Eckstein's home than at participating in this questionable project. She was dressed in a modest skirt and blouse, and she made a point of locating Simona and smiling broadly at her. When she realized that Eytan was standing there in his underwear, she blushed and looked away.

Benni pulled her inside and shut the door. He rubbed his hands together and strode to the middle of the room, then he motioned with his arms for everyone to gather in close. They set down their equipment, briefs and files and crowded together so he would not have to raise his voice.

"Tov, chevrey," Benni began. Then he turned to the burly stranger of the group and said, in English, "Excuse the Hebrew, Arthur. This is a legal formality that should not worry the CIA." Arthur nodded, and Benni continued on in Hebrew as the group eyed the American with some surprise.

"I am commencing this operation under Article IV of the 1956 Security Laws of the State of Israel, permitting unilateral initiation of a secure mission by a senior intelligence officer, myself, and my second-in-command, Eytan Eckstein." He looked over at Eytan, who just watched the performance with amazement. "I am ordering full compartmentalization as deemed necessary for the security of this operation. No details shall be revealed to fellow employees of any body, nor shall approval of VARASH, the Committee of the Heads of the Services, be sought until I determine such necessity. Are we clear?"

Benni looked around. All heads were angled toward him to hear his low tones, and no one expressed surprise or consternation.

"I might remind you, as volunteers," he continued, "that as the old saying goes, 'Success has many fathers, while Failure is a lonely orphan.' All those who wish to withdraw may do so within the next thirty seconds."

Then he looked down at his watch, following the sweep

second hand without raising his eyes, until half a minute of silence had elapsed.

"Good!" He clapped his hands together. "Now, speaking of fathers, I have just discovered that Eckstein here will be one in less than nine months!" He slapped a palm onto Eckstein's naked shoulder. To the accompaniment of some congratulatory whoops and shouts, Benni asked Yudit to help Simona round up a sufficient number of glasses from the kitchen.

When the wine was poured, and as ten mismatched glasses converged to clink together, Baum made his toast.

"To the 'new' Eckstein. And to the success of *Operation Flute*. *L'Chaim*."

———

By the time Eytan emerged from a cursory shower, his home had already been transformed into a bustling satellite of AMAN's Special Operations. Wearing blue jeans and a grey T-shirt, he walked barefoot along the second-floor landing as he toweled off his hair. The bedroom telephone had been pulled into the hallway, its white wire taped down to the old carpet and its handset also secured to the cradle with silver duct tape, to prevent anyone from disturbing the communications link. A second black wire continued from the telephone and along the floor to Eytan's study at the far corner of the flat. He followed it and poked his head into the office.

Horse and Sylvia did not even look up. The small bald man had cleared Eytan's desk and set up a portable fax machine. He was busy setting a fresh roll of paper into the platen. Sylvia had pulled a chair up to the fold-out guest couch, where she was laying out the intercept files that came from Horse's massive "accountant" cases. The intercepts were all decodes and translations on thick stacks of folded, perforated computer paper. They were color-coded, each according to its source—foreign embassy, overseas illegal intercept, local telephone land line, satellite transmission.

Eytan wondered what bluff Baum had used to get twenty kilograms of top-secret material out of the building. He stepped quietly over to the iron railing of his second-floor landing and looked down. Baum was seated directly below at the round common table, his great bald head looking like a science model of the planet Mars, replete with sunburned patches and meandering scars. Typical of Benni, he had no paperwork spread out beneath his meaty hands. He was keeping the table cleared for the landing of steaming coffee cups, melon slices, cakes and whatever else Simona might concoct.

Eytan smiled. Baum was sticking his neck way, way out on this one, and again Eytan chastised himself for his temporary lapse of trust. Just after the toast, Benni had taken his arm and escorted him up the stairs, suggesting a refreshing shower before beginning work. It was simply an excuse to get Eytan alone.

"Just listen to me, Eytan, because there isn't much time," Baum had said as he turned on the shower taps and closed the bathroom door. "When Pearlman had his accident in New York, I didn't think much of it. But when Samal died, I got on your 'frequency.'" He held the bath curtain open. "Go ahead, get in." Eytan stepped out of his underwear and welcomed the spray of hot water. Baum poked his head inside the curtain, ignoring the residual spray that beaded on his rotunda. "I started putting this thing together right there and then, but I didn't tell you in case I couldn't muster the support. Then I turned around, and you were off to Europe." He scratched his head and laughed. "That was a crazy move, Eytan, but it did the trick. I hope you understand that I couldn't back you up in Itzik's office. It would have tipped him off."

"You *not* backing me might have tipped him off."

"No chance. His ego is too enormous."

"Who's the American?"

349

"Arthur's the deputy CIA station chief over at the U.S. consulate on Nablus Road."

"So what the hell is he doing here?"

"He's a good man, I've known him for a long time and he has a double motive. First, he's pissed off because of his government's impotence on the TWA 206 case."

"And second?"

"Second, a close friend of his was a case officer at the U.S. embassy in Frankfurt. He was coming home for Christmas, on Flight 206. Arthur wants Kamil, too."

"Now there's a motive I can understand," said Eytan grimly as he rinsed himself of soap.

"I'm going to call in every favor I can," said Benni. "It's about noon in Washington. Even later in Europe. We'll have to work fast, and we'll work all night."

"What do you expect to get?"

"Just enough to prove our case when the shit hits the fan, Eytan. Not a miracle—just a little *mazal* and one break. That's all we need. Now dry off and come on down."

Eytan looked out across his salon. The main telephone line had been stretched across the room to the low pass-through that accessed the dining room. The wire had been spliced through a switch box, so that the phone would still ring, while a secondary line ran to a modem on the dining table. Yablokovsky was in there, hooking up a portable GRID computer. Yudit was setting up behind a portable electric typewriter.

In the middle of the salon, Danny Romano and Arthur the American were working over a powerful cellular telephone set. Romano chewed enthusiastically on his empty pipe stem while Arthur screwed a large antenna into the base unit. They appeared to have hit it off, having discovered some mutual history. They were conversing in a Sicilian dialect.

Over by the television set on the far wall unit, Uri Badash

was busy unhooking the roof aerial and effecting a connection to a powerful field radio—a modified AN PRC unit which he usually used in his car to contact security units around the country.

Eytan dropped his towel on the railing and came down the stairs. He joined Benni at the round table and poured himself a cup of coffee. Already the room was beginning to go blue with cigarette smoke.

"Are you clean?" Baum asked as Eytan sat down.

"As a virgin bride."

"Now, I've already taken the liberty of handing out assignments."

"Brief me."

"Basically, we're putting out requests to personal contacts at CIA, MI6, Scotland Yard and SDECE."

"Asking for?"

"Updated information on all recent Kamil sightings, or even speculations."

"The sightings will come up negative."

"Probably."

"Why do we need speculations?" Eytan asked.

"To cover our bare asses. We'll keep the ones that match our theories and throw the rest out."

"Very bureaucratic of you, Benni."

"Don't insult me, boy."

From the dining room, Yudit's electronic typewriter began to clack.

"What's she doing?" Eytan asked.

"Keeping the record."

"More ass-covering?"

Benni wagged a finger at Eytan. "Extreme bravery should always be based on meticulous preparation."

"Okay," said Eytan impatiently. "What else?"

"Listen," Baum instructed as he pointed at Danny and

Arthur. The CIA agent was sitting on the couch, pressing the cellular handset to his ear.

"Jerry? Hey, buddy. It's Art. Got anything for me yet?" The American waited for a moment. The connection must have been weak, for he inserted a finger in his free ear. "Okay, pal. Soon as you can, call me back at—" He leaned over the base module. "Oh-two, five, five, niner, zero, one, niner. Roger that. Out."

"He's talking to CIA station in New York," said Benni. "They're working on Zvi Pearlman's case."

At that moment, Arthur got up from the couch and walked over to the table. Eytan stood up to offer his hand.

"Art Roselli," said the American. His grip was calloused and powerful.

"Friendly cover name," Eytan grinned as he switched to English. "Eytan Eckstein."

"My pleasure," said Roselli. He examined Eytan's blond hair, light eyes and European features. "You don't *look* Israeli," he said.

"You don't *look* like a spook," said Eytan.

Roselli laughed and clapped Eytan on the shoulder. He grew serious for a moment.

"I want this bastard, too, Eytan."

"I know you do," said Eytan. "We all do."

Arthur turned to Benni. "Well, Baum. It'll be a while. What else can I do?"

Baum looked up at the American and rubbed his jaw.

"Look, Arthur. I don't want you to get burned. But we could use Langley's latest pickups on anything related to Kamil or TWA 206. Even seemingly unconnected intercepts. Can you do that?"

Arthur smiled. "Can Special Forces kick ass?" He had been a Green Beret in the early days of Vietnam. He turned and walked back to his phone.

Yablokovsky came out of the dining room, cleaning his glasses with his T-shirt. He was tall and bony, looking like he played too much basketball and didn't eat enough. His hair was mussed and stuck up all around his head like untrimmed grass.

"Okay, Benni. I can talk to Paris," he said proudly.

"Fine, Yablo, but very careful now." Benni continued, "First, ask for an Eyes Only contact with Pierre Chandesais. When you have him, call me."

Yablokovsky walked back into the dining room and sat down at his GRID.

"What's he using?" Eytan asked.

"Telex software."

Simona came out of the kitchen. She had brushed her hair and changed into jeans and one of Eytan's shirts. Eytan smiled at her, wondering what she would look like all bloated and waddling.

"Can I do something other than cook?" she asked.

"Apparently so," said Benni and he gestured at her stomach.

"No, really." Having worked in the Hole at General Headquarters during her army service, Simona was used to the atmosphere of feverish operations. Actually, she was somewhat enjoying the nostalgic feelings brought on by having her house commandeered.

"As a matter of fact," Eytan said, then he turned to Baum. "Is the phone working?"

"Yes."

"Mona," Eytan said. "We don't want any surprise visitors."

"Oh!" She put a hand up to her mouth. "That's a real possibility. Especially with our recent news."

"You'd better call everyone around who might just pop on over tonight. Yael, Shlomi and Lisa. And your folks. Tell them everything's okay, but you're feeling lousy and you're going to bed."

"Good idea," said Baum.

"And not too far from the truth," Simona said as she touched her stomach. She pulled a chair over to the dining room pass-through, picked up the phone, and began to dial.

"Shhh!" Benni hushed everyone in the room as he gestured toward Simona.

Eytan leaned toward Baum and whispered, "What's on upstairs?"

"Horse is handling MI6. Sylvia's got her work cut out for her. She has a week's worth of intercepts, the routine red flags marked by Tel Aviv for investigation."

"It'll take her all night."

"So what? She's not going dancing."

Uri Badash walked over from his radio set and sat down at the table. He poured a cup of coffee and lit a cigarette. "Well, can't do much more. Every border unit and investigation team has been ordered to report to me with details of all male detainees. I couldn't give them much to go on. I just said males, not necessarily Arabs, between thirty and forty years old, 180 centimeters in height."

"Thanks, Uri," said Eytan.

"Anything to fuck your commander, my friend."

"We don't need to fuck him," said Benni. "We just want to go around him."

"Then leave the fucking to us," said Badash with a malevolent grin.

Simona finished her last call and came slowly over to the table. She was holding her forehead.

"I didn't have to do much acting," she said. "I think I'll throw up, just for fun, and go to bed."

Eytan began to rise, but Yudit came out of the dining room and took Simona's elbow. "I'll help her," she said.

"You're a sweetheart," said Baum. "When you're done, Yudit, canvass everyone and update your files."

Simona kissed Eytan on the head and the two women went up the stairs.

The cellular telephone rang with an electronic burbling. Arthur answered, said a few cursory thank yous, and hung up.

"Ninth Precinct in New York says Pearlman's death was hundred-percent accident," Arthur said with some apology. "And my office has checked out the driver, up, down, and sideways."

"Okay." Eytan gave the CIA man a thumbs-up. Kamil may have had nothing to do with 'Harry Webber's' death, but to Eytan it was as if Zvika's final act—stepping out in front of an errant taxi—had been a warning to his compatriots of an oncoming storm.

"I've got Chendesais," said Yablo from the dining room.

"Tell him Hans-Dieter Schmidt would like to discuss an old matter in private," said Benni.

"*Ruth,*" said Yablo, using the Israeli Army radio term for *Roger*.

Horse came bounding down the stairs, which amazed Eytan, for he had never seen the little man even walk quickly, let alone scamper. He was rubbing his hands together.

"We're going to get a description!" he announced.

"What?" said Eytan.

"MI6 has been 'loaned' the Scotland Yard file on the murders of Samal and the Indian store clerk. Apparently a bus driver gave a description of a man who accompanied Serge into Kensington. Three days ago, they took that sketch around to every hotel in London. A pension clerk recognized it and filled in the rest of the detail. The sketch'll be faxed to me within thirty minutes."

"*Mitzooyan, Soos!*" Benni stood up and pinched his little

355

brainstormer on the cheek. "Fabulous. Get back up there."
Horse turned and trotted back to his post.

The joy was temporary, as Yablo reappeared wearing a
hangdog look.

"No go, Benni. Pierre Chendesais says he can't end-run
any information around your commander. Apparently his
C.O. and Ben-Zion party together in Paris on a regular basis.
Their fathers were together at Suez in '56. Says it's too risky."

"Damn!" Benni slammed the table.

Danny Romano ambled over. "Fucking French," he said
as he tapped his cold pipe. "Want to let me have a go at the
Italians?"

"Negative," said Eytan. "No offense. They look beautiful
but they're full of holes."

"No argument," said Romano.

"Excuse me," said Art Roselli. "Give it to me in English.
Maybe I can help."

"Arthur," said Benni. "The French won't cooperate with
us."

"What a surprise," said Arthur. "Fucking Frogs."

"*Securité* is usually okay with us," said Eytan. "But we're
asking for sub-channel stuff."

Roselli ran his fingers through his curly hair. "Why don't
you let me try them via Langley? I'll false-flag the request."
He meant that he would disguise the inquiry as a purely
American one.

Uri Badash looked up at him with surprise. "Now you're
thinking like an Israeli," he said.

"Too much falafel," said the CIA man as he returned to
his telephone.

Uri Badash's field radio hissed. He had the speaker on
very low volume, so he walked over to the set to receive the
communication.

In less than half an hour, Horse came springing down

the stairs again, holding a piece of fax paper in his hand as gently as a butterfly wing. He lay the sheet on the table and everyone gathered to examine it.

It was a standard police sketch—well executed but aesthetically wanting. The best-remembered features were emphasized, the curly hair, strong jaw, slim nose and narrowed eyes. The image caused all the men to furrow their brows, for something about the face jogged synapses of memory. Yet gradually, one after another, they all shook their heads.

"Looks familiar," said Uri Badash. "But not from any of the Shabak files."

"Yes," said Baum as he held his chin and studied the fax.

Eytan released an exasperated sigh. "It's no Amar Kamil I've ever seen. Not that I'd expect it to be."

"You have another page," Sylvia's voice croaked from the landing above. Horse ran back upstairs and returned with the second transmission.

"It's the description on color and details," he said. Then he read the English. "Hair: red-blond. Eyes: green. Skin: ruddy with some freckling. Curved, one-inch scar beneath right occipital."

As Baum listened to Horse he picked up a pencil. The fax of the sketch had come over somewhat smudged, as such transmissions are wont to do. With the lead point he drew in a curved line just beneath the right eye.

"*Ya Allah,*" Uri Badash whispered. "That can't be." He lifted his head and took a step back.

"What is it, Uri?" Eytan demanded.

"That's Rami Carrera," the GSS agent whispered.

"Who?" said Benni.

"I swear, that's Rami Carrera. He's a major with Planning and Logistics."

"*What?*" Romano's usually cool demeanor was punctured by his own gasp.

"He's an advisor to the PM," said Badash. "I see him all the time, whenever I'm checking out our team at the Knesset."

Eytan snatched the sketch from the table and stared at it. Years back, when he was an officer candidate, Rami Carrera had been a staffer at Training Base One. "It sure as hell *looks* like Rami Carrera," he said.

Benni took the sketch. "I would say you are all out of your minds, if I did not also have a memory for faces. But what is Carrera's face doing on this transmission?"

"Shall I cite precedents?" Horse had taken a seat and was eating a piece of Simona's coffee cake. He slurped from a glass of tea.

"What did you say, *Soos*?" asked Benni.

"Do you want me to cite historical precedents for agent-doubles posing as other individuals? Plastic surgery is no longer just a science, you know. In Switzerland, it's an art. There's the Oswald case—still speculation, of course. There's Beckman in Germany, and that remarkable Degaulle double in the sixties. Then—"

"Cut to the chase, Horse," said Eytan.

"Well," said Horse as he picked some crumbs from his shirt. "If *I* were inserting a man into your military environment, I'd double him as one of your officers. Of course, I'd have to eliminate the original. . . ."

"Yudit!" Baum yelled. The girl came scrambling out of the dining room. "Drop what you're doing. I need a photograph. Take my car and go to the office."

"Wait," said Eytan. "Change that, Yudit. Stay away from H.Q. Go to Beit Agron, the Government Press Office. Tell them you need a photo of Major Rami Carrera. Tell them he's being promoted or something. Don't use your ID card unless you have to, and get it back here in half an hour."

"Major Rami Carrera," said Yudit.

"Yes. Go."

She stepped quickly out the door.

"I'll get a team to Carrera," said Uri and he made for his radio.

"Yes," said Baum.

"No, wait." Eytan gripped Baum's arm and shot him a look. "Uri, we can't risk that yet. We might blow it. Let's wait till we fax the Brits our own picture for confirmation."

"I can't wait on this, Eytan," said Uri.

"Please. Just for a while. But in the meantime you can have your office check Carrera's recent movements. If he's been anywhere outside the country. Just in case."

"Okay," Badash relented.

Benni gave Eytan a quizzical look. Eckstein just turned the fingers of his left hand upward and touched them together in the Israeli gesture that demands patience.

During the next half hour, twenty cigarettes died and a liter of coffee was consumed, but nothing of significance transpired.

Before Yudit returned, Sylvia made her first appearance since secluding herself with her intercept transcripts. She limped slowly down the stairs, for her arthritis was flaring and her lungs were as black as a coal miner's. She was holding a single sheet of yellow computer paper.

"Well," she croaked. "There's only one piece of any interest." Then she looked at the round table, the ravaged cups and saucers. "What's the matter? You can't bring an old woman something to eat?"

"What do you have, mother?" Baum asked impatiently.

Sylvia hacked for a moment. "We have one item of some interest, a pickup from the PFLP station in Tunis. It was an intercept of a telephone request to the station, in French. Courtesy of Mossad, I might add."

"*Nu?*" Eytan tried not to scream at her.

"A Mr. Theodore Klatch requested that the station

broadcast a Christmas carol, on three mornings running. The song was 'We Three Kings.'"

"So what's so strange about that?" Uri Badash asked.

"It's not even September yet," Sylvia scoffed. "Policemen," she added as if spotting a cockroach.

On hearing the song title in English, Arthur rose from his post by the cellular and came over to the table. "May I ask?" he said.

"It's a wild card, as you might call it," Baum told him. "Possibly a coded message. A song called 'We Three Kings.'"

"I could send someone to the American Cultural Center to get a copy," Eytan suggested.

Sorelli saved him the trouble. He began to sing slowly in a deep, pleasant baritone.

"We three kings of Orient are, bearing gifts we've traversed afar. . . .'"

"Yablo," Benni called. "Arthur will dictate a lyric to you in English. See what you can do with it."

Sorelli joined Yablo at his GRID.

There was a soft knock at the door. Benni rose and doused the lights while everyone else froze. Eytan checked the peephole and admitted Yudit, then flipped the lights back on. She proudly handed over a black-and-white glossy of Rami Carrera, and Horse ran with it to fax London before it was too late.

"Just the face!" Benni called. "Cover the uniform!"

Yablo printed out five copies of "We Three Kings" on a small dot matrix and handed them out. Then he hunched to his machine and began trying to break the possible cipher.

Arthur's telephone rang. He answered it, listened for a while, then he covered the mouthpiece and spoke to Benni.

"It's my boy in Virginia. We duped the Frogs, but they really don't have anything. However, Vienna station does have one item of possible interest, but they can't give it to us over an open line."

Baum thought for a moment. "Can he telex?"

"Hold on." Arthur turned back to the phone. "Can you telex it? Come on, Chuck, just give it to me in a simple One-Time. I don't know, use your imagination for Christ's sake."

Benni snapped his fingers and Yablo wrote his GRID modem number on a pad and handed it to Arthur.

"Yeah, now you're cookin'!" Roselli said into his phone; then he recited the number for his co-worker in Virginia. "Encode it and send."

Yablo switched back to his telex software, and after twenty long minutes a paragraph of gibberish appeared on his screen. Arthur was pacing next to Yablo's computer.

"All right," said the American. "It's like this. My boy says, 'Back up the value of the last digit when Boston won the Pennant.' That was 1975, so take each letter and back through the alphabet by a value of five."

Yablo saved the gibberish to disk and loaded a word-processing program. Then he pulled the enciphered message onto the screen, typed out the English alphabet, and wrote a simple macro that would take each letter of the message and replace it with the proper value.

After a few minutes, he handed Arthur a printout. Roselli smiled as he read the decoded transmission aloud.

HI ARTY. FUCK YOU. MARK THIS. RECENT INTERCEPT VIENNA STATION OF PHONE CALL TO MOTHER.

"That's the Russians," Arthur interjected.

CALL INITIATOR, MAJOR V. KOZOV, FOR-EIGN AGENT RUNNER DEPARTMENT VIII. CALL RECIPIENT, COLONEL I. STEPNIN. RELEVANT QUOTE: "HE CAN'T LAST LONG WITH THAT FACE. THEY WILL EITHER PROMOTE HIM OR KILL HIM." END OF SHAREABLE INFO. HAVE A NICE DAY.

Arthur lowered his paper. Benni and Eytan stared at each other.

Uri Badash responded to the crackle of his radio and picked up the handset. He signed off and spoke to the room.

"Rami Carrera has not been out of the country in eight months."

Horse appeared above them, leaning over the railing. He was also holding a piece of paper, but he did not need to read from it.

"MI6 responds to our fax of the photograph. That's him. That's the killer."

It was no easy task convincing Uri Badash to leave Rami Carrera alone. The Shabak agent did not believe that Carrera was a double or a mole, but he wanted to pick him up for questioning just the same.

Benni and Eytan stalled him, calling a break in operations while they went upstairs and out onto the veranda off Eytan's study, where they conferred quietly in the eerie silence of postmidnight Jerusalem. Then they asked Badash to join them.

They begged him to do nothing about Carrera until after 7:00 A.M., at which time he would be free to act as he saw fit. In the meantime, they asked him to accomplish another difficult mission.

Benni explained that a prisoner in Atlit might still hold the key to the Kamil case. He wanted George Mahsoud transferred to the Russian Compound in Jerusalem, and only a GSS man of Badash's rank could effect such a transfer. And he would have to do so in person.

Badash reluctantly agreed, not bothering to disguise his skepticism.

"This had better not be a wild-goose chase, Baum," he said as he packed up his communications gear.

"I promise to invite you for dinner when the goose is cooked," said Eytan.

As no more pertinent intelligence was forthcoming from any contacts, Benni ordered one and all to work on the "We Three Kings" code. They did so until it was after 3:00 A.M. and everyone was thoroughly drained. They produced a lot of gibberish and some interesting poetry, but nothing of operational value.

Finally, Baum gathered them all together in the salon.

"Okay," he said. "Fine work. Wrap it up and sweep it. Don't leave a scrap. Go home, get some sleep and keep your mouths shut."

One by one, the agents and analysts left the apartment. Arthur shook hands all around, sorry that he could not join them for the remainder of developments. He was promised a discreet postoperation briefing by Baum.

Danny Romano was the last to leave. In the doorway, he turned to Benni and Eytan.

"And what are you two up to now?"

"A few hours' rest, we hope," Eytan answered.

"Sure." Romano smiled over his pipe stem and left.

Alone now in the apartment—except for Simona, who had slept peacefully through all of the ruckus—Benni and Eytan put up a fresh pot of coffee.

Sleep was a luxury they would have to forswear.

It was just another beautiful summer morning in Jerusalem. The violet sky was paling to a robin's-egg blue, the air was still cool and dry with the desert night, the branches of the trees were heavy with dew-dampened leaves and dancing starlings.

In the northern hilltop suburb of Ramat Eshkol, Major Rami Carrera stepped out from his quaint stone cottage. As usual, he was wearing a crisply ironed dress uniform, his black combat boots highly polished, his black beret tucked under his left epaulet and his Ray Bans perched in his curly red-blond hair. The Jerusalem summer had brought out the freckles on both sides of his slim nose, and the stretched tissue of the curved scar below his right eye—souvenir of a near-fatal jeep accident—was burned to an even deeper red than usual.

Major Carrera carried the usual pile of rolled-up maps under his left arm, and with his right hand he jauntily swung the leather briefcase that never left his side. He stopped as he often did, to take in the fresh scent of Jerusalem pine. Then, once more thanking his lucky stars for his career-making posting to the Knesset, he marched down his slate walkway, opened his wrought-iron gate and headed toward his parked Ford Escort.

Carrera stopped short as two men emerged from another parked car and blocked his way. They were both in uniform, wearing officers' field ranks. He could not see their eyes for their sunglasses, but they were polite as they showed him ID cards designating them as IDF Field Security agents.

The men asked him to confirm that he was indeed Major Rami Carrera, Planning and Logistics. Carrera produced his own ID, and the two men informed him that they had been instructed to escort him immediately to General Headquarters in Tel Aviv. When Carrera asked the reason for the summons, the men replied in typically cryptic fashion, "This is a matter of national security," and they produced a typewritten order on army letterhead.

Carrera wanted to take his own car. The agents politely declined his request, and he reluctantly joined them in their vehicle, which promptly sped off out of Ramat Eshkol. Yet the car made a left turn on Sderot Eshkol, instead of a right, which should have been evidence enough. . . .

The men were not simple Field Security officers.

And Rami Carrera was certainly not headed for Tel Aviv.

13

Bethlehem

AMAR KAMIL WAS ALMOST HOME.

Through the swirling dust of an Israeli army convoy he could see the church steeples, domed mosques and minarets of his city of birth. The shining stone structures shimmered in the distance, poking through a long swatch of filigree cloud that was part morning fog and part residue from a dying Negev storm.

The army convoy stretched for a full kilometer along the Hebron road, dipping into a shallow bowl of scattered shops and houses before rising toward the city. Amar had no other choice but to wait his turn, for the customary Israeli roadblocks were out in force and there would be no skirting the issue. Still, the image of the city seemed to float in the morning air like a mirage from an Arabian fable, and Amar feared against all logic that it might suddenly disappear.

For years he had trained himself to ignore emotion, scorn

longing and repress love. Yet as he sat behind the wheel of the car and stared out into the bright morning, he could feel his heart begin to swell within his breast.

It had been twenty years.

The line of vehicles began to move more quickly now, for most of them were jeeps and trucks of the Occupying Powers, and they would be quickly waved through at the checkpoints. The traffic halted only whenever an Arab vehicle, identified by its blue or green license plate, was stopped and searched by the soldiers. *All* of the Arab vehicles were inspected, their drivers and passengers humiliated, no matter how polite or tactful the process.

Amar was driving a white Siat he had rented in Tel Aviv. The plates were Israeli, and that fact, along with the army's desire to decongest the morning traffic, would probably work in his favor.

Now that he was actually on the ground in Israel, wearing the face of a well-known cabinet advisor, Amar had to take some further precautions. He sported a large khaki bush hat to cover his hair, and he had purchased a pair of teardrop sunglasses of the type worn by helicopter pilots. The lenses drooped sufficiently to hide his scar. Upon arrival in Tel Aviv he had quickly destroyed his purloined American passport. Then he staked out a Bank Leumi cash machine, selected a proper citizen who carelessly dropped his wallet into an open shoulder bag, and followed the man onto a crowded bus where he lifted the precious ID cards with relative ease.

He reached the roadblock before the main entrance to the city. Folding gates of vicious tire spikes had been stretched prone across the road, forming an obstacle that required slow, careful driving and tight turns. Six young soldiers toting assault rifles herded the cars through, peering in the windows with that sharp cruelty of youthful power. On the far side of the roadblock, two battered cars with West Bank plates had been pulled over, all of their doors ajar, trunks open, their *kaffieh*ed drivers and *jallabieh*-draped women standing aside under the blazing sun while the Jews rummaged through their belongings.

An officer, no older than a college freshman, pointed at Amar and motioned for him to drive around the teeth and bear to the left. Amar slowed, expecting to be questioned, but then someone yelled, "Sa! Sa!" and by the added flurry of waving arms he realized that he could drive on. He touched his hand to his hat brim as he depressed the gas pedal.

When Amar had last seen Bethlehem he had been too young still to drive a car. However, like most urban children he had spent his playtime in fantasy adventures that took him through the city's streets and alleyways, day and night, discovering secret cul-de-sacs, shortcuts and side roads. Despite the passage of time, the city had hardly changed, the only obvious difference being the blight of television antennae where none had existed at all in 1967. The layout was certainly unaltered, and it returned to him now like a suppressed childhood memory extricated by a hypnotherapist.

For some reason, Amar decided not to penetrate immediately to the heart of the city. He felt the anticipation of a man being reunited with an old lover, and he wanted to intensify the ecstasy by prolonging the act. He turned left off Derech Hebron and cut over to Manger Way, a long mountainside road that wound around the city like the hem of a pleated skirt.

The traffic was thin here, just the occasional taxi and the scratched and dented vans and pickup trucks common to all the Arab laborers on the West Bank. Amar had to concentrate hard to keep from driving off the road and into the sharp gulley below, for his gaze was riveted to the old stone houses, shops and mosques that spilled up and over the high hills to his right. Boys in dirty dress trousers and white shirts chased soccer balls through the narrow streets; girls in skirt uniforms marched in little groups, hugging their books and giggling as they watched the boys. Old farmers and peddlers prodded their flea-bitten donkeys, overburdened with wood piles, petrol cans, burlap rice bags and anything else their masters saw fit to torture them with. Outside of each small grocery or café, groups of men sat at rickety wooden tables, taking long drafts of smoke through the rainbow tubes of their *narghile* pipes while they tossed tiny ivory dice onto *Sheshbesh* boards from their sun-blackened hands.

Amar suddenly felt a stab of something in his heart, an emotion that took him by surprise. Though he had dreamed for years in exile of returning to the womb of his birth, its face unaltered in any way brought on a feeling of frustration and rage. His people were prisoners, their homes occupied by cruel and arrogant infidels, yet here they were going about their daily lives as if all that really mattered was a good game and a smoke. He had spent his youth fighting for them, killing for them, yet they seemed to have done nothing to better themselves.

He hit the brake as he realized peripherally that something was blocking the road, and he turned his attention forward. An Israeli armored personnel carrier was lumbering up the avenue from the direction of Beit Sachur. The hulking iron monster was covered with white-yellow dust, and it sprouted black machine-gun barrels from every orifice. Atop the vehicle, a squad of soldiers sat brandishing their weapons, grinning arrogantly beneath their helmets and goggles, waving the civilian traffic aside.

One of them clutched a torn Palestinian flag in his hand, and he waved it over his head like a conquering Crusader. Amar wondered if the Jews had killed some unarmed teenager to capture their prize, and he quickly turned his anger on those who deserved it.

He was suddenly ashamed of his harsh judgments of his own people. How could they better themselves under these conditions? How could a prisoner hope to improve his lot when his life was composed of iron bars, a worn mattress and an open toilet?

No, he thought then. *Don't make excuses for them. Love them as brothers, but don't allow them the luxury of sloth or surrender.*

Amar had long since cleansed himself of delusion. The Jews, while under British occupation, had built magnificent museums, schools, gardens, settlements, and a secret, powerful army. *His* people lacked something of that stubborn ego. That was a fact. If he ever returned to Bethlehem as a leader, a *Muktar*, he would change all of that. He would change it by force if necessary.

The image of himself as a returning hero brought on a renewed surge of love for his fellow Palestinians. This was where he belonged, among his compatriots, side by side, liberating Palestine from the grip of the foreigner.

Alone in the car, with no one to witness his weakness, he almost allowed the tears to well up and fall from his eyes.

Amar was certainly running on a tight timetable, but he decided that he could afford the luxury of one nostalgic detour. When he reached the fork to Beit Sachur, he turned right and drove up the steep hill and into Manger Square. Though it was still early morning, already the courtyard before the Church of the Nativity was filled with groups of Christian pilgrims. Pushcart vendors were hawking ice cream and fruit drinks, and soldiers patrolled in pairs, while others walked along the high parapets atop the buildings.

He parked the car in the tourist lot, for to drive an Israeli rental deeper into the city might draw undue attention. He walked out of the square, carrying only a slung camera, then he headed west toward the marketplace. Before he reached the stalls, he cut south down a long stone staircase between rows of claustrophobic dwellings. When he stepped out onto Kanah Street, he had to think for a minute, but then he remembered and walked east along the road until it merged with Jubaya.

Without even realizing it, Amar was walking very quickly now, almost at a run, his heartbeat growing faster, his throat constricting in anticipation. Would it still be there, the small stone house that had seemed like a castle to him? Would the green iron railings where his mother had hung her wash still stand on the little balconies outside the upper windows? Would the little sheep pen still be in the front yard, its chicken-wire fence still bent where Jaja had jumped from the roof and broken his arm? But what about the smells? Would the air around his house still be thick with the spiced chicken and yellow rice dishes his sisters concocted?

And what of love? Could a memory of his love for his little brother still permeate the atmosphere? And what of hatred? Was his bitterness toward his father burned like a sign from *Allah* above his doorpost?

There it was! He had found it! Yet as he stopped short to just stand a moment and look, he realized that he was not alone. He turned to see a group of about ten Arab boys, none of them older than twelve. They also drew to a halt as he did, but their feet continued to move in the dusty street like the paws of restless wolves. Some of them wore *kaffiehs*. They all clutched stones or small bottles in their hands, and their murmuring voices were unpleasant. The largest boy stepped forward.

"Ma atah rotzeh?" He demanded to know the nature of Amar's business. In Palestinian-accented Hebrew.

Amar instinctively looked down at himself. He almost had to laugh, for his disguise was working *too* well. Commando sneakers, blue jeans, an epauletted shirt, a camera. Of course they thought he was an Israeli intruder.

Suddenly the front door of Amar's house opened, and a young man in his early twenties stepped out. He was muscular beneath a purple paisley shirt, and when he saw Amar and the boys, his expression revealed vicarious pleasure.

All at once the misidentification was no longer humorously ironic. What could Amar do, address them in fluent Arabic? The territories were crawling with Israeli agents and informers. One could be observing him at this very moment. What could he say to the young man and the boys? "I am the great Amar Kamil, come to liberate you"? "This was once my home, and I only wish to touch it"?

"Ma atah rotzeh po, Yehudi?" (What do you want here, Jew?)

The gang leader shouted at him again in Hebrew, and assuming that Amar's lack of response was the result of fear, he stepped forward and spat in Amar's face.

Kamil reacted instinctively. He lunged for the boy with a growl, but he stopped himself in midaction as he realized what he was doing. In another moment, he would have to defend himself, he would have to kill.

He turned and ran.

The boys chased after him, throwing stones and cursing in Arabic. He slipped and fell as a rock bounced off his back, the camera strap broke and the Nikon smashed against a rock.

Amar got up and sprinted down Jubaya, stones ricocheting off the walls around him, bottles smashing and throwing shrapnel as he fled the epithets of rage. He turned right and ran along a street that curved back up toward Kanah, with the pack close on his heels. They began to fall back as they ran out of ammunition, for they had to stop to collect more stones, yet they still followed him as he took the stairs to the marketplace three at a time, the sweat pouring down his neck as he turned again and broke into Manger Square.

The momentum of the chase carried the pack of boys to

the lip of the square. But the soldiers on patrol had been serving in Bethlehem for a long time. They saw Kamil, the pursuing boys, and acted quickly to quell the potential riot. Six of the young soldiers immediately turned and charged for the southern entrance, and the boys flipped around and ran away, their pursuers chasing them with drawn batons.

Amar leaned back against a parked tour bus. Heaving, he bent over and spat into the dust, trying to catch his breath.

When he straightened up, a young soldier was offering him an open canteen. He smiled at Amar.

"You should be more careful," the soldier said in Hebrew. "You can't just wander around here." He shook his head and clucked his tongue. "An Israeli isn't safe in his own country anymore."

Amar took an Arab taxi from Manger Square to Beit Jalla. It was too dangerous for him to remain out in the streets. His broadcast from Tunis should have been running for three days now, and he had to have faith that it had produced the desired results.

This time he had the driver drop him only three doors from his destination. Carrying an empty gym bag from the trunk of his rental, he got out and began walking in the wrong direction, and as soon as the taxi was gone he doubled back and hurried along the narrow road. Beit Jallah was a small section of Beit Lechem that relied on the skills of its carpenters. The air was always filled with the sweet smell of olive wood sawdust and the piercing whines of the lathes. Ironically, whenever the rioting in the West Bank grew to newsmaking proportions, the Palestinians in Beit Jallah were the first to suffer. When the foreign tourists were frightened away from Israel, there was no one to buy the carved camels, crucifixes, and multitudes of Marys and Josephs.

He found the little wood shop easily, for he had spent

the afternoons of his childhood at Abu Kaddoumi's lathe. He did not fully expect that the old man still lived, but he was sure that Kaddoumi would have passed on his skills—and his commitments—to whomever inherited his business.

He knocked on the green wooden door. From inside, the slow methodical crack of a mallet stopped, and after a few moments the door creaked open.

The withered face was lined with a hundred deep crevices, the beard and moustache white as goose feathers, and one eye half closed and clouded with cataracts. Yet there was no mistaking Abu Kaddoumi's once fierce and regal visage.

The old man stared at his strange visitor, looking him up and down, eyeing his folded duffel, and apparently deciding that he was a tourist or wholesale buyer.

"Good morning, meester." Kaddoumi's voice was as harsh as one of his steel rasps. "What can I help you?"

"Boker tov, adoni," Amar greeted him in Hebrew. *"Efshar l'hikaness?"*

The old man pulled on the door and admitted the Israeli stranger. Carpenters in Beit Jalla were accustomed to having the owners of Tel Aviv tourist shops appear in person to wheel and deal.

Once inside, Amar closed the door and leaned back against it. Kaddoumi was shuffling over to his workbench when Amar spoke again, in Arabic.

"Kayf haalak, Baba?"

The old man froze in his tracks. He did not move in the slightest; even his breathing stopped. No one had greeted him that way in nearly twenty years. Certainly no one had called him *Father* using that particular endearment.

Slowly, the old man turned to face the stranger. He reached up and fingered the dusty *kaffieh* around his neck, which he used to cover his nose and mouth when he worked at his lathe. He squinted through his one good eye.

"How are you, Baba?" Amar asked again. He reached up and removed his bush hat and sunglasses, which certainly did nothing to alleviate Kaddoumi's confusion.

The old man had never seen this fair-haired Jew before, yet there was something about his voice, and the words he chose. It was more than likely that this was a trick, an agent of the Israeli secret services sent to baffle and entrap him. However, he would give nothing away. He edged a bit closer, for the light in the shop was stronger near the door, and he stared up into the stranger's eyes. The eyes were windows to the soul. You could peel a man's flesh from his face, but you could not change the truth in his eyes.

"*Al'ism, min fadlak?*" Kaddoumi asked.

"If I say my name, you will not believe me," said Amar. "But I will tell you this: On the loop of your belt, you kept a silver watch. The watch stopped working in 1965, but inside the cover, you had a picture of your daughter, Samira. Had I not left Beit Lechem, perhaps I might have married her." Amar watched as the old man's eye widened slightly. "In the drawer of your lathing table, you kept a simple key." He pointed to a tall olive-wood statue on a pedestal in the corner of the shop. "In the back of the base of the Christ, there is a keyhole. Inside the door you kept a box. In the box, you saved my wages for me."

The old man's breath began to quicken, and he fought the blood that was draining from his cheeks.

"All these things can be learned," Kaddoumi whispered.

"Yes," Amar agreed. "They are only facts, secrets between godfather and godson, and secrets can be broken." Amar lifted his shirt, pointing to a small puckered scar in the flesh near his navel. "Even this could have been created by a surgeon, although we know that it happened when I did not heed your warnings and pulled a drill through a crucifix, and you carried me in your arms all the way to the Epheta Hospital."

Kaddoumi's legs began to shake, and his lips quivered as he tried to battle the torrent of memories. "Even this . . . ," he tried to say. "Even this . . ."

"Yes, Baba, even this could be learned. But can love be learned? Could anyone but you or I know how I loved my brother Jaja? Can hate be learned? Could anyone on earth but you know how I prayed each day for my father, though I despised his every breath?"

"Amar?" the old man croaked.

"Yes, Baba."

"Amar?" Kaddoumi staggered forward.

"It is I, Baba."

They fell into each other's arms, the old man's sinewy muscles nearly crushing the breath from Amar's body as Kaddoumi cried and kissed his godson on his strange face.

"You are home!" Kaddoumi cried. "I knew you would come!"

"Shhh, Baba. Shhh."

The old man's joy sprang forth like a desert flood, and he babbled and danced as he squeezed Amar's hands and felt his face, searching for the lines and scars that had turned him into a stranger.

Amar laughed and joined Kaddoumi in his pleasure, and he was hard-pressed to keep the old man from running out into the streets with his news. In his own house in Beit Lechem, Amar was still a stranger. But here at the feet of his godfather he was a conquering hero.

After a few glasses of hot tea and an hour of reminiscence, the old man was finally able to calm himself. Amar alluded to the many hours they would soon spend together—for it would take a week of nights to relay all of the adventures of twenty years—but that would have to wait. Amar was "working," and he did not have much time.

Kaddoumi proudly confirmed that he had recently been

visited by "three wise men." Amar was pleased, and he politely asked that Baba go to Bethlehem's Omar Mosque and say his midday prayers. The mosque was at the city center, and it would take Kaddoumi some time.

Baba complied with proud pleasure. "Your treasure is in the hole," he said as he patted Amar's cheek and made to leave.

"Baba . . . ," Kamil began.

"You needn't say it," Kaddoumi assured him. "I will tell no one. Today I am a happy mute."

"*Ma'assalama*," Amar said.

"*Allah isalmak.*"

Amar locked the front door and closed the steel-shuttered windows. It was already growing warm in the shop. He stripped to his waist, carefully set Kaddoumi's current wood project aside and hauled on the lathing bench until he had moved it two meters to one side.

The sawdust on the floor was so deep that you could not see the frayed rug beneath, but Amar knew it was there. He coughed on the dust as he rolled the carpet back, and the itchy particles of olive wood settled into his back, already shining with sweat.

There was a small trapdoor in the floor. He pulled it open and lowered himself into a black hole. He pulled a box of matches from his damp trouser pocket and lit one just long enough to see what he needed.

His hands emerged from the earthen foxhole, placing a musician's case, a plumber's tool box and three huge watermelons on the shop floor.

He lifted himself out and carried the objects over to the lathing table. He found Kaddoumi's water jug, standing where it had been for twenty years, and he finished half the contents and used a cupped hand to wash the dust from his stinging eyes. Then he found a rag, a small screwdriver and a can of machine oil, and he began to work.

The mechanical effort did not take very long. When a man was weapons-trained by professionals, his hands quickly become their own masters. They flew over the steel tubes, the springs, the safeties and sights, cleaning, checking, oiling where necessary. His fingers worked from a motor memory unconnected to intellect, following a pattern that had been burned into their nerves by repetition.

When he was done, he held a fully assembled, Russian Rocket-Propelled Grenade–7D in his outstretched hands. It was a collapsible antitank rocket launcher, a modification of the original RPG7, retailored for the use of paratroop forces.

The RPG was a weapon much feared by Western armor troops, for the Arabs had proved that it could penetrate the heaviest of main battle tanks at close range. The Israelis, always preferring practicality to national pride, had themselves adopted the weapon. Its ugly shaped-charge warheads could take the turrets off of almost anything, and make ground meal of the crews of armored personnel carriers. If a warhead exploded near a human being, there would be nothing left but his shoes.

Major Kozov had arranged for Amar to recover a high-powered pistol from an agent in Jenin. However, Amar was determined to steer well clear of any potential trap that might be sprung by his Russian master. Though he had pretended to comply, he knew already on the train in Germany that he would never attempt to get close in for a pistol shot.

He also knew that it would require no great brains to kidnap a high-powered rifle, for the modern sidearms of Israeli soldiers—M–16s and Galils—could easily be used as sniper weapons. But Amar was a skeptical student of history, deriding the notion that a lone sniper, his eyes filled with sweat and fingers trembling, could effectively dispense with a head of state. Besides, the Israeli Prime Minister was practically a midget, constantly surrounded by bodyguards who obscured his puny frame. Amar would have to penetrate that cordon of flesh.

The RPG–7D would serve his purposes much better. Having long ago been stolen from an IDF armory—after being captured by the Jews from the PLO during a raid into Lebanon—the weapons parts and their human babysitters had been put to sleep almost eight years before Amar's near debacle in Munich. Now the deadly dragon, with its three heads, was back in the hands of its rightful owner.

Checking the action as best he could, Amar unscrewed the two halves of the launcher and placed them, along with the rockets, into his gym bag. Still, he was not a man who left things to chance, and he knew that he would have to test-fire the RPG at the earliest chance.

He replaced the gutted melons, the musician's case, and plumber's box into the cellar hole, closed the hatchway, and pulled the rug back into place. With a worn broom, he shifted piles of sawdust over the floor until once again the rug had receded, like a desert highway beneath shifting dunes. Then he pulled the lathing table back into place.

He poured the remains of the water jug into his hands and washed his face and torso. Then he turned on the lathe and let the small breeze from the fanbelt cool his heated body. He looked at his watch, realizing that Abu Kaddoumi would soon return.

He knew that he should not let the Ancient One live, yet he also knew that he could not harm his godfather. He decided that he would still need the old man, though he wanted to be gone before Kaddoumi reappeared, lest his professional judgment get the best of him.

He pulled on his shirt, his hat, his sunglasses, and he hauled the strap of his heavy bag onto his shoulder. He realized that he could not return to his rental car, for the soldiers at the square might choose to search him. Well, that was all right. The car made for a perfect dead lead.

He examined his watch once more, this time squinting at the date. He had less than sixty hours before the Prime Minister would appear at the Western Wall for the ceremony. And he still had much unfinished business to conclude before then.

Mars was still out there. And *Jupiter*.

And *Venus*.

There were still too many planets in Amar's universe.

14

Jerusalem

Later That Day

EYTAN WAS SURE THAT HE WAS GOING TO MILITARY PRISON.

Moshiko, the young security guard from the office, solemnly led the way down the stairs from Eytan's apartment. Ben-Zion had been smart to send a familiar face; otherwise, Eckstein might have blown his head off right through the door. Two "gorillas" from Peaches—AMAN's internal security department—brought up the rear. The giants did not say anything, and they didn't have to. Eytan could feel their looming power, underscored by the fact that their footfalls were nearly silent as they descended along behind him.

Yesterday he had been suspended without pay, all but a de facto dismissal from the Service. Today he was being summoned to Headquarters, and the appearance of an armed escort did not bode well. Given his participation in a renegade counterintelligence operation, he hardly expected to receive a commendation. The Israeli military system encouraged bold improvisation, even insubordination when absolutely warranted—but if you were bucking your superiors you damned well had to be able to prove your motives pure and your results brilliant.

Colonel Ben-Zion frowned on anything short of blind obedience.

Eytan was not shocked by this latest turn of events. He had half expected it, and he told Simona not to worry too much about him. However, he then kissed her goodbye, handed her his Browning and two full magazines, and instructed her to shoot anyone who tried to enter the apartment.

"But I have to go back to work *sometime*, Eytan," she had protested, waving the pistol with a carelessness that made Eytan wince.

"You're pregnant and you're not feeling well," he coached. "Your boss is a doctor. He'll understand."

"Half the damn country is pregnant," she continued to argue.

"Please, Mona. Please." Something in his tone caused her to sadly acquiesce.

The silent, plainclothes quartet walked out into the bright sunlight of Eytan's parking lot. As they headed toward a row of cars, Eckstein tried to break the mood.

"So he's finally giving you something interesting, huh, Moshiko?"

"This is more like punishment, Eytan," said the young man. "Believe me."

Eytan gave up making small talk.

Colonel Ben-Zion's private car was waiting with the engine running. It was a long black Oldsmobile, driven by a war cripple, which was a cynical selection that allowed Ben-Zion to tool around in a gas-guzzling boat of a vehicle.

All of the men fit easily inside, even though Benni Baum was taking up much of the backseat.

"Ah!" Baum clapped his hands as Eytan fell in beside him. "Prisoner Number Two."

"*Et tu,* Benni?" Eytan winced as he tried to adjust his stiff knee.

"We're in the same leaky boat." Benni slapped him on the leg. "Save the Shakespeare for Itzik."

The car pulled out of the lot and headed up past the Promenade with its spectacular view of the Old City.

"*You're* in a bright mood today," Eytan said.

"Well, it's a beautiful afternoon," Benni replied. Then he squeezed Eytan's thigh, signaling his captain to shut his mouth.

They rode the rest of the way in silence. Benni smoked a cigarette, then snuffed it out in a rear-door ashtray. However, he then field-stripped the butt and dropped the debris on the floor of the car. One of the gorillas shot him a look. Baum just smiled at him. . . .

They arrived at the door to Ben-Zion's office. Heinz pulled it open, wearing the expression of a firing-squad commander. The two gorillas took up posts in the hallway, while Moshiko excused himself after giving Eytan a shy, apologetic look.

Colonel Ben-Zion was standing in front of his large picture window, his hands clasped behind his back, his head angled downward as if he were watching the sidewalk traffic on Jaffa Road. His khaki-colored civilian shirt was wrinkled and sweat-stained, and the hair at the back of his head was rumpled and flattened to his skull, as if he had not managed to shower in recent days. He did not turn when Eytan and Benni entered the office.

His secretary was sitting at her dictation post next to his desk. She looked up at the summoned officers and said, "They're here, Itzik," as Heinz closed the door.

"You may go, Ariella," said the Colonel.

The girl was always happy to be dismissed from her boss's

high-voltage environment, and she gathered her notepads quickly.

"You too, Heinz," the Colonel added.

The Aryan-looking captain seemed not to have heard correctly, for he just stood there without moving.

"Yes, Heinz," Ben-Zion reiterated. "That's what I said."

Heinz trotted out reluctantly after Ariella.

When the three men were alone, Ben-Zion turned from the window. His usually tanned, handsome features looked jowly and haggard. His eyes were bloodshot.

"Did you think I wouldn't find out?" the Colonel asked quietly. His voice had none of the bluster of his frequent harangues.

Eytan said nothing, waiting for a cue from Benni. But Baum just lit up another cigarette, and Eckstein put his hands in his pockets.

"There is no such thing as compartmentalizing from me," Ben-Zion said. "From each other, yes. But not from me."

The Colonel walked over to his desk. With his finger, he touched some papers, yet he did not seem to be really reading anything. Eytan thought him somewhat sobered, drained of his usual acerbic lexicon. Despite his own motives, Eytan suddenly felt somewhat ashamed, like an errant child standing before a disappointed father.

He was amazed at how quickly their effort had been blown. Who had leaked it? Romano? Never. Sylvia? She was hard as a walnut. Horse? He was Benni's man—first, last and always. Badash? The GSS man would more likely double for the Syrians than squeal to Ben-Zion.

Arthur Sorelli was certainly an unknown quantity, yet Benni would never have brought in a foreign agent unless he was absolutely sure of him. Yudit and Yablokovsky were the most likely candidates. They were young, and they had never been field agents. They could be easily frightened.

"Don't bother looking for scapegoats." The Colonel

seemed to be reading Eytan's mind. "You can't run a *peoolah tachtit* right under my nose." He used a derisive term for *underground action*. "It's like your own daughter fucking her boyfriend in the basement. . . . You can smell it." There was actually some hurt in his voice.

Eytan and Benni still said nothing. They were both somewhat shocked by Itzik's tone of resignation and surrender. They had expected an explosion, a screaming match, and they were ready to shout right back. Yet they were unprepared for this.

Ben-Zion moved behind his desk and sat down. He poured himself some orange drink. One of his telephones rang, and he looked at it and it stopped. Ariella was smart enough to know when to intercept.

"The Kenya team has nothing," he said.

Eytan held his breath. Colonel Itzik Ben-Zion was openly admitting an operational failure. He wished to hell he was recording the event, for he hardly believed his ears.

"Neither does Cairo." Ben-Zion finished the juice, then he picked up a pencil and tapped it on his desk without looking up. "Our people in Larnaca have circumstantial items—a dented VW minibus, purchased sight unseen, of course. Nothing of any value yet. Dagan was Mossad now, as you know. They're giving us everything they can."

The Colonel looked up at Eytan, and he held his captain's gaze for a long moment as he twirled the pencil. He could not come out and admit that perhaps Eytan's Kamil theory had some merit, but something in his look told Eytan that this was not, after all, going to end in a dank prison cell across the courtyard of the Russian Compound.

Ben-Zion rose from his chair. He put his hands behind his back again, and he spoke as he paced slowly before his window.

"I must ask you, gentlemen, about an additional matter.

And I expect a truthful answer." He turned and faced his officers. "An advisor to the Prime Minister, a Major Rami Carrera, has been reported as missing by his wife and co-workers. He failed to show up to work today. I don't suppose you two know anything about this?"

Eytan felt his heart begin to race. He used every physiological trick he'd ever learned to focus all of his energies on keeping his blood pressure down and his skin cool. Getting Rami Carrera to a safe house in Maalé Adumim had been no small effort for him and Baum. They had raced along the Jerusalem–Jericho highway at breakneck speed, just to keep Carrera from jumping from the car, while they pleaded, cajoled and offered the barefaced truth. Unflinching, they even allowed him to threaten them with a loaded pistol, a fact which ultimately convinced the major that he was not being hijacked by Arab terrorists. Finally, Eytan's rapid-fire sputtering of place names, army exercises and fellow soldiers from their mutual officers' candidate school served as proof to Carrera that his escorts were truly "AMAN-niks."

"What was that name, Itzik?" Baum asked with blatant innocence.

"Carrera. Rami Carrera." Ben-Zion stared at the pair suspiciously, but they had been trained to lie like rug merchants, and he did not really expect to read anything in their faces.

"Does he have a girlfriend?" Eytan asked.

Ben-Zion waved the question off. "So you know nothing about it," he stated.

Eytan and Benni looked at each other and shrugged. They wanted Itzik to order an all-out search for Carrera, but the idea had to be his own. All the same, Benni could not help prodding.

"There's a standard drill for these things, Itzik," he said with just enough condescension.

Eytan took his cue. "He sounds like a sensitive asset. It could be a PFLP snatch operation. Or even Hezbollah."

Ben-Zion seemed not to hear. He walked back to his desk again, sat down, and picked up an internal phone.

"Get me Liaison," he said. Then, "This is Ben-Zion. That Carrera search I told you to set up? It's a go. Contact all the necessary police and GSS people. Make it countrywide, and get it moving quick." He hung up.

Eytan let out his breath, swallowing the urge to expel a victorious whoop. He was tired of standing. He had not slept much since the morning, and his knee ached. He limped over to the couch, sat down, and lit up a Time.

"I will make an arrangement with you two," Ben-Zion suddenly said. "As you well know, this is not the first time that I *may* have ordered an operation to be conducted 'off premises.'"

The Colonel was hinting that he might allow Eytan and Benni to continue their work. They listened, waiting for the other shoe to drop.

"It would also not be the first time in the history of intelligence work that an agent has been 'dismissed.'" He angled his head at Eytan. "Only to be asked to continue his tasks as a free-lance."

Eytan smoked in silence.

"I have the authority to bless your operation," Ben-Zion said in full voice. "Or dismantle it, if I wish. If you can show me, now, that you are being productive, I shall reconsider."

Baum turned and walked to the window. Eytan watched, wishing he could read the major's thoughts. Ben-Zion's challenge was really directed at Baum, for the two ranking officers were of equal experience and bull-dogged tenacity, while Eytan was more the junior whose career hung in the balance. Baum would have to act carefully, for Itzik could well be bluffing, entrapping the men into revealing their insubordination firsthand. Baum made a move that relegated Eytan to the role of messenger.

"Eckstein," Benni ordered. "Get Shabak on the line and have them patch you in to Uri Badash."

Eytan got up. Ben-Zion gestured at a telephone, and Eckstein asked an AMAN operator for GSS headquarters. When he had Badash on the line, he waited for Baum's next instructions.

"Ask him to pull all red-flagged foreign passports from the past three days."

Eytan relayed the message, then he told Badash that he was in Ben-Zion's office in Jerusalem. He rang off to wait for the return call.

The port services in Haifa, Ashdod, Ben-Gurion Airport, Gaza, Eilat and the Allenby crossing would have recorded all foreign entries into their data banks. Passports that matched alert codes from allied intelligence services or Interpol would have been flagged for investigation.

After a few minutes, the phone rang. Itzik took the call himself, which made Eytan's spine go stiff. The Colonel's conversation with Badash was all business, the distrust barely disguised. Mostly, Ben-Zion listened. Then he hung up and recited the information.

"Two passports are suspect," he said. "One belongs to a Belgian woman who may be a PLO mule. She was detained at Ben-Gurion. The other is an American passport. A backcheck through the U.S. State Department indicates that it was stolen in Munich six months ago. The registered owner is one Mr. Roger Goldstein. Mr. Goldstein is presently at home in Philadelphia. However, his alter ego came on through, and the idiot control clerk cannot recall a description."

Though the summer sun had defeated Ben-Zion's air conditioner, the certain knowledge of a penetration chilled the room to silence. At last Ben-Zion rose from behind his desk, though he did not feel compelled to actually mention the name *Amar Kamil*.

"You two gentlemen must have work to do," he said, as if Baum and Eckstein were lagging about. "As you may be somewhat vulnerable, Mr. Eckstein, I will assign two baby-sitters to you."

Eytan thought that Ben-Zion just wanted to keep tabs on him. He tried to wriggle out of it.

"Itzik, I'd much rather you put them on Ettie Denziger." As he said it, the words confirmed his nagging fears for his surviving teammate.

"Unlike you," Itzik sneered, "Tamar Shoshani can take care of herself."

Benni took Eytan's arm to keep his captain from screwing up the whole deal. He walked Eytan to the door.

"And gentlemen," Ben-Zion said before they could exit. "If you find something, I will take the credit," he assured them. "And if you don't, I'll have your balls."

———

Baum and Eckstein were conversing in Bavarian dialect, which deeply annoyed Eytan's babysitters. One of the giants actually spoke German well, but the officers' exchange was doubly shrouded in Municher slang and encrypted references, making it about as comprehensible as whale song. There was nothing the bodyguards could do about it. They walked along behind the pair, their stature reduced to that of a couple of toddlers on a playground, left out of the game because they couldn't speak Pig Latin.

The strange quartet moved along the corridor on Floor Two and then down the stairwell to the main entrance. Benni squeezed Eytan's shoulder.

"I'll be here," he said.

Eytan turned and bowed to his escorts. "Take me home, gentlemen."

They rode back to Eytan's apartment block in a grey Opel Kadett, the two young toughs in the front bucket seats, identical sunglasses, big arms hanging out the windows, like college ball players in a carnival bumper car. Eytan sat in the back and smoked. He only asked one question.

"Haven't seen you two before. You from Jerusalem?"

"Tel Aviv," said the driver.

"Uh huh."

Eytan did not go upstairs. He wanted to, but he was not going to pop in, see Simona for a minute, and then leave her again. He had the keys to his Fiat in his pocket.

"I'll take my own car now."

The babysitters jumped out of the Opel to join him. He turned on them.

"Now boys," he lectured impatiently. "We're not going to travel as an entourage, like nervous Italian cops."

"We're supposed to stay with you."

He stepped a bit closer, shaking his head and lowering his voice. "I'm a *decoy,* people. A *target*." He was improvising, yet as he said it the truth rang home like the big bells on the Church of the Holy Sepulchre. He was exactly that, which was why Ben-Zion wanted him operating again. "How do you expect me to function with you two holding my hands?"

"We're supposed to stay *with* you."

"So stay with me." Eytan got into the Fiat and started the engine. "Just not too close."

The giants made to run for their Opel. "Where to?" the driver called to Eckstein.

"Wingate." Eytan pulled out of the lot.

He lost them at the first major intersection. The light was going red at Derech Hevron, and he rolled to a stop behind a taxi, letting the Opel creep up behind him. Then he gunned it, jumped around the taxi and cut through a blur of enraged drivers as he careened around an Arab bus and zipped down into Gonen. He sped over the railroad tracks, left on Ben

Zakai, all the way around to Herzog, up Ben Zvi. He was already exiting the city for Tel Aviv, while the two out-of-towners still foundered somewhere in the industrial zone, cursing and spitting.

The babysitters were sure of only one thing—Eytan surely was *not* going to Wingate.

That, of course, was precisely his destination.

———

Boaz was pleased, and actually quite surprised, to see Eckstein again. The instructor was out on the sand lot near the obstacle course, putting a platoon of paratroop commandos through their paces. Half of the young men held M–16 bayonets in their hands. The other half were trying not to get stabbed.

Boaz walked away from the group. He pointed at Eytan's head.

"Nice haircut," he said, perusing the blond spikes that Eytan had attempted to comb flat. "Very modern."

"I need a refresher," Eytan said without ceremony.

Boaz looked at his student's eyes. "Oh?" Like most martial artists, he was a student of body language, facial expression. Eyes. "Now?"

"Yes."

Boaz glanced over Eytan's body. "Where's your pistol?"

"My wife has it."

The *Krav-Maga* instructor raised an eyebrow. He was not about to ask for the details. He had been in the business long enough.

"Then you'll be needing another one, I think."

"Afterward."

"Fine." Boaz turned to his students. *"Chadal!"* The paratroopers stopped battling one another and dropped their tired arms. "That's it for today. Tomorrow at seven." They walked off toward their barracks, speculating optimistically about the odds of getting an evening pass into Netanya.

Boaz and Eytan walked across the course, trudging quietly through the sand of the big dunes and down onto the beach. The sun was low above the Mediterranean, a light breeze carrying gull voices. Gunfire popped from the ranges.

"You want a uniform?" the instructor asked.

"Don't have time."

They walked again in silence. At last they faced each other at the lips of the sea.

"So, Eytan." Boaz looked at his student, sorry for him that this was suddenly so important. It was clearly no longer an ego-building exercise. Something was up. Something very bad, from the way Eytan clenched and unclenched his fists. "What *do* you have time for?"

"Pistol work."

Boaz reached back and drew his Browning. He withdrew the clip, cleared the breach, and pointed it at Eytan's chest.

"Take it from me, and it's yours," said Boaz.

They worked for an hour, until Eytan's knee was near to exploding and his hands were scraped and bloody. He returned to his Fiat, his clothes soaked with sweat, and the Browning holstered to his waistband.

Armed. But not dangerous enough.

———

The Café Alaska was situated on Ben-Zion Street in central Tel Aviv, at the south side of a big square that held the Habimah National Theater. The irony of the shady avenue's name had never registered before, because Eytan had not been in the café for many years. He had been recruited by AMAN in the Alaska, while he was still a paratrooper. Young Eytan in uniform—replete with silver wings, operational pin, a perfect maroon beret cocked over one eye, nervously fingering the barrel of his Galil while he read the same paragraph in a copy of *Life* magazine over and over again as he waited. His bosses-to-be—large men in open-necked shirts, bristling chest hair, briefcases, and eyes that never stopped watching his.

They met there several times while he was being vetted. He—always the edgy candidate, wanting so badly to say the right things, to be accepted. They—always cool, solid, professional, used to examining anxious candidates, trying to put him at ease while throwing him off his guard. Then, as it went on, there were other meetings, in other places, with other men—psychologists, medical doctors, desk men who gave him long written tests, one who spoke to him in flawless German, one in American English. In a dark, empty import/export office in an industrial zone of Givatayim, he first met Danny Romano, who even then sucked on an empty pipe as he recorded Eytan's biography for two straight days.

It went on for months, with Eytan taking test after test, interview after interview, never knowing if he'd passed until he was called in again. Always circling the periphery of the Service, never meeting another candidate, until he was finally cleared and the gate was opened, admitting him only to his basic training and many more months of tests.

So he was back at the Alaska. He sipped his *café afooch,* thinking of himself as a wounded animal searching for its birth cave, a comfortable place to die.

The café seemed much smaller now, though it had twenty tables arranged in cool darkness near a long mirrored bar, and there were ten more tables on the sidewalk beneath shiny white umbrellas. In his memory, as with all such things, it had grown into a vast, bustling cabaret. Yet now there were hardly any customers, and that was how it had always been. It returned easily into a clear cocoon of reality.

Ettie Denziger came in off the street. Her hair was cut short, a sort of blonde pageboy. She was very tan, wearing a white Izod shirt and jeans, sandals, carrying a small brown shoulder bag.

He had always wondered if AMAN used a whole string of cafés for its recruiting drives, or if they had a favorite spot, a regular "office" of milk shake and espresso machines, agent-waiters, and armed cooks. Did the Alaska make its monthly rent on the expense accounts of case officers? Or did every candidate have a different restaurant stamped on the cover of his or her vetting file?

Ettie pulled up a chair and sat down. She looked around and smiled, lifting her palms up and answering his speculations with a question.

"Capestrano?" she said.

"Cappuccino," he answered, toasting her with his cup.

She laughed briefly, then rummaged through her pocketbook for a cigarette and lit up. She blew out the smoke and looked at his head.

"Terrible haircut," she said.

"Thank you."

"It matches your complexion."

"Another compliment."

She reached out to touch his hand, then hesitated and put her fingers on the table. She looked at the white tape around two of his knuckles.

"What's that?" she asked.

"I'm still visiting Wingate."

"You should try tennis, my dear."

"That gives blisters, too, I hear."

Ettie got up and came around the table. She pulled another chair over and sat next to him, elbows touching. It was an old habit from Europe, faces to the door, but that wasn't why she did it. They watched the people passing on the sidewalk, soldiers, summer students, old brown men, young mothers with prams. It was growing dark.

"This nostalgic return is very sentimental, Eytan," she said, like a wife suddenly discovering a bouquet of flowers.

"I didn't know you'd ever been here until you said so."

"Oh!" She pinched the skin of his wrist, hard. "You tricked me! Good for you."

"I thought I owned the place. Me alone."

"That's what we all thought. But then I worked in Recruiting for a while. Remember? It was after Morocco. The Alaska was it for a long time, then the Rondo. Now it's probably the Central Bus Station, given the budget."

Eytan smiled, but he was thinking about Morocco. Her skin in the moonlight. Her cheek against his. Her breath.

"Let's walk," he said. He put some money on the table, and they went out into the cooling evening, the breeze from the distant sea.

They began to walk west, down toward the Mediterranean and the big avenues where the crowds would be lining up for movie tickets and taking over the cafés on Dizengoff. The holidays were coming soon, the schools would reopen, the ocean would cool. The atmosphere was compressed, hurried, the voices raised and the cars and buses faster it seemed, as if lives were being stuffed into envelopes of insufficient time.

Eytan walked with his hands in his pockets. He felt the Browning heavy on his hip beneath his untucked shirt. Ettie took his elbow.

"I'm leaving soon," she said.

A mission, Eytan knew. Hopefully, it would take her very far away for a long time. Safely into a lesser danger.

"Good," he said.

She put her hands behind her back. "Always the diplomat." She was an expert dissembler, but it failed with him.

"*Flute* is here."

Ettie stopped walking. This time, Eytan took *her* elbow, and they continued after a few awkward steps.

"What do you mean, 'here'?" she whispered.

"Ba'aretz." The expression meant *in the land*—a common tribal endearment of the common citizen. Yet now it also meant *in our house.* As he said it, he felt the hairs on the nape of his neck.

Ettie said nothing for a few moments. They reached Dizengoff Square, the fountains in the raised round overpass sputtering up into plumes of pink and yellow lights.

"You lead," Ettie said, like a fatigued dance partner at a marathon. And Eytan took his cue. From then on, as they moved slowly northward, she would follow in step as he doubled back without warning, grabbed a cab for a few blocks, boarded a bus and got off before it left the curb. It was automatic—improvisational yet predetermined. Graceful but erratic, like the meanderings of a senile, indecisive couple.

He told her everything, some of it in German, Hebrew, English. When he got to the part about Mike Dagan and Cyprus, she took his hand and squeezed it, and she did not let go. The telling made his heart beat faster, bringing the truth up, looking at its danger in the passing lights of city night. Their coupled palms were slick with sweat.

At last they were back on Dizengoff, having doubled back over from Ben Yehuda, walking north where the cafés thinned and the shops were closing as the tourists looked for drink and entertainment in the south, having spent their jewelry and Judaica budgets. Ettie's voice was thick though steady as she reasoned aloud.

"It is him," she said, having juggled all the pieces of Eytan's story. "But I'm not so sure he's inside."

"He's inside," Eytan said.

"It's not hard evidence, Eytan. Penetrations happen every month. No one has a description to go with the passport."

"It's him."

"Why?" Her voice rose a bit. Anger, or maybe panic. "Why does it have to be him?"

395

Eytan stopped walking. He turned to her beneath the light of a streetlamp. He was still holding her hand.

"We're all gone, Ettie. Everyone outside is dead. Harry, Rainer, Mike." He slipped into their cover names. "Francie has been 'locked up,' wherever she is. Now it's just you, me, and Hans-Dieter. We're all here. Where else would he want to be?"

"But why, Eytan? The man is a professional. Why would he want it?"

He looked down at her, the eyes so wide and blue. He suddenly hated it all—his country, his superiors, the Service. She should have been married, carefree, studying art at Bezalel. She should have been happy somewhere.

"I don't know, Ettie."

They began to walk again, this time with Eytan's arm around her, his hand gripping her shoulder. He could feel the tightened muscle, the shiver in her spine.

They moved toward Arlosorov, then Sokalov, their eyes darting now, beneath the trees of the quiet streets, examining the shadows of the doorways. Eytan's free hand hung loosely near his hip. Ettie clutched her pocketbook, the zipper open.

They mounted the stairs in silence. Eytan did not want to think. She turned her key in the lock. He was always thinking, always. Thinking, planning, anticipating. They were inside. Ettie bolted the door and walked through the rooms like a stranger in her own home. He couldn't do it anymore, think for so many, double-thinking, triple-thinking. He wanted to stop, to rest, to just let it happen.

Her hands were shaking as she poured straight vodka into simple cut glasses. Eytan watched her, seeing the open suitcase on the floor, the folded clothes, careful selections. There was a pile of books in French—dictionaries, *Vol de Nuit,* maps of Paris. Ettie saw him looking as she handed him the glass. She drank quickly, watching him until he also took the burning liquid.

"Would you have wanted me as a brunette?" she asked, a false playfulness.

He saw her then, as she would look soon, her blond pageboy black, her eyebrows arched and plucked like a Parisian model's. They could dye her whole body, but to Eytan her being was blond, golden, sunlit, thin like the mountain blood of Europe that ran in her veins. How would they cover *that*? He hated them all.

She put her glass down somewhere, without bending. He felt his chest swell, his throat, his mind paralyzed, pushing Simona down and away while he tried with all his might to remember her face.

Ettie reached down for the tails of her shirt. She lifted it over her head, the blond hair flying and then clinging to her raised face. He tried not to look at her, almost thankful that she came to him, to press her soft breasts against him so he could not see. Her mouth was soft and wet, then harder as it pressed against his and he took her in.

Her hands gripped his head, her fingers in his hair, clutching. His own hands struggled against the thick air, drawn to the skin he had to touch. And then she was unbuttoning his shirt, almost frenetic; she groaned as their tongues met.

She was leading now, dancing a clumsy waltz toward the double white doors yawning into her darkened bedroom.

"Ettie," he tried to say. "Ettie."

"We're going to die, Eytan," she cried between the flesh of his lips. "What difference does it make? What difference?"

Yes. What difference.

The telephone rang. Like a boxing bell after the first round. They stood still, mouths together, eyes half-open. She was a professional. Her master called. She responded like a Pavlovian experiment.

She put an arm across her breasts, her back heaving as she stepped to the phone. She answered, then held the instrument in the air without turning to him.

He took it, trying to control his breathing like a sniper before a kill.

"Ken?"

"I've been trying you there for an hour." It was Benni. There was no admonition, simply information to underline the importance. "You'd better get back here. Now."

Eytan hung up. He turned. Ettie was standing there, holding her shirt to her chest. She knew the spell had been broken, but she still hoped.

Eytan had never seen her cry, her restraint a horrible curse cast by unknowing parents. Yet now her tears welled; they ran over, across her tanned cheeks.

He wanted to come to her, to hold her again, to be lost. But it was past. He was thinking again. He had lied a thousand times, killed and killed again. Perhaps the only good thing left to him was to be true to Simona. The one good thing.

"I want you to go under," he said, his voice hoarse. He buttoned his shirt.

"I can't." She took a step forward. "I'm leaving soon."

"Go on in," he said desperately. "Until this is over."

She came closer, shaking her head, the wisps of her hair sticking to her cheeks. He reached out then, taking her head in his hands, kissing her once more.

"I'm alone, Eytan." Her voice broke. "I'm so alone."

"I love you, Ettie," he whispered. "I always did."

He turned and walked out quickly, closing the door, the white wood echoing in empty rooms.

Ettie stood there, holding her dampened shirt. Shivering. Breathless.

15

The Dead Sea

AMAR KAMIL WAS CLIMBING A MOUNTAIN.

He did not need ropes, carabiners, or pitons, for he had chosen the face well. It was only sixty or seventy degrees at the worst spots, with plenty of solid hand- and footholds, and unless you were going straight up a vertical slab you would not need the accoutrements of a team or a free climber. He had cheated much more treacherous slopes, in Switzerland, in the Urals, where the ice and snow were like nature's time bombs, threatening to explode from under your boots without a clue as to the delay of the mechanism.

Here, in the Judean desert, your most formidable opponent was the sun. It was bright like the heart of an atom, yet as it sucked the liquid from your body you hardly seemed to sweat, for even as the water gushed from your pores it was instantly evaporated. That apparently cool breeze was a devil's lie.

399

The sun could turn good muscle to jelly without warning. It could sear the areolae of your lungs. Beneath the shade of a hat brim, it could cause a condensed rivulet to wash an eye with salt, making you see true rock where there was only sand, forcing your hand to reach for false security.

What you needed here was knowledge, experience, the fatalism of the Bedouin. You needed good legs, a little water, and the will to keep putting one foot carefully above the other.

Amar smiled as he climbed. He had everything he needed.

He wore the gym bag like a knapsack, his arms slipped through the nylon straps, the heavy webbing cutting down into the flesh over his collarbones. Although he had wrapped the RPG sections and the rockets inside a large beach towel, the metal warheads and iron tubes were as heavy as a field mortar, and they banged against his spine with every step.

At a roadside kiosk near Jerusalem—the kind where every summer boy scout rounded out his inventory—he had bought a pair of khaki shorts, a cheap web belt and plastic canteen, and a green T-shirt with a large Society for the Protection of Nature symbol on its chest. His white sneakers were brown now with dust, his legs and arms were already going pink with virgin burn, and his hands were scraped and bloody with the climb. He savored each new pain. He would not be getting much sleep, and the physical discomforts would help him remain alert.

He reached the summit of the mountain. It was a long, narrow razorback, and he did not stand up to take in the view like some amateur hiker. He stayed low and walked quickly to the other side, slipped down onto his rump and lay back, shaking the gym bag loose for a few moments of relief. He tipped the sun hat back and turned to look north.

On the far side of the gorge he could see the small parking area at Mitzpeh Shalem. Though it had seemed like quite a climb in his Siat from the Dead Sea to the popular overlook, now he was even higher, and his car resembled a white cold capsule on a giant, spiky anthill.

He had changed his mind about the car. It was not, after all, a good idea to abandon it in Bethlehem's Manger Square. With nightfall, all but Israeli military vehicles would have to clear out, and then his rental would stick out like a goat dropping on a fruit plate. The Jews would suspect it, perhaps even calling in their sappers to check it for explosives. At the very least, they would trace it.

So, he had left Abu Kaddoumi's shop and looked for a café. It was a careful selection, and he finally settled on a small, rundown counter with a few tables and, most important, a portrait of Nasser on the wall. The owners were not happy with the Egyptian–Israeli peace accords.

Amar was the only customer, and he spoke to the proprietor in Arabic. When he was reasonably sure about the man, he suddenly offered him one hundred U.S. dollars to go and fetch the Siat. Then he waited across the street.

Within twenty minutes, the man returned alone with the car.

With the RPG in the trunk, Amar drove back through Jerusalem, then down toward Jericho, turning south for the Dead Sea. It was not that he mistrusted the integrity of the PFLP-SC cell members—he doubted that they would have fiddled with the weapon parts. He was simply cognizant of the fact that his people were not always proficient in their assessment of military hardware. If the Middle East wars had proved anything, it was that painful fact.

Besides, he had learned from hard experience that you never accepted the word of another that your weapon was in good working order. He had to test-fire the RPG. If one of the rockets worked, then the chances were good that at least one more would function. He only needed one.

However, when he performed the test, he needed to be well out of range of any Israeli citizens. The Judean desert was a perfect spot. Since the Jews had given back the Sinai, they had been forced to turn nearly every remaining plot of open desert into military training grounds. The Judean days and nights were full of the echoes of tank cannon and small arms. If he was out of sight, one more bang would hardly raise an eyebrow in this Hell's Kitchen.

He lifted his gaze from his distant car and slowly scanned to the east, his eyes resting briefly on every shadow that might be a human figure. The wide oval of the Dead Sea entered his frame, a waveless flat plate of green steel, laced with salt lines like the sweat stains on a soldier's tunic. Neither a boat, a buoy, nor a bird dared rest on this tepid broth of natural corrosive.

When his head had completed its rotation he was facing south again, satisfied that no one observed him. He looked down into the deep crevice far below his feet. It was the crotch of a dry wadi, scalpeled into a burning wound by the years of winter floods and summer winds. The walls rose high into the desert air, almost touching where the wadi turned sharply north again into ever higher peaks of chiseled rock. The lazy pop of small-arms fire echoed from behind the mountains, the short bursts separated by long intervals, as if the soldiers' trigger fingers were made arthritic by the heat.

He reached back and pulled his canteen from the canvas pouch, taking a small gulp of warm water. Then he worked the plastic bottle back into its pocket, slid his arms through the pack straps and started down.

His heels dug into the steep decline, raising small clouds of dust and spurting mini avalanches of stones that fled from between his feet. The echoes came back to him like running water, and for some reason, perhaps a burst of optimism made

foolish by his airy freedom, he began to hum *"La Marsellaise."*
"Allons enfants de la patrie-eh. . . ."

He directed himself down toward a jutting slab of granite marked by a mushroom of thorny bush. He stopped at the outcropping a hundred meters below the summit he had left.

Breathing. Searching. No one in sight.

He shrugged off the bag and laid it on the flat table of rock. He looked across the wadi to the facing incline, perhaps two hundred meters away, and quickly found what he needed—a target. There was a pile of blackened stones clustered upon a cut in the mountainside. Most probably a cold Bedouin fire. Next to it stood a rusting jerry can, probably long emptied of its water or petrol.

He unzipped the bag and folded back the towel, lifting out the two halves of the RPG. They screwed together easily. Next, he removed a pair of rocket sections. The heavy metal warhead piece threaded quickly into its booster.

He rested the splayed bell of the RPG launcher on his left sneaker, gripping the metal mouth with his left hand, and he carefully slid the rocket down the tube. Just below the conical warhead, there was a small protruding nipple. He turned the rocket until the nipple slid home into an open notch at the mouth of the launcher. Now the exposed primer of the booster would be sitting directly over the hole in the steel tube where the firing pin could pierce its fulminate.

He carefully hefted the weapon, laying it across his arms like a napping toddler. It was heavy now, and very long, menacing in its black and brown and green repose.

He did not have an optical sight, but that did not disturb him. The missing telescopic range finder was designed for field use against moving armor, complete with a graded windage scale and night illumination. He remembered that the RPG had one quirk in its design. When the rocket burst from its cocoon, a tail of spindly aluminum fins unfolded. With most other weapons, a crosswind would carry the projectile along with it, and you had to compensate by aiming into the source of the wind. With the RPG, these fins would act like sails, turning the rocket on its axis, its warhead back toward the source, so you had to compensate in the *opposite* direction.

If your target was a moving vehicle, this could get quite complicated, and RPG men had to be well practiced. However, Amar's target would not be a tank racing along at forty kilometers per hour.

The simple iron sights would suffice. Besides, as every combat veteran knew, when the blood was racing and the brain was crushed by gunfire, you aimed instinctively, like a shotgun artist on a skeet range.

He decided to quick shoot. He raised the flip-up sights as he cradled the weapon. Then, he reached out to the tip of the warhead and removed the fuze cup. He wrapped the fingers of his left hand around the rearward wooden grip, curled his right arm under the heavy tube, reaching past his left, pushing his palm against the forward trigger grip. With his thumb, he slowly pulled the hammer down until its heavy spring was locked by the sear. He pushed the safety button off and rested his index finger on the trigger.

He looked up, scanning the high ridges of the deep notch. Except for a trio of vultures sweeping wingtips to the sun, nothing moved. He felt no eyes upon him. He squinted across the wadi at the distant jerry can.

In a single sweeping motion, he lifted the RPG to his shoulder as he thrust his left foot out into a fencer's lunge. The crossed wires of the rear sight met the hole of the forward sight and the can appeared amid them like a cube of brown sugar as he pulled the weapon into an iron caress against his neck and fired.

The first explosion deafened him, crushing his eardrums as he remembered that he'd neglected to protect them. But he followed through, allowing only his brain to flinch as he kept the tube frozen and the second bang came almost instantly, heels upon the first like a two-round cannon burst as the jerry can exploded into a thousand shards of spinning steel, thrust upward on a plume of dust and rock that hammered off the distant face. The acrid cloud of rocket smoke swatted his eyes and burned his nostrils, a glorious stench as he raised his head from the weapon, watching the shrapnel of his power tumble slowly back to earth like flaming hail.

The campfire rocks were gone. The jerry can was gone. There was only a wide gouge of blackened sandstone, emitting wisps of smoke like cooling lava.

Amar smiled. Even a near miss would do.

———

It took him less than thirty minutes to return to the car park at Mitzpeh Shalem. The concussion of the explosion had temporarily deafened him, making his ears feel like they were stuffed with wet cotton, and his head still rang with a high-pitched squeal like the death throes of a shortwave radio. Yet he knew that the physical effects would soon pass, and he was spurred on by the rush of adrenaline that came with the successful test.

He got into the car and drove it out of the dusty lot.

By the time Amar reached Meshoor Adumim, on the highway rising from the Dead Sea to Jerusalem, he had developed a raging thirst. Up ahead, off the left side of the two-lane blacktop, he spotted a small rest area. A mini tour bus was parked on the unpaved lot, and a group of Swedes was taking turns mounting an old camel that whined and spat as its master, a brown Bedouin boy, coaxed it up from its scabbed knees beneath the weight of giggling European flesh.

There was also a restaurant, a low stone building adorned with strings of red plastic Coca-Cola pennants. Amar cut across the highway and pulled into the lot, parking next to a line of cars facing a tourists' Bedouin tent. He got out of the Siat, pulling the gym bag with him. He dropped it into the trunk and walked into the restaurant.

It was dark and cool inside despite the summer heat. The windows had been covered with some kind of smoked plastic, giving the interior the tones of a building wearing sunglasses. The Judean winds slapped hard at the pennants outside, and he could hear them snap like firecrackers, yet here inside the penetration through cracks and slats made for a gentle breeze.

A few sunburned Scandinavians sat at the wood-topped, metal-legged tables, chattering in sing-song tongues and swigging bottle after bottle of soft drinks. Amar did not want to be there for long. He walked straight for the snack bar and ordered three bottles of grapefruit drink. The boy behind the counter was an Arab. Amar spoke Hebrew. He finished the liquid in less than a minute.

"*Yesh po shirutim?*" he asked the counter boy as he paid.

"Outside. Around the corner," the boy answered with ill-concealed hostility.

Amar walked out and turned the corner, finding the door to the men's room. There was one stall in the corner of the dusty latrine. The door was closed, two black shoes on the floor draped with collapsed tan trousers. There was one long porcelain urinal, wide enough for three men to piss at once. There was a sink and a shard of broken mirror.

He stepped up to the sink, removing his sunglasses and his hat. His hair was thick with dried sweat and gluey chunks of Judean dust. His face was chalky below his eyes and streaked with lines of salty rivulets. He opened the faucet, bent to the porcelain, and washed his entire head, using palmfuls of the tepid water and letting the filth run off a number of times. With each splash, he felt more refreshed, awake, and clearer in thought.

His hearing was almost back to normal now. As he

washed, he began to review the checklist of his operation.

There were four main points remaining. Three of them were his original targets, Venus, Jupiter, and Mars, preferably in that order. He had not been able to access the other girl in Cairo, but even before arriving there he had known he might have to miss her. She had served well as a decoy to make the Israeli agent founder, show his hand, expose himself recklessly. Predictable.

He still had almost thirty-six hours in which to access those remaining three. That would be difficult but, with the information he had, not impossible.

The last and final phase was the Prime Minister. That would be the most difficult target, yet if his cover held and he moved like lightning, he would be relaxing with a drink at the bar of the Jerusalem Hilton while the storm raged around him after the kill.

All of the elements were interchangeable in chronology, some of them disposable. He wanted Venus and Jupiter, but he would dispense with them if necessary. He *had* to have Mars, and he *had* to have the PM.

For the plan to be perfect, a work of political catastrophe and aesthetic vengeance, the PM had to go before Mars. And Mars would have to know it before he himself died.

Escape? It was not likely. However, it was really only a matter of twenty kilometers. He had to get as far as Abu Kaddoumi's shop. How long could he live in the hole beneath Kaddoumi's floor? He decided that he could survive it for a very long time, eating and drinking once a day, passing his waste up in a bucket, thriving off the knowledge of his coup.

One year, he decided. *I can live in that hole for one year.*

He raised his head. His face was clean, his cheeks healthy and sunburned, the scar a half moon of thin rubbery flesh. His hair was not pristine, but it was free of dust and the curls glistened with cool droplets. There were no paper towels anywhere, so he reached down and pulled up on the cloth of his T-shirt, rubbing it over his face as he smiled into the damp cotton.

"Say, aren't you Rami Carrera?"

Amar froze. The voice came from behind him. An inquisitive baritone in Hebrew. He slowly lowered the T-shirt, seeing his own face in the cracked mirror, and over his right shoulder, another face. It was that of a young Israeli in his late twenties, open, relaxed, a look of pleasure. The face was topped by a visored hat with a silver badge on its peak.

Amar turned to the policeman, measuring the distance as he did so, continuing to wipe his hands, seeing that the man was relaxed. The right hand was resting on the butt of a Webley, although lacking threat, a simple policeman's posture. A strike to the throat with a right knifehand, and it would end there. However, it could also send Amar's planets spinning into unreachable orbits.

"Why?" Kamil asked as he reached back with his left, picking up his glasses and hat off the sink.

"The whole goddamn force is out looking for you, Major," said the cop, obviously pleased now that he had made his catch of the day. "Where the hell have you been?"

Amar's mind began to race through his options, like a computer speed-probing a data bank. What did this mean? Why would they be searching for Carrera? He hadn't touched the officer yet. Had Major Kozov blown him for some reason? That made no sense at all. Kozov's primary mission was still untouched, an unconsummated act.

Play it out. See what happens.

"*Ya Allah,*" Amar shook his head, displaying the annoyance of a film star constantly badgered by his public. "Can't a man fuck his girlfriend in peace in this goddamned country?"

The policeman laughed. Amar brushed past him, stepping

out into the bright sun, donning his glasses, slapping his hat against his thigh. The policeman followed.

"Well, everyone seems pretty upset," said the cop.

"Who's *everyone*?" Amar snapped as he headed for his car. The policeman tagged along.

"The army, for example."

"I'm entitled to a day off, you know."

"Shabak is putting muscle on, too."

"Fascists," Amar said, trying to lighten his voice now. The cop laughed again. "Well . . ."

"Look *comrade*, my wife's a wife. Jealous type. So she sniffs some pussy on my hands and turns the whole fucking country on its head?"

The policeman was a bit embarrassed now. "I'm sorry, Major Carrera. Just following up as instructed. You know how it is."

"Yeah." Amar had reached the car. He opened the door. "Listen, officer." He smiled easily now, yet retained a hint of disdain in the eyes. "I'm on my way home to Jerusalem. In half an hour, your search will be canceled. But *my* troubles will be just starting."

He got into the Siat and started it up. The officer tipped his cap back. "You'll be okay?"

"Of course I will."

"Okay. Sorry again."

"Thanks for your concern," said Amar, and he backed the car out, turned it quickly, and broke out onto the highway, heading up for Jerusalem.

Amar gripped the wheel with both hands, feeling like he might snap the heavy black plastic. His teeth were set hard, and when he was sure that the stupid cop was not in pursuit, he floored the gas pedal and fixed his blazing eyes on the winding road. The car picked up speed. He shifted, again and again, making the engine roar.

Someone was on to him. Already.

He had indulged his self-confidence like some amateur, allowing his activities to fill gaps of time which he could not spare, even detouring into unforgivable nostalgic meanderings. While he frolicked in the desert like some half-crazed ascetic, his enemies burrowed like rats, uncovering evidence, tracking him, unmasking his plan.

Now he had to adjust, raise his blood to the boil of *Jihad,* move like a tornado of whirling sand.

As he drove, he reworked his plan, laying out options, dismissing some, predicting reactions, countering them. In his mind he lay out a timetable, hour by hour, sparing no seconds, placing actions into slots, yet budgeting with room to maneuver.

In less than an hour, he burst into the door of Abu Kaddoumi's shop. The old man was finishing up for the day, sweeping his lathe table with a whisk broom. At first Kaddoumi's face registered impatience, for he wanted no more customers today. Then he recognized his visitor and threw up his hands.

"Amar! I thought I might not see you—"

"Hush!" Kamil locked the door and put the gym bag on the floor. He advanced on the old man and reached out for his wispy shoulders, gripping hard.

"Baba, did you tell anyone?" he whispered.

"What?"

"Does anyone know I've returned?"

"Of course not." The old man pulled away, reaching up to adjust his dusty *kaffieh*. Amar stared into the milky eyes, searching for truth.

"What is wrong with you, Amar?" Kaddoumi asked, as if Kamil had just returned from school in a sullen mood.

"We must work, Baba."

"Do you want some tea?" The ancient one turned to light the gas stove.

"No! I don't want tea!"

Kaddoumi froze. Perhaps in another year, another life, he would have slapped the boy. But the tone brought the old man sharply up to the present. *This* Amar was not the young one of their youth. *This* Amar was a warrior, a terror of terrorists. He was a new man, a new face, a generation of pain.

"What must we do, Amar?"

"I need you now, Baba. More than ever."

"I am listening."

"Fine." Amar took one of the old man's hands and held it, feeling the raised spots and callouses, the withered flesh. "You must find me three men."

"What men?"

"PFLP-SC men, Baba. They must be fighters, all of them. Can you do that?"

"I know a father of one of the boys, but we never speak of this."

"Good. You must speak of it now. And there is more. The three men must be of height and weight like my own. If possible, they must look like me."

"As you looked?"

"As I look *now*, Baba."

"This will be very hard."

"Yes. Find me three, and I will choose. Their hair and skin color is important, for we do not have much time. Look at me. We need the body and the face, some bastard Western blood. As close as you can."

"It will be difficult."

"And they must be very brave, Baba. You must tell them that this is full of danger, yet full of honor for their families. You must tell them much, but tell them nothing."

Amar spoke in the winding, circuitous Arabic of the Koran, full of hidden intentions whose veiled poetics inspired an ancient warrior.

"I understand," said Kaddoumi, his eyes brightening with enthusiasm.

"Two of them must be armed, Baba. One with a pistol. *Not* a revolver. A pistol." Amar mimed the loading of a magazine with his hands.

"A pistol."

"Yes. And there is more."

"What more?"

Amar produced a piece of crumpled paper. He had written up a list in the car.

"Take this to an apothecary."

"They will all be closed."

Amar ignored the practicality.

"Take it, find one, bring me the items."

The old man looked at the paper. He squinted. "My eyes. . . ." He clucked his tongue.

"No matter. Give it to the store owner. Tell him your daughter is to be wed. She has many handmaidens. He will understand." Amar produced some money and stuffed it into the old man's hand. "And there is more, Baba."

"What more?" The old man was smiling now. It was almost like a game, a fantasy. Yet it was also a challenge, and so high a compliment that Amar had such faith. He could do it. Yes.

"You must find three items. I don't know where."

"What items?"

"A tube of steel, at least fifteen centimeters long, by at least two and a half wide. Then, at least ten washers to fit inside the tube, their holes at least a centimeter."

"A tube, fifteen by two and a half. Ten washers, at least a centimeter hole."

412

"And finally, a pair of asbestos gloves."

"Gloves?"

"Like a blacksmith's gloves."

"A blacksmith."

"Can you remember, Baba?"

"Of course I remember!" said Kaddoumi, and he began to mutter to himself. "Three men, the pistol, an apothecary, a tube. . . ."

Amar reached down and took Kaddoumi's face in his hands. The old man looked up as Amar bent and kissed him hard on both cheeks.

"Move your ancient bones quickly, Baba." His tones had love and fear, pleading and threat rolled into a growl. "The revolution has little patience."

Kaddoumi said nothing. He reached up and touched Amar on the cheek, as if to say, *I will do this, and I forgive you your voice, for you were once as my son.* Then he wrapped his *kaffieh* and left the shop.

Amar closed the door again. Then he turned and leaned against it, grinding one fist inside the palm of the other.

Yes. Someone was on to him already.

And he could guess who that someone must be.

16

Jerusalem

Three Hours Later

THE WARM EMERALD SPIRES of the Russian Orthodox church had turned cold and blue with the night, their gently curved cones of sunlit grace now sharp and threatening under the pale glow of the Compound's spotlights. The stately towers that held the onion tops now reached from inky shadows toward an even darker pitch of desert sky, and the coils of white smoke from a nearby incinerator transformed the holy architecture into a Soviet moon rocket, complete with the vapors of liquid oxygen roiling around its boosters.

Eytan walked across the Compound, heading northwest from the Special Operations building toward the squat rectangle of the police prison at the far corner of the square. The vast parking lots were nearly empty now, the tarmac silent and still where it usually reverberated with the hum of engines and the hurried trod of detectives' footfalls. A few weak lamps threw yellow shafts of light from the barred windows of the municipal courts, yet they offered no more practical illumination than would the rays of a flashlight to the floor of a Scottish loch.

He shivered as he walked, the stiff breeze that rustled the cedar leaves bringing hints of an early autumn chill. Benni Baum stripped off his brown leather jacket and draped it over Eytan's shoulders.

Eytan did not resist, concentrating on the sheaf of papers in his hands, squinting to see them as Baum briefed him, while adding to the pile.

"This one is from the Chief of the National Police, permitting temporary transfer of the prisoner." Baum slipped the coarse white page beneath Eytan's thumb. "And this one is a guarantee from the army, stating that the prisoner will only be moved across the Compound for interrogation. So you'd better not lose him."

Eytan took the form and held it close to his face, trying to make out the details.

"This looks like Ben-Zion's signature," he said, and when no reply was forthcoming he added, "Is it?"

"Itzik is no longer concerned with our methodology," Baum said, evading the issue of forgery. "He needs results."

Eytan grunted as his toe caught a crack in the blacktop. Horse reached out for his elbow and kept him from going down.

"Be careful, young man," Sylvia croaked. "Try not to break the other leg for a day or so." She coughed from behind him and he felt a drop of spittle strike his neck.

The quartet moved across the black expanse, whispering to each other like monks beneath the great shadows of the church. A small bald man, a waddling white-haired matron, a burly bull-necked wrestler—they resembled a crew of circus freaks briefing a limping pilot as he headed for his night fighter.

George Mahsoud was now sitting in a solitary cell below the holding pens of the police prison. He could not know that Eytan Eckstein was about to spring him, and Eytan was not wholly convinced that Mahsoud's guards would surrender their charge.

"Are you sure we've got enough paperwork, Benni?" He was already holding a pile two centimeters thick.

"I'm sure."

"Yeah? Have you ever tried to renew your driver's license?" The Israeli police were notorious for their bureaucratic hyperbole.

"Don't worry, Eytan. This will work."

"So, Horse." Eytan turned to the little analyst. "How did you break the code?"

"There was no code." Horse's high-pitched voice was usually flat of emotion, yet now he showed a hint of professional pride. " 'We Three Kings' is just a simple activator, as far as I can determine. It was the 'author' that was significant, the guy who put in the request. *Theodore Klatch.*"

"Theodore Klatch," Eytan repeated slowly, not getting it yet.

"Forget Theodore," said Horse. "What's *Klatch?*"

Eytan did not have to think long. *Klatch* was the IDF slang for the famous Russian assault rifle, the Kalachnikov.

"AK–47," said Eytan.

"Right. Drop the 47."

"AK."

"And . . . ?"

"Amar Kamil." Eytan snorted a short laugh. "Shit. It can't be that simple."

"It's not simple at all," Horse said defensively. "When a man knows you'll be searching for complexity, his simplicity becomes the most complicated code of all."

Horse was right. A computer could have batch-processed

the song itself for a month, while the name of the "author" sat out there like a string of fireworks, ignored for all its noise and flashing lights.

"There's more," said Baum. "Tell him about the intercepts, Sylvia."

The old woman was already struggling to keep up. Now she had to pump her stubby legs into a half trot to pull abreast of Eytan.

"Last night I asked our friend, Uri Badash, for the West Bank dailies," she said. She was gesticulating, and the glowing tip of her cigarette made firefly arcs in front of her heaving chest.

"What 'dailies'?" Eytan asked. "You mean the Arab newspapers?"

"No, you young fool." She had to stop for a moment while she coughed up a great glob of phlegm and spat it out into the wind. Baum sidestepped nimbly to avoid being hit. "I mean the regular intercepts."

"What kind of intercepts?" Eytan was familiar with the standard intelligence operations, but most of his focus was not domestic, and he had been out of it for some time.

"Ain li savlanoot." Sylvia muttered a complaint and Baum stepped in.

"GSS has a program, Eytan. It's a random intercept of West Bank telephone lines. Every night a midnight shift transcribes the tapes onto computer. Then you can run a quick search for names, codes, times . . . *You* know."

"So they're finally entering our century," Eytan said. Shabak had been bugging domestic phone lines for years, but it had been a primitive operation using roomfuls of operators and switchboards.

"We took four days of files," Sylvia continued now, "and put in a search for *Klatch, Christmas,* and all the major nouns, adjectives, and verbs of 'We Three Kings.'"

She stopped walking again while she coughed, bending over her dark, shapeless dress as her head bobbed with the spasms.

"*Nu?*" Eytan said impatiently.

Sylvia wiped her mouth and they continued on. "Only one thing came up. Day before yesterday, an Arab plumber in Hebron got an early Christmas greeting by phone." She reached into the pocket of her dress and produced a slip of paper. "Here's the name. And he's not a Christian."

Eytan put the paper into his shirt pocket without looking at it.

"A GSS team is on the way to watch his house," said Baum.

"Why a GSS team?" Horse actually showed some territoriality.

"You want them to do half the work but not take any of the credit?" Eytan commented with surprise. "Horse, I'm impressed. This must mean you're optimistic."

He tried to say it with humor, yet the piecemeal fitting of puzzle sections did not give Eytan much comfort. It was all too slow, even though they had drafted an impressive troop of brains and talent and were problem-solving at record speed. So they had confirmed that Kamil was already "inside"—Eytan had suspected as much when he left Cairo. So now there was an activator signal, author verified, setting agents running here in Israel—so what? Was that supposed to make him feel more secure? This wasn't some trainee exercise of capture the flag. Amar Kamil was a killer, operating with support. He moved like a whirlwind, and whatever discoveries they made, Eytan knew they were always three steps behind him.

"And one more thing," said Baum. The group was nearing the police prison now, so they slowed their pace and lowered their voices even further. "And it's a jewel, maybe your best card with Mahsoud." Benni opened the flap of his shirt pocket and pulled out a folded sheaf of telex paper. From his pants pocket he produced a handful of keys, where a mini flashlight dangled from the ring. He opened the paper and shined the spot of light on it so Eytan could read. The quartet stopped moving. Sylvia and Horse stood back as if of good manners—but they had probably already read the message. "It's from Arthur, and it's confirmed."

Eytan squinted at the page, his eyes going wider as he understood the significance of the English sentences. "*Ya Al-lah*," he said quietly.

"Now you have something to bargain with," said Baum.

"If only I could—"

"You *can*. You can make him an offer."

"Can I?"

"You can deal."

Eytan thought for a moment. For the first time, someone had something to offer George Mahsoud. Something that could persuade him to talk. Yet Eytan did not want to make any phony promises. In order to be convincing, he had to believe his own words. Mahsoud was too smart to buy bullshit.

"Can I?" he asked Baum again.

"Anything within reason. I'll back you." Baum reached out and snatched the paper back as he grinned. "Just in case he gets the best of you, I'm sure CIA would prefer that I kept this."

"Thanks."

"Which reminds me. You left your pistol with Simona."

Eytan lifted up his shirt tail and the leather jacket. The Hipower gleamed in the window lights from the prison. "A donation," he said.

"So it's true what they say." Baum clapped him on the shoulder. "You're a charity case."

Eytan smiled as he began to walk again. He realized that

he was proceeding alone when Baum stopped him with his voice.

"Just one more thing."

Eytan turned. His "crew" stood in darkness, watching him, measuring him. They seemed a sad family, with no choice but to pin their hopes on a faulted son.

"Badash set George up for you pretty well," Baum said, making it all too clear that the ball was now in Eytan's court. "Uri had two men with him when they brought Mahsoud down from Atlit. They never called him by his name. The whole way, they referred to him only as Amar Kamil's *friar*."

In Hebrew, the word *friar* was meant to bring a man's blood to boil. It meant *sucker,* yet in the most derogatory sense. A man who is used by another, taken advantage of, a lowly dupe to be exhausted by work and then discarded for another, similar fool.

Eytan nodded, assessing his armory of psychological weapons.

"*B'atslachah,*" said Benni.

"Good luck," said Horse.

Sylvia coughed.

Eytan turned and headed into the police building.

———

The road from Beit Jala to Husan was not well lit, and once they left the Hebron Road there were only the yellow lamps of Eytan's Fiat and the pinpoints of Judean stars by which to navigate. He could well have stayed on the two-lane black-top until the Gush Etzion intersection, but he did not want Mahsoud to know their destination. Not yet.

It was cold inside the box of thin stamped steel, and both men were hunkered down inside their leather jackets. They fixed their eyes beyond the dirty windshield onto the twisting mountain path, no more than a cracked sinew of dried tar flanked by swirling shoulders of white dust. The roadside fell away into deep ravines of spindly pines and rock-terraced vineyards, and when you turned at a crest you could see the distant clusters of huddled village lights, floating weightless on the blackened hillsides, like lost spaceships searching for friendly landings.

For a long time, neither man spoke. Eytan had informed Mahsoud quite simply that he would shoot him if he tried to escape. The warning was somewhat gratuitous, for George's wrists were cuffed, the short connecting chain of the manacles having first been passed through the metal handle of the passenger door. Mahsoud could not grab the steering wheel, nor could he do much damage with his feet, and if he did manage to open the door and jump, the ensuing keelhauling promised nothing more than a painful suicide.

The prisoner's forced posture made him look as though he were recoiling from his driver, although he did attempt to retain an air of resigned pride as he kept his head erect and his knees splayed in affected repose. Mahsoud was sure that the Israeli was going to stop somewhere and torture him. He assumed that Eytan was a GSS agent, and Shabak had a reputation for "creative interrogation." Besides, it was the one thing his captors hadn't tried yet.

They had been driving since Jerusalem for half an hour, and Eytan had worked hard to keep his peace. He wanted Mahsoud to think, to feel the open road, to smell the mix of pine and dust, of cooking fires and scythed hay. He wanted Mahsoud to sense the warm proximity of his own Arab village, to know that he was very close, within an arm's length, that he could change the course of his wretched life. That he could go home.

Eytan kept the radio off, the heater silent so as not to dilute the discomfort, the windows open just enough to let the dreams of Beit Fajar fill the car.

"I know what you're thinking," Eytan finally spoke, in Hebrew.

George said nothing. He continued watching the

darkened shapes of the craggy mountains that twisted like a paper panorama as the car followed the curving road.

"I know you speak Hebrew, George," Eytan stated without annoyance. "But if you prefer, I can say it all in English, or French, or German. My Arabic stinks, but we can converse like *goyim* if you wish." It was not a derogatory term as Eytan spoke it. It simply meant "non-Semites."

George still said nothing, though he turned his head away and watched a passing cluster of Arab homes. Perhaps he knew someone there, for he released a small sigh.

"I know what you're thinking," Eytan said again, patiently.

"What am I thinking?" George whispered, almost to himself.

Eytan felt a stab of optimism, yet he made sure not to smile, nor to alter the tone of his voice in any way.

"You're thinking just what I would be thinking, in your place."

A moment of silence.

"And what is that?"

"That I'm taking you to a safe house. That we'll torture you there. That I might just shoot you and leave you for the dogs."

Another long stretch of silence. Eytan glanced sideways. He thought that Mahsoud's mouth was set into something like a closed smile.

"*Safe house* is a funny word for this part of the country," George said.

The West Bank, at night, was certainly no place for a leisurely drive. If you inadvertently stumbled through an army roadblock, some nervous kid might open fire *before* he yelled, "Halt!" Alone in Palestinian territory, driving with Israeli plates, you were also a fine target for bricks or Molotovs. There was no spot in this no-man's-land where you could feel comfortably secure.

"Yes, it's the wrong word," Eytan said. "But still, none of those things will happen."

"What will happen?" Mahsoud had been dealing with these people for a long, long time. He had no reason to believe.

"I'm taking you home, George," Eytan said.

As he said it, he felt the atmosphere shift. Peripherally, he saw Mahsoud's body stiffen, his head reaching back just slightly. Eytan knew that it was anger, for Mahsoud had every reason to suspect the cruelest of jokes.

"To Beit Fajar," he added. Then he turned to look at Mahsoud, and he kept looking at him, driving on instinct, shifting as the tires scrabbled over loose stone, waiting until Mahsoud finally turned to stare back at his escort.

Their eyes met and locked. Eytan saw the fatigue then, the mask that never cracked, yet had become so brittle in its forging that it could well shatter like over-fired steel. A lock of Mahsoud's hair, just above the bridge of his nose, had recently gone white like a deer's tail. The eyes were dark and glistened with longing.

"Yes," said Eytan. "This time, just a visit." He turned back to the windshield so they would both survive the night. Then he fired his best shot. "But I can make it permanent."

George shifted in his seat, as best he could considering his manacled hands. He touched his knees together and twisted a bit. It was not a posture of surrender, just a statement. *I am listening.*

"First of all, I am not Shabak," Eytan said. "Yet I am also not the simple analyst that I said I was in Atlit." He did not want to rush it. It could not sound rehearsed. He reached into his pocket and took out a pack of Time, pulling one out with his teeth. He lit up with the car's lighter, and offered to place the cigarette in George's mouth. The Palestinian shook his head, once. "Let's just say I'm counterintelligence. And I am only interested in Amar Kamil."

"*How* can you get me off?" George whispered.

423

"We have just received a piece of vital information. It pertains to TWA 206."

As was customary with major government prosecutions, upon Mahsoud's capture he had been charged with many counts of sabotage, subversion and terrorism. However, the conviction that had sent him up for life was one of mass murder, for direct complicity in the downing of the American airliner with all aboard. The prosecution had proved beyond reasonable doubt that Mahsoud had actually passed the suitcase bomb from the hands of the technician to Amar Kamil. "We convicted you as a direct accessory. Correct?"

George said nothing.

"For delivering the bomb. Correct?"

George was frozen. He imagined the tape recorders in the car, the microphones, the little reels whirling around, waiting to record his heretofore unrecorded confessions.

"Well," said Eytan. "British Intelligence says that you *could not have done it*." He instinctively false-flagged Arthur's information. There was no reason to expose the CIA or one of its deep-cover agents. "You couldn't have been in Frankfurt, and you couldn't have been with Kamil. Because at that time, and for two weeks before that, and one week after that, you were in Ireland."

The handcuffs rattled. Mahsoud had laced his fingers together, gripping them to keep his hands from shaking. He was hearing the defense that he could never have used, but it was all true. He had not even been included in the planning or operation of TWA 206, for he was attending an IRA-sponsored intelligence course near Belfast. Doubly unlucky, his only alibi had not been the kind you could use to throw yourself on the mercy of an Israeli court *in camera*. At the time of the trial, he had not even bothered to tell his attorney. How would they have produced a witness? Through an ad in the *Belfast Telegraph*?

"We know this to be true, George," Eytan pressed on.

"Because the Brits had a deep-cover agent who also attended the course, and his report is now sitting in my boss's safe."

Eytan stopped talking. They were passing Husan where the road took sharp turns over crumbling razorbacks. He concentrated, reviewing what he'd just said, letting Mahsoud think.

"The cigarette." George's voice was hoarse.

Eytan lit a fresh one and reached out, placing it in the corner of George's mouth. The Palestinian drew in deeply, blew out a long stream of smoke, then bent his head down to take the white stick with his fingers.

"So?" George said. He was admitting nothing, yet his next question said a great deal. "Are you the Attorney General?"

"I can get you off, George."

"How can you?" George said quickly. "Who *are* you?"

"I can. It isn't me alone. It's my department. I'm just the messenger."

"*What* department?"

"It doesn't matter." Eytan fought to convince him. "We're top intelligence. Powerful. I can make this deal."

Mahsoud thought for a long time. He could talk, and then something might happen. Or he could talk, and then nothing. Back to Atlit. How much did it really matter? After all, just as the GSS men had said, he was only Amar Kamil's *friar*.

"What do you need?" he said.

"Help," said Eytan.

"What is the price? How much do you need?"

"As much as you can give."

"The payment?"

"Freedom."

It was all very clear now. In the fashion of barter and bargain that had been born in these very hills.

"What do you wish to hear?" George asked.

"Amar Kamil is among us," Eytan began. "He is some-where in the country, and he is running a mission. At least part of the operation is to kill me, and some others of my department."

"So this is only to save yourself?"

"And others."

"Why? Why would he want you? Who are you?"

"I don't know why," Eytan said.

"You're lying," George snapped. Having decided to buy in, he quickly turned on Eckstein. "If you want help, then give something."

"I tried to kill him once."

"You tried to . . ." George stopped. He bent to his cigarette, took a drag, and sat back. "Oh, no."

"What?" Eytan said.

"Was it Bogenhausen?" George's voice was a whisper again. He stared through the windshield, into the past.

Now it was Eytan's turn to be silent. He was torn, know-ing that to get anything of value he had to give something up as well. Yet every bone in his body ached at the idea of exposing an operation to this Palestinian.

"Was it *Munich,* for *Allah's* sake?"

"*Yes,*" Eytan said.

He turned the car sharply to the left, taking the turn toward Kfar Etzion. It was clear now to George that they really were headed back toward the Hebron Road. In a while, they would come to the highway. If they crossed it, only another kilometer lay before Beit Fajar, and the house of his mother, his sisters, his nephews.

"You truly do not know why Amar wants you, do you?"

"No."

"Then listen carefully," said George. He gripped the cig-arette again with his lips, and this time he left it there, the bright nub vibrating as he spoke. "I am going to assume that you are an intelligent man, not just a man of intelligence. If you will do the same for me, then we can dispense with flimsy denials for the sake of the game. If I am on track, say nothing. Agreed?"

Eytan complied by remaining silent, just nodding his head once. He was gripping the wheel hard, waiting.

George continued.

"All right: You say that you tried to kill Kamil in Bogenhausen. If that is true, then you were part of one of the Israeli teams. Mossad, or AMAN."

Eytan continued driving, his mouth set hard.

"If that much is true, then you already know a great deal about Amar Kamil. However, what you *don't* know is the most important part. The part that might get you killed."

Eytan realized that George was still bargaining, building his own case. He certainly had the right to do so, so Eytan kept silent, letting the Palestinian tell it his own way.

"Kamil confounded the Western intelligence services for ten years, didn't he?" George stated with some irony. "We knew that NATO Intelligence called him Houdini, and we were proud, we of his cell. He would commit some audacious act, like the Hans Bremmer killing in Berlin, but at the same time he would be positively spotted in Paris. Correct?"

Eytan just listened.

"He was photographed outside the Palace Hotel in Copenhagen, just after the explosion at the EEC meeting, remember?" George said with some nostalgia. "But Falaci swore that on that very day, she interviewed him in Rome. The discrepancy made headlines."

Having set the stage, George smoked for a minute. Eytan felt a strange pressure building in his chest. He knew it was coming, yet he didn't know what it was.

"Did you know that Kamil had a brother?" George asked.

If Eytan had wanted to say something, he could not have.

His throat was thick, his breath labored. Yes, it was in the records. Kamil had had one brother, a boy who had died in a refugee camp in Jordan.

"Jaja was his name," George continued. "In '67, Kamil took his brother with him to Jordan. Amar had murdered an Israeli officer, to prove himself, and to spite his father. But he was afraid that the Jews might find him, might harm his beloved brother. He was clever even then, Kamil. He made Jaja 'die.' There is even a false grave near Amman."

Eytan was a bit lost now, though temporarily relieved that George was off on a tangent. "A brother," he managed.

"Yes. And Jaja was alive, of course. Kamil had sent him to Cairo. In the seventies, after Kamil's first hijacking, he began to gain a reputation in the community. Hadad started to funnel money to him. He gained power. He pulled Jaja out and brought him to Europe. Are you following?"

Eytan nodded again.

"We were all amazed. All of us! Jaja was four years younger than Amar, but it didn't show at all. They could have been twins. He was not a fighter, Jaja, he was just a sweet, handsome, rather simple young man." George's recitation had changed. He was lost in the story, the tones of nostalgia bent with remorse. "At first, Amar resisted the idea of using a decoy. But we convinced him. We set up a system of guarding Jaja that seemed foolproof. Amar kept him happy. He gave him money and cars and women. Jaja was living like a king. All he had to do was show his face on occasion. The right place and the right time."

The constriction was back in Eytan's throat. He was trying to concentrate on his driving, yet his palms were now slick with sweat, the wheel slipping.

"But Jaja was hard to control. Kamil really loved him, let him get away with things, spoiled him. We were all careless." George's voice became suddenly weaker, the confession of a guilty parent, rather than a convicted terrorist. "It got away from us in Bogenhausen." He bent his head to his cuffed hand and took the cigarette away, dropping it on the floor of the car. He stubbed it out with his shoe. "Mohammed Najiz was just a cover name," George said as he turned to Eytan.

"Whoever you are, may *Allah* help you, mister. It was Jaja you killed in Bogenhausen. You murdered Jamayel Kamil."

Eytan slammed the brakes and the car skidded, the rear wheels fishtailing into the dusty shoulder. He straightened it out and caught the road again, but he pointed the nose of the Fiat away and pulled off the road, stopping in a spray of gravel. He sat there, gripping the wheel, frozen, trying to catch his breath.

Of course. Why hadn't he seen it all before? It had to be something like that. Amar Kamil was a professional, a stone killer. Only something so personal could have driven him to a suicidal vendetta. Throughout Eytan's career, over and over again they had said it, the catchphrase of field operations, words to live by: *"Ma she'galui, lo chashood."* The most obvious, is the least suspicious. What a fool he had been.

His remorse at killing Mohammed Najiz had always been there, suppressed, reasoned away like the survivor's guilt after a fatal car accident. These things happened. Yet now he knew. His victim was his enemy's brother, his enemy enraged by love. Eytan understood that, identified with it, utterly, completely. He felt a blinding pain in his heart, a sorrow that joined with Amar Kamil's. For *together,* they had murdered Jamayel.

Somewhere out there was a man fueled by an emotion even more dangerous than simple vengeance. Amar Kamil was himself driven by guilt, a truth he could probably never flush from his soul no matter the rivers of Israeli blood he spilt.

After a while, Eytan began to drive again. Slowly now,

for he did not trust himself. They passed the turnoff to Kfar Etzion and continued on. When they crossed over the illuminated Hebron Road and were once more climbing into the dark hills, Eytan spoke again, his voice shaky.

"What happened after Bogenhausen?"

"Well, I know that you people had some difficulties," said George. "One of you was captured."

"Yes."

"Were you wounded then?" George looked down at Eytan's leg. He had noted the limp.

"A chase team shot us up."

"Bulgarians. We used them sometimes, courtesy of the KGB. But I am sure you know that."

"Yes."

"They were sloppy that day. They should have been closer to Jaja. You killed him, and then they had to try for you."

"What happened to Kamil?"

"The Russians picked him up."

"For what?"

"Training." George's recitation had changed again. His sentences grew short, his tone hard, reluctant. Yet Eytan sensed that it was not the reticence of secrecy. It was something else.

"What kind of training?"

"I don't know!" George suddenly shouted in the car. "I wasn't there after that. They probably wanted him for something, a mission, I don't know. They planted all kinds of stories. He's dead, he's in Yemen, he's in Libya. But they had him."

Eytan remembered now what Baum had said. Badash had preset Mahsoud's state of mind, sowed the seeds of resentment. Yet if Mahsoud *did* resent Kamil, it was already there and had been festering with him in his cell in Atlit for a year and a half. Eytan had to nurture it, bring it out.

"They've been using you Palestinians for years," Eytan said. *"Friars,* all of you."

"Oh!" George shouted again; his handcuffs rattled. "And I suppose *you* are not used? The Americans adore you, just because you're Jews? They give you billions because you're pretty? Every single American weapon system since 1973 has been tested by Jews in battle, and not a drop of Christian blood spilled for it. Do you think that's love?" George would have spat, but he remembered where he was and swallowed the foul bile.

"It seems to me a few Arab boys have died in Russian tanks as well," Eytan said quietly.

"Yes. So we are all of us fools," said George. "We are all *friars.*"

"Perhaps."

They drove on in silence for another minute. Up ahead, the pasty walls of low Arab houses began to appear, clustered together on a hillside, falling away from both sides of the road. The village of Beit Fajar was serviced by an Israeli power company, yet most of the lights were dimmed, as if the Palestinians did not want to pay the Jews any more than was absolutely essential.

"Go straight," said George. "I'm at the end of the village." The joy that should have been in his voice was simply not there.

"Why didn't Kamil take you to Moscow?" Eytan asked. "Weren't you his second?"

"I was his second, his first, his best," George shot back. "I was loyal like a dog. I don't know why he left me. Maybe it was because of Jaja. Maybe the Russians didn't want me."

Now George was dissembling, but his reticence was a matter of honor and pride.

The truth, a source of great pain, was that Amar had

431

refused to allow the Russians to "repatriate" George to Moscow.

As chief of Kamil's security team, George had been responsible for Jamayel's safety as well. But he had failed, choosing instead to focus that fateful day on ensuring Kamil's escape from Munich to Berlin. Yet instead of expressing gratitude for that, in his grief Kamil had vented a rage that he usually reserved for the enemy.

In full view of a KGB major who was offering *both* men a means of escape, Kamil had denounced George, derided him for incompetence, foisted blame for Jamayel's death upon him. Kamil had actually slapped George and thrown him out of the KGB safe house, swearing to take vengeance upon his deputy as well.

George could have accepted Amar's explosion as emotionalism on the heels of a tragedy, but he knew Kamil too well. Such an oath, though patently psychotic, could not be taken lightly. George knew now that if Kamil survived, then he himself would be doomed, and his family would fare no better.

The equation was simple. For the sake of The Cause, George would have accepted a life sentence. But he was not going to spend his days in a cold cell because of Amar's misplaced sense of guilt-racked vengeance.

"He could have insisted," Eytan pressed.

"He could have," George said. "He didn't."

"No, he didn't."

"Don't think that I am a fool, my friend," George snapped. "I cannot be led like a dog anymore. Your people got me, so now you have me. Yes, I am angry, even without your help, thank you."

Eytan did not respond. The man was too smart. If he wanted to offer more, he would do so without the clumsy prodding.

"And you can also be sure," George continued, "that the KGB did not spend a year on Kamil so he could come here and finish you off. Don't flatter yourself. The Russians have their own reasons, their own agenda, and they don't give a fuck about Kamil, or you, or me, or any bunch of pathetic Jew and Arab patriots out to battle for god and country. Kamil has a mission. Something else. A man like Amar, it must be something that will throw us all into another whirlwind of terror. I assure you, it is something *horrific*."

The road ended, turning from splintered tar to a turnaround of powdered earth. Eytan stopped the car facing a large, low house of milky stone. There was a cement porch beneath an overhang of carefully manicured wood. A few dried plants hung below in baskets, thirsty for winter rains. A mangy yellow dog got to its feet before the wide green door. He barked once at the Fiat, weakly. George sat in his seat, staring. Eytan looked at him for a moment.

"I'm going to take the cuffs off, George," he said. "But please. I'm not a very good shot."

The images of wild bullets flying around inside his mother's house were not lost on George. He turned his wrists and lifted them as he nodded.

———

For an hour, Eytan sat in one dark corner of the family's common room. There were no chairs, only soft rich pillows lining the floor along the walls, and a single large low table of polished olive wood. *Neft* lanterns threw flickering shadows across the ceiling. None of this was an indication of poverty. In a wealthy *Muktar's* home, it would have been the same.

The house had belonged to George's father, and after his death, George's mother reigned. But with the return of the eldest and only son, George was king again.

His mother and sisters cried, hugging him, kissing him, while his six young nephews hung from his legs and pulled him to the floor. Eytan watched the Palestinian transformed, laughing, almost having to push away the piles of food and fruit that were thrust upon him.

Someone handed Eytan a glass of boiling tea, and seeing that it was poured from a common *finjon,* he drank it. Other than that, the family ignored the presence of the Israeli "policeman."

After some time, neighbors began to appear. The word spread quickly, and when too many strangers came to knock at the front door, Eytan rose, went to George, and whispered something in his ear.

George nodded, gave a command in Arabic, and the strangers withdrew. Eytan resumed his lonely, intrusive vigil.

He knew enough about the Palestinians to leave George with his pride before his family, so he waited patiently. At last, George rose and took his leave, moving to the door with Eytan close behind, as his mother and sisters stroked his cheeks and held his sleeves, keening softly as he reassured them with a courageous smile.

Eytan kept his hand on the butt of the Hipower as he escorted George to the car. He did not think that George would break and run, but Mahsoud was clearly a village hero, and surely his neighbors were watching, their intentions inscrutable.

Eytan drove three hundred meters, well out of sight of the village, before he stopped the Fiat and cuffed George to the door handle. They were out on the highway, driving fast and nearing Bethlehem, when he spoke again.

"Whatever Kamil's mission," Eytan ventured, "it can't be good for the Palestinians."

George laughed. "How could it be worse?"

"We are all trying for a settlement, George," Eytan said, feeling foolish as he did so. "In our own ways. Even Arafat wants it."

"But does that insane little man in the Knesset want it?"

"In his own way."

"On his own terms, you mean."

"Look," said Eytan. "I can tell you only this. My own department, the analysts, the experts, tell him he will have to deal with Arafat. And I don't mean by killing him."

"Yes," said George, somewhat impressed. "You will have to deal. If you don't, this will all explode soon."

"And do you think your Amar Kamil is going to appeal to our sense of reason?"

"He is no longer 'my Kamil,'" said George. It was clearly a decision he had made in solitary, though perhaps his mother's tears had allowed him to voice it. "We grow older, and we find other heroes."

Eytan told George nearly everything. Without revealing the operational details, he described the progress of the investigation. He told him about the murders in Europe, Rami Carrera, Theodore Klatch and "We Three Kings." He fumbled in his pocket and produced a slip of paper, reading the name of an Arab plumber from Hebron.

George listened, his eyes glittering, for some of the details were familiar. He had helped plant many of Kamil's sleepers, in various parts of the globe. And although he was not privy to all the details, nor the final objective of any of Kamil's projected missions, he could piece together parts of the puzzle.

"The three kings," he said thoughtfully.

"You know it?" Eytan asked.

"I can help. But what assurances do I have?"

"You only have my word," said Eytan.

"As an Israeli officer and a gentleman?"

The scorn was not lost on Eytan. He said nothing.

"What is your name?" George asked suddenly.

Instinctively, Eytan reached for a lie, a cover. It was automatic, the cornerstone of an agent's training. He heard the voice of his very first instructor in his head. *When I am done with you, you won't even remember your real name.* Yet against all reflex, without a clue as to why, he responded like a simple human being.

"Eytan Eckstein," he said.

"That's a nice one," said George. "It will do. Tell me, Eytan. Do you have a wife?"

"Yes." Simona's face appeared in Eckstein's mind.

"And do you have a child?"

"My wife is pregnant."

"*Mazal tov,*" George said in typical Israeli fashion. "*Allah* willing, it will be a son."

"Thank you," said Eytan. He did not care what the child would be. He wanted it to be born, to be healthy. He wanted to live to hold it.

"Swear on the life of your son."

Eytan hesitated. Now they were past it all, far from the game of wits and battles, treachery and vengeance. They were no longer blood enemies, trying to outmaneuver one another. They were two simple men of the Levant, and to swear on the life of your unborn son . . .

"If I live," said Eytan, "I swear on the life of my son that I will get your sentence commuted."

The Fiat turned round the curve of a mountain, and Bethlehem rose from the night like a mirage of jewels. The yellow lights of the clustered houses sparkled through a cold mist, the minarets and church steeples silhouetted like stalagmites against a froth of synthetic glow.

"I will help you," said George as he watched the city of Christ appear. "But given your chances of survival, I shall prepare to spend the rest of my days in jail."

17

Tel Aviv

That Same Night

ETTIE DENZIGER'S LEGS were as smooth as the belly of a lamb. Their long curves of suntanned muscles rose from a shiny pair of ebony heels and up into a black spandex miniskirt, whose hemline threatened a breach of the obscenity laws. The material, tight across her hips and buttocks, rippled like the skin of a thoroughbred as she walked, and her hands, tipped by freshly clear-lacquered nails, flashed past her thighs like racing flags. A wide, patent-leather belt girded her narrow waist, its silver-tipped tongue falling through a round buckle. Her white, sleeveless cotton blouse was frothy, and it did not cling to her skin despite the sultry evening heat. Yet the straps were slim and she was braless, two buttons open at the chest, the curves of her breasts distinct, her nipples pushing at the cloth.

She moved with the easy, erect posture of a tropical bird, her blonde hair bobbing at her neck, her blue eyes gleaming

437

under long dark lashes, her lips a parted bow of oiled crimson.

If you were looking for her—or even if you were not—she would be very hard to miss.

She did not turn every head on Dizengoff, but for a woman who usually craved anonymity, she was shattering her own record. The sidewalk cafés were jammed. Plumes of cigarette smoke and espresso vapor drifted from the restaurants, across the gesticulating heads of patrons and out into the street. Waiters weaved between the tables like overwrought nurses in an intensive care unit, while mannerless fingers snapped at them, as they tried to save the olives that rolled from their jostled trays and the drinks that slopped over onto plates of pita, rice, *shishlik* and *baba-ganoosh*.

Groups of young soldiers, unable to sit in patience for long, wandered through the crowds, tapping their dusty rifles, hoping against all odds that some charitable girl might take them to her bed. For who knew what the morning would bring? Strangers engaged each other in heated political debates, and friends called out to other friends and waved them in to their tables. In Tel Aviv, everyone knew everyone.

Ettie walked, trying very hard to recognize no one. She carried a yellow leather purse, hung from her right shoulder by a long strap. It tapped against her hip, full of mundane conveniences pertinent to an attractive woman primed for an amorous encounter: lipstick, mascara, tissues, address book, pencil, a condom and a .22-caliber Beretta.

She was, in fact, looking for a man. She had an image in her mind. Someone she wanted. No one she knew. At irregular intervals, she slowed to look in shop windows, read a posted menu, examine a movie ad. To give him time. She might find him, alone, sipping *café turki* at one of the hundreds of alfresco tables. However, in this society it was more likely that he would find her, should she decide to alight.

She stopped at a white wooden kiosk to buy cigarettes.

Captain Heinz was in the lead car. It was a grey Peugeot taxi, and he rode in the back like a passenger. He had a big five-watt Motorola on the seat next to him. It had a push-button collar mike on a long curled cord so he would not have to conspicuously lift the walkie-talkie to his head. He reached up and depressed the button.

"Eagle Two, Eagle Two, this is Eagle One. I am stopping to cover."

Heinz's expert driver immediately slowed, selecting a newspaper stand as a reason to pull to the curb. Heinz edged close to the right window, his fingers touching the barrel of a shorty Galil assault rifle tucked between his knees.

Due to an intrusive café umbrella, he could see only Ettie's legs and the yellow handbag, about thirty meters along the sidewalk. A wooden match trailed smoke to the pavement as she stopped to light her cigarette. Then her feet moved on.

Two young men passed the Peugeot on foot. They wore blue jeans and scuffed sandals. The one on the left had a green knapsack hanging from the shoulder of a ragged T-shirt. His hair was brown and curly, with the wet oily texture of a day in the sea. The one on the right wore an oversized teal oxford, the tails hanging over his rump. His hair was long and blond, falling well past his collar. The wire that ran up past his neck and behind his ear was completely concealed.

Heinz looked across the avenue. A Number 4 bus rumbled by, and then he could see another couple moving well out ahead, fifty meters past Ettie's position. The boy and girl, arms wrapped around each other, stumbled along as if drunk with beer and passion. The boy turned his head to look back, just for a split second. Then he leaned in to suck on the girl's uplifted lips.

Heinz looked out the rear window of the taxi. The *Aleph* and *Bet* pairs would have to continue past Ettie, so the *Gimmel* trio was quickly crossing the thoroughfare to take up the slack. They looked like young reserve soldiers, appropriately sloppy, fatigue shirts rumpled, combat boots scuffed, their slung M–16s too filthy to pass the inspection of even a blind master sergeant. Two of the soldiers were clutching bottles of Goldstar, and the three of them clung to each other for support. They laughed and bantered, though not excessively. They accosted a group of high school girls at a sidewalk table, making their victims giggle as one of the men maintained a position so that he could glance ahead.

Very good. Heinz smiled. They were all Special Operations trainees, though well advanced in that phase and nearly ready for foreign operations. The six men and one woman were already good trackers, and each one was an excellent shot.

He pressed the mike button again.

"Apple One, Apple One, this is Eagle One. Do you read me? Over."

The case of the fat Motorola squawked back to him. "Eagle One, this is Apple One. *Ruth*, I read you. Over."

"Little wheels forward," said Heinz.

It was a perfect evening for Itzik Ben-Zion's aide. For once, he was not flying a desk. He was actually running an AMAN operation. Even sweeter, he had a GSS team attached to him as well. Three of the Shabak agents were cruising in a panel truck. He kept them well behind the primary team, as backup. The fourth was riding a Vespa.

As per Heinz's instructions, the motor scooter passed him now, the white-bowl-helmeted driver weaving his machine between the traffic. As he moved on up, Heinz could see the outline of a pistol butt beneath his flapping shirt.

Heinz was extremely pleased that the Colonel had decided to tackle the matter head-on. He had feared that Ben-Zion might allow Benni Baum and his crippled sidekick to run the whole show into the ground. So, while Baum and Eckstein dragged the Kamil case through the quagmire of a plodding investigation, Itzik Ben-Zion was going right to the heart of the matter.

Denziger had agreed to act as bait. It seemed brave on her part, and foolish, but Heinz knew there was no real danger. He had her completely covered.

Given her operational history, Denziger was an expert when it came to Kamil's modus operandi. She had seen him close up in Europe and thought she knew what to look for. However, Benni Baum was not the only one with cronies in MI6. Itzik Ben-Zion *also* had friends in foreign intelligence services, and he had concluded that Kamil was running with a face that closely resembled that of IDF Major Rami Carrera. The major was still listed as missing by the internal security forces, despite a policeman's report of a sighting near Jerusalem. These facts were well-concealed from the Israeli public, but Itzik had Denziger quickly, yet fully, briefed.

Heinz was aching to pounce.

By now Ettie had moved far north, away from Dizengoff Center, where the crowds thinned and the sidewalk atmosphere was more civil, rather like the quiet clusters of a springtime Parisian boulevard. She tried to affect a sense of solitude, while projecting availability, although knowing she trailed an entourage of bodyguards did nothing to relieve her tension. How she wished that Eytan were with her! Yet from the moment he had rushed from her apartment, she knew that it would be impossible to reach him. She had not even tried.

Yehezkiel Heinz made her skin crawl, but he had always had that effect. Actually, the whole set-up gave her the shakes; it was too spontaneous. Yet she wanted it all to be over, so she had jumped at Ben-Zion's ploy, if only to be done with it.

Nearly an hour on the street and nothing had happened.

If Kamil was following, she had to give him his chance. Up ahead, the Café Stella looked right. Just a few scattered tables, pastel umbrellas folded for the evening, romantic couples bent over milk shakes and toasted cheese. An empty table.

She sat down and immediately lit up another cigarette. She tried not to look around her, blurring her focus, staring thoughtfully at the passing cars. A waiter took her order, then brought her a cup of *Nes*. She did not touch the steaming coffee, afraid that her hand would tremble.

She tried to relax, forcing herself to sit back against the white metal chair, crossing her legs, tapping the toe of one black high heel against the air. She picked up a menu and looked at it, seeing nothing. She smoked.

At least it was a "blind track"; she did not know any of the people following her. That was the best way—you could not inadvertently make eye contact, focus too long on a fellow agent. People passed in both directions—a girl on a bicycle, an elderly man walking a dog, a kissing couple, a slow-moving cab, a pair of European hippies. Any of them might be her people—or none of them. Heinz would be well concealed. She did not fully trust him, but she had to.

A shadow passed over her menu, then remained there for a moment. Ettie raised her eyes. A man was standing a meter from her toe, silhouetted in the high light of a street lamp. He was not looking at her directly; rather, he seemed to be perusing the tables, looking for a seat. The streetlight formed a halo that softened his curly hair and outlined the broad shoulders of a cream-colored blazer. His slacks were of a dark cotton, pleated and fashionable above soft leather loafers. The cuffs of his blazer were rolled back over muscular forearms. She reread the menu for the fifth time.

"Efshar l'hitstaref?" His voice was deep, soft and quick, friendly yet tinged with a certain reserve.

Ettie looked up. He was facing her now, one hand in a pants pocket, the other gesturing at the empty chair at her table. Was this him? She had to make a snap decision. So far, he fit the general description. If she selected the wrong man, then the right one would not approach. If she rejected the right man, then he would not likely try again on this night.

"Vakashah." Ettie smiled and tilted her head across the table.

His face entered the light now as he pulled the chair out and turned to sit. Ettie watched him, her slight smile planted on her lips, her hand still steady as she took a drag on her cigarette, her crossed foot tapping the air more quickly. She began to pray that her blouse front would not flutter with her beating heart, that sweat would not begin to roll down from her armpits.

His jaw was strong and very angular, ending in a square chin with the hint of a mandibular cleft. The mouth was full, set in a smile not unlike her own, yet the corners were rigid and caused shadowed creases that ran up alongside the nostrils of a sharp, aggressive nose. His eyes were large and bright, although the color seemed to be chestnut, which did not fit the description. However, with the advent of soft-tinted contacts, Ettie knew that the actual iridic color meant nothing. The long eyebrows were bushy and reddish blond, like the full head of strong, curly hair.

None of that really mattered. What *did* matter was the short, curved scar just below the right eye, which stood out under the harsh lamplight like a razor slash on the cheek of a fashion model.

Ettie stubbed out her cigarette and forced herself to speak.

"It's a lovely evening, isn't it?" She dropped her right hand to her side.

"And you are a lovely girl." His Hebrew was fine, yet there was something mannered about it. He was flattening the tone, slurring the consonants. Hiding something.

"Thank you." She would have liked to blush, but the

heat was already flooding her face. She lifted the small purse onto her lap, the zipper just below the table edge. "Do you smoke?"

"Don't we all?" He was trying to be friendly, yet his smile was fossilizing with the passing seconds. He was leaning into the table, as if he might pounce and devour her at any moment. While he opened one hand for a cigarette, the other withdrew toward his body.

"Kent?" She opened her purse, removing the cigarettes, measuring the angle of the butt of her nestled Beretta. Was Heinz watching? Were his people ready? She sensed no other presence. Her throat was going dry, her lungs working hard.

"Fine," he said. His eyes were fixed on her hands as he waited for the smoke. The smile was gone now and another expression was clouding his face. It looked like a tumbling, irrepressible fury.

Ettie felt the panic come. She could not stop it. It was like an orgasm. Once triggered, there was no way back. Where the hell were they? Couldn't they see him? She was in the middle of Tel Aviv, a thousand people, yet alone with her killer. Alone with Amar Kamil.

"What is your name?" The words came from her throat in a choked whisper as she struggled with the pack of Kent.

"My name?" His voice was mocking now, heavy, a distinct corruption of the vowels. An unmistakable Arabic accent. "My name is not important," he said. "But *your* name is Ettie Denziger."

Ettie dropped the cigarette pack and launched herself out of the chair as if stung by a high-voltage current. Her right hand dove into her purse even as the terrorist's fingers darted to his own jacket, pulling it open, reaching inside.

They were on him like a typhoon.

Someone shouted. A fist and forearm looped around his throat and he went backward off his chair as the blond hippie

444

dragged him while knifing down onto his collarbone with an open hand. A second man appeared, spinning on one leg like a ballet dancer as he back-kicked his heel into the killer's solar plexus. The chair banged onto the sidewalk as an engine roared and a white Vespa sprang over the curb from the street, the driver slamming the heels of his boots onto the concrete as he pushed the flailing motor scooter onto its side and leaped headfirst into the fracas. Three soldiers came sprinting up the street, sober as policemen, their weapons thrusting out like spearheads down into the mass of screaming flesh as the café patrons scattered like spooked pigeons.

A dark van screeched to a halt at the curbside. The side door flew open and three men in plainclothes, pistols drawn, tumbled out. Moments later, the entire group of adrenaline-poisoned men were dragging their captive toward the van. Another ten seconds and they were all inside. The door closed, the van sped away, and everything was gone, like the finale of a magic act at the Moscow Circus.

She stood there shivering in the evening heat, looking like a jilted, vengeful lover. Her pocketbook was at her feet, both of her hands gripped around the butt of her Beretta. She would have cried, had her survival instinct not shut down every emotional valve of her psyche.

She jumped when she felt the hand around her shoulder. It was Heinz. He was pressing against her, trying to lead her gently away from the scene. His face was close and he was grinning like a boy who had just rescued the pigtailed girl from the schoolyard bully.

"Come, Ettie. It's over."

Her eyes darted. People were staring at them. Someone pressed her yellow pocketbook into her stomach and she took it. She felt herself taking steps on wobbly legs, succumbing to the pressure of Heinz's encircling arm. She heard whispers. Someone asked, "Who was he?"

"Bank robber," Heinz answered over his shoulder. He was still grinning.

There was a grey taxi parked twenty meters up the street. They walked toward it. The driver was holding the door open. From inside, the sounds of excited electronic voices crackled from a radio set.

"We got him!" Heinz squeezed her shoulder. "You were terrific!"

She said nothing. She felt herself resisting his pull.

"We have to move," Heinz said. "They'll start the investigation without us."

Ettie stopped walking as they reached the Peugeot. Yes, it was over. She had done her part, and now she didn't give a damn what happened. She didn't need to be a part of the backslapping and strutting that was about to transpire. She only wanted Eytan—and Eytan was not to be had.

"Heinz." She put a hand to her forehead. "I'm not going. I need a drink."

He looked at her and smiled wryly. "I have to be there. They can't do it without me."

She realized that he thought she was extending an invitation. She almost laughed, but managed an expression of disappointment instead.

"Well, they can certainly do it without *me*," she said as she touched his arm. "I need to relax now."

Heinz shrugged. He reached out and took the pistol from her hand. "Well, if you're going to get drunk, I'd better take this." He pocketed the Beretta. "I'll give it back to you tomorrow, okay?"

She raised her hands. "Sure."

"Lunch?"

"Sure." She backed away.

Heinz winked at her, saluted and dove into the car. "Move!" He shouted at the driver and the taxi screeched away from the curb.

Ettie walked for a long time. She walked without direction, no destination in mind, yet with every step her posture changed, her shoulders dropped, her muscles warmed and the evening air began to penetrate her pores. She was still wound with tension, but as she moved farther away from the sight of the "snatch," it began to ease. For the first time in weeks, she felt free, released from the manacles of dread.

It was over. No more of her comrades would die. Eytan was safe. Soon she would be in Paris. Other perils would replace this one, yet moving and working again would bring relief. It was like any dangerous sport. You were scared until you started, then it was fine.

She stayed away from the cafés now, walking west on Ben-Gurion toward the sea. She took off her heels and strode through the trees on the dark center island of the thorough-fare. There were few people here, but in Tel Aviv, even an attractive single woman was safe on the streets.

She reached Kikar Atarim and trotted up onto the plaza, where hundreds of tourists sat out at the open-air pizza par-lors and teenyboppers spilled out from the door of the big disco that looked like a flying saucer about to take off. Colored strobes flashed inside the huge frosted windows and rock and roll blared from the doors. She kept on, across the plaza, down the wide flights of cement stairs to the beach.

The fine sand between her toes was like aloe cream to sunburned flesh. She moved buoyantly, swinging her purse from the strap in her hand, tossing her hair back and opening her mouth to the black sky, sucking in the salt air as the Mediterranean crashed over the breakwater at the marina.

She looked to where the waves lapped at the flat shore,

the pools of rushing water slithering under the moonlight. There was no other light here, and she squinted at the scattered dark shapes of couples wrestling in the peppered dunes.

She felt a pulling at her thighs, her own private gravity, a sharp longing. Her tension still gnawed at her. She did not know exactly what she wanted, but she knew what she needed.

She looked up to the left at the massive towers of the beachfront hotels. A thousand lights, a thousand beds. Perhaps relief was there inside, even an hour of headlong passion to wash it all away and start over again with tomorrow. Yes, anonymity was there as well. On the streets, the public cafés, she was vulnerable. Inside one of these expensive oases, she would be in another country.

There was a ramp leading up to the Ramada Continental. She stopped at the base, brushed off her feet, and put her heels back on. She found her lipstick and touched up her mouth without a mirror. Then she marched up the walkway and entered the main lobby at the front of the hotel.

It was perfect. Full of strangers. A busload of American tourists was poking over three long rows of suitcases in the middle of the shiny slate floor. Bellhops in purple jackets loaded hand trucks and pushed toward the elevators. Tour guides shouted at the desk managers. A cluster of Italian pilots, still in their sweaty UN flight suits, interrogated a short, flustered bell captain as to the best night spots and the fastest women.

Ettie pushed through the crowd. The lobby dropped off into a large lounge, dotted with low glass tables, stuffed armchairs and secluded banquettes around the perimeter. At the far wall, before a panorama window that faced the sea, a long mirrored bar was lined with foreigners perched on rattan stools. Ettie suddenly felt her raging thirst.

She moved to one corner of the lounge. There were a

few empty tables cocooned by curved, high-backed couches. She selected the farthest one and sank into the soft sofa, facing the room.

A waitress appeared quickly. Where there were dollars to be had, the service was decidedly un-Israeli. Ettie ordered a screwdriver, specifying foreign vodka. It arrived and she finished half of it in one long pull, put her head back on the soft velour and lit a cigarette.

It was not her first time inside the Ramada. As a trainee, she had been in all the major hotels. The teams often came here to practice their covers, striking up conversations with tourists, lying about everything from birth to concocted ambitions, perfecting their foreign tongues and accents.

She watched a man come across from the lobby, taking a table near the bar. There was a discotheque on the lower level, and its curved stairway broke open near the man's seat. Just as he settled, the loud beat of a rock-and-roll band thrummed up from the opening, and he quickly abandoned his position.

He looked around, searching for a quieter spot. He came toward Ettie's banquette and sat down at another table a few meters away, with his back to the lounge.

Ettie looked at him. He was tall and well built, with jet-black curls and eyebrows. He had chiseled features, yet his eyes were obscured by a pair of large, heavy-framed tortoiseshell glasses. However, he was not a tourist. He wore an open-necked simple blue shirt rolled at the sleeves to his biceps, black jeans, and sandals. Almost immediately, he set to reading from a book of Hebrew poetry by Abba Kovner.

Ettie sipped her drink, snatching glances at the stranger. She found herself smiling. Here, in the midst of this circus, he was cutting out all the cacophony and reading Kovner. Probably a kibbutznik, although a farmer at the Ramada was certainly not likely. At any rate, he was obviously here on business.

A waitress approached the stranger. He ordered soda water, and then he called her back and smiled shyly, begging for two aspirin as well. She walked away and he rubbed his temples with his fingers.

Ettie found herself staring at the man, yet he did not even glance at her. Then she shifted her body, crossed one leg and bore her eyes into the side of his head, trying to force him to notice her.

He did not comply. He continued reading.

The band on the lower level took a break, leaving only the chatter of ten different languages echoing in the lounge. Glasses clinked. Hotel employees called to each other.

"Tomato juice," Ettie heard herself say.

The man looked up from his book, turning his head toward her with an expression that was uninviting.

"*Slicha?*"

"Tomato juice. It's good for a headache."

He smiled politely. "Thanks." He returned to his book.

The waitress brought the stranger his soda water and a plate with a pair of white tablets. Ettie motioned to her.

"I'll have another." She tapped the rim of her glass. "And bring my ill friend here some tomato juice, please."

"*Vakashah.*" The waitress left.

The stranger looked at Ettie. His smile was slightly warmer now, although he merely nodded his head in thanks.

" 'A Canopy in the Desert,' " she said.

The man looked at his book, then back at her, his expression showing surprise.

"You know it?"

"My favorite poem."

"I thought no one read Kovner anymore."

"There are a few of us romantics left, I'm afraid," said Ettie.

450

The man looked at her for another moment. Then he slowly closed the book. She got up, taking her drink with her, and sat down across from him on the small divan.

"I'm Ettie," she said, extending her hand.

"Ronni Grossman," said Amar Kamil. It was so easy. So unbelievably easy. Even the most highly trained agent, at the right place, the right time, the correct point of weakness in her life, was open to the simple gambit.

He had tracked her all evening, carefully, at a considerable distance. At some point he had concluded that she was un-accompanied, yet not alone, moving with a discrete entourage. Then he sent in his sacrificial decoy, and they snapped him up like famished piranhas.

The rest of it was elementary, for all of her defenses were down. He shook her hand very briefly now, maintaining the teasing air of reluctance. Just a bit shy.

"And what brings you to 'Sodom,' Ronni?" Ettie asked playfully.

He sighed. "Oh, one of those stupid bankers' conventions." He shrugged as if embarrassed to be seen here. "Believe me, I'd rather be home."

"Thank you *very* much." She put her fingertips to her chest and bowed her head to the executioner.

He laughed. "Not at this moment," he said. "In general, I mean."

"Where is home?"

"Petach Tikva."

Ettie looked at his face. He was very tan, and behind the glasses she could see that his cheeks were patched with peeling, reddened skin.

The waitress brought the drinks. They did not look up at her.

"You look like you've been at the beach," Ettie said.

"Lebanon," said Kamil quietly. This was the only dangerous juncture. He had carefully patched his scar with spirit

451

gum, then dyed it with tea. He had done the same to the other cheek. Now he reached up to the left eye, behind his glasses, and peeled away a small patch, rolling it between his thumb and finger. "It was hot."

Ettie nodded. Unfortunately, this was not unusual. Most combat reservists were spending their thirty-day stints in the security zone of southern Lebanon.

"Yes, we've been having quite a spell," she said.

"Lebanon is hot even in January," he said sadly. He looked away.

Ettie felt him drifting, his thoughts wandering back up north, back to wherever he had recently lain in ambush and fear. She did not want to lose him.

"So, Mr. Grossman," she said brightly. "When you're not soldiering or banking, what do you do for fun?"

They talked for half an hour. For Ettie, at first, it was a bit like pulling teeth. Ronnie was inherently shy. He was clearly an intellectual type, and his Hebrew was complex and showed an education. But he was no social butterfly. He had recently endured a painful divorce and confessed that he had been avoiding women. That was fine, Ettie thought. She wasn't looking for a wedding.

She lied fluently about her own life, mixing fact with fantasy. She expressed her artistic ambitions, and Ronni knew quite a bit about art. It turned out that they shared a love of music. However, when the subject came up Ronni sneered at the banging noise that flooded up from the disco. He said that he was going through a Greek phase, listening to a lot of old Aris San records.

Ettie told him about the Rondo. It was usually a common disco, but Yehudah Poliker was appearing now. Poliker was gaining popularity with his full band of Bouzoukis and his Hebrew renditions of wild Athenic tunes.

"Do you dance, Mr. Grossman?" She finally asked.

"I haven't in a long time," said Kamil.

They walked along the promenade, south toward the Rondo. Ettie took his arm and chatted, ignoring the stiffness in his body. When they mounted the stairs into the large cabaret, the pounding of the tambours and the snapping fingers of the spinning crowd seemed to break his mood.

Ettie took him straight to the bar. When he had finished two brandies, she got him out onto the floor.

It was here that Kamil quickly shed Ronni Grossman's reserve. He let Poliker's basso Greek tones surge through his body, joining a hundred others spinning and stamping, flailing their arms and crying "Yassoo!" as they twirled their partners. Ettie laughed with pleasure and kicked off her heels. She tossed her purse behind the bar and clutched his big hands, driving her body in toward his and then back again before they touched. They joined long lines of hora circles, split off and danced with strangers, then found each other again, laughing and covered with sweat, their shirts as limp as summer bedsheets.

At last, Poliker broke the frenzy. His lead female singer took the floor, and she began a soft, mournful, haunting tune about a woman who wished she had died in battle with her lover.

Ettie slid her arms around her partner's waist. She looked up at him. He rested his fingers at the curve of her back, and they began to sway. Ettie pressed her chest against his, feeling the heat. Her hips locked with his legs. All four of their hands slipped lower.

"Take me home," she whispered hoarsely.

"I will take you," he said.

In the taxi, they kissed. Clothes wringing wet, tongues intertwined. She tried to remove his glasses; he said he was blind without them.

She took his hand and pulled him up the stairs to her

flat, laughing as she fumbled with the keys, her vision blurred by alcohol and the rush of blood that came with her anticipation.

She flicked on the light and he immediately flicked it off. She took his hand and started toward the bedroom, but he stopped at the couch and turned her, pushing her down. She grabbed at his shirt, pulling herself up, covering his mouth with her own, driving her tongue inside. Then she tore the shirt open and slid down again, carving her nails through the hair of his chest as he began to breathe in hoarse rasps.

She snapped his belt open and groped at his jeans, yanking them down over his hips as she pulled her heels up onto the edge of the couch and her spandex skirt slid up to her waist. She reached toward him and groaned as his flesh sprang into her mouth. And then he was reaching down, pulling her blouse over her head—she fighting to keep what she had at her lips, squeezing with her hand, pumping with her mouth as he tore her panties from her and grabbed her hair. He pulled her head away, growled, bent at the knees, and plunged into her.

She reached around and up under his shirt, digging her nails into his back as she bit down hard on his nipple.

Ettie Denziger was rough.

Amar Kamil was even rougher.

18

Jerusalem

Later

IT WAS BENNI BAUM'S TURN to answer the door with a pistol.

The hammering of the brass lion's-head knocker was violent and incessant, yet it did not cause Baum to go crouching through the darkened rooms of his stone Turkish house in Abu Tor. He was too old and too proud to play commando in his own home.

He threw on the lights and came rumbling through the salon, his slabby feet whip-cracking on the cold tiles, one hand holding the drawstrings of his blue cotton pajama bottoms against his hairy belly, the other hand swinging a heavy, oily, Colt .45 automatic. His "house" gun.

"Koos eema shelchah, tafseek kvar!" he cursed as he reached the big wooden door. He was not worried about disturbing the neighbors—the Baums had owned the two-story villa for many years, and it stood alone on a hillside plot of land. But Maya had already been awakened by the racket, and his wife's

wrath was potentially much more deadly than the venom of some political fanatic. The banging stopped. "Who the hell is it?" Baum growled.

"Eckstein."

Baum turned the key, and Eytan came barreling into the room as if he had been about to ram the door with his shoulder. Baum sidestepped like a blasé toreador as Eckstein blurred past him, the breathless captain quickly recovering his footing as he stopped short and turned.

"Benni," Eytan rasped as if he had just run a full kilometer. "It worked."

Baum reached out and flicked the door shut, and his pajama trousers fell to his crotch. He pulled them up again.

"Take it easy, Eytan."

"It worked, Benni."

"Where's Mahsoud?"

"In the compound." Eytan waved the question off with his hands. His face was flushed and he reached down to rub his knee as he grimaced. "In his cell."

"You took him back?"

"Yes, for God's sake!"

"Good." Benni motioned Eytan toward a large European couch, unconsciously using the barrel of his .45. "Now, have a seat. Calm down, and tell me."

Eytan stalked over to the couch, but he could not sit. He was about to explode.

"Was ist passiert hier, Bernard?" Maya came into the room, squinting at the light and smoothing her hair with a hand. She was wearing a pair of worn furry slippers and a yellow terrycloth robe. She still had the flaxen blond hair of her youth in Germany, and despite her weight you could still see the form of a buxom, powerful *Fräulein*.

"Eytan needs a drink, Maya." Baum's tone was a shrugging apology, something his co-workers never heard. "Would you mind, *Liebchen?* Some schnapps?"

456

"Natürlich," she said, and as she walked past the two men she reached up and patted Eytan on the head. "Poor boy."

"Now." Baum lumbered over to Eckstein and pushed him down onto the couch. "Sit." He placed the .45 on the glass coffee table, careful not to make a scratch. "Tell me. Slowly." He fell into a large armchair.

A brandy glass appeared in front of Eytan's face. He took it and drank some of the powerful white liquid.

"Danke schön." He looked up at Maya.

"Bitte. I'm going back to bed." She waved and disappeared. She was no stranger to midnight callers.

"I took him all the way home," Eytan said. "He was already talking, he started before we got there, but I think his mother was the last straw."

"Good," said Baum.

"Benni . . ." Eytan looked at Baum carefully. He did not want to miss the reaction, to compare it with his own. "We killed his brother."

Baum's eyebrows furrowed. "Mahsoud's brother?"

"Kamil's brother. We killed Amar Kamil's brother."

It took a moment, but then Baum's expression changed, the realization washing over his face like a torrent of icy river water. He lifted his head and leaned back into the chair, yet he did not shout. He whispered.

"Gott im Himmel," he sighed in his native tongue.

Eytan said nothing. He just watched Benni's brain working.

"Mohammed Najiz?" Baum was barely audible as he looked at the white stucco ceiling.

"Yes," said Eytan. "But not Mohammed Najiz." He paused for the effect. "It was Jamayel Kamil."

Baum shot out of the chair. He walked around, holding his pajamas with one hand, his face with the other. "Is that right?" he asked himself, scouring records in his memory, trying to put it together. "Is there a Jamayel in his file?"

"Just a dead one," said Eytan. "But he was not dead, until we killed him."

Baum paced some more, still reviewing history, comparing events, reaching for conclusions. Finally, he faced Eckstein from across the glass table.

"Yes," he said. "It would make sense. It would explain everything."

"Yes," said Eytan.

"But could it be a bluff?"

"No."

"No. You are right. It fits too well. It explains everything."

"*Almost* everything," said Eytan.

Baum moved back to the chair and sat. He looked at Eytan anxiously, like a puzzle master awaiting the answer to a crossword that had eluded him for years. No sign of remorse had crossed his face. Only curiosity.

"What else?" he asked. "Tell me all of it."

"There isn't time." Now Eytan stood, lighting a cigarette as he began to walk around the huddle of furniture. He drained the brandy. "Forget about the brother for now, Benni, and consider the three kings."

"What?" Baum was so involved in the solution to Kamil's quest for vengeance that he'd forgotten about the Christmas carol.

" 'We Three Kings,' " Eytan said. "Kamil was in Russia, Balashikha maybe. They probably had his face changed, set him up for a penetration."

"*This* penetration?"

"Yes." Eytan paced, concentrating as he smoked. He was very tired, functioning on all his reserves and a pool of noxious adrenaline. "George doesn't know all of it. They were good with compartmentalization. But he can guess, and his guess is as good as ours. The three kings are sleepers. Mules. A piece of Kamil's old network."

"And what are they muling?" Benni asked.

"He's not sure, exactly," said Eytan. "But he thinks the parts of a weapon."

"A bomb?" Benni's voice dropped to a whisper again.

"I don't think—"

"A nuclear device?"

Eytan stopped and frowned at the major. "You've been reading too much fiction."

"I *never* read fiction," Baum snapped.

"Not a bomb, necessarily," said Eytan. "Probably a personal weapon of some sort. Maybe a Sagger. Something small, but uncomplicated, not perishable."

"So then what's the target?" Baum knotted the drawstring of his trousers until his girth poured over the cloth. He began to wave his trunklike arms as he got up and walked in small circles. "What's the target? A vehicle? Can't be a facility. Not enough power. An aircraft? Maybe the thing's a Strella, but they don't disassemble well. What the hell's the target?" He began to massage his great bald head.

"You've already said it, I think." Eytan was standing still, smoking.

"What have I said?"

"A vehicle. An aircraft."

"That means nothing."

"Unless someone is inside."

"*Who's* inside?"

"Benni," Eytan said. "George thinks that the Three Kings Operation was designed for one mission only. Assassination of a head of state."

Baum stopped moving. He looked at Eckstein. Then he yelled. "May-yah!" From somewhere above, a pair of heavy feet hit the floor, and a muffled reply rippled through the ceiling. "Get me my clothes!" Baum yelled again as he marched toward a telephone that sat on a corner wooden tea table.

The instrument was strangely modern for Baum's

European taste; a Tadiran scrambler. He quickly dialed the number to the night desk of the General Security Services.

"Get me Uri Badash," he snapped. "Then find him and patch me in! This is Major Benni Baum."

Benni waited. He turned to Eytan, snapped his fingers and opened his hand, catching the cigarette pack and the box of matches. He dropped his great head to his shoulder, squeezing the phone there while he lit up.

"Are you sure about this, Eytan?" His eyes had the look of a Grand Inquisitor.

"Of course not," Eytan said.

"Humph," Benni snorted. It was a simple reality check. Whenever an agent claimed to be 100 percent positive, you halted operations for reevaluation. Eytan apparently still had his wits about him.

"He could be bluffing you," Benni said, meaning Mahsoud. "Having one over on you."

"Very possible," said Eytan. "But I don't think so."

Baum put up a finger as someone came on the line. The voice was clear, as the sophisticated Tadiran had none of that gurgling interference common to most scramblers.

"Badash?" Benni said. "Baum. Listen, Eytan has broken the prisoner . . . Yes, Eytan. No, he didn't *have* to damage him." Baum rolled his eyes. "Now, *listen*. I think we have an emergency here."

Benni went on to explain quickly about the three kings, the unknown weapon, and the potential targets. He and Badash agreed that a man like Kamil would not likely be sacrificed for anyone less than a head of state. Badash said that the Foreign Minister was currently on his way to London. The Minister of Defense was in Washington.

The Prime Minister was in Jerusalem, with no pending travel plans.

They talked for another minute, until finally Badash

agreed to go to a full alert. He terminated the conversation so he could begin issuing orders, and Baum hung up.

"Badash says we have to assume that the target is the PM," said Baum. Maya appeared holding a pair of trousers, a shirt, underwear, socks and shoes, all in a perfectly neat pile in her outstretched hands. Baum smiled at her briefly, then began to dress. As he spoke, his wife stood there with an utterly flat expression, like a deaf valet. "He is pretty sure he can get the man to postpone all public appearances over the next ten days. Except for one. Tomorrow night, there is a swearing-in of elite troops at the Western Wall. Badash says no way will the PM cancel his speech."

"Why the hell not?" Eytan demanded. He felt an over-whelming surge of panic, underscored with anger. He had done everything he could—solved the puzzle, broken the codes, proved his points, alerted the world. It was as if he was shackled to the responsibility for Amar Kamil's actions, and no one would allow him to rest. He wanted desperately to sit back now and watch while the big boys took over. Yet even the Prime Minister would not allow it. "That crazy midget doesn't *have* to be there," he exploded. "He can send the Chief of Staff, or Sharon, or some other fucking hero, for God's sake. He can just stay home for once!"

Baum zipped his fly, kissed his wife and bent to tie his shoes. "No he can't," he said, looking up at Eckstein. "His grandson is a paratroop recruit. He's one of the kids being sworn in."

Eytan slapped himself on the forehead. "*In al deenak*," he hissed.

The secure line rang, an electronic warble. Baum grabbed for it.

"Speak," he said.

He listened for a moment, mouthing "It's Horse," to Eckstein as he did so. Then he said, "Okay, I'll be there in ten minutes," and hung up.

"What now?" Eytan asked.

"I don't know," said Baum. "But he was very excited. And when Horse gets excited . . ." He pulled his Browning from the tea-table drawer and stuffed the holster into his hip. "Let's go."

"No. Wait, Benni. I can't." Eytan suddenly had on a look of frantic indecision. "Simona. She must be going crazy."

Baum stopped at the door. "Call her," he said.

"*Call* her?" Eytan snapped. "There's a fucking maniac out there."

Baum thought for a second. Then he went back to the phone and called in to Headquarters. He got on a line to Peaches, the AMAN security detail, and ordered two armed men over to Eytan's apartment immediately.

"She has my gun," Eytan said.

"And make sure it's someone she knows," Baum instructed into the phone, "or she'll shoot them right through the door."

Baum hung up and made to leave, but Eckstein seemed frozen to the floor. His face was drawn, and suddenly sad.

"Now what?" said Benni.

"I have to talk to her," Eytan said.

Baum looked at him. Then he cocked his head at Maya and said, "I will wait in the car."

Maya touched Eytan on the arm and went on upstairs, while Baum went out the front door.

Eytan looked at the phone. He reached for it, hesitated, then picked it up. He wanted to go home. He wanted to be with her, to lock the doors and windows and crawl into bed, pull the covers over, disappear and wake up as someone else, in another life, light years away.

"*Shalom,* honey," he whispered as Simona came on the line.

She was crying, frantic with worry over him. He tried

462

his best to soothe her, racked with guilt as he was, she fearing for her sanity and the health of their unborn child if this nightmare did not end soon. He promised her that it would. In a couple of days, they would take their vacation. They would go down to Eilat. They would swim, and eat, and make love and lie in the sun and the silence.

She said nothing.

He told her about the two security men, that they would be there soon, and she would be safe. They would watch over her.

"And who will watch over you, Eytan?" she said through her tears.

There was no answer to that question. At least none that would allay her fears.

"I love you," he whispered. But she had already hung up.

———

The midnight security shift was on duty at Special Operations. As with most institutions, government offices or private businesses, there was an employee pecking order. If you were new, you had to suffer through a trial period of distasteful assignments.

So the daytime guards had been replaced by kids, stiff-backed AMAN recruits who examined every detail of your ID cards and checked and double-checked the computer. It took Eytan and Benni too damned long to get through the main entrance, and their annoyance was inflamed by the surety that they were being summoned to another of Ben-Zion's egotistical dressing-downs.

As they reached the Floor Two landing, Eytan was surprised to see Moshiko manning the post. The young man was sullen, hands folded on the desk top, eyes dark with fatigue, his black hair mussed by constant finger combing.

"What happened?" Eytan asked as he flashed his ID. "I thought you were promoted to Peaches?"

"I was," said Moshiko with disgust, "until you lost those two idiots in Talpiot."

"But you weren't even there."

"That's what the Colonel said. I should have been there."

"But he didn't *send* you."

Moshiko smiled weakly. "Are you talking about logic, Eytan? Or about Ben-Zion?"

Eytan patted the poor young man on the shoulder.

"Sorry, Moshiko."

"It seems like as long as you're here, I'm fucked."

"Believe me, I'm trying to quit," Eytan said as if talking about his cigarette habit.

"I suppose the commander wants to see us," Baum speculated.

"He's not here," Moshiko said. "Neither is Heinz. Or anyone else, for that matter."

A motion from down the darkened hallway caught Eytan's eye, and he looked up. Horse was standing outside of Communications, waving them on madly.

Baum and Eckstein passed through, hurrying along to meet the little bald figure. Except for the clacking of the telex and cipher equipment, the floor was empty and silent.

They reached Horse and he motioned them to follow, disappearing into the empty personnel office like some playful dwarf in a fairy tale.

"What the hell's going on, Soos?" Baum demanded as soon as the three men were alone.

"We have him." Horse blurted it out quickly, unable to stand it anymore.

Eytan stood dead still, just looking at the analyst as the little man shifted excitedly from one foot to the other.

"What's that?" Benni said, bending down as if he were losing his hearing.

"We have him! We've picked up Amar Kamil!"

"Where?" Eytan said in a gasp. He did not believe it. "How?" He wanted *desperately* to believe it. "Where is he?" He grabbed Horse by the arm without even realizing it.

"They got him in Tel Aviv, tonight, on the street." Horse was talking very quickly now, afraid that Eytan might strangle him if he didn't get it out fast enough. "Itzik set it up with Heinz. They used Ettie Denziger as bait, and they got him."

"Where?" Benni grabbed Horse's other arm. "Where is he, Horse?"

"At General Headquarters!" Horse was squeezing his eyes shut now, screeching. "They're starting the interrogation!"

All at once he stopped babbling. He opened his eyes. His arms hurt, but he was alone and the door swung on its hinges while Baum and Eckstein's pounding footfalls receded down the hallway.

Horse backed up and lowered himself into a chair.

"I've *got* to find another job," he sighed.

———

Victor Gate was never dark. As the main entrance to the *Kiria*—the Command General Headquarters of the Israel Defense Forces—there were always vehicles and personnel passing through the long, counterweighted railroad gates just off Kaplan Street in Tel Aviv. General Headquarters itself was not a single building, but a myriad of streets and structures laid out over many square *dunams* of concertina-wrapped property.

The Kiria always reminded Eytan of the back lot of a Hollywood film studio, for nothing was uniform here, and the atmosphere changed radically from block to block. There were buildings of every size, shape and period, stone Turkish villas and British corrugated barracks, low wooden Quonset huts and towering steel-and-glass communication towers.

Military vehicles from every service branch clotted the narrow roads, and civilian cars with black IDF plates snuggled up on the sidewalks. Men and women hurried to and fro, wearing Air Force khakis and Armored Corps class A's, filthy Paratroop tunics and Navy dress whites. There were bustling canteens on every other corner.

All of the highest-ranking officials had office suites here, including the Prime Minister, Chief of Staff, and Minister of Defense. As major conflicts would be conducted from inside the facility, much of the complex existed underground in cavernous steel honeycombs. All of the major intelligence branches leased various buildings for committee meetings, action planning, security screenings and high-level investigations.

It took Baum and Eckstein less than forty minutes to speed down from Jerusalem. Once through Victor Gate, they drove directly down the hill, taking a right at the incongruous Tudor castle that held the PM's Tel Aviv offices. They parked next to AMAN's low, flat, railroad-style barracks that were usually used for interviewing and polygraph screening of new recruits, declining agents and the occasional suspect spy.

Coming in from the dark, they squinted their eyes before the blinding white walls, which had apparently just been painted. The main hallway of Building 17 was jammed with AMAN personnel. Uniformed officers and men in rumpled civilian clothes milled about, talking excitedly, drinking coffee, and grinding cigarettes into the floor. Except for the lack of TV cameras and flash guns, it looked like an emergency room to which the body of a celebrity had just been delivered.

"Eckstein, Eytan," he said and flashed his ID at an armed sergeant blocking entrance to a pair of double doors.

"Baum, Major." Benni poked his own ID across Eytan's shoulder. The sergeant opened one of the doors, stuck his head in and repeated the names like a maître d' at a dinner dance. He pulled his head out and allowed them to slip through.

They entered a small briefing room. Rows of chairs sat behind banks of connected work tops, facing a large steel desk at the far end, just below a giant pane of two-way glass. Usually there was a pull-down map covering the observation window, except during interrogation exercises, when trainees would sit there in silence, watching the procedure in the secondary chamber while they listened through earphones like diplomats at the UN.

The briefing room was nearly dark, lit only by the dimmed bulbs of overhead bank lights. No one sat in the chairs, as all of those present were crowded together near the two-way panel, peering through into the interrogation chamber.

Itzik Ben-Zion stood in the middle of the group, towering above the rest of the men. He had one foot up on a chair, but his excitement was obvious by the uncharacteristic gesticulation of his hands. The other men, about ten in all, were field rank officers from his various departments. They were all wearing civilian clothes, except for one—a short muscular general who was Deputy Chief of Staff of the IDF. Heinz was also there, pacing back and forth in small circuits, coming to tiptoes to see over everyone's head, then coming down again and smiling to himself in utter self-satisfaction.

As Baum and Eckstein walked forward, Eytan gripped Benni's arm. He squeezed hard, to steady himself, and he felt Baum stiffen as well in anticipation. Eytan felt his heart rising into his throat, beating at the root of his dry tongue. He did not care who had captured Kamil, and his fury over the risking of Ettie's safety was all but gone now, for none of it would matter if what he was about to see were real. At last it would all be over. At last.

He staggered forward through a cloud of cigarette smoke

and pushed up behind the huddle of excited men. Ben-Zion felt his presence and turned his head, looked briefly at Eytan and Benni, then turned back to the window without a word. Heinz swiveled his head as well, shooting Eytan an expression of arrogant triumph as he jerked a thumb toward the captive animal on the other side.

Eytan's eyes widened.

The small interrogation chamber was as bright as an operating theater. Its snow-white walls were devoid of all fixtures. At its center, a steel chair was welded to the floor. Two young men stood well back from the chair, leaning in the corners of the room, arms folded across their muscled chests. Silent.

In the chair sat a man. His ankles were shackled to the steel legs, his wrists to the iron armrests.

Eytan's head stretched forward, straining his neck muscles, the veins beating in his throat.

The prisoner was tall, you could see that even though he sat. His posture was erect. He was well-dressed, European style, wearing a blazer that was torn at one shoulder. His head was crowned with curly, red-blond hair, yes. His jaw was angular, the nose sleek, not necessarily Semitic, yes.

Eytan squinted.

Yes, there was the scar, a curved red scythe beneath the right eye. The eyebrows were full and fair.

Yet the actual eye color, it was hard to make out.

A man suddenly passed before the window. Eytan had not seen him yet, as he had been out of range to one side. He was small, well built, with short blond hair and a pair of cold blue eyes. He was wearing jeans and a white dress shirt, an empty holster in his waistband. Eytan recognized him as a veteran agent named Mori. He was a decorated field man who had been employed, at various times, by both Mossad and AMAN. His specialty was psychological interrogation. It was said that Mori could get a man to surrender his own mother without laying a hand on him. In training sessions, he had often made recruits piss in their pants.

There was a small speaker on the wall of the briefing room, and suddenly Mori's whispering voice came over in fluent Arabic.

"Once again, please," he said as he paced. "What is your name?"

Eytan locked his eyes on the prisoner. He wanted to hear the voice, as if that would confirm the reality of the event, no matter what the man said.

Yet the prisoner said nothing. He did not even move. He did not blink. He stared straight ahead, his nostrils flaring in defiance.

Then something clicked in Eytan's brain, something that caused him to begin to shake his head, slowly, back and forth. It wasn't right. Yes, the prisoner had all the physical markings, the correct colors. The hair. The scar. But he also had a single, glaring trait that Amar Kamil would never, ever have displayed.

This man looked *frightened*.

And those *eyes*.

"Wrong," Eytan blurted. He tore his gaze from the window and turned from the group. He started out of the room, knocking over a chair, ignoring it as it clattered to the floor.

"Eytan," Baum called out.

"Something's wrong," Eytan said as he pushed through the double doors. He shouldered through the cluster of men in the hallway, hardly hearing the growing commotion behind him. He turned left, then down the hallway, then left again until he found the flat recessed door to the interrogation chamber.

He flipped the handle down and walked in, ignoring Mori's startled reaction as he barreled forward, straight for the prisoner's chair. He could see the head turning, the man trying to see what was approaching, but Eytan saw only the red-blond hair.

Before anyone could react, he reached out and placed his left hand on the back of the prisoner's head. Then with his right, he grabbed a lock of curls between his thumb and forefinger and pulled with all his might.

The prisoner screamed. One of the guards yelled, "You fucking maniac!" and lunged forward, but Eytan was already holding the tuft of hair up to the light, for if this really *was* Kamil, there would be bottle-colored light tones turned dark at the roots.

"Wrong!" he snapped as a pair of hands reached for him, but he sidestepped and shook them off, jumping in front of the prisoner's face.

The man was recoiling now, trying to turn his head away, cursing in Arabic. Yet Eytan managed to lock one hand around the prisoner's jaw as he zeroed in on the curved scar with his free fingers and pinched the flesh hard. He quickly raised his thumb, sticky with a gummy residue, and smelled it as Baum, Heinz, Ben-Zion and the entire group from the briefing room tumbled into the chamber, all of them yelling at once.

"What the hell are you doing?"

"Eckstein, you fucking maniac!"

"Get him out of here!"

Eytan felt his arms being pinned behind him, but with one last burst of strength, he yelled "Wrong!" once again, wriggled free, and cocked his left arm as far back as he could. With one great sweep of his hand, he smacked the prisoner on the back of his skull, sending the man's head whiplashing forward over his chest.

"Goddammit!" Itzik's voice boomed through the commotion. "Get him down!"

"It's not him!" Eytan yelled as he was tackled once and for all. He fell back in a pile of flailing arms and legs, with the strength of three agents who feared for their jobs combining to hold him down, like orderlies in a mental ward.

"It's not him, you idiots!" Eytan screamed, waving his arms to break free. "That's his *real* hair color! And it's a spirit-gum scar!"

"Chadaaal!" Benni Baum boomed the command, and all at once the madness ended. Everyone froze. They were all ingrained military men, and a major had just yelled "Cease fire."

Baum stepped over the pile of prone bodies, holding his hands aloft to maintain the temporary break in hostilities.

"What did you say, Eytan?"

"It's not Kamil!" Eytan was still shouting with fury. "Let me up, damn you."

Benni reached into the pileup and grabbed Eytan's arm, hauling the wincing captain to his feet. Eytan immediately charged over to the prisoner again, but this time no one stopped him.

The man was slumped in his chair now, looking at his feet, breathing hard. He tried to pull away as Eytan reached for his face again, yet when the Israeli said, "It's over," in Arabic, the prisoner slowly lifted his head.

Eytan stared into his eyes. Then he groaned.

"He isn't wearing contact lenses."

"So what?" Ben-Zion shouted at him, furious as his nightmare returned like an unexorcised curse.

"He has brown eyes, Itzik," Eytan snarled as he jabbed a finger toward the prisoner's face. "Amar Kamil has *green* eyes, for God's sake!"

No one in the room spoke. The twelve men stood there, staring at Eckstein like dumbfounded schoolboys caught at mischief by their headmaster.

Eytan was breathing like a pneumonia patient. His shirt was torn, his knee in flames, his fists clenched.

"Where is Ettie?" he whispered.

No one answered him.

Heinz turned away.

The prisoner looked up at him and smiled.

A sound like a keening father sprang from Eytan's throat. He launched himself toward the door, splitting the crowd like bowling pins, racing from the building with Baum and an entire entourage of agents fumbling for their car keys as they shouted impotent orders to each other and preyed at his heels.

Ettie Denziger was dead.

By the time Eytan reached her apartment, Itzik had already radioed ahead for a Shabak team to investigate. The GSS men were waiting in a small cluster on the landing before the open door, and he could tell by their faces.

Benni tried to stop him from going in, but he tore away, crashing into a scene that would never leave his memory, no matter the horrors that lay in ambush in his future.

The apartment was a shambles. The liquor cart was on its side, the floor covered in shards of torn labels, broken glass and the wretched stink of unimaginable cocktails. The cushions were thrown from the couch, the wooden coffee table in splinters. One of the French doors to the bedroom was off its hinges, a pane of glass broken through by face or fist.

She had not been an easy kill.

Eytan stepped forward, his legs like putty, his breath a train of whines that he could not hear. The bedroom was dark, but as it grew ever near, he could see the fringes of her white coverlet. They dripped a slow crimson stream onto the parquet floor, and he could see one of her small bare feet pointed at the ceiling.

He felt two hands on his shoulders. The strength against his nauseous weakness halted him.

"Let me, Eytan," Benni whispered.

Baum walked past him, into the bedroom. Eytan strove to hold himself together, his body quivering from head to foot, his fingers stiff and cold as he watched Baum, graceful now, delicate. The lumbering major tiptoed into the darkness, bending silently over the bed. He moved his hands across the light shadows of her bruised and bloodied skin. He looked once more, then reached for the coverlet with his fingers, and laid it gently over the shell of a memory.

Baum came out. He was pale and his lips trembled. He walked to Eytan and stood before him, head still, eye to eye. He did not speak, but reached up to touch Eytan's shoulder, then encircled his captain and began to lead him away.

Eytan moved his feet, his eyes trailing over the ruined room. He could feel the silent presence of many others, but he did not see them.

A trail of blood meandered across the floor, from the bedroom, through the pool of mixed alcohol, and to the door.

Among the assembled mourners, only Eytan had ever slept with Ettie Denziger, and only he knew that she always kept a short commando blade tucked between her mattresses.

At least she had wounded her murderer.

They were almost into the hallway when Eytan suddenly stopped. He turned back and walked quickly into the apartment. Baum followed, concerned that Eytan would, on impulse, reach the horrid scene before he could be stopped.

But he did not go for the bedroom. He lunged for Ettie's white European telephone.

Hands shaking so that he almost could not dial, he

steadied himself and tried to remember his own telephone number in Jerusalem.

It rang seven times, and he waited for Simona to pick up.

It rang seven more times.

There was no answer.

19

Jerusalem

The Last Day of Ramadan

THE SOLDIERS' HOME IN JERUSALEM was certainly no Grand
Hyatt Hotel. If the International Society of Travel Agents
had been forced to rate its facilities on a scale of one to five
stars, it *might* have appeared as a dusty, wobbly meteor in
some forgotten galaxy of youth hostels and sherpa way stations. The guest rooms were barren, with cold tile floors,
rickety wardrobes, low iron beds and thin, lumpy mattresses.
There were no writing desks, televisions or telephones. The
bathrooms were communal, with rows of metal shower stalls,
seatless toilets, and pig-trough sinks with bare piping and
free-flow spigots. Bring your own towel, soap and shaving
mirror. The board was hardly nouvelle cuisine—three meals
a day, served kibbutz-style in a massive mess hall of long
wooden tables and plastic chairs. Take as many helpings as
you dare. Bellhops? Carry your own kit bag and your rifle.
Room service? If you wanted a snack, there was a grocery
store down the street.

The one great thing about Soldiers' Home was the price. It was free.

There was such a *Beit Hachayal* in every major city in Israel. They were run and subsidized by the Israel Soldiers' Welfare Association, and exhausted troops en route to their units were glad to find them and grateful that the Israelis showed their appreciation in deeds rather than accolades. Sometimes, an entire company of soldiers would be brought to a Soldiers' Home for rest and recreation. After a stint in southern Lebanon, it was like a paid vacation on the Riviera.

To the logistics personnel of Military Intelligence, the second best thing about Soldiers' Home was that, when absolutely necessary, the facility could be commandeered. And so it was today, that all of the guests and staff had been invited to relocate. The protests of the tired troops went quickly mute when trucks appeared to take them across town to the Ramada, whose manager was more than happy to have the army foot the bill for filling so many of his rooms left empty by the declining tourist trade.

Colonel Ben-Zion could well have held his briefing at the Ministry of Defense, or Camp Sneller, or even the old film auditorium at Beit Agron. However, he argued well that none of these facilities was completely secure, his mission was ultra-secret and there would be no way to prohibit the curious observer. He needed a completely pristine building, devoid of all but invited personnel. Taking over Soldiers' Home was perhaps the best solution. It was also an act of theater, the solution of an empire builder.

Throughout the early morning, staff cars had been entering the long curved drive off Ben Zvi Avenue, quietly discharging their passengers, then parking in the lot next to the large stone pyramid that served as a monument to Jerusalem's fallen sons. The drivers had been told to do their smoking at the wheel, so as not to attract attention by milling around in groups. At each ground exit from the main building—a three-story structure of Jerusalem granite—a pair of GSS men in civilian garb barred access.

The "invited guests" were men and women of various service branches, all of them carefully selected for their talent and discretion. The Mossad, AMAN, Shabak and National Police people arrived in civilian clothes. The Paratroop, Navy and Air Force officers appeared in their dress uniforms, hardly distinguishable from field battle dress.

Eytan had managed to snatch a few hours' sleep in one of the vacated "suites." With his brain racing as it was, he certainly had no desire for slumber, but his body had finally rebelled, and Baum had practically had to carry him into the building. Now, after four cups of Turkish coffee and an egg sandwich, he stood with Benni in an empty hallway some distance from the big double doors that opened into a large auditorium. The three-hundred-seat theater was the Soldiers' Home's newest renovation, its rows of cushioned movie-house seats raked sharply back from a wide wooden stage. It was usually reserved for military and historical lectures by the Education Corps. Today it would be used in an effort to prevent catastrophe.

Eckstein and Baum smoked their cigarettes, watching the officers as they entered the theater—recognizing each other, shaking hands, chatting as if they were about to attend another boring lecture by some fossil of the military community. They had every reason to be nonchalant, for their orders were devoid of the nature of the business—just the place and time.

On the other hand, for Eytan it was like the first public appearance of a political official who had not really wanted to be elected. Itzik Ben-Zion, though wrong at every turn about Amar Kamil and his objectives, had not lost his Machiavellian edge. He had now dropped the entire operation in Eytan's lap. Numbed as he was by recent events, Eytan felt the weight of the responsibility, yet he was unscathed by the cruelty of Ben-Zion's foisting of the assignment. At least he could now think clearly without fretting over his comrades or loved ones. They were, all of them, either dead or under round-the-clock protective custody.

"Do you think she's really safe?" Eytan said as he squinted down the long hallway. He watched Danny Romano coming through the double glass doors of the main entrance, followed by Horse, who hurried after him like a reluctant leprechaun.

"Of course she's safe," Benni replied. "Itzik's so spooked now, he probably choppered her down to Dimona and had her billeted in the bomb room."

"That's comforting," said Eytan.

Half-crazed with worry, Eytan and Benni had raced from Tel Aviv, back to Jerusalem and Eytan's apartment. Upon their arrival, they had nearly engaged the Peaches people in a gunfight. Some quick explanations revealed that Ben-Zion, upon realizing his terrible mistake regarding Ettie and Kamil's decoy, had dispatched a team directly from the Kiria to pick up Simona and spirit her away from Eckstein's apartment to an airtight safe house. He had also attempted to have Baum's wife picked up. However, the pitiable agents assigned to this risky mission had suffered some bruises and black eyes before succumbing to the *Hausfrau*'s refusal. Much to Baum's delight.

Needless to say, Eytan was not crazy about the arrangement. Ben-Zion had refused to reveal Simona's whereabouts, but at least that retention of professional ethics gave Eytan some comfort that she was truly out of harm's way.

Romano walked up to Eytan and Benni. He took his dry pipe from his mouth and placed a hand on Eytan's shoulder.

"I'm very sorry," he said.

Eytan waited a moment, until he was sure that he could speak.

"I should have made her come in, Danny."

"No one ever made Ettie do anything she didn't *want* to do," said Benni.

"You're not a fortune-teller, Eytan," said Romano.

"Then what do they pay us for?" Eytan's voice cracked.

"Educated guesses, luck, and hopefully harmless mistakes," said Horse.

Eytan looked down at the little man. No wonder Benni kept him around.

"Where's Sylvia?" Baum asked.

"Working with Shabak on the latest intercepts," said Romano. "How about Badash?"

"He's inside already," said Eytan.

Romano looked around, back at the main entrance. "I think we're the last ones. We waited outside. I didn't see Heinz."

"And you won't," said Baum. "He's probably on his way to Marj Ayoun."

Eytan did not join in the satisfaction over Heinz's demise. He doubted that Ben-Zion had been so kind as to just ship the captain off to a field assignment in Lebanon. It was much too pathetic to induce any joy. Heinz had simply echoed the Bogenhausen Fiasco, almost step for step, believing he was braying at Kamil's heels while he pounced on a well-placed look-alike. He had inherited the Feldenhammer curse, and the Colonel had quickly dispatched him, like a leper.

Baum looked at his watch.

"Let's go in," he said.

———

There were about fifty officers inside the auditorium. Rather than gathering down front, they were scattered across the rows of seats, feet propped up, jackets tossed, some tired heads resting back on laced fingers. A few drank from steaming paper cups; a lot of them smoked. At the back of the stage two Air Force lieutenants were up on chairs, pinning a large *Tatsah*—an aerial recon photo—of Jerusalem onto the heavy blue curtain that was drawn across the film screen. In the middle of the stage, General Zamir, the Chief of AMAN, was bending over a long wooden table and examining some materials as he spoke to Itzik Ben-Zion. Both of them were wearing their dress uniforms. In any other army, the presence of a brigadier general would have caused the junior officers to sit bolt upright on their hands, stiff-spined and silent. Here, the Israeli men and women chattered on.

Romano and Horse found seats, and Baum and Eckstein walked down the long aisle. Eytan scanned the morning-scrubbed faces. He recognized the Chief of the National Police, then Uri Badash, and a senior Mossad officer known only as 'Pierre.' Many of the men and women of his own age group also looked familiar, but in the IDF that was a common déjà vu.

"Eckstein, come on up here." Itzik spotted him and snapped his fingers, then he pointed at three young men in civilian clothes at the back of the auditorium. "Security," he called, "lock it up. No one out, no one in." They jumped at his command. Then he waved his hand over the room like Moses parting the Red Sea. "All of you, close it up down front. We don't want to shout here."

The sleepy officers struggled up and out of their comfortable nests, bitching and moaning as they marched forward to crowd uncomfortably together.

Ben-Zion moved to the front of the stage. The triple bronze "falafels" on his epaulettes looked as if they had been spit-shined. His black boots were polished, his belt buckle a mirror. His dress uniform was pressed and creased like an American Marine officer's. His secretary had worked overtime. He placed his fists on his hips. The open dialogues fell to a few low whispers.

"Good morning," Itzik began. "You have all been summoned here to aid in an ongoing AMAN operation called
Flute." This seemingly mundane statement was actually
loaded with meaning. Ben-Zion was taking control, making
sure to clarify right off the bat just which branch was running
this mission. However, for the record, he would also note
that *Flute* had been a concoction of Baum's and Eckstein's,
and if it all went wrong he wanted that "credit" to go where
it was due. "I will now turn this briefing over to my officers."

Ben-Zion had not intended to actually leave the stage, but
when General Zamir climbed down to take a seat in the front
row, protocol demanded that the Colonel follow suit.

Stiff-kneed and all but reluctant, Eytan hoisted himself
up. Then he reached out for Baum's hand and leaned back,
until the major huffed his girth up and over to stand beside
his captain.

"Just tell it straight," Baum mumbled.

Eytan looked out across the expectant faces. As a young
paratroop officer, he had always enjoyed addressing his troops.
Now, that naïveté of young ambition had been burned away.
This was his first briefing in a long, long time, and he hoped
his last. He put his hands into his pockets.

"Ladies and gentlemen," Eytan began. "We are here to
prevent the assassination of the Prime Minister, by an Arab
terrorist called Amar Kamil."

He stopped talking and looked at them. They looked at
him. Someone snickered in disbelief.

"Why would we want to?" an anonymous voice joked
from the farthest row. Someone laughed. General Zamir
turned his head. The perpetrator coughed.

"Politics aside," said Eckstein.

"Uh, excuse me Eytan." A dark-haired woman wearing
army major ranks raised her hand. Eytan recognized her as

a communications expert he had known from field operations. "Is this a training exercise?" It was a common enough question in the military, meaning, "How seriously are we supposed to take this?"

"This is not an exercise," said Eytan.

"Oh, shit," a Mossad officer exclaimed in American English. As if on signal, four dozen notepads and pencils rustled out from pockets and briefcases.

"We have Amar Kamil as deceased," offered one of the police officials.

"The coroner made a mistake," said Benni Baum, causing a momentary rumble of excited voices that quickly died to a cold silence.

"All right, now listen up," Eytan said. He took his hands from his pockets and lit up a cigarette. He blew out a stream of smoke. "We're going to share with you everything we know, and most of what we suspect. I'll begin at the beginning, and I'll try to keep it short. We have a lot of work to do."

He began with the destruction of TWA 206, the operational decision to take out Kamil and his cell. He moved quickly through Europe, omitting only the proper names and places that might breach AMAN security and networks. He described his own solo efforts on the continent with some embarrassment, but he knew that he faced an assembly of fine minds, and together they might pick up something he and Baum had missed. When he summed up recent events and revealed Ettie's death in a carefully controlled voice, a female Mossad agent who had known 'Tamar Shoshani' gasped and covered her face.

"So this is where we are now." Eytan was relieved to be able to escape from the horrors of history, to lose himself once more in the game at hand. "These are the conclusions of myself, Baum, the informant, and Uri here from GSS."

Badash shot him a thumbs-up. "Kamil is going to go for the Prime Minister. He probably wants me and Benni as well, but we think that's secondary now. He has the aid of an old PFLP-SC network in the territories. He has an unidentified weapon—larger than a small arm, smaller than a tank—so the exact choice of technique remains unknown."

"*Ya Allah,* could you be a little less specific?" someone remarked.

"*Shtok,*" Ben-Zion boomed, silencing the sarcasm.

Eytan ignored the interruption.

"According to Badash here, Kamil will have only one opportunity left during the next two weeks. The swearing-in ceremony at the Western Wall."

"That's tonight," a Paratroop officer blurted incredulously.

"Yes," said Eytan, gesturing at the bug-eyed Airborne colonel. "That's why you're here. The PM will arrive by helicopter directly from his residence. He has agreed to wear a ballistic vest."

"Oh, *that'll* help," someone commented.

"Get him to cancel, for God's sake!" someone yelled.

"*You* get him to cancel," Baum retorted loudly.

"*I* will." The Chief of the National Police stood up, puffing out his chest. "I know him personally."

"Sshh." Eytan lifted his palms to calm the outbursts. He pointed at the Paratroop colonel whose battalion was being sworn in. The officer was slumped in his chair, shaking his head. "Tell them, Colonel," said Eytan.

"His grandson's one of my trainees," the colonel said sadly. "The PM won't cancel."

"Stubborn fool," someone mumbled.

Uri Badash stood up, exploding over the assembled heads. "Now listen, all of you! Our job is to provide security for whoever needs it, not to send the government to the bunkers.

If you want to do that then let's just roll up this fucking country and go back to Europe!"

Badash stared at them all for a moment, while they hushed to an embarrassed retreat. Then he sat down.

"All right," Eytan continued. "Before we go on, let's have a look at Kamil's face." He nodded at Uri, who picked up a small walkie-talkie and issued an order.

The double doors at the back opened, and all heads turned as Major Rami Carrera came in, escorted by two men from Peaches. He had spent the last few days locked up in an apartment in Maale Adumim, guarded by two ex-AMAN-niks whose loyalties to Benni Baum were undiluted by their retirement to the private security sector. He looked tired, his uniform rumpled, yet he was clean-shaven and exhibited no annoyance. After all, upon his "kidnapping," Baum and Eckstein had fully briefed him, and he had quickly realized the importance of being kept underground.

Ben-Zion, on the other hand, was shocked to his groin and instantly furious. However, he quickly realized that he could not publicly reveal his having been duped. He turned straight in his chair and stared at Baum and Eckstein with undisguised loathing.

Eytan waved Carrera to join him. The major walked up to the stage and mounted it, letting Eytan take his elbow.

"So, people," Eytan said. "This is the face that Kamil has now."

"But *he* knows that *you* know." Someone's mind worked quickly.

"That's right," Eytan said.

"So he'll try to change it again," someone else called out.

"Or not," said a third voice.

"Why don't we just shoot Rami?" one of Badash's GSS officers suggested. "Just to avoid confusion."

Carrera smiled and shot him the finger.

"Okay," Eytan waved his hands. "You're beginning to think like Kamil, and that's what we all have to do. Let's work, but let's try to do it with some structure, all right?"

The suggestion was idealistic, but impractical. In typical IDF fashion, the orderly briefing quickly dissolved into a heated tactical discussion. Ranks were ignored, manners nonexistent. The officers rose from their chairs, marching around, smoking, calling out suggestions and proposals, supporting each other, deriding one another.

"He knows there's a massive manhunt for him," someone said.

"So he has to try and stand off, use a long shot of some kind," another chimed in.

"If it's a sniper weapon, he has a chance."

"He has never used such a weapon on operations," Eytan said.

"There's always a first time."

"Could be a Stinger, or a Strella."

"No way. They're infrared. He'd more likely hit a hot truck."

"Hard to get something like that past us."

"Tonight, you won't get a *flashlight* past us," declared a GSS man.

"The whole *thing* could be a decoy operation."

"Can't risk that."

"The PM will have his gorillas on three sides when he gives the speech. So the bastard can only take him from the front, from the Jewish Quarter."

"Good point."

"*Bad* point. A helicopter has no bodyguards!"

"The chopper will tree-top it through the wadi," an Air Force officer said. "Not a chance of hitting it."

For a full hour, the men and women argued. They took hard positions, then had their theories trashed. A group of them climbed onto the stage, and they pointed at various structures on the huge aerial photo, drawing on it with markers, scratching their heads furiously.

Eytan and Baum sat down at the long wooden table. They were joined by Romano, Horse, Badash and the Paratroop colonel. A naval captain also participated, as a company of his Naval Commandos would also be included in the ceremonies. The seven men pored over maps and photographs, made checklists and deleted most of the items, then began again.

Finally, General Zamir mounted the stage. He clapped his hands together until everyone resumed their seats. Ben-Zion made to join his commander, but Zamir waved him back into his seat as well.

"All right," said the tall, grey-haired officer. "I have listened to most of your arguments. I believe we have distilled this operation as best we can. We have to move, so we will assume the following—with room for brilliant improvisation, I should hope. I will summarize."

The general held out a hand and counted options on his fingers.

"One: Most of us agree that this will be a ground-to-ground attempt. Two: Given the security cordon, the most likely attempt will come from the front, the western ring of the forecourt, during the PM's address. It is here that most of our forces should be concentrated. Three: We all concur that Kamil now realizes that his Carrera gambit is blown, so he *must* attempt to penetrate us disguised as the exact *opposite* of an IDF officer."

The general waited, yet no one raised an objection. This was not out of respect. They simply agreed with him.

"And finally. Four." He turned to Eytan. "Unfortunately for you, Eckstein, it appears that you have become the world's best expert on Amar Kamil. Take a moment, if you must, and issue the Order of the Day."

The general hopped down from the stage. The notepads appeared again, pencils poised. Itzik Ben-Zion leaned over his knees and gripped his rippling jaw with one hand.

Eytan did not need a minute. He had already decided.

"All right, people," he commanded. "These are my orders . . ."

———

From the pale desert sky above Jerusalem the night came on quickly, a rushing indigo curtain unfettered by any clouds that might have stubbornly retained reflections from the sun, as it submerged into the distant Mediterranean. To most Jerusalemites, the evening brought a cool, welcome relief from the harsh days of a dying summer. To Eytan, the descending dome of ink was a cold shroud. He watched it from the parapets of the Jewish Quarter of the Old City, feeling like a seasick sailor in the rigging of a wooden fourmaster, observing the purple billows of a gathering typhoon on the horizon.

He rubbed his arms to stay the chill, and he looked down into the great forecourt before the Western Wall. The huge courtyard was flat, like the floor of an ancient, open vault, a thousand squares of Jerusalem granite sanded and polished like the steel deck of a great ship. In the center of the floor, a large square area was cordoned off by lengths of brocaded ropes on black metal stands. Inside the ropes, along the near three sides of the square, rows of steel gun racks held gleaming Galil assault rifles, racked in perfect symmetry, their deadly mouths open to the sky. Beyond each flock of rifles stood a wooden table, and on each table a pyramid of army Bibles, bound in rich blue leathers.

Farther on, a wooden stage had been erected. It held a semicircle of metal chairs to bear the weights of dignitaries. A wooden podium stood at the lip of the stage, a small speech lamp glowing over the top of the lectern and single microphone. The stage was rimmed with Israeli flags and unit pennants, giving it the character of an old man's birthday cake.

From below the stage and to its left, a cacophony of low, bleating sounds rose from another cluster of metal chairs. Members of the Israel Defense Forces marching band, wearing their olive dress uniforms and British-style peaked caps, forced warm air through their cold instruments. Behind the musicians and looming above them and the stage, stood a large, temporarily erected steel structure. It was a giant version of the silver parachute wings of the IDF Airborne Corps. The parachute canopy and the wings were wrapped in kerosene-soaked burlap, as were the meter-high Hebrew letters that proclaimed, Swifter than Eagles, Braver than Lions. When the troops swore their allegiance, the phoenix would burst into flames.

As Eytan stood on the high ramparts of the western rim of the courtyard, almost nothing was beyond the range of his vision. To his left, the only visitors' entrance that led from the Arab quarter had been sealed by Border Police. Along the high parapets of the old Ottoman wall that sealed the northern half of the forecourt, seasoned paratroopers walked in full battle dress, poking their way between the banks of floodlights that spilled down into the square below. Directly across the forecourt, the giant stones of the Western Wall itself rose to meet the flat expanse of Harim es Sharif, the Moslem holy place from which Jewish troops were barred by national authority, in order to avoid clashes between Israelis and observant Palestinians. From the center of the Moslem holy ground, the enormous gold cap of the Dome of the Rock gleamed under starlight like the private observatory of a billionaire.

Normally, at the foot of the great vertical slab that had once been called the Wailing Wall, hordes of black-clad Jews bobbed and prayed, touching the holy remnants of King Solomon's Temple, scribbling notes to God and tucking them into the ancient cracks. Tonight, due to the incursion of the pagan military ritual, only a few old men were gathered at the wall. They bent over rows of heavy wooden tables, studying their Torah in the failing light.

To the right of the military ceremonial enclave, a long, curving stone ramp led from the forecourt up to an arched gateway, and into Haram es Sharif. Due to the political sensitivity of the disputed area, only a handful of loyal Israeli–Arab policemen guarded the gate. However, they had been warned thrice over to allow no one to pass this night from the Mount down into the courtyard. And just to make sure, another contingent of Border Police guarded the foot of the ramp.

The only open entrance to the forecourt lay to the right, the Dung Gate at the southern side of the roofless vault. A steel checkpoint had been built there, like an old border post between East and West Berlin, where a long stream of visitors slowly filed forward to fill the ceremony.

Eytan had always treasured his visits to the *Kotel*. Since being sworn in there himself—younger by fifteen years, an emaciated, sleep-starved, proud recruit—he held it as doubly hallowed ground. Despite the throngs of visitors, it was always a quiet place, filled with the hush of prayers, the reflexive whispers of Jews close to God. He was not a religious man, but the Wall seemed to him like the soul of his people's history. And if he did not exactly come to pray, it was a fine place to meditate, to reevaluate and reabsorb the reasons for his being.

It was a place of piety.

A sealed sanctuary.

A killing ground.

"Knife One, Knife One, this is Fork, over."

The crackling voice startled him, vibrating against the

right cheek of his rump. He pulled the small walkie-talkie from his rear pants pocket.

"This is Knife. *Ruth,* go ahead," he said into the small black box.

"*Knos.*" It was Benni's voice, summoning him down into the forecourt.

"*Ruth,*" Eytan said, and he replaced the radio. He took a deep breath. The Prime Minister was on his way. He looked around at the stairways and ramparts and rooftops of the Jewish Quarter. There were many figures silhouetted in the shadows. They were all AMAN, GSS, Police or Mossad. Snipers, scouts, communications people, pistol marksmen. Many of them carried night vision scopes or goggles. Half of them peered down into the forecourt, the other half into the nooks and crannies of the residential district of deep alleyways and winding walls.

Eytan started down the wide stone staircase that led to the forecourt. With each tread on the hard granite, he was losing hope, while he tried to keep his wits alive.

The courtyard was filling with soldiers, the fresh-faced, expectant recruits forming up at the southern end to begin their march to glory.

Dignitaries and the soldiers' families waited alike at the single entrance. It was slow going, as on Eytan's orders every participant or visitor, including ranking statesmen and politicians, had been cleared during the course of the day and issued color-coded identification cards. At the gate itself, Horse sat hunched over Yablo's portable GRID. The particulars of each Paratroop and Naval Commando recruit had been downloaded from the data base of the central recruiting depot at Tel Hashomer, and as each family member arrived, he or she had to supply the name, address, and birth date of his or her soldier-candidate. If the information checked out against the details that appeared on the yellow screen, the civilians were likewise issued colored ID cards and instructed to pin them to their clothing.

No Arabs were admitted to the ceremony—neither Israeli citizens nor residents of the West Bank. Even so, pairs of plainclothes agents wandered through the gathering crowds, discreetly interrogating anyone who remotely matched Kamil's build.

All of the ranking officers seemed quite satisfied with Eckstein's precautions. The perimeters were hermetically sealed—it would require wings and a cloak of science-fiction invisibility to penetrate the security shield.

Yet Eytan found little comfort. He felt like a blind elephant battling a scorpion.

His one remaining hope was that despite arguments to the contrary, he still believed that the Prime Minister was safe, as long as he himself had not yet been killed. To that end, he and Benni had spent the entire afternoon on the streets of Jerusalem. They had wandered back and forth through the most public areas, along the packed sidewalk cafés on Ben Yehuda Street. Eytan out in front, Benni a few meters behind, hoping that Kamil would make his move. Praying that he would not.

Nothing. A day of spent exhaustion, waiting for gunfire that never erupted.

But there was still the remote chance that Amar Kamil's obsession with 'Tony Eckhardt' would overpower him. Eytan reached the floor of the courtyard and turned right, heading toward a brightly lit area somewhat removed from the gathering throng. Beneath a bank of small floodlights, perched high atop photographers' lamp stands, stood General Zamir's Chevrolet command wagon. It bristled with antenna array, and its radios crackled with the calm staccatos of field officers.

Normally, a whole contingent of aides and intelligence officers would have surrounded the vehicle. However, they had all been ordered to stay well back, out of the circular pool of light that spilled over the polished stones.

Alone in the glaring spot, like a master of ceremonies on a massive stage, stood Benni Baum. He had one foot up on the running board of the command wagon, and he shielded his eyes from the artificial glare as he stared up at the turrets of the Jewish Quarter. Eytan walked up to join him. They exchanged glances, but no greeting. Alone together under the white-yellow beam, they looked like the imminent victims of a kangaroo firing squad.

Here we are, was the message. *Take your best shot.*

It had been difficult getting Zamir to agree to this last-ditch effort, yet in the end he had no choice. It was the duty of his soldiers to protect the nation from disaster, and if such self-sacrifice could cause the terrorist to reveal himself, there was no good reason to resist the tactic.

The flesh over Eytan's chest crawled, the roots of his hair charged as if by an electrical storm. He could not help moving every few seconds, but he stayed within the light. Benni hardly seemed to be breathing heavily.

A crash of cymbals made Eytan's heart leap, and he spun toward the Wall. The band began to play the hymn of the Israel Defense Forces, a British-style marching tune full of brass and drums. The formations of troops stepped off, tramping down toward their gun racks and bibles. The crowd burst into applause.

Eytan turned his head to the south and the Dung Gate, where another, different roar rose to match the outburst of familial enthusiasm. A bright light flashed over the metal security checkpoint, and an Air Force Bell 212 helicopter popped up like a gigantic, angry wasp. It hurried over the barriers, its spinning rotor tilting forward as it angled down and quickly settled into a cleared square of stones from which landing flares hissed and spat pink flashes. The skids had hardly touched the earth when two identical black limousines raced forward, pulling up short on each side of the chopper. Their doors opened, dome lights extinguished, and groups of large young men in civilian clothes bent beneath the wind and flashing blades as the helicopter discharged its passengers to both sides. It was impossible to tell into which vehicle the Prime Minister was hustled—if at all. Both cars, taking separate curving courses, headed down toward the ceremony.

Eytan tried to think. The marching band, the thunder of applause, the whine of the helicopter. It was impossible to concentrate. He covered his ears. . . .

High above the vault of the Western Wall's forecourt, the Dome of the Rock stood on the vast plot of the Temple Mount, a slab of stones larger than a square kilometer. The Mount was lined on three sides with groves of tall trees. At the far eastern edge of this religious roof—from where Mohammed had ascended to heaven, and upon which Abraham had nearly sacrificed Isaac—the sounds of the military ceremony were muted by distance and the evening wind.

At this edge of the Mount the thick Ottoman walls dropped forty meters straight down to the darkened valley below. The dry moat was uninhabited, peppered with scrub, broken tombs, and fallen stones from the Mount of Olives, which rose high to the east.

At the foot of the wall, soldiers in full battle gear had been placed at fifty-meter intervals. The wall was a precipice, an unscalable array of giant vertical slabs, but the army was taking no chances.

Most of the cold, lonesome soldiers were fairly alert. They were all bored.

One of them was dead.

His throat had been crushed by a single, knifehand blow. Actually, he appeared to be still of this world, albeit a bit sleepy. He sat on the ground, back against the wall, rifle across his splayed legs, his head resting back comfortably. Only a close look at the bulging eyes would have revealed his condition.

Amar Kamil climbed. Once again, he needed no ropes, carabiners, or pitons. There were large cracks between the stones. Plenty of handholds. The soles of his combat boots gripped the rocky lips, his splayed fingers found sufficient points of tension. The gym bag hugged his back as he moved slowly up through the darkness, noiseless, barely breathing, hardly dusting the uniform of the officer whose naked body was by now going stiff in an olive grove near Bethlehem.

He rolled onto the top of the wall and dropped down to his feet, moving quickly behind a tree. His dyed black curls gleamed in the starlight. He shucked off the gym bag and slowly opened the zipper, placing the maroon beret on his head, cocking it over one eye and ear. He withdrew the pistol, his homemade silencer permanently welded to the barrel. It was primitive, but at the most he might need a trio of defensive shots. He tucked it into the belt of his dress tunic, at the small of his spine. The deep knife wound there was a gouging fireball, and it still bled despite the tight wraps of surgical tape. He ignored it.

Finally, he removed the two halves of the RPG, screwed them together, and lay the weapon back inside the bag. Inserting and arming the rocket would take but a few seconds.

He poked his head around the tree.

To his right, the great Dome of the Rock was magnificent, silent, not a soul in sight since the daily prayers were long over. Ahead, the wide stone porch of the Temple Mount lay open to him. At the far side, the lights of the ceremony played skyward from the vault below like the closing night of a carnival in Monaco.

The marching band had stilled. The troops must have

received their rifles, for he could hear the echoes of parade orders and the stamps of hundreds of metal butts on the cold stones.

He stood up, picked up the bag, and began to walk. The Jews would not be on the Mount. Despite the open hatred that flowed their way from every Palestinian soul, they still showed respect for the Moslem shrines. That would be their undoing.

He walked. Casually, as if he belonged, a conqueror. Between himself and the distant top of the Western Wall, a pair of Arab policemen stood talking and smoking. They were desecrating the holy shrines, but Amar was not offended.

The wind blew across the vast square, the leaves of the tall eucalyptuses rustled. The Arab policemen turned toward him, staring at the brazen Israeli officer in wonder.

He walked, and he smiled broadly.

Eytan tried to think, his brain aching with the strain. All around him there was chaos. Engines hummed, people applauded, rifle butts slammed the stones and orders hammered off the walls. Yet nothing was happening.

He spun around, searching the high parapets, straining to see beyond the shapes and shadows. It could not be that he was wrong, that it would not happen here at all. If his concept was deadly foolishness, and Kamil surprised him again, accomplished his mission, Eytan could not live with it. He began to squeeze his fingers in his hair, praying for a gunshot, almost wanting the bullet to tear through him, to prove that he was not a madman.

The ceremony grew suddenly silent. The troops had their rifles, their bibles. A sergeant-major was speaking to them, reciting their code of allegiance, asking them if they would swear to it.

He had to *think*. At every turn he had been one step

behind Amar Kamil. Now he had to think like Amar Kamil. Now, if ever, he had to *become* Amar Kamil. He had to out-think *himself.*

"Ani Nishbah!" Three hundred troopers shouted their allegiance in a unified thunder of youthful innocence that shook the stones beneath his feet.

And then he saw it. He was wrong. The idea that the PM was safe as long as *he* lived was wrong. No, Kamil wanted Eytan to witness this final coup, just as he had suffered through the deaths of his comrades. This would be Kamil's most vengeful blow. The simple killing of his brother's murderer could wait. Maybe until tomorrow. Maybe for ten more years!

Another flash inside his brain. Itzik Ben-Zion was right. Kamil was not suicidal, and if he did intend to kill the Prime Minister, while retaining any hope of escape, there was only one disguise he could choose. He *had* to be dressed as an army officer, for in the ensuing melee, anyone else who was running from the scene would be brought to the ground like a hunted gazelle.

The troops, the band, the officers, the audience. They were all hushed now to a respectful silence. Eytan turned his head. Upon the stage of dignitaries, a small crowd had gathered at the front, behind the lectern. It was a semicircle of giants, all of them men over two meters tall. All of them shifting, watching, eyes twitching. The Prime Minister's gorillas.

The little man stepped up onto a low podium of wood. His old grey head entered the light of the lectern; his silver tie gleamed. He cleared his throat, smiled, and began to speak.

Eytan turned back toward the Jewish Quarter. Now. It would happen now. He began to be drawn from the pool of light, then he stopped. They all expected a shot to come from the front. No! It was the exact opposite, *always*, of what they expected.

496

He heard a voice, the crackle of a radio from inside Zamir's command wagon. A piece of a sentence.

". . . the trooper's dead. We just found him at the foot of the eastern wall of the city, over."

Eytan spun back to the light, his mouth open to shout. Baum was gone.

He raised his hands and turned, frantic, searching. His eyes caught the movement, on the ramp leading up to the Temple Mount. Benni was sprinting like a bull. Alone.

Eytan ran, pulling the walkie-talkie from his pocket. "Camel One, Camel One," he hissed. "This is Knife, come in." The Arab cops on the Mount were on his radio tether. They did not answer.

He was running blind, breathless before he even started, unable to call to the Border Troops as he passed them, his knee blazing as he sprinted up the ramp.

At the top, the slim door to the Moroccan gate was open. He ran through it, onto the wide expanse of the Mount, his heart hammering, leaping even farther into his mouth as he saw the crumpled bodies splayed across each other like Romeo and Juliet.

He heard the sharp cough to his left and spun on it, running again as he dropped the radio and it exploded in a hundred shards of plastic and transistors across the stones of the Mount as he drew his pistol and cocked it.

Where the Mount ended at the lip of the Western Wall, the ground was submerged in long rectangular shadow. Another retaining wall, two meters high and leading to a second wide parapet, jutted up from the darkness. A figure sat at the foot of the stone embankment.

Eytan ran to the wall and crouched. He put out his left hand and braced himself as he moved along it, leaving palm prints of sweat.

Baum sat there, breathing slowly, his head back against the cold granite, one hand over his belly. A river of blood ran over his fingers and into his crotch. It was already seeping out from under his trousers, across the stones. His suntanned face was as white as a full moon.

Eytan moved to him, his teeth set in a skull's grimace. As he approached, Benni slowly turned his head. There was no sign of pain in Baum's face, yet his eyes were glazed. He looked tired, worn, almost ready to surrender.

He lifted his right hand from beside his leg, slowly, and as Eytan neared, Benni gripped his captain's arm with his last vestige of power. He opened his mouth, and Eytan bent his face to him.

"He is much faster than you, Eytan," Benni whispered. "But you must beat him. You *must*."

Eytan tried to speak. He could not. There was no time for it. He pulled his arm away and looked up. The wall was high, too high. He looked down at Baum, then lifted his right foot and placed it on Benni's shoulder. Baum quickly raised his hand and wrapped his fingers around Eytan's ankle, to steady him.

In one swift movement Eytan launched himself upward, slamming his stomach down onto the top of the wide wall. He held on to his pistol, scrabbling with his free hand as he swung his legs up, rolled over, and came to his feet.

Amar Kamil was waiting. He stood only two meters away, his back to the low edge of the top of the Western Wall, the lights haloing his silhouette. He was wearing the dress uniform of a Paratroop captain. The triple bronze bars shimmered on his epaulettes, the silver parachute wings a bright slash over his left breast. The maroon beret was cocked over his right brow as if he had been born to wear it.

Next to Kamil's feet lay the rumpled form of an empty gym bag. Next to that, resting on the lip of the wall, the silent black tube of a Rocket-Propelled Grenade launcher gleamed. The ugly warhead was loaded, the cap of the charge removed, the hammer pulled down, ready for the strike.

Even so, it was hard for Eytan to make the mental leap. Kamil looked so much like an Israeli, his costume perfect, his red-brown boots placed easily apart, so hard to imagine that this was the man who had starred in all of Eytan's nightmares. So calm, so relaxed.

Except that he was pointing a silenced pistol directly at Eytan's face.

Eytan was frozen in his half crouch, his mouth suddenly dry as sand, his breath like waves of liquid gas, the pulse pounding in his throat. He stared at the shadowed face, immobile, only the eyes blazing like a panther's. Nothing of Kamil's body moved, except for the mouth of the silencer, which dipped twice at the ground, quickly.

Eytan bent, slowly, like a man under water. His eyes on Kamil's face, he lowered his Browning toward the stones, wanting to try it anyway, knowing that he'd be blown off the wall and into Baum's lap if his hand even twitched.

He rose again, without the weapon, turning a bit now, facing full to the front, his limbs shivering, coursing with blood and adrenaline.

From somewhere, he heard the falls of footsteps, yet so far away. They would never make it. He heard another sound, the drone of a distant voice, slightly metallic, the speech echoing in the great vault below.

Unbelievably, he felt his body moving forward, rebelling against a mind that tried to compel him to stop. Yet Kamil's form did not waiver.

"Do not worry, *Mr. Eckhardt,*" the voice said in perfect, controlled Hebrew. "You will only have to witness the assassination of your Prime Minister. And then I will end it for you, as you ended it for my brother."

The silenced pistol began to drop, slowly, its trajectory changing just slightly. He was going to shoot Eytan, not kill him yet. Just enough to immobilize him, while he then stepped to the wall and used the RPG, blowing them all back into a ghastly twilight of tribal revenge. He was going to shoot Eytan in the legs. *In the legs*.

"*You* killed Jamayel." Eytan was amazed that he could find his own voice, harsh and hoarse as it was with terror. "*You* killed your own brother." He moved his right foot forward, almost dragging it. "You used him like a tethered goat. And I was merely the punishing hand of Allah."

He hit the mark. Kamil lifted his head, the eyes narrowing to burning slits, the rage crawling over his face. For that crucial millisecond, he raised the pistol to fire at Eytan's head, and Eytan made the only move he could: the only technique he had ever managed to do half-well in *Krav-Maga*.

He lunged with his left foot, snapped his left hand forward, up, over, catching the silencer and sidestepping as it exploded next to his face. He yelled as he struck out with his right fist, but Kamil snapped his head over and the punch went wild. He felt a sharp blow to his knee but still he held on to the gun, yet in that split second he knew that he could never complete the move, could never turn the weapon on Kamil and use it. An open hand chopped down into his face as he twisted to the left with all his might, swinging his right hand over toward the pistol, slamming into it, wrenching it from Kamil's grip as he followed through and hurled it high and away into the night.

For the length of a brain synapse they stood, empty-handed. But it was no match. Eytan did the unthinkable.

As Kamil's eyes bulged in disbelief, Eytan yelled Simona's name, launched himself forward, gripped his nemesis in an embrace of hatred and took them both over the edge of the parapet, to fall the length of a long hollow scream into the stone forecourt far below. . . .

20

Hadassah Hospital

One Week Later

THE CORRIDOR WALLS OF THE MILITARY WING were neither
white nor green. They had instead that mustard hue which
looks like the aged, spotted skin of some other, youthful color
long forgotten. The floors of the hallways were dark and
speckled, like the backs of river salamanders, the tiles close
together to prevent the grating sounds of gurney wheels over
cracks. They were clean, these floors, wet mopped and dried
each day before the dawn, although the hallway windows
were left open to the breeze that tunneled up from the distant
Mediterranean and brought a talcum film of dust that dulled
the shine by noon.

It was the IDF's private wing of the hospital, yet more
than that, the security section of the military wing. Pass
upon pass, release over permit you would need to get in
here. No reporters, photographers, candy stripers, or magazine hawkers. No civilians, except the cleared family visitors

and the doctors and nurses, who were all reserve duty officers anyway. No matter the national crisis—all-out war, terrorist massacre, tragic multiple traffic accident—the wing never bustled.

It was on the top floor of the northwest building of Hadassah, which itself sat far away from Jerusalem's center, jutting out over the sloping valleys of Ein Kerem, framed by high peaks bristling with pines. The breeze was always mint fresh, and in the evening with the setting sun, the old mustard walls and shoe-burnished tiles glowed orange-pink like the seeds of summer pomegranates.

Benni Baum moved slowly along the hallway, wearing a pair of worn leather sandals whose soles hardly left the floor. With his left hand he clutched the drawstring of his baggy blue pajama bottoms. With his right, he gripped the silver pole of an IV stand, whose metal casters squeaked as it rolled along beside him like an alien pet at heel. The tube from the hanging bag of glucose snaked down into his forearm, and through the open shirt of his pajamas the wide stomach bandage was as fresh and white as goose down.

His head bent low with the painful effort, sweat beading on his great bald brow. His pace could only have been called a trudge.

He thought, as he walked, that perhaps he should have been more careful with Eytan Eckstein. He wondered if his own influence on the young man had gone unrealized for its intensity, if it could, somehow, have been checked. And yet, he reasoned, Eytan's drive had a soul of its own. Who could have imagined a heart that would choose such a final, desperate act? Benni knew that, even in his own foolish youth, he would never have done it.

Still, he promised himself, the next time, if there would ever be such an opportunity, he would more closely monitor the unexpected, spontaneous heroics of the young.

He stopped walking and touched the tender spot where the bullet had been removed. It was hardly healed, but he could not wait to escape the silent, miserable ward.

He looked up and squinted down the long hallway. At the far end, three men approached the nurses' station. One tall man in uniform, carrying a large bouquet of flowers. The other two were muscled, fidgety, sunglassed kids in civilian clothes.

Itzik Ben-Zion, and a pair of his Peaches.

Benni began to hurry forward, anxious to reach the room before the Colonel did. He shuffled faster, maneuvering around the chair in the corridor where Moshiko sat, pistol in lap, reading another Graham Greene. Baum pushed the heavy door aside and went in.

"The Prince of Darkness is paying a visit," he announced.

Eytan looked up from his bed and grunted, an ugly sound like he was smelling flatulence. He lay on his back, stretched out along the large hydraulic unit near the far window. He looked rather like a burn victim. The sheets were starched and dry bone white. Both arms were lifted toward the ceiling, fixed to metal braces and cocooned in heavy plaster casts. He wore white pajama bottoms, and his trunk was swathed in many lengths of gauze and adhesive. His head was also wrapped above the eyes, though with only a single band so that his hair stuck out, giving his pain-marked face the air of a kamikaze pilot.

At the foot of the bed, Simona sat in a green upholstered chair. She was wearing jeans, already going too tight, the fly button open to relieve the pressure, a loose pink blouse untucked to cover her casual repose. She was knitting a tiny sweater of yellow cotton. Israeli women never had sonograms just to know the gender of their babies.

She looked up at Benni as she understood his warning. "Too bad," she said. "And it was turning into such a nice evening." Then she looked at Eytan and smiled. He lifted his head from the pillow and returned the expression.

"Do you want me to raise you up?" Simona asked.

"No. Just cover me with a sheet and pretend I'm dead."

The pains had receded now to something of a dull ache. The drugs that dripped into his hand did most of that, though at times it still surprised him, coming in waves from all the compass points of his immobilized body.

He was still as amazed as everyone that he had survived the fall. In those last two seconds of twenty-meter plummet, no inkling of a future had crossed his mind; his adventurous history had not passed before his eyes. He had only seen Simona's face behind his squeezed eyelids.

They had crashed together onto one of the large wooden prayer tables at the base of the wall, smashing it into a pile of kindling. Kamil landed on his back, sandwiched between Eytan and the wood and stone, crushing his spine and snapping his neck. He had died instantly.

However, Kamil's body and Eytan's own protruding elbows had kept the captain from mortal injury. Even so, his arms had fractured in many places, he broke six ribs and his forehead was split like a sliced grapefruit.

His leg, on the other hand, had never felt better.

The first ones to the bloody wreckage—members of the IDF marching band—did not initially know what to make of it. To them, in those few seconds before the crowd of security forces came tumbling through the forecourt, it looked as if a madman had taken a paratroop captain with him in a suicidal leap from the Western Wall.

Which was actually the proximate truth.

Eytan regained consciousness after eight hours of surgery and another thirteen submerged in a dark sea of dreams. With his first words, he lied to Simona. He told her only that he had grappled with Kamil, and they had gone over the

Wall. She would be furious if he revealed the truth, and he decided to keep it to himself. To himself and Benni Baum.

Even when the Prime Minister had come to visit, heaping accolades on this Brave Jewish Soldier, Eytan had found it easy to remain self-deprecating. The bloody memories that were laced through *Operation Flute* prevented him from joyful indulgence.

"I only did it to earn my combat bonus, sir," was all he said. The remark caused roars of laughter in the roomful of officers and politicians. But Eytan did not join them. . . .

"Maybe I should go?" The voice came from the corner of the room, where Francie Koln stood quietly tucked away, reading a magazine. She looked quite pretty without her drab field disguises, her long brown hair washed and pulled into a ponytail, her contact lenses liberating her from her plain spectacles, her skin healthy from the Egyptian sun.

"Don't you move," said Eytan. Besides Baum, Francie was the only member of his team who had survived the ordeal, the only one he had managed to save. She was living proof that it had not all been a waste. "You can stand right there," he said. "Night and day, until I get out of here."

She smiled at him.

"Ahalan!" Itzik Ben-Zion crashed into the room, holding a tasteless burst of flowers more appropriate to a Mafia funeral. "My warriors!"

Baum was already sitting on his bed, smoking a cigarette. He glanced up at Ben-Zion, then dragged a book onto his lap and thumbed the pages. No one else responded to the Colonel's bellicose greeting either. Eytan turned his head to look, but Simona kept on knitting, and Francie simply folded her arms across her chest.

Ben-Zion's two guards frowned like angry courtiers of the king. But Itzik was not offended. Nothing could dampen his jolly mood, for as promised, he had taken full credit for Amar Kamil's interception and demise.

"So?" Itzik slammed the vase down onto the food cart at the foot of Baum's bed. The water spilled over and ran onto Benni's sheets. Baum turned his head and watched it drip. "How's my captain? Or maybe I should say *major?*"

Eytan did not take the bait. Simona looked up from her knitting and said, "How much?"

"Pardon me, madame?" Itzik bent his head to her, a wide smile fixed on his lips.

"How much does a major make?"

The Colonel laughed. "Spoken like a true mother-to-be," he said. "Well, everything is negotiable, of course." He turned so that he could see both Eytan and Benni at the same time. "Gentlemen, my congratulations. Everyone is ecstatic. The media is hounding me for names, but naturally I will continue to lie to them. *LaHaDam.*"

He used the acronym of deniability favored for media response: *Lo Hayu Ha-Dvarim Mi-olam*—These things never happened.

He waited for some kind of acknowledgment, a crack in the ice. When it failed to thaw, he just pressed on.

"Eckstein," he boomed. "Your suspension is rescinded—"

"With full back pay," Simona said quickly.

"Yes, of course."

"And a bonus."

Itzik laughed again. "And a bonus."

"For Benni, too, I imagine," said Simona.

Itzik looked at Eytan and jerked a thumb at Simona.

"She's a tough one." He winked.

"You're lucky Benni's wife isn't here," Simona warned.

"*Very* lucky," Baum agreed, his face still in his book.

Itzik cleared his throat.

"Anyway, Eckstein. Naturally, full reinstatement. In addition, if you wish, you can take over the Training staff. How's that?"

Eytan said nothing. He just looked at Ben-Zion as he drummed the fingers of his right hand on the metal traction brace.

"Well, you can think about it." Itzik grew a bit uncomfortable with the chilly atmosphere. He looked around. "So, everyone is okay?"

Now they all lifted their faces to stare at him, waiting.

The Colonel looked at his watch. He mumbled something about getting back to the office. Then he stepped to Eytan's bed, looking for a safe place on which to rest his hand. He found it on Eytan's thigh, the only obviously undamaged part of his body. He squeezed the flesh, leaned closer as he said conspiratorially: "Once in a while, Eckstein, you kill the right man."

He patted the leg hard, and laughing at his own joke, he nearly made it to the door.

"No, Itzik," Eytan called out, and the Colonel stopped and turned. "If I had done that, *you* would be dead. And if you don't honor my deal with George Mahsoud, you *will* be."

Itzik and his two guards stood there, frozen, mouths agape. The Colonel's face went dark, brooding, all self-congratulations gone, measuring the value of his captain, and his threat.

He dropped his head just slightly, turned, and departed. For once, without another word.

EPILOGUE

Three Months Later

THE JUDEAN MORNING WAS A BRILLIANT ONE, its dark dawn clouds and showerstorms of cold rain dismissed now by a determined December sun, and a spearhead of high frothy cirrus rushing across a cobalt sky. The heat of Ramadan had long since passed into the cold clear breezes of Jerusalem's welcome winter, her citizens relieved to air their hats and sweaters, to huddle inside the street cafés and caress hot mugs of coffees and onion soups. To have their cars and streets and houses washed each night by downpours of pure waters, then polished to a lacquer glow by the piercing rays of a high Mid-Eastern star.

It was the kind of winter day that carries sounds more crisply, in an air unfettered by wafting clouds of desert dust. It was the kind of day that casts aside the fetid smells of summer-heated foliage and frees the scents of pine and bougainvillea, to make the act of breathing a heady, intoxicating pleasure, instead of a burden of survival.

It was, in fact, Christmas Day.

Eytan drove his Fiat past Bethlehem, skirting lines of Christian tourist buses, their windows filled with the proud heads of habited nuns and the excited faces of foreign pilgrims. His arms were still encased in plaster casts, though only partial now. They ended just above the elbows, and his thumbs and fingers were free and mobile. There was still quite a bit of discomfort, especially around his tightly bound ribs. The doctors had warned him not to drive as yet, but he had insisted, so they had given him a small packet of pills in case the pain became too much. He had thrown the medicine away. The wash of perfumed air and the freedom of the roads were all he needed.

As he left the southern outskirts of the city, he pushed the Fiat into fourth out on the open road, then cracked his window just enough to hear the pealing bells from Manger Square. He turned his head to the right and lifted his chin, for in the wide valley below—its summer scruff now rich and green with winter waters—a Bedouin in flowing robes led a long train of camels through the wadi. Their caramel furs were shiny and wet, their long necks bowing snout to tail as they swayed unhurried through the valley. Their caboose was a giant albino, his rare lush coat unsaddled, glowing like a polar mirage.

Eytan turned his head farther, to look at George Mahsoud. The Palestinian sat proudly in the passenger seat, this time unshackled by any manacle, his dark uncertain future swept clean by the onrush of certain freedom. George sensed the eyes upon him, and he pulled his own gaze from the camel train, to look into the face of a man who was his enemy, his jailer, and his liberator. George was still confused by the unfolding of events, promises that actually came to pass, deals that were not merely tactics of deceit. It was certainly *not* the way of things in this ruptured, painful place. He was hard pressed now to assign a title to this Israeli. Perhaps he was, just simply, an honest man.

"It is a beautiful day, isn't it?" George said.

"Yes, it is," said Eytan.

They turned their eyes back to the open road. They had hardly spoken a word since leaving Jerusalem. For George, the months of waiting had been only that. Something he was accustomed to, an expert at. He had kept his hope in check.

For Eytan, the promise had not been simple to fulfill. There were lawyers, judges, procedural battles. Even when it all was finally pushed through, Ben-Zion had made one final, feeble effort to resist. However, the threat of a "palace coup" by Baum, Romano and Sylvia, coupled with Uri Badash's intimation of a leaked exposé, had caused the embittered Colonel to quietly relent.

Even then, they had to wait for an appropriate event to cover George's release, for if so much as a hint of his "collaboration" were breathed, his liberation would only catalyze his execution. At last, the remains of an Israeli pilot were offered up for barter in Lebanon; the list of Palestinian prisoners to be exchanged proved fortuitous. And George was free.

Eytan drove faster now, imagining how he would feel in George's place. He took the left-hand turn at Gush Etzion, and headed up the winding road to Beit Fajar, the summer powder muddy now, the wandering goats pulling their hooves from the sticky earth.

The low stone houses were bright with their fresh rain showers, the blue-green doors painted anew. Through Badash, Eytan had gotten word to George's family, for he wanted the Palestinian to be welcomed properly. On the distant roof of the Mahsoud house, sitting alone at the top of the village hill, a pair of outlawed Palestinian flags whipped in the wind. The cement porch was festooned with flowers.

Eytan stopped the car some distance from the house. He would not participate in the revelry, intrude on the joyous homecoming. He did not need to.

George sat there for a moment, his breathing shallow, staring. It would not do to show emotion, neither before his "driver," nor before his village.

"You are going to have to give it to us, you know," George said quietly.

Eytan did not have to ask what George meant by *it*.

"I know it," Eytan said.

"There is an ill wind blowing." George said it sadly, devoid of warning or threat. It had more a tone of regret. "I can feel it in the people's minds, their whispers in the cells."

Eytan nodded. There were, in fact, rumors of a gathering storm. The Palestinians were not going to wait for Arafat much longer. Uri Badash spoke about it often now. His agents in the territories were nervous, like farm animals before an earthquake.

"It may still take some time," Eytan said. "The Danes and Swedes fought for three hundred years, you know."

"They had only axes and arrows," said George. "We do not live in such a luxurious world."

Eytan turned to him.

"If it were up to me, George, I would give it to you. But would you settle for that?"

Mahsoud smiled. "Maybe." He straightened his shoulders, opened the door, and got out. He had no belongings, only the leather jacket that he had polished as best he could with a damp handkerchief.

He crossed in front of the car, and Eytan rolled down his window, sticking his head out.

"George," he called.

The Palestinian stopped. He turned, and he saw that Eytan was about to offer him the typical Israeli farewell. He put a hand to his lips.

"Don't say it," he said. "And I will not say it in return."

Eytan was a bit taken aback. "Why not?" he asked. "It's our only word of optimism."

"But it is not a part of our histories," George said. "Not yet." He lifted his hand and waved. "Until then."

He walked up the long muddy road, and Eytan watched him. He reached his house, the old dog got to its feet and barked, the door opened, and a throng of hands pulled him inside. The door closed.

Eytan put the car in gear and turned it around. He stopped for a moment, lit a cigarette, and smiled as he began the long drive back toward Jerusalem.

George was right.

Shalom. It was only a word. *Salaam.* Not a part of their histories. *Peace* . . .

Not yet.